Toria

King Medus II – King of Toria and the Torian Empire
Ophelia – King's Orator
Jason – Algus – King's Sword

Other

Archimedes – deceased goman commander of Torian army
Aristippus – Regent of Xavala
Amid – deceased brother of Darius
Omid – deceased slave of Ismene
Waif Magician / Shirin – Half-algus, half-goman hermit

Escorts

Lyra – Darius's panther
Paris – Selene's pteron
Tiro – Lex's peregrine falcon
Xenia – Nikolaos's dormouse

VIRIDIAN LEGION

Andy Blinston

Book 2 of the Rakkan Conquest series

Falbury

Viridian Legion

First published in Great Britain in 2020 by Falbury

Copyright © 2020 Andy Blinston

The moral right of the author has been asserted.

Part 2 in the book series Rakkan Conquest

First Edition, 2020, Andy Blinston

A CIP catalogue record for this book is available from the British Library

ISBN: 978-1-9993139-5-1

Falbury Publishing

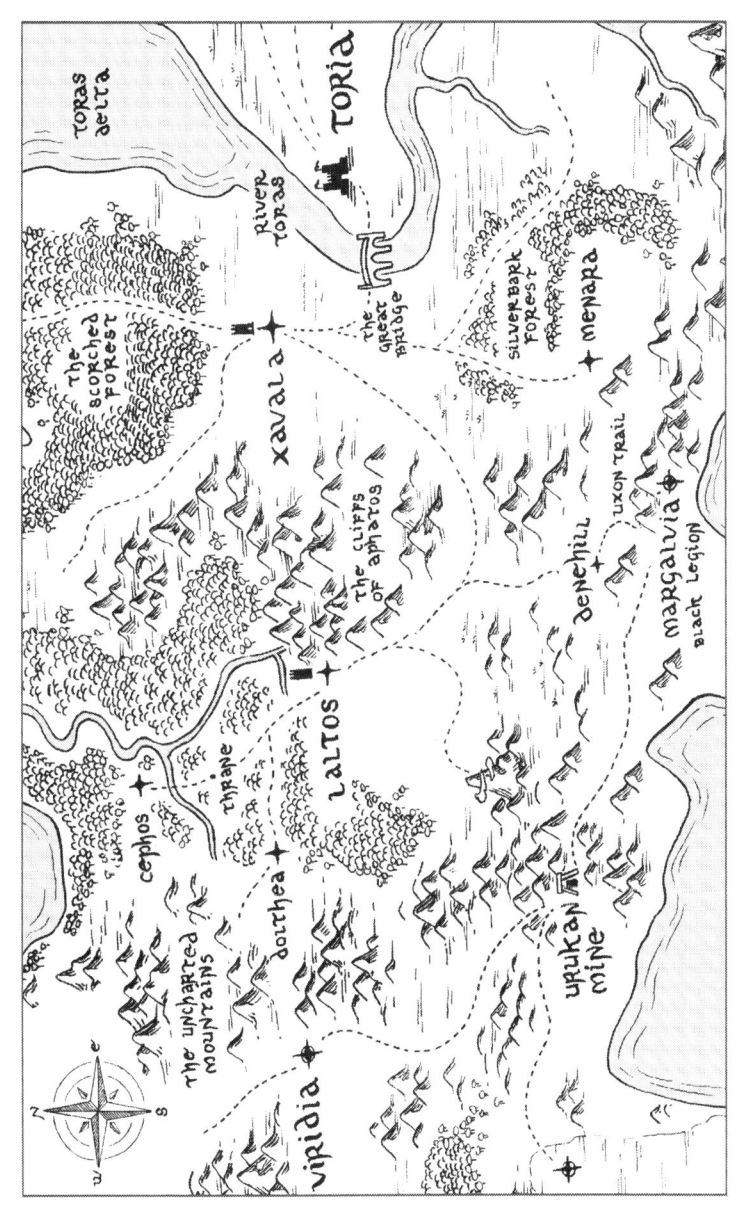

Character List

Margalvia
Varro – Warlord of the Black Legion
Julius – Black Commander
Brutus – Black Centurion
Darius – Black Legionnaire
Sulla – Red Militia
Flora – Friend of Sulla

Laltos
Theodoros – Regent of Laltos
Lex / Alexandra – Algus – House of Theodoros
Selene – Algus – House of Theodoros
Gorgias – Algus – House of Hera
Nikolaos – Algus – House of Hera

Viridia
Hadrian – Warlord of the Viridian Legion
Cordus – Viridian Commander, Second-in-command

Prologue

Lex – West of Laltos

Before setting out on a quest for revenge, you should dig two graves—at least, that's how the saying went. But so far, Lex had dug tens of thousands, and not for her enemies. Although that number swelled by the day and loaded her with an ever-greater burden, she still wasn't ready to give in and be buried. Her revenge would save the lives of more people than it had taken so far.

Blood streamed between the cobbles in the road and left no pit or nook untainted. Heavy rain lashed down as it had all evening, but the ground stayed crimson. The water swept down the sloping road, over the grass and into a swollen red river.

Overlooking the water, Lex stood tall on the only bridge into the town left standing while she counted the moments until the evening's light deserted her and her army.

At least it would spare her the sight of slain civilians, butchered children and charred women. Her hatred burned. Every town looked the same after a Viridian Legion assault.

The ring of steel swords clashing joined the thrashes of rain in the streets ahead. Smoke billowed from the closed shutters of the buildings, sending dark clouds with fiery bursts to fill the sky.

Only the odd soldier and invader were visible through the haze, but by the echoes of the screams, she knew how outnumbered the humans were.

Dark, thick kuraminium cuirasses encased the Viridians' torsos, while scratched plates shielded their wrists and shins. Helmets hid their heads with only slits for their ravenous eyes and mouths. What hope did the human soldiers have with only thin scales to cover their backs?

A few dozen algus and hundreds of soldiers from the Laltos Guard stood behind her and awaited orders with the same silent, fatigued grimace that must have soured her own face. She'd marched them quickstep for days, only to arrive late.

They had no choice but to battle tired.

So many settlements had fallen since the death of Archimedes that she didn't dare learn the name of this place, didn't dare add another to the list of failures in her mind.

If only she hadn't been forced to deal with the goman to save Darius. If only they hadn't lost the Staff of Arria…

But this town would be different. *I won't fail.* She'd save as many as she could.

Most of her fighters were peltasts, good at tossing spears but torn through at close range. But humans had few options against rakkans. It wasn't like their armour made a difference against warriors with the strength of giants.

Overhead, her escort, Tiro, swooped over the streets and surveyed the horrors. She didn't see it as if with her own eyes, but knew every detail the falcon observed. A few surviving civilians ran into a large town hall in the centre. Women carried their young, covering every inch of them they could.

Men ushered the women. One man pushed his wife through the doors as the blade of a Viridian Legionnaire sliced through his spine. His mouth gaped wide in pain for a beat before his body was dragged away and hacked.

The woman screamed as a defending soldier pulled her inside. A few algus then burst out of the hall and fought off attackers at the door, but the black helmets of the Viridian Legion only grew in number as they rushed in from nearby streets, as endless as the rain.

Back on the bridge, Lex ripped her sword from its scabbard. "We need to reach the town hall. Show them no mercy. Slay them as the savages they are." She flared algor to send a bright blue film across her blade that would slash metal and bone.

The other algus followed her lead. Behind her, each hoplite raised their shield and readied their spear. *Brave men, to fight without my powers.*

The straight road from the bridge to the town hall was tightly packed with buildings at either side. They'd use the roofs to avoid being massacred.

With a yell of fury, Lex burst forward. Blood splattered under her boots, followed by the swift footsteps of the other algus. Two hands tightly gripped the hilt of her sword. A roar swelled behind her from the charging men as she left the bridge and raced into the smoky town.

As they entered, the blare of a rakkan horn sounded above the shouts and screams. Her soldiers quickly raised ladders to the first houses while the algus charged to clear the street.

A Viridian Legionnaire ran from a side road. His helmet turned as Lex sliced her gleaming blade through his neck, her pace unfaltering.

She and the other algus sprinted side by side. Every invader that charged forward met with a swift blade through exposed limbs, necks and shoulders.

But soon, an impenetrable mass of black armour came into view. A wall of shields met them with sharp spears jutting from the gaps, tips wet with rain and blood.

The other algus skidded to a halt, but Lex veered to the side, leapt to grab hold of a second-storey windowsill, and hoisted herself up.

As she kicked open the shutters and steadied herself, her mind shifted to what Tiro now saw. The town hall was overrun. Doors hung loose from their hinges in a charred mess. A hole had been smashed through a wall.

Tiro. How many are left alive?

Her escort darted inside as she pulled the bow from her back, nocked an arrow, then began a barrage from her perch. She flicked the end of each arrowhead with armour-piercing algor before letting it loose while other algus and peltasts joined the attack from the rooftops as they arrived.

The Viridian testudo formation, the turtle of shields, faltered for a moment before it ignited in fire as the legionnaires flared ferven. Raindrops hissed and fizzled to leave a rising steam from the shields fixed in place.

How long before they jump up? How long until they use the weighted nets?

A few of the algus had remained in the street below and now tossed algor-coated javelins through the gaps in the shields. Some legionnaires fell with cries of pain, but Lex was now distracted by the screams Tiro heard.

The bottom of the town hall was like a red lake. Piles of men lay strewn across the floor with limbs twisted and snapped. A sword through the heart of each would have been an easier method of subduing civilians, but the Viridian Legion found it too merciful.

The swords would come later. Men and boys were broken but left alive. Their screams of pain were drowned out by the screams of the women and girls, now so loud Lex didn't need her escort's ears to hear them.

All Lex could imagine was her own daughter shrieking alongside them. Lex clenched her jaw; hatred burned inside her as she turned her attention back to the street. She shot arrow after arrow into the testudo of shields below, but it did nothing to quell her fury.

Rows of legionnaires behind pelted rocks, human limbs and heads at the roofs, defiling the brave fallen.

Lex's father was the Regent. It was her family's duty to protect their people, and every day they failed more and more.

No more. As Lex loosed more arrows into the necks and eyes of Viridian Legionnaires, her thoughts shifted onto Darius, onto the half-rakkan she knew could turn Laltos's fortunes around. But he sat far away in his own rakkan city. *We need you.*

While she prayed, a spear smashed into the shutter beside her. The testudo was up against the wall below. Arrows darted into it from the roofs. But worse, through the haze behind the algus and peltasts on the rooftops, Lex saw charging legionnaires.

After a quick scan below, she saw it—warriors in the quieter streets jumped two storeys to grab hold of the roofs with ease.

She pointed. One of the algus opposite saw and whirled to give orders to the men as Lex slung her bow over a shoulder and grabbed hold of the wet roof above. She pulled herself up. The clay tiles were slippery and thin, with the slightest of inclines, made to hold up the rain and little else. *Hope it collapses under their heavy armour.*

Once up, her gaze met with two of her algus, and she signalled towards the town hall. "We have to move. They'll all be dead soon."

A musclebound algus nodded and barked orders to surrounding peltasts.

But Lex didn't wait. She darted across the tiles and leapt from roof to roof.

A few legionnaires had climbed up and threw weighted nets towards her and other charging algus. Some dodged too late and became tangled and pinned by the kuraminium balls. But Lex powered on.

One algus ahead of her sidestepped to avoid a net and slipped on the wet tiles, smashing through the roof to leave a gaping hole.

She dodged around and sprinted faster for the roof at the centre that stood higher and wider than any of the others. Screams from the hall grew, a horn of shrill pain from people young and old. Tiro still watched from his perch inside, helpless.

Now only one roof away from the hall, Lex glanced over her shoulder and counted half a dozen algus following. *Hope it's enough.* She leapt from the last roof and onto the top of the next, deliberately driving a heel through the clay tiles. She then kicked aside the debris and watched it fall to be swallowed by the bloody hall below.

Kneeling, she looked at the swarm of black helmets that now lifted to look up at her. The red floor was interrupted only by bodies, and screams quietened one by one.

They'd already started the slaughter. Had Lex's arrival hastened the act?

An algus knelt beside her and ripped out more roof tiles. She took off her bow and loosed arrow after arrow, her quiver lighter by the minute with little to show as a result.

The invaders' helmets burst with fire. Arrowheads bounced off.

What can we do? Unable to fight on the ground, what hope did the humans have? Damn the King. How could he demand they pay for assistance?

They needed powerful warriors, rakkans against rakkans to halt the charge across the Empire. They needed Margalvia. Lex had practically begged on her knees for the city's warlord to aid Laltos, but to no avail.

One of the Viridians below gazed up with a grimace of pure loathing. She recognised the blackened signet ring on his finger at once and spied the two green bands on his bicep. His large nose showed a kink from being broken one too many times, and its flattened tip matched the flatness of his hate-filled face.

Lex snarled.

Second-in-command of the Viridian Legion, the red-headed Cordus was responsible for more atrocities in the last year than she'd seen in a lifetime.

The commander scowled. He grabbed the hair of one of the screaming, broken men and cut off the head with a single slash of his flaming gladius. He held the bleeding head out. Muscles bulged in his tattooed arms. Then he lobbed the head towards Lex as if it weighed less than a nut.

She dove to the side as it crashed through the tiles and shook the ones beneath her. She crawled to the hole again, grabbed one of the exposed wooden beams and glared.

The screams ceased one at a time as legionnaires at the edges of the room put blades to the people's necks and ended their pain. Soon, the only movement was that of the Viridians.

Lex held her sword, sharp and ready, twitching to jump to her death just to take the fiend Cordus with her.

Whilst she held back tears of rage, a hand grabbed her shoulder and gently pulled her away.

"It's over," the algus cried. "We need to flee."

She nodded, vision blurred with tears. Hope was lost. *Again.* She'd lost too many men in the past through not retreating when she should.

The algus blew a horn, and all the figures that had been making their way across the rooftops turned and bolted in the opposite direction.

Lex stood and glared into the hall below one last time, meeting the eyes of the Viridian Commander.

She spat. *One day, I'll end you. And your warlord.*

Setting off at a sprint, she followed the flapping cloaks of her algus across the rooftops. Her escort soared out of the hall through the hole in the roof and glided over her. The odd Viridian still harried men on the roofs, but she cut down every rakkan in her path with angry swings.

Another day. Another defeat. Since Archimedes's death, the King and his regents hadn't the stomach to aid until their own lands were threatened. Soon the Viridian Legion would push all the way to Laltos. The whole west of the Empire would crumble, and her father, brothers and sisters would all fall to join the rest that she'd loved and lost over the years.

Loose tiles slipped from the roofs under her rapid footsteps. She overtook a few soldiers with a quick glance back at the rakkans in pursuit.

Margalvia was their best hope, as unpalatable as rakkans were to the rest of her race.

They needed Darius. He'd listen. Who better to create the First Alliance, a human and rakkan city working together? After all, it had been the old Darius's idea. Only then might she see a world where a human and a rakkan could live together without fearing the other kind, a world where her daughter could grow up safe. *If only.*

1

Darius – West of Laltos

Darius spied through the tangle of branches, catching his first glimpse of the Viridian Commander responsible for much of the carnage he'd witnessed of late. There were times when he wished he could unsee what was before his eyes, and today was one of those days. He was used to taking blows from swords, spears and axes, but unlike a weapon, a sight or a memory could leave a wound that time did not mend.

Now, his eyes were drawn to the man before him, the broken nose, shaggy red mane and the large signet ring on the rakkan's tattooed finger that confirmed his mark. *Cordus. A clean death would be too kind for him.*

But that would go against his warlord's direct orders. "Observe; don't interfere," Varro had said. "I want information—troop numbers and locations, not bloodshed." It had been easy to agree at the time, but now that he'd seen what Lex had described, it wasn't so easy.

The armoured Viridian Commander sat eating, reclined against a ruined home on the outskirts of the village he and his warriors had raided earlier that night. It was three towns over from where Lex had said he was last seen, and all three lay burning.

The once dull, orange clay wall behind the Viridian Commander was splattered with red and split in two by a fracture from the floor to the roof tiles. Bodies littered the ground, severed into so many parts they were impossible to count.

If the commander was moved by the horror, his greedy, satiated face did nothing to show it. The corpses were the fortunate ones, judging by the survivors Darius had seen. Despite the gore that would usually turn his stomach, he couldn't look away.

The perennial forest around was shorter than most, but the thick overlapping branches and needles gave Darius the cover he needed. It was too bad the dense bushes killed the breeze, made the stink of smoke and ash from the smouldering homes linger. It took all his restraint not to cough and give himself away.

He eased through the thick branches an inch at a time, kuraminium sword ready in his hand and helmet heavy on his head. Morning dew wet his arms as he slid through. Despite the thick, humid air, his muscles were tense and hard. *Varro should have ordered me to slaughter them all, just as Lex urged.* This was Darius's fault. He'd killed Archimedes. The voice in his mind was now replaced with Lex's begging, along with the memory of the pain in her alluring eyes that still turned his insides.

Lyra followed every footstep stealthily at his heel, so close her black fur pressed against him. She was always affectionate when he was troubled. *I don't deserve a girl like you.*

A few yards away, a handful of Viridian Legionnaires collected equipment and loot from a few huts around—anything metal, coins, clothes, weapons—and dumped them into a heap at the centre of a clearing.

When only a few inches from breaking cover near them, Darius paused. His debate with Lex replayed in his mind. "We need an alliance," she'd insisted, "and there's only one way. Slaughter as many Viridians as you can. Help us defend. Ignite war between the rakkan cities."

Perhaps their shared humanity was why they were the only ones eager to intervene.

Some of the many proverbs his mentor, Brutus, had shared with him came to mind. *Margalvians defend their brothers. Better to die loyal than live false-hearted.* But weren't the dead men before Darius also his brothers?

"Hurry," the commander grunted as he bit another chunk of meat from the bone clutched in his hand, a bone from no animal… "I'm already sunburned because of your sluggishness yesterday, and who knows how long this cloud-cover will last." The rakkan's skin once would have been as pale as chalk but was now covered in red, raw patches.

In contrast to the well-groomed commander, the five scraggly haired legionnaires had skin covered with weeks old blood and dirt.

"It's the right thing," Lex had insisted. "Trust your heart, not your head."

Six rakkans wouldn't be much trouble for him, and he'd give them the same grisly end they'd condemned this village to. Two wrongs didn't make a right, but perhaps six did…

He looked at Lyra. *Am I a fool for considering this?* Her amber eyes narrowed slightly, teeth bared. As if her feelings were his own, a second anger rose inside him. She wanted these rakkans dead as much as Lex, or perhaps through loyalty to the old Darius.

Leaves rustled as a gust swept through the trees. Darius swore he saw shadows behind Lyra, but a few seconds later, nothing moved as the wind died down. Perhaps it was the ghosts of the dead, waiting to see justice.

A few jeers from the rakkans drew back his gaze. A lanky human boy, young but with the thinning hair of a weathered man, limped towards the commander with a waterskin in hand. Chained at the ankle, one of his eyes shone a deep shade of purple and was practically swollen shut.

Judging by the boy's height and slender but toned arms, he was just shy of a teenager and no stranger to physical labour. Darius had once known a slave boy of a similar age and now recalled watching that boy die far before his time.

That day, Darius hadn't been strong enough to save him. Now he was.

After the boy handed over the waterskin to the commander, a legionnaire picked a stone from the ground and rolled it between his fingers, conjuring ferven on it until it became a ball of flame. Then, he lobbed it at the boy, narrowly missing him.

Another legionnaire took a spear from the central pile, pushed the boy over, then drove the spike between a link in the chain with a laugh, anchoring him to the ground.

"Please, not again!" the boy cried.

Darius clenched his jaw. The indignant rage he often felt had once seemed irrational, but it was now impossible to ignore.

"I wonder if the Warlord will like another human sacrifice…" the commander mused.

The more Darius watched, the easier his decision became. He wasn't disloyal. Loyalty given deserved loyalty in return. But neither would he do nothing.

He reached down and tugged the black band across his bicep until it snapped off. The visor on the front of his helmet would conceal his human eyes, but he'd leave none of them alive to tell of the carnage, regardless.

He surveyed the axes and swords within the stack of equipment, confident they were wedged in and out of easy reach of his foes.

It's time, Lyra. She slinked to his flank as he closed his eyes for a moment. He focused his attention on his skin, sensing every shift in the movement of air, which readied his heightened rakkan reflexes. Blood pumped into his muscles, priming rakkan strength enough to crush bone.

Then he burst from the overgrowth. Ferven blazed from his sword as he let his rage flow out, and he swung the weapon towards the commander's midriff. The rakkan dove to the side, leaving Darius's blade to only graze his skin while the legionnaires gaped.

A second later, the five scrambled to get weapons as the commander rolled and ripped a sword from the pile.

Before the rakkan could regain his feet, Darius leapt and stabbed for the neck with all his algus speed. But the commander rolled away again and sprung stealthily to his feet.

Slippery bastard.

A heartbeat later, the other five rakkans grabbed weapons and dove into the fray.

Lyra pounced from the undergrowth and sank her fangs into the ankle of one legionnaire. The rakkan cried out and turned his head enough to expose his neck. With a thanks to his escort, Darius lunged and slashed through the rakkan's veins.

Averting his eyes from the gushing blood, Darius ducked as the other legionnaires responded by swinging their swords and axes. He smashed one rakkan across the helmet with his sword and tripped another with a quick sweep of his leg.

Lyra pounced on the fallen rakkan and sank her fangs into his face. He screamed and flailed but couldn't get a grip on her before his strength waned.

The commander stood grimacing at Darius with only a few of his men left. "I know you," the commander spat. "No rakkan moves that fast, Margalvian mongrel."

Good thing the dead can't talk.

Darius focused and let algor creep down his sword, icing it to the tip so it would cut more than flesh. Then he darted in and unleashed a few swift strikes at the rakkans' thighs that the commander parried with a ferven-raging sword.

But two of his legionnaires failed to block. Their slashed bodies fell to stain the earth as the others countered.

Darius parried their strokes while stealing a glance at the captive boy now sat up, gaping. *Free him, Lyra.*

When another two of the legionnaires' heads fell to Darius's sword, the commander and the others paced backwards.

"Why?" the commander asked, fear in those obsidian eyes—fear that the men and women had felt, fear the survivors had felt.

Darius paced forwards slowly, savouring their terror as the rakkans backed out of his way.

Meanwhile, Lyra ran towards the boy, snapped her jaws tight on the chain holding him and dragged the spear up from the dirt.

The boy watched her, paralysed.

"Run," Darius said.

The boy almost tripped over the chain in his hurry to race away and into the forest.

"You're welcome." Darius grunted as he trained his eyes on the two remaining rakkans. Lyra paced wide to protect his flank.

The final legionnaire lunged forward and gasped as Darius's blade sunk into his thigh. Gasping turned to howling when

Darius twisted and ripped out the blade, then cut across the rakkan's neck for good measure. That left only the commander.

"Scum." Cordus spat. "What kind of rakkan fights for humans?"

"I can assure you I've killed as many humans as I have rakkans." Darius eased forward with careful, menacing steps. "People say I'm an indiscriminate slayer, a miserable bastard who takes out his ire on others. But while the latter may be true…I'm not indiscriminate."

Cordus scowled. "You should want the humans dead as much as us. They starved your people like they did to us."

Darius scanned his eyes across the corpses, the broken shells of homes that would rot with their owners.

"You live for revenge," he said. "And now you'll die for it."

With a thrust too rapid for Cordus's defences, he stabbed his sword into the commander's groin until the point hit bone. Blood oozed. Although the slow flow told him the wound wasn't mortal, Darius dropped back and swallowed before sickness gripped him.

The desolate village filled with the commander's howls. But, despite Darius's lust for retribution, the pain brought no satisfaction.

Before the tension could ease from his muscles, branches snapped and footsteps sounded within the forest. *More legionnaires?* But as suddenly as the sounds had appeared, they silenced.

Scanning through the foliage, he swore he saw shadows moving again.

He watched. Every sway of the trees dragged his gaze away, but he found nothing there except the wafting air.

Lyra. She stood only a few feet from where he'd seen the shadows. *Come close.*

Before she could respond, a net sprang from within the forest. The metal balls tied to it snapped branches and leaves as they hurtled towards his escort.

Darius willed her to run, but she dodged too late. The metal weights slammed into the surrounding mud with a heavy thud that only kuraminium made. She writhed inside the netting, only tangling herself further.

I've got you. Darius moved towards her, sword drawn and ready to cut her free, when a deep-bellied growl broke through the trees in front of them.

"You dare come into my lands?" came a sonorous voice. Shadows grew between the foliage near Lyra, like passing clouds blocked the sun. A second later, the darkness formed into countless figures who wore the black, terrorising helmets of the Viridian Legion.

At their centre, a colossal rakkan emerged and stepped over Lyra, clad in a kuraminium cuirass so thick it would take a battering ram to shift it.

Darius's heart pounded.

Three viridian bands circled the rakkan's bulging arm, and his helmet had wide horns like a bull or demon—the marks of a warlord.

It could only be one, whose name Darius knew only from lore. *Hadrian.*

Darius had never set eyes on Hadrian before, but as he surveyed the Warlord's figure, he realised the rumours were true: arms the size of a normal man's legs and likely just as strong, a large jaw, and a glowing stare terrible enough to bring most men to their knees.

A thick layer of grime and ash shone on his pale face that, together, made him look carved from stone. But his heavy, grunting breaths bared the life within. Grey hairs mixed with the rusty stubble on his chin.

Around the Warlord, Darius counted at least a dozen other armoured rakkans with green tattoos that covered their entire arms, just like Cordus's.

Under normal circumstances, Darius would fancy his odds. But he couldn't help feel nervous in front of the rakkan that gave even his own warlord concern.

Hadrian grabbed Lyra by the scruff of the neck through the netting and handed her to one of his legionnaires, who clamped a forearm around her neck. Then, he knelt beside the commander Darius had just stabbed and touched the oozing wound.

"This won't go unpunished," the Warlord said. "I know who you are, Darius the Dreaded."

That's what they call me? Darius wasn't the one ready to crush a panther's neck.

"You dare attack one of my blood?" Hadrian roared and punched the ground so hard Darius felt the shock in his boots. "My bloodline is divine." Hadrian stood up tall. "You don't have the right."

Not only giant but unhinged. Darius stepped back and looked from side to side, desperate to get Lyra from their clutches and escape the encircling rakkans, but they stood close together, spears at the ready.

"You Margalvians are so weak," Hadrian said. "Too afraid to face us in battle. Drop your weapon, half-breed." The Warlord's helmet angled down towards him.

A tightness grew around Darius's neck as if his own windpipe were being crushed by a rakkan. *A warrior's weapon is his life.* In his mind, the horrid memory replayed of the first time he'd failed to drop his weapon when cornered, when his baby brother had bled to death in his arms.

26

Hadrian turned to the legionnaire holding Lyra. "Kill her."

Before another thought entered Darius's head, his fingers relaxed, and his sword hit the ground.

The Warlord's gaze shifted back to him. "Hold that order. Secure him."

The line of rakkans came towards Darius, spears pointed with sharp heads. Only Hadrian and the legionnaire gripping Lyra stayed put.

Darius's mind refused to function.

Rakkans approached from each side. His only weapon was on the ground. If they restrained him, there'd be no escape. It was fight or die.

The spear of the legionnaire to his right prodded his armour, and the rakkan moved behind to secure his arms. As he did, Darius's gaze dropped to the dagger hung sheathed on the rakkan's belt. *I just need to save Lyra.*

Five more spear tips pricked his neck.

The legionnaire behind took one of Darius's wrists, then moved closer to get the second. But before he could, Darius dropped to his knees.

Spears scratched up his helmet as he reached out and grabbed the knife from the rakkan's belt. With a single sweep of the arm, he tossed the dagger between two legionnaires in front.

It flew towards the man holding Lyra.

The rakkan tried to dodge, but the knife stabbed into his upper arm, weakening his hold, and Lyra landed on the ground in a tangle of netting and weights that she writhed against.

Meanwhile, bodies piled on top of Darius until he was pressed deep into the soil. Only his metal cuirass gave him space to breathe. He wrenched his head as free as he could, eyes fixated on Lyra whose head had found a gap in the net and desperately bit at it.

Before she could free herself, Hadrian dove and caught her tail.

Darius cried out as her legs poked out of the net and skidded on the ground, claws ripping dirt into the air but failing to help her escape.

In the wrestling, Darius felt the squeeze of many hands on his arms and legs, restricting his movement so much he may as well have been wrapped in chains. Soon after, they grappled his arms behind his back.

The Warlord roared and pulled Lyra up, slapping a palm to her neck before standing and pointing to the heap of warriors. "Get that mongrel to his feet."

Against his ineffective struggles, they picked Darius up and faced him towards the Warlord, painfully twisting his arm. All Darius could do was lock eyes with Lyra. *I'll save you.*

The emotional bond they shared told him she knew it was a lie.

Hadrian's eyes seethed white-hot inside his helmet. "I don't know what your game is, but if Margalvia wants to send assassins and spies, then we'll respond with swords and spears. In our lands, the law is a hand for a hand. You try to kill my kin, I'll kill yours." Hadrian glared down at Lyra.

2

Darius – West of Laltos

Darius twisted, squirmed and flared algor over his entire body, bursting in a flare of brilliance but still unable to shake off those restraining him, who conjured ferven in defence.

One legionnaire tore the helmet from Darius's head, giving him a full view of Lyra convulsing in the net.

Darius felt her terror seize him, felt her pained gasps trying to drag in air through her constricted neck. He kicked one of the rakkans holding him and tried to wrench his arms loose, but they held him tight.

Hadrian stepped closer until his helmet squashed Darius's nose. "I'll break you," Hadrian said.

"We should sacrifice his panther," one of the legionnaires said with a greedy laugh, "in tribute to you, Warlord."

"Take your hands off her!" Darius shouted.

"Good idea." Hadrian grabbed hold of one of Darius's wrists. "Give him a knife. I want him to be the one to do it."

What the…?

A legionnaire prised Darius's fingers apart while another pushed the hilt of a knife into his hand with a chuckle. Then Hadrian squeezed his hand into a fist so hard the hilt pressed against the bones in his palm.

With quick thrusts, Darius strained to bury the dagger into any part of Hadrian he could, but the Warlord's hold overpowered him. How was he to escape such monstrous strength?

"You'll sacrifice your pet to me," Hadrian said. "Maybe then my divine wrath will be eased."

"She's not a *pet*!" Darius tried to force his fingers open to drop the blade, but Hadrian's grip was too strong. One finger snapped, sending a jolt up Darius's arm.

With his other hand, Hadrian brought Lyra's body to brush against the dagger.

Lyra, try to get free!

She squirmed. She writhed. Her amber eyes widened with fear and Darius felt the rush of his heart as it mirrored her panicked beats.

"You're going to feel the blade pierce her skin," Hadrian said, "cut into her and feel the blood you hate so much flow out of her. Then, I'll keep you in a hole with her body rotting next to you."

Darius tried to butt the Warlord, but Hadrian dodged back. There was nothing Darius could do but yell in fury. Ferven crackled in his throat as he screamed. This couldn't be happening…

Hadrian pressed the dagger into Lyra's belly, pricking the skin and causing a trickle of blood to dampen her soft fur. Her high, desperate screech pained Darius more than the hands grappling him.

She wriggled, roaring as the dagger sank deeper. Her fear threatened to overwhelm him.

Blood flowed hot over his hand.

As he stabbed, a sharp pain lanced his own abdomen, as if someone was cutting through him. It was a pain he knew *he* deserved, but it was his escort that bore the wound.

His throat rasped with his yells until he barely made a sound.

Lyra shuddered, convulsed.

The Warlord held her higher, choking her. For once, Hadrian's eyes turned black as the ferven faded, leaving only a satisfied stare.

Feline blood flowed down onto Darius's arm. He cried out, so enraged it overwhelmed the nausea and terror stemming from his escort.

The flow grew heavier by the second. He had to act now.

Think! An idea finally struck him. Summoning whatever calm he could to form algor in his mouth, the cold mixed with the spittle inside.

Sacrifice this. He spat and sprayed the algor into Hadrian's eyes.

The Warlord jerked back, dropped his arms and flared ferven across his head, shaking it.

His break in concentration relaxed the hold on Darius's arm. Darius flared algor on the knife as he thrust up, slashed through the netting then stabbed the dagger into the eye slit of a legionnaire's helmet.

Lyra writhed weakly, spun her head enough to sink a tooth into Hadrian's thigh.

He roared, ripped her away and tossed her high and far to crash into the branches of the trees.

Right arm now free, Darius slashed at Hadrian, who stepped back to dodge. A legionnaire tried to grab Darius's arm, but his algus speed helped him weave around and stab into the rakkan's thigh.

Hold on, Lyra. I'm coming. She was still alive, clinging weakly to life with dread. *I won't let you bleed out.*

One legionnaire tried to wrap their arms around him in restraint, but Darius twisted and jabbed the knife into the rakkan's neck.

Hadrian lifted his head, now free of algor, then charged, head low and fists clenched.

Darius writhed, finally ripped both arms free of the rakkans, then dove to the side and rolled away just in time to escape Hadrian's charging figure.

No sooner had Darius turned to face his foe again than blood splattered onto his face. He shuddered. Before he could wipe it, a boot slammed into his cuirass and punted him several feet across the ground.

He landed, winded, wondering how these rakkans fought so aptly. He hobbled to his feet while wiping as much of the sickening liquid from his face as he could. Thankfully, light-headedness hadn't taken over, but how long before they drenched him?

Hadrian bent and cupped some more of Lyra's blood in his hand while the others readied their spears. "Want more? I know you fear it."

The Warlord was faster and more cunning than Darius had thought. It would take more than a few swipes to beat him and his men, and the longer Darius delayed, the longer Lyra bled out.

Darius eyed the Warlord, wanting nothing more than to sink his dagger into the rakkan at least a dozen times.

But Lyra.

If he left Hadrian alive, there would be retaliation. Varro would know he'd disobeyed orders.

But Lyra may die.

He growled under his breath. As much as it pained him, there was little choice.

"When I see you again, only one of us will walk away." Darius gave Hadrian one last scowl before turning. He bolted into the forest, headed for the place he'd seen Lyra crash through the branches.

"Margalvia will pay for this!" Hadrian roared.

Booming footsteps thudded. Darius panted. *Keep running.*

Those cold, foreign feelings inside told him Lyra was still alive, but for how long? Branches snapped and leaves scattered from the bushes and trees as Darius bashed them aside, searching.

Finally, he caught sight of black fur.

He stopped by her panting body and ripped off the remnants of the net. *I've got you.* Lyra's fear eased as he gathered her into his arms. By now, he no longer felt her pain, but he knew it was great, and their flight would only hurt her more.

Sorry, girl. While pressing a hand hard into the open wound on her belly, he set off at a pace Hadrian couldn't match. The thuds behind soon quietened, but that brought little relief. His real race was with the timer in his hands, oozing warm blood through his fingers.

Memories of his baby brother bleeding in his arms flashed back to mind. The screams. The smell. Failing to save him. The blood sent fierce shudders through his body. Every time he dwelled on that memory, it made the sight of red overwhelming.

He wouldn't let it happen again. But even running at the pace of an algus, Margalvia was far away.

The town of Dolthea was closest. *Hold on, Lyra. I'll get you help.*

All he knew of Dolthea was the lodge he'd stayed at a few days prior.

With the clouds and overhanging branches, he only got brief glimpses of the now-rising sun, but it was enough to discern which direction was east. He ran and ran; faster than he knew he could sustain. As he did, he shed his heavy armour, piece by piece, until running in only his sweaty linen tunic and boots.

The dense forest forced him to constantly duck and weave. Soon he'd reach the road and follow the trail, but the longer time dragged on, the more he checked overhead in fear that he'd taken a wrong turn.

Fatigue slowed him further until he burst through a clump of grass as tall as him to find well-trodden dirt underfoot—the road.

His laden breathing made Lyra squirm in his arms. *Easy, girl. I'll get you there.*

3

Darius – Dolthea, West of Laltos

He didn't know how he kept sprinting with Lyra for however many miles it was to Dolthea. He followed the trail of hard dirt, arms whipped by branches that had grown out across the path.

Thick forest towered over him at each side like a narrow leafy canyon. Each mile looked the same as the last, but he soon entered through a set of wooden gates into the town.

Inside the stone walls were rows of tall, thin wooden buildings which flew past him block by block. He raced around, bumping into men and women as he did, and he eventually found himself in a wide street under a wooden sign with an herb symbol on it and the name "Thaliea's".

Herbalist. Not a surgeon, but worth a try.

Fidgeting with nerves, he kicked the door twice. No sounds came from within, so he kicked again, harder.

After a few more silent moments, the door of the neighouring building slowly creaked open, and a young man with long, silver hair flowing over his shoulders leaned out. "Is something wrong? Thaliea's is closed today."

Darius walked across to the man and conjured a thin coat of algor in his eyes, the proof of an algus. "My escort needs help. She's been wounded."

The youthful man glanced at Lyra's wound and frowned. "She needs a miracle, not an herbalist."

One more snide comment and she won't be the only one. Darius looked more closely at the wide doorway the man stood in and noticed a symbol etched into the wood, a man holding an axe in one hand and a balancing scale in the other. Darius vaguely recalled the figure which always hung around Lex's neck—her God of Justice.

"Where can I find a surgeon?" Darius asked. "Or a stable master?"

The young man stared with eyes as silver as his hair. "Not for two towns over. But perhaps I can help. It so happens I work miracles."

It was all Darius could do not to roll his eyes. Something about the man's aged hair yet youthful, wrinkle-free skin made Darius curious if he hadn't cheated death himself. "Get help if you need to. Money's no barrier." Lex had given him enough silver crests for such matters.

"Come in. My name is Aran, by the way." The man ushered Darius through the door and into a room with rows of benches pointed towards an altar engraved with doves and crows.

Aran pointed to the altar, and Darius laid Lyra down with his hand still pressed into her bleeding wound.

"We haven't even used this altar yet," Aran said. "The first temple in the west, and it's going to open blood-stained."

"I'll buy you a new one," Darius said, "just mend her."

"That won't be necessary." Aran placed his hand above Darius's and switched quickly. "You can wait in the side room."

"I'll stay here," Darius said.

The man simply looked at him.

Darius stared back. "I'm serious."

"I'd rather not work the divine dance under watchful eyes."

"I'd rather ensure you do it right."

Aran's eyebrows arched. "You don't have much faith in people, do you?"

And with good reason. "Fine, but if anything happens to her, I'll—"

"Gut me? Castrate me?" Aran nudged him towards the door to the side of the altar. "I know better than to play loose with someone's escort. After all, it's the Order that bonds human and beast in the first place."

Darius was vaguely familiar with the Empire's newest religion, and searching Aran's eyes, he saw no malice or malevolent intent. Aran continued watching until Darius slowly made his way across the room and through the side door.

Once he'd eased the door closed, he reached out, touched the rough wood with his fingertips that felt like it separated him from Lyra by miles. Perhaps he should just trust the man.

Turning around, he took in the bare room Aran had relegated him to. It contained only a wooden stool and a bottle of firewater next to it. *I'm sure Aran won't mind if I help myself.* He sat and grabbed the bottle, then picked the wax seal from the top and took a few gulps while listening carefully.

The thin wooden walls should have let him hear everything in the next room, yet it was oddly quiet. It was only now he felt the sweat that had soaked his tunic and wafted it to cool off.

How could he have been so foolish? What would Brutus, Sulla and Varro say when he arrived home with an injured escort?

He shouldn't have got involved in this war unless ordered to. A warrior had no place taking matters into his own hands.

To pass the time, he gazed around the room at the shelves on the walls. Despite only having attended the Order's services occasionally with Lex in the past, he recognised the incense burners and sacred scrolls that told of the God and Goddess's bond. A few figurines of the couple caught in an embrace seemed worth a minor fortune, as well as roused a little envy in him. What did a perfect relationship feel like?

Surprisingly to him, the Order didn't partake in animal sacrifices but instead practised grain offerings and abstinence from the most pleasurable indulgences.

He continued sipping firewater, trying not to take too much given where he was and his previous pondering, but so much time passed that the bottle was almost empty when Aran threw open the door and stepped into the room.

"I've done what I can."

Darius shot up and craned his neck to see Lyra still lying on the altar without moving so much as her tail. "She's well?"

"She'll live at least another few days."

Darius glared. "Days?"

The man frowned. "You don't seem impressed."

Darius took a step forwards until their foreheads almost touched. "Days? That's it?"

"As far as I'm concerned, I just worked a miracle. I've stemmed the bleeding, but she's badly wounded. That blade cut her liver, and she needs a surgeon. But there's none here. The bag beside her has some herbs to prevent rot from setting in, but the bleeding is still—"

Darius pulled a silver crest from his pocket and pressed it into the man's chest. "I pray you've done enough." He pushed past and gathered the bag of herbs and Lyra's limp body in his arms. At least the man had bandaged her, but a few days wasn't enough to run to Margalvia and its surgeons.

"Are there any swift horses in this city?" Darius asked.

"Yes, I believe so."

With the supernatural speed of a swift, Darius may make it home in just under a week. Along the way, he'd have to call at other towns and surgeons.

He was halfway out of the door when Aran put a hand on his shoulder. "One more thing," the man said, concern creasing his brow.

Darius paused. "Yes?"

"Just remember, he who seeks revenge keeps his own wounds green."

What the hell does he know? "Thanks for the advice." Darius wasted no more time and sprinted outside.

Hold on, Lyra. He could only pray Margalvia didn't hear of his blunder before he arrived.

4

Sulla – Margalvia

Sulla counted through the silver coins in his hands. They'd bought his sister's body and felt dirty, but his real concern was over who had paid with them.

He laid back on the straw mattress. The last coin made ten crests with the human king's ugly insignia stamped in—useless in Margalvia but could bribe a human or two.

The stone hovel Sulla called home had only one circular room with two beds and a few chairs round a fire in the centre. In it, charcoal kindled as Flora and Julius sat drinking firewater so cheap you had to scrape your tongue after every mouthful.

Flora curled strands of her long, golden hair around her finger while whispering and smiling at Julius.

Sulla cursed to himself. No man liked to see his sister used. He'd warned her that Julius was a philanderer. The women all fell for those cheek dimples and thick black hair. Sulla contemplated kicking Julius out there and then but knew better than to tell his sister who she should and shouldn't invite home. He'd just hang around so they wouldn't get up to anything. *Wish she'd invite Darius home instead.*

Sulla caught his sister's eye, and she stopped whispering and frowned. "Please don't be mad I accepted the crests. Someone will trade rations for them."

Sulla shrugged. "I'm not mad."

"You sure?" Julius sniggered. "It's easy to tell when you're annoyed."

"How's that?"

"You stop making jokes. It's a relief, really."

"I have a joke." Sulla sat up and leaned towards the rakkan. "You, thinking you can work your charms on Flora."

She chuckled as Julius frowned and shook his head. "I wasn't trying—"

"You were, but I forgive you. At least you'd pay with actual money."

His sister stood and pushed Sulla backwards onto the bed. "Don't be churlish and stop sulking about those crests."

"It's not so much the crests but who paid you. Still not going to give me a name?" He raised an eyebrow at her.

"My customers are *my* business."

So it was with such a disreputable profession. Sulla had to admire her loyalty; after almost a century, she'd still never given him a single name. That wouldn't stop him from trying though.

"Surely I've given you enough of my rations over the years to earn a name. Is it Darius?" It was Sulla's hope that the girl he'd grown up with on the streets would marry someone with honour. And she'd take excellent care of the half-rakkan. It was one way Sulla could repay the man for saving him from his former life. Too bad Darius had shown little interest. *What a fool. She's gorgeous.* The payment in crests made him wonder though.

His sister shook her head. "You? Earn rations? Since when?"

Sulla grunted, aware he hadn't seen a day's full pay in months. "Not my fault the Warlord refuses to send us to battle." He'd complained enough to the Militia Chief but understood the rakkan just followed the Warlord's orders.

It had been a rare time that Margalvia hadn't been fighting for its survival. Their enemies held back and gave them a chance to enjoy a little peace. Is this what life would be like without war? *How dull.* No wonder war was rife. Peaceful life was a bore.

"And how many rations did you earn when we were on the streets?" His sister pointed her finger. "Your thieving wasn't too profitable."

Julius raised an eyebrow and smirked. "Sulla was a thief? Wait until everyone hears that a commander in the Militia was a pickpocket. Ha!"

"Best not to mention that in company, sis," Sulla muttered. He stood and walked past her to grab a cup of firewater. "I did my best." Pity it wasn't enough to spare her toil.

"Don't call me 'sis'." With only a frown, Flora relayed all their previous arguments. But just because they weren't related by blood didn't mean she wasn't family.

"Sounds like you'd have been better off whoring yourself out too, Sulla." Julius laughed. "Why not do that now and earn your keep?"

"Who said I don't?" Sulla shot back. "Last night, in fact. Just ask your sister."

"Ha!" Julius clapped his hands. "I don't have a sister."

Sulla held up his cup and grinned. "You will in nine months."

Flora snorted and spat out the firewater she'd been drinking.

Julius rolled his eyes and murmured under his breath. "I don't know how a poseur like you managed to rob anyone."

"Do you want me to thump you?" Sulla said. "I could give you a few more dimples on those cheeks."

His sister grabbed a rag and wiped the drink from her chin. "Oh, stop fighting. I think I preferred it when the Red Militia and Black Legion were away at battle, and I didn't have to put up with your childishness. Will you be leaving any time soon?"

"Who knows?" Sulla shrugged. "The humans are too busy squabbling amongst themselves to take us on in battle, and the Viridians keep the west busy while the other cities stick to their ambush tactics here in the south."

"Really?" Flora frowned, brushing her hair behind her ear. "We hear nothing of what's happening in the human cities. I thought they were all part of the Empire, not fighting each other."

Sulla chuckled. "They may be called the Torian Empire, but as far as I've heard, the regents of each city have no more love for each other than the warlords of the rakkan cities do. We're not in outright war amongst our race, so long as we share a common enemy. The humans are busying themselves selling off their daughters to gain allies. There's so much intermarrying those regents must all be inbred by now."

Julius scoffed. "Most of those daughters are adopted."

"Ignore him. Take it from me, by the cross-eyed look of some of those regents, they're inbred."

"At least humans are united under an empire with a king," Flora said. "People must like that. The King bonds them."

"Ha," Julius scoffed. "The King rules through fear and apathy, not popularity. As long as the cities pay their taxes and keep his army bolstered, he leaves them alone."

"But he forces the cities to work together." Flora bit on her lip, furrowing her brow in thought. "Maybe *we* could use a king to straighten out those Viridians."

Sulla nearly spat out his own drink. "Nonsense. Rakkans have survived so far without one."

Julius leaned over and took the clay bottle of firewater from beside Flora. "Aren't the rakkans that took the Blades and became overlords the same thing?"

"No. Rakkan overlords never demanded taxes or made laws. They took up the Blades and led in battle."

"So what? Isn't commanding the legion of every rakkan city enough to call them kings? Five legions, just imagine…"

Sulla dipped his head. "Four, now. The King had Archimedes raze Gerunda, remember?" Rakkan scribes had never recorded such a mass slaughter in their lengthy history.

Julius took a long look at his drink, then set it down by his feet. "It's too easy to forget."

An awkward silence of the kind Sulla loathed threatened to follow, so he broke it with the first thought he had. "Good thing that goman is dead, or it might have been two or three cities razed by now."

"I hear Laltos is doing their best to destroy Viridia and leave only three legions," Julius replied. "Good luck to them, I say."

Sulla scoffed. "More like Hadrian is doing his best to destroy Laltos. Lex says they're getting no help from the King, so she's trying to ally with other human cities. So much for the King bonding them…"

"That's what she's up to? Too smart for comfort that woman if you ask me."

Sulla muttered under his breath, "Even a potato is too smart to make you comfortable."

The three continued drinking together and Sulla lingered as long as he could, despite the occasional dirty look from Julius. As the hours went by, they downed enough to suffer the next day, until they were disturbed by a knock at the door.

Sulla opened it with a loud greeting, ready to offer a deep drink to the visitor, but the smile fell from his face as he was confronted by a rakkan wearing a long apron with fresh blood soaked through.

"Yes?" Sulla asked.

The man sighed. "You need to come with me."

5

Sulla – Margalvia

After a brisk run across the city, Sulla's vision was soon filled with hacked and haemorrhaging bodies as he burst into the largest room of the garrison. It spanned more yards than he could count and was open except for the odd stone pillar that held up the high ceiling. Rows and rows of straw beds had been hurriedly laid out in a manner they did only following a battle.

Surgeons, or "butchers" as Sulla liked to call them, scurried around with saws and knives, seeing to the dozens of beds occupied with warriors that clutched their bleeding wounds and howled. It seemed like there was a mix of Black Legionnaires, Red Militia and even…miners? The grime and dust covering the skin of most made him suspect they'd come from one place—the Urukan Mine.

Those not severely wounded were left to sit or lie on any floor space they found while wrapping bandages over their lacerations cut straight and clean. *What in hell happened?* A cave-in wouldn't slice men open like this. The heat and humidity in the room sent beads of sweat down his temple.

"Where's the Militia Chief?" Sulla asked a carer running past.

"At the back," she replied over her shoulder as she scurried.

Sulla pushed through the bodies. *Please don't be laid bleeding on a bed.* Although ranking below the Warlord, there wasn't a rakkan in Margalvia Sulla trusted more than his chief.

He finally spotted the rakkan at the back of the room near the corner, lying as he'd feared and looking so pale it was as if he had only a pint of blood left in him.

Stood by his head, a cleric chanted messages to the Creator in a long-dead tongue that few still uttered, and none knew the literal meaning of. Blood stained the man's usual plain white robes, but Sulla didn't let it stop him, nudging the man away as he came and stood beside the bed. *He's not dying on my watch.*

The cleric grunted but went back to chanting while a carer arrived and laid a hand on the Chief's sweaty brow. Even without touching, Sulla could tell the rakkan ran a fever, and judging by the stench from the bloody sheet covering his legs, rot had set in.

The Chief's gaunt, sunken eyes held nothing of the fire and steely grit they once had.

"Sulla?" the rakkan croaked.

Sulla grabbed his hand and brushed aside the damp, brown fringe falling into his eyes. "Claudius. What happened?"

"The Viridians, they came through our tunnels from deep in the mine, started slaughtering everyone and caving in our entrances."

Sulla frowned, struggling to think of reasons the Viridian Legion would do such a thing. As deplorable as they were, even they hadn't violated the Urukan Treaty set up decades ago to ensure an uneasy peace in the world's one source of kuraminium. "Why would they do this?"

The Militia Chief coughed weakly, trying to clear his throat a few times. "They were roaring things like 'death to the traitor' and 'vengeance is ours' as they cut us down."

It made little sense to Sulla, but then he wasn't the sharpest rakkan. "Why call us traitors?"

"They mentioned a name." The Chief's voice weakened to a rasp. "The Dreaded One."

No… Few others besides Sulla knew that Viridian moniker. He whirled around, casting his eyes across the beleaguered warriors and miners biting down on folds of cloth to bear the pain. Only then did he realise how many weren't here and were likely dead. *It can't be Darius's fault.* "How many of our tunnels are still open?"

"None," the Chief said, voice now so faint Sulla had to lean in to hear him above the shrill cries of a rakkan in the bed next to him.

This couldn't be happening… How would they arm themselves or make goods to trade without a source of kuraminium? What did the Viridians blame Darius for that warranted *this* affront?

With a fit of coughs, the Militia Chief's head slumped to the side, like every breath required effort.

A surgeon walked by, and Sulla grabbed his arm, pulling him to one side and out of earshot. "You need to help Claudius. He's growing weaker by the second."

The surgeon looked over. "I'm sorry, but I think he already has one foot in the afterlife."

"No!" Sulla squeezed the surgeon's arm tighter. "You need to do something now!"

But the surgeon yanked himself free with a grimace. "These wounds are a day old and badly infected. Even if I cut off his limbs, the rot has spread."

Damn him. Legend said rakkans had once been immune to infection, that ferven killed the rot as it took hold. Why not now? Why was the rot not killed by the fire? *What can I do?*

Sulla turned, ignited his hand with ferven and punched a hole into the wall. His hand shook, and his breathing became shallow and fast. Despite the shouts and cries of pain filling the room, those around paused and stared at him, the familiar faces the ones most shocked at his outburst.

"Sulla," the Chief called.

"Yes?" He turned back to the rakkan and knelt beside him.

"I know I don't have long—"

"Don't talk like that." Sulla grimaced, but as he looked into his friend's dark eyes, he saw an unexpected peace and calm that he couldn't share. Whether or not he liked it, Claudius was succumbing. Sulla turned and pulled the cleric back to the Chief's bedside. Those prayers were necessary.

"Don't blame him," Claudius said.

"Who?" Sulla suspected he knew the answer to the question, but clarity mattered.

"Your friend. Whatever he did, it doesn't excuse this treachery."

True. But it didn't make the truth any less sour.

"Before I..." the Chief said feebly. "This is important. I want you...Chicf...Red Militia."

A few of the rakkans around exchanged glances at the Militia Chief's words. If they hadn't, Sulla would have sworn he misheard.

He scoffed, shook his head, and fumbled for words. "Me? Chief? I'm just a warrior. You do the thinking and I charge in. I know little of tactics." He'd be half the leader Claudius was and wouldn't take too kindly to taking orders directly from Warlord Varro. "I'm not worthy of the rank. Find someone else."

The Chief smiled. "You're a commander, not a warrior. I've chosen."

Taking one of the rakkan's hands, Sulla gasped at the hot skin. It took restraint not to punch more holes in the wall and instead put on a smile for his friend. How could he deny a dying man his last order?

He leaned down and whispered, "I always knew your judgement was lousy."

The Chief laughed weakly. "You'll do…well."

Sulla sighed and squeezed Claudius's hand.

The Chief's mouth curled slightly as he exhaled, shoulders relaxed, and his grip loosened. "Good. Now, go…don't watch me die. It'll be ugly."

As proud as ever. Sulla considered whether to ignore the order, but again he couldn't deny his friend's wishes. So he leaned across and kissed the Chief's forehead for the last time, curses screaming through his mind while his lips tasted the salty fever stealing his friend.

"You." Sulla caught the cleric's eye. "Speak louder. Make sure the Creator hears you and guides him to the afterlife."

The cleric gave a nod of respect that Sulla probably didn't deserve then went back to his chanting.

Meanwhile, Sulla turned and strode out of the room, blocking out the screams. What the hell had Darius done to warrant this?

Sulla needed to speak with Warlord Varro. Their retaliation had to be swift and forceful, because nothing else would give the Viridian Legion what they deserved. Margalvia had to be merciless.

6

Sulla – Margalvia

Sulla cracked open the door of the commanders' room and peered inside. A few bright specks broke the darkness, from clay oil lamps along the wall between hanging black banners. Two rakkans stood muttering in the shadows at the far side, and only when they turned did he recognise the Warlord and Brutus. *Finally.*

Both had stern faces with the same tension that gripped Sulla's innards. It was fortunate for him that Varro was with his older brother, as Brutus had always been a good mediator. Sulla and Varro's discussions of late often turned into arguments—that's why Sulla held a sword in his hand.

"Sorry to interrupt your brotherly bonding," Sulla said.

Varro turned his head towards Sulla and brushed the hair out of his eyes. "Sulla, come in."

"I assume you've heard," Sulla replied, marching in. The two brothers stood to the side of the circular stone table that dominated the heart of the chamber. Varro wore a tight leather tunic while Brutus was wrapped in a cloak as black as the darkened corners of the room. Despite being the oldest, Brutus was a foot shorter and had thick stubble across his head and chin in contrast to the blond-haired, clean-shaven warlord.

"Any news on Claudius?" the Warlord asked.

Sulla grimaced. "As good as dead."

Brutus murmured and took a seat at the dimly lit table. "We need to get the commanders and weigh our options."

"Claudius named me Chief of the Red Militia," Sulla said firmly. "Our next move should be between me and you, Varro. We don't rule by committee."

"*We* rule nothing." Varro narrowed his eyes. "I do. But I also listen to my subordinates."

Who always disagree, so nothing gets done. "Then listen to this," Sulla said in a hushed tone. "I say we retaliate within the day, dig our way back into the mine and cave in *their* tunnels."

Brutus cleared his throat and traced his fingers through the carvings on the table. "Let's not be rash. We don't even know why they've dared to break the Treaty. Open war is a big step, even for Hadrian."

"Does he need a reason?" Sulla pulled out a chair and sat down, resting his face in his hands. "He's a crazed despot that only responds to a show of force."

"I'm with Brutus." Varro began pacing around the table. "I refuse to send the Black Legion to battle, leaving us vulnerable to the King attacking."

Yet again, only Sulla saw what needed to be done. "Don't tell me you've been talking more with our prisoner."

"He's an algus, isn't he? He has valuable insights."

"You can't trust a word he says. The King hasn't attempted an attack since Archimedes fell. Viridia is our biggest threat. How

52

do we arm ourselves for a war without the mine? How do we eat when we have no weapons to trade Lex for food? Our last farms have dried out from this damned summer."

"Varro's right," Brutus said, with a solemn look of apology. "The King is the kind to bide his time until an opportunity presents itself. One of our legionnaires claims to have seen his algus nearby just a few weeks ago."

"The King wouldn't dare attack Margalvia," Sulla said. "Without the Staff of Arria, he couldn't win a battle against the Black Legion."

"He could if we're off fighting Hadrian."

Sulla scowled. "We can't afford to be timid."

"This isn't—" Brutus was interrupted as the door crashed open, and in stormed Darius wearing only a bloody, filthy tunic, boots and scabbard. Just the sight made Sulla's body tense, as if he didn't know whether he wanted to see and speak to the man or not. *Is it true?*

Darius strode up to the Warlord and grunted. "I've just returned, and they said I had to report to you immediately."

"Yesterday." Varro looked him up and down with a frown. "What happened to you?"

Darius's fists were clenched so tightly his knuckles were white. "Can this wait?" He looked back at the door.

"Careful of your tone with your warlord," Brutus said, his voice more concerned for the man than threatening.

"What's wrong, Darius?" Sulla asked with trepidation. Perhaps there was a reasonable explanation for it all.

But Darius didn't answer, just paced around to the other side of the table.

"Where have you been?" Varro's voice dropped low.

Darius shook his head. Was that a tear in his eye? "She's been wounded," he whispered. "The surgeons are stitching her up as best they can."

"Alexandra?" Varro asked, a rare hint of fear in his voice.

"No. Lyra."

How dire. The last time Lyra was injured, Sulla hadn't seen Darius leave her side for a week. She'd been one of the few keeping him from becoming an amoral monster when Archimedes altered his mind. Yet the fact made Sulla all the wearier that his chief had been right.

Brutus stood and placed a meaty hand on the half-rakkan's shoulder. "By the Creator, what happened, son?"

"I…" Darius took a deep, shaky breath.

"You what?" Varro asked with a twitch of his eye that Sulla spotted. The Warlord was always calm and patient…until he wasn't.

Darius shook his head.

Giving the man a few moments to compose himself, Varro steepled his fingers and looked down at the table, where the web of engravings on its surface laid out a map of Margalvia and its surroundings. "Double the scouts in the north. I want warning if the King intends to strike. As for Hadrian and the mine, I want more knowledge of what his plans are. We'll send a spy to infiltrate the Viridian Legion."

Darius frowned and took a step closer to the table. "What do you mean, 'Hadrian and the mine'?"

"He attacked our designated tunnels," Brutus explained.

"Killed our warriors and miners stationed there," Sulla added, "including the Militia Chief." His voice almost broke as he studied Darius for any reaction to the words.

Darius fidgeted, scratched at his tunic, then his stubbled chin before stepping back and turning away from them all. The room froze in silence, so still Sulla felt Darius's heavy breaths. The man leant against the wall and grimaced as if he'd heard his own family had been killed.

Taking a step back, Sulla looked away and clenched his shaking fists. *He did something.*

Meanwhile, Brutus lit a pipe with the tip of his finger and began puffing smoke while his eyes trained on Darius without blinking. "Come along, lad. Spit it out, whatever it is."

Darius gave a lengthy sigh that sounded more like a groan by the end. "I…locked horns with the Viridians."

The curse from Brutus was only half as foul as the steely glower of Varro, or the curses in Sulla's mind.

"I gave you specific instructions," Varro said.

"I know," Darius said. "But they attacked me first. I had no choice but to fight."

"You couldn't have run?"

"I…could have." Darius lowered his head.

"Your instructions were clear on what to do if you were discovered. You must have killed countless men for them to construe it as an act of war."

"They deserved death. You weren't there; you didn't see the depravity…"

"I'm sure I've seen worse in over a century as a warrior," Varro said. "But go ahead, enlighten me."

Darius paused and looked at them all in turn. "I did what you asked. I gathered their locations and numbers."

Sulla couldn't stay mute any longer. "We didn't ask you to fight them. We didn't ask you to invite them to begin open war with us!" He took a step towards the man, fists still clenched, but then stopped a few feet away, remembering the mercy the old Darius had once shown him when he'd been guilty of far worse.

"Tell us everything that happened," Brutus said softly, the disappointment plain on his face.

"One moment I was hidden," Darius began, "the next, they ambushed me." Darius went on to relay his version of the events that had transpired, including the sights he'd witnessed before. Tales of Viridian depravity were nothing new to them all, but Sulla and Brutus still winced at the details that Darius focused on so intently.

"I would have killed them all," Darius said. "Viridia would be none the wiser if Hadrian hadn't come."

"But he did," Varro uttered, "and you should have fled. You disobeyed me."

"Come, brother," Brutus said. "The lad didn't intend for war."

"It doesn't matter. His actions led to it, and *cannot* go unpunished." Varro's flat words brought a finality to the conversation for now, and his gaze returned to the markings in the table. It was a paralysed state that Sulla had seen one too many times, and he suddenly remembered his reason for being there. Darius's misdeeds could wait.

"I say we should be aggressive." Sulla's voice rose. "We need the mine, the kuraminium."

"We've enough to trade with Alexandra for now," Varro said. "I'm sure she'll take a promissory note if need be."

"I'd rather not be Lex's lapdog."

"Watch your tone," Brutus said, as Varro glared.

"I've given my orders," the Warlord said. "This is no longer a discussion."

Sulla stood and pushed back his chair so hard it toppled over. "Wouldn't want to risk growing a pair of balls, would we?"

Brutus choked, coughing up a cloud of smoke. "Sulla!"

"I want the Viridians dead," Sulla continued. "I don't want information. I want my sword soaked with their blood. I want to hear their screams. I want them to rue the day. Damn it, Varro, why aren't you angrier?"

Varro's stare darkened, cold and unrelenting in a way Sulla had only seen before on the battlefield. When he finally spoke, the Warlord's tone was quiet and low, yet so threatening he may as well have had his swords drawn. "Insult me again…"

It took all Sulla's restraint not to open his big mouth. A sword to the gut didn't faze him, but being foolish would achieve nothing.

Varro shot up from his seat, body so tense his tunic stretched at the seams. "You think I don't want to strangle Hadrian with my bare hands? Take it from me, this betrayal won't go unpunished, and neither will *your* actions." His furious gaze shifted to Darius. "This city has already forgiven you once. Do you think they will a second time? I won't help you escape the noose again."

If the fear in Darius's eyes was anything to go by, he doubted he'd be forgiven, and Sulla wasn't sure either.

"Our enemy is Hadrian," Brutus interrupted, stepping around the table, between Darius and the Warlord. "We should direct our hate towards him."

"Don't think mine isn't." Varro straightened his back, flared his nostrils in disgust. "The swine will pay."

All Sulla wanted was justice, retribution for Hadrian. Otherwise, all he could do was mourn, the sad thoughts circling his mind endlessly as he lay idle.

Action was far preferable, and Sulla wouldn't labour the point. He knew to leave now before stretching Varro's patience. But before doing so, he looked over to Darius, who had sunk to the floor with his head buried in his hands.

"How many are dead?" Darius asked in a muffled voice.

"At least a hundred legionnaires," Sulla said. "More miners."

Darius clasped his head tighter.

Sulla wanted to console the man, but his anger was only rising by the second. "Just remember, Varro, if you hang him, you're killing our best assassin." That was as far as Sulla could get to standing up for the man at the moment. "Now, if you'll excuse me, I'm going to check on my men."

Varro gave him a last glare before turning away.

With a nod to Brutus, Sulla turned and left, the frustration he'd expected to leave with now predictably right at the surface.

At least Varro was sending spies. *It's a start.* How Sulla would persuade the Warlord to launch a full-on assault, he didn't know. Yet.

7

Darius – Margalvia

Darius stumbled. His knee hit the ground and splashed into the inches of blood he'd stepped through—a training pool twenty feet long. *Keep going.* He had to beat this weakness.

Pig's blood stank no different to a human's, just like that of all those he cared about that had needlessly fallen because he was too weak to save them. And now more were dead because of his mistakes. The disgusting, cold fluid seeped into his trousers.

He swallowed. It wouldn't beat him. He pictured Hadrian, summoning anger to fuel him on.

"Push yourself, Darius," Brutus urged, watching along with Julius. The pair stood shirtless, built with thickset muscles yet opposite in almost every other way. Brutus had short hair over his head, chin and neck while Julius was clean shaven with thick tufts on his scalp which swayed in the wind.

A few yards away, Sulla sat with folded arms and a furrowed brow, watching Darius's every move like each one concerned him more than the last.

Behind the three rakkans, the rock-strewn mountains that Darius had once looked at in awe now seemed barren and distant. High on the plateau, where the clouds touched, was the best place to train, the only spot Darius would do his desensitisation training. Located just outside Margalvia, the only unfamiliar face watching and judging his weaknesses was that of the full moon.

He stood again and trudged, the wet soaking his bare feet and making him shudder. The last blood he'd seen was Lyra's, along with all the butchered corpses the Viridian Legion left. All those months he'd spent caring more and more about others, and now he wished he could turn it off again. So much anger, so much hurt.

His mind wandered to his baby brother again, the sight of the red filling his vision. Legs trembling, light-headedness overcame him, and he collapsed onto all fours, splattering blood over his torso.

Brutus grabbed his arm, pulled him out of the pit and onto the rocky surroundings that felt more bearable despite the jagged stones that dug into him.

"You've got worse," Julius said with a hint of a grin. "You'll be no use on the field of battle in this state."

Darius wished even more than usual that Varro hadn't asked Margalvia's most insufferable commander to train him.

"Don't you need to shave your chest again?" Darius asked, casting his gaze across the rakkan's flaunted muscles. "If you're not careful, you'll end up looking like a man."

Julius clicked his tongue. "Get back in your bloodbath, baby."

Perhaps the constant jibes at Julius's physique hadn't done Darius any favours in forming a mutual bond, but, given the commander's vanity, the temptation was always too great to resist.

Darius ripped off his bloody clothes, tearing his tunic, and threw them into a pile until he was left in just his underwear. "I don't care about battle." He worked best as an assassin.

"You should," Brutus said. "I raised you to be a warrior, and that you were."

Darius cursed. Even though the blood was one of many regular trials in his training, the new daily regimen was his first punishment, and more would follow. Still, he wanted to conquer this fear more than anything. "I don't understand. Why am I worse than when we started?" What had happened to all the progress in the last few months? Circling around his head for the hundredth time that day were the events with Hadrian, the feeling of the dagger sinking into his escort, the foolish decision he'd made in taking on those Viridians, as if going behind his friends' backs was ever a wise move. He'd already heard a few hiss "traitor" in the streets to him. *Thought I was past that.*

Brutus sauntered over to him, picking up a cleaning rag from the pile of training supplies nearby. He offered it out. "Do you think this has anything to do with Lyra?"

Darius waved away the cloth and gritted his teeth. "Why? She's still alive." *But for how long?* He drove the thought to the back of his mind. The reasons for his hatred of blood were irrelevant. All that mattered was conquering it, and that required repeated exposure. "Again."

"Wait," Julius said. "Varro's coming."

Sure enough, a solitary Varro walked up the mountainside path towards them, dressed in his usual understated, sleeveless tunic with swords hanging from his waist. It looked like training was over, and hopefully he wasn't coming to give Darius a death sentence.

As the Warlord approached, Darius grabbed a cloth and began wiping every trace of blood from his body.

Sulla stepped forward and helped him with his back, though roughly enough Darius suspected he meant to cause a little soreness.

"You should take it easy, Dar," Sulla said. "Stay with Lyra until you're more clear-headed."

Where I can't drag us into any more wars, he means. "I can't be with Lyra all day. The anger festers inside me." And the guilt.

The scars on Sulla's forehead deepened with his frown and he stepped away, tossing the bloody rag aside. "I know the feeling."

Varro arrived, and the four of them bowed their heads. "I've been speaking with Alexandra," he said.

"She's here?" Darius couldn't help but feel annoyed Lex hadn't bothered to come and see him. Did she know about Lyra?

"Yes. We've been completing the latest trade and had a brief discussion about Hadrian. Now she's visiting Lyra in your quarters."

The panther would like that. It didn't shock Darius that she prioritised her scheming over him and his panther, though. "So, what's your plan, Warlord? Kill Hadrian?"

"Not quite. Alexandra has proposed to unite the Red Militia and Black Legion with the Laltos Guard to attack the Viridians."

"You've agreed to an alliance with Laltos?" Julius gasped.

Varro looked out across the jagged mountains, behind whose peaks stood the thick-walled city of Viridia. "That's what I've told her."

The evasion of a "yes" made Darius suspect he was about to get caught in more webs of lies.

"But," Varro continued, "I don't entirely trust her. Usually, she does everything to avoid talking with me. I sensed she was keeping something from me."

You have no idea.

"Lex, keeping secrets?" Sulla gasped sarcastically. "Next you'll tell me ferven is hot."

A sinking feeling started in Darius's stomach, this time unrelated to blood.

"Lex wouldn't betray us," Brutus said with a wave of his hand. "She's reticent, yes, but she'd never do anything to harm us. I know everyone else is enamoured with her, but if she ever brought harm to you or Darius, I'd crack her skull. And she knows it."

Darius pressed his lips together, the unease turning into a stone in his belly. *Glad I never mentioned her whisperings in my ear.*

"She's calling it the First Alliance," Varro said flatly, giving no clue of his feelings on the idea. "To secure Laltos's blessing, we need to convince the Regent, and she knows the way to win over her father."

"It'd be much faster to kill Hadrian," Darius said.

Julius nodded. "Maybe there's a reason a rakkan and human city have never allied before."

"I don't see how we can get to Hadrian," Brutus said.

"I was an assassin, wasn't I?" Darius replied, trying to keep his voice sounding indifferent to the task when really, it was all he'd dwelled on for days.

"No," Varro said. "You can't do it."

"Says who?"

"Me. You can't beat him and all his guards."

Darius looked each of the three rakkans in the eye to find every one of their doubt-filled faces showing they were of the same mind, even Brutus.

"I have algus speed and rakkan strength," Darius said.

Varro raised an eyebrow. "You can fight, assuming there isn't too much blood involved. Hadrian obviously knows of your weakness."

Darius straightened his back and frowned. "A weakness I won't rest until I conquer. This blood-pit isn't for revitalising my skin. Soon I'll tolerate even a large-scale battle."

"Prove it." Varro drew a sword from his scabbard. "Score a hit on me, and I'll send you to Viridia tomorrow."

Darius's frown deepened while Brutus and Julius exchanged wary glances. Sulla's eyes widened and blinked a few times. Varro had never sparred with Darius before yet showed more confidence than Darius assumed was merited.

"You never make wagers," Darius said, searching Varro's expression for clues to his motives, but the Warlord's face was as plain as his unblemished skin.

Varro ran a hand through his blond hair and slicked it back. "Correction: I never make a wager I can lose."

"I have no armour."

"My sword won't need to touch you for you to know I've won."

"I presume I get a weapon."

With a nod, Varro motioned his approval for Julius to hand Darius his sword. The kuraminium spatha was longer than the short and agile gladius he was most comfortable with, but Julius had trained him to exhaustion in both.

"There is one thing." Varro walked over to the pool of blood. "I don't think you'll ever vanquish your fear. So let's assume Hadrian will take full advantage." He submerged his sword until even the hilt was coated red, then withdrew the dripping metal.

"It's not a fear. I just hate it." Darius raised his spatha, trying in vain to not focus on the dribbles of red.

Varro stepped forward, the intensity in his eyes bearing a striking resemblance to those of Lyra on the hunt. Then the Warlord raised his sword with a flick.

Specks of blood splattered onto Darius's face. He grimaced but made no move to wipe it clean and instead raised his spatha until their blades touched. *Push through it.*

The three watching rakkans fidgeted and folded their arms, a glint of eager anticipation in their eyes as if they'd waited decades to see this.

Despite Darius's will, he couldn't stop focusing on the blood.

Without a tell to give away an attack, Varro suddenly lunged forward, stabbing at Darius's chest and sending a splatter of red forwards. Darius dodged to the side, shocked when the blade skimmed him and narrowly missed the skin.

Giving Darius no time to reel, Varro slashed the blade across and forced him to bring the spatha up to block.

The blow sent more splatters on his torso, so Darius flared ferven, burning the liquid away, and summoned his algus speed before unleashing a flurry of strikes aimed at the Warlord's midriff. Slash after slash that would have landed on any other rakkan were dodged, blocked, and parried by Varro, before Darius stepped back with a grimace.

I'm slower than usual. Despite his flaming body, he couldn't take his eyes from the blood dripping down Varro's sword, the thought of it touching his skin again sending a shiver down him.

Varro's eyes narrowed at the sight.

The only thing that would get rid of the blood was if Varro conjured ferven on the sword.

So, summoning calm, Darius sent a thin film of algor sliding from his hand an inch at a time until it coated the spatha. If Varro wanted to block it, he'd have no choice but to flare ferven.

Darius waited.

But the Warlord merely stared, motionless. His cold, black eyes watched with the same predator intensity, but his weapon remained cold and red.

Looks like I'll have to force it. Darius drew his sword back and lunged forward.

In response, Varro flicked his sword, splattering more blood towards Darius's face.

He blinked.

When he opened his eyes, Varro had already dodged to the side, allowing Darius's spatha to slice through the air. The Warlord then thrust his sword until the point came within an inch of Darius's neck and stopped dead before landing a mortal wound.

The pair froze. Varro's sword dripped onto Darius's shoulder.

Damn. Darius flung the spatha to the ground and stomped away, wiping his skin frantically. Varro was right. Darius was in no shape to battle at the moment.

Julius snorted a laugh, but Varro silenced him with a glare.

"This isn't funny," the Warlord said. "His failure is yours, sword-master. Margalvians defend their brothers."

Julius looked to the ground, failure weighing heavy on his head.

All Darius had wanted since Lyra's incident was to return and kill Hadrian, but that now struck him as unwise. "So, what now? Am I to serve my punishment?"

"Alexandra has requested your help to convince her father," Varro said. "You're to go to Laltos. She'll explain the rest to you."

Darius groaned. Laltos and the western front was where all this had begun, and, despite his eagerness to evade the noose, Laltos was too far away from his injured escort for comfort. Plus, the last time he'd been in the city they'd tried to kill him.

"I can't leave Lyra yet," he said. "The surgeon said it's half and half whether she'll survi…" He tried desperately not to imagine her lifeless body.

Brutus stepped forward and put a hand on Darius's shoulder. "Surely, it's best for him to get his head together first, Varro?"

"We'll take care of Lyra," Sulla said with a forced grin.

"We don't have the luxury of time," Varro said.

"I guess it's best for Darius to be out of Margalvia for a while," Brutus muttered.

"And what if Lyra doesn't recover?" Darius asked, the thought already bringing an exhausting sadness to the surface. He couldn't be away if she…

"I won't lie," Varro said, "it's possible. But your city needs you. You can't do anything for her that our carers can't. Look how readily you'd leave if I sent you to kill Hadrian."

Darius shook his head, feeling torn between too many needs and wants. He wanted to sit by Lyra's side. He wanted to kill Hadrian. He wanted to kill anyone at this point. What he didn't want was to be ordered away from them all.

"Think of it like this," Varro said. "If we join forces with Laltos against Viridia, I'll face Hadrian on the battlefield myself. I'll end the brute."

Darius paused, ashamed at the hint of pleasure he felt at the words. Was this his best chance to avenge Lyra, to end the war?

"Will I stand with you?" Darius asked. "Or am I to get the noose?"

"I haven't decided. For now, your orders are to leave with Alexandra for Laltos."

Darius looked to Brutus, seeking his mentor's opinion, and received a consoling nod in reply. Sulla's lips were pressed together tightly, unusually holding back whatever he wanted to say, but disapproval was clear on his lowered face, regardless.

Mulling the order, Darius gazed at the dark sky. Perhaps Laltos was the best place to be until his fate was decided. If any of them discovered that he'd bent the truth over who attacked whom first in his encounter with the Viridians, he didn't really want to be around until they'd cooled off.

It would be much easier to go unnoticed in Laltos than last time, now the humans weren't actively hunting him. He could even help them stem the invasion and be useful for once.

His warlord was right about one thing. Every time Darius visited Lyra, he felt the sting of powerlessness. The connection they had would stretch over any distance, and in that sense, he was always with her. Although his place in the Black Legion now felt insignificant compared to Lyra's life, he owed them loyalty.

With a sigh, he bowed. "Yes, Warlord."

8

Lex – Margalvia

How can I break the news to Darius after this? Lex knelt on the corner of the thin rug that lay between Lyra's body and the cold stone floor. A tiny flame from the lamp in her hand was the only source of light in the room. Usually, she hated the darkness the rakkans survived in, but this time she was glad the shadows spared her a clear view of Lyra. A wounded animal tugged at the heart.

A trace of warmth lingered in the air for now, not enough for Lex, but enough for Lyra without the risk of her overheating. In front of the empty hearth was a woollen rug where a man could lie outstretched without touching the black stone walls. Judging by the deep folds and wrinkles, someone had laid or slept there for days. *Darius, you sensitive soul.*

Lex hadn't felt the cat yet, but given they'd placed her in a cool room with a draughty chimney, it was likely she was running a fever. For now, she slept, her only movement the deep breaths that stretched the stained bandages around her abdomen.

From the little the rakkans had told Lex, Darius's part in this was known, and her pleas to him seemed to have worked. But she didn't take any pleasure from the fact. *Another one hurt because of me.*

She reached out and wrapped her hand around Lyra's paw. Hot, as she'd expected. "I'm sorry, girl." Her own peregrine escort had been injured a few times, but not so badly. Darius must have been so worried. If she'd known it would have ended like this, she'd never have asked him to help her. And to think she'd come to Margalvia hoping it was the right time to break grave news to him…

She placed the lamp down on the floor and lay next to Lyra, so they were nose to nose, glad her leather tunic saved her from the cold emanating from the stone underneath. As she stroked the fur on Lyra's front paw, the panther fidgeted but seemed to relax after a few seconds. Lex hoped her presence helped, though she suspected it wouldn't help as far as Darius was concerned.

He'd blame her. Perhaps she deserved it. Yet, underlying it all was the fact that his affection for her often led to frustration and anger. But what more could she do about that? She'd told him, as hard as it was, not to hold out for her. Maybe her painful news would finally crush his hopes. Marriage to another man would end his interest.

The hard stone pained her hipbone, and she shifted her weight with a curse. It didn't relent and instead spread to the familiar chronic stabbing pain. Once started, it rarely went away, the constant reminder of losing a loved one.

She went back to stroking Lyra's fur, letting the soft touch distract her. "How do you think Darius will take the news?" she whispered. "I hope you'll stay and take care of him for me. He needs you, Lyra. Don't leave him now."

The panther fidgeted again but remained unconscious.

Lex's thoughts drifted from Darius to the man she'd arranged to marry—Aristippus, or the "Silk Regent" as he was known. *Why did that reprobate have to ask to marry* me *and not one of my sisters?*

Unfortunately, she had no other offers to choose from. Many failed attempts to secure alliances with other human cities had left her with only marriage as an option if Laltos was to survive the war. None of the spineless regents of the cities in the Empire were prepared to have a thought independent of their king unless there was something in it for their…manhood. The King seemed happy to allow Laltos to burn, so what else could she do? For the thousandth time that question lingered in her mind, but still no answer came.

The thought of the Silk Regent's hands on her sent a shiver through her. She sighed and wrapped her arm around Lyra's fevered body. As much as she longed for a man like Darius as her husband, she knew the price of real love wasn't worth paying. When you treasured them, the pain was too great when they cheated, left, or died.

The thought took her back to a time she'd tried hard to forget, when at only eighteen her husband had laid succumbing to his mortal wounds.

She pulled her arm away and rolled onto her back. Her breaths became sharp. Cold stone below sent chills through her. When they'd found him, the burns had left his face so horrifying it would never leave her mind. He'd had no skin left to even blink.

No one knew how many rakkans it had taken to break through his algor, but they had. His throat was so badly damaged he could barely speak, but she still remembered the deep, raspy voice he'd used to repeatedly call out "Alexandra." Her algor had spared him some pain before death. Nothing had spared her own, not even slaughtering every Viridian warrior she crossed paths with in the days since.

As she relived her ordeal, the latch on the door snapped up.

She bolted upright, blinking her eyes and praying the tears didn't show.

When the door swung open and Darius entered, he jerked to a stop. "Oh. Sorry, I didn't realise you were still here." His voice was hushed, and his gaze went straight to Lyra. "How is she?"

"I don't know." Lex shifted out of his way and leaned back against the wall. "It looks as if her bandages need changing."

"I'll find some clean ones." Darius knelt beside his escort and stroked her head.

"Stay with her. Get a slave to do it."

Darius turned his head with a sullen look. "We don't have slaves in Margalvia."

"Right…I meant servant." Indentured servitude wasn't too far removed from slavery as far as she could see, the only difference being the servants were freed after a decade whether or not their debts to their masters were paid.

With a grunt, Darius returned to giving Lyra all his attention. "What brings you to Margalvia this time? Trading? Seeing my grandfather again?"

He never realised she was here to see him. Meeting others hadn't been her motivation for coming, but while she was here, she'd planned to see his grandfather to check on her daughter again. Not that she'd let Darius in on the secret. Watching your son die made a parent protective of the one child they had left, and she saw nothing wrong with that.

"I also came to see you," she whispered, "if you can believe that."

He grunted, much like the guarded Darius she knew and loved before. "Wanted to check I'd done what you kept pushing me to do?"

"I didn't push you. I asked you."

"You convinced me, manipulated me." His voice rose.

"I *never…*" She trailed off as he turned and glared with ferven swelling in his eyes, giving more light to the room. His short, dark hair was spotted with dried blood, and his beard was a little longer than the half-inch he'd kept it at recently.

"How are you?" she asked. "Are you eating?"

He scoffed. "Why? Ready to send me out to kill again?"

"I…" She dipped her head, feeling the anger rising in her but unwilling to vent it on an anguished man. The truth was she did have another request of him, whether or not she liked it. "I think it's best I give you some space. I don't want—"

"They all know I fought the Viridians." Darius looked up hesitantly. "But they don't know I started it. I'm still unsure how they'll punish me."

She gasped.

"I didn't mention your part in it." Darius turned back to his escort, clutching her paw.

"I…" Lex didn't know what to say. Was the war she wanted worth the pain it brought Darius and Lyra? After witnessing the rivers of blood, she couldn't answer.

Considerations passed through Lex's mind too fast to make sense of them. Surely, they wouldn't execute or banish Darius…

The two of them could flee, forgetting about alliances and revenge and living a life away from the conflict. It would ensure Darius was safe, but then she'd be giving up everything she'd worked towards in her adult life.

The image of her late husband's seared face returned at the mere thought of abandoning justice. She reached to her neck and grasped the pendant that always hung there, the axe-wielding God of Justice—the final executioner. *We can't let tyrants kill without retribution.* It went against every instinct in her.

Darius turned and frowned at her, his pupils wide and black in the dim light. "So? Nothing to say?"

"I won't let Varro kill you."

"You didn't see how angry they were, how many Margalvians died because of me." Darius scratched his head, not noticing the dry blood he hated falling from his fingernails. "If not killed, I'll be spat at, whipped and exiled. Not that it matters if Lyra doesn't pull through."

As much as she wanted to believe it wouldn't happen, once you lost the trust of a Margalvian, you never reclaimed it. "Don't fret." She placed a hand on his, but he snatched it away.

"How can I not?" He stared back at Lyra and became so still it looked like he'd stopped breathing. "If I'm to be exiled, or worse, there are things I need to do. Will you finally let me speak with my grandfather?"

Lex yearned to let him and get some connection to his former family, but there would be a time and place for a reunion—only when it was safe for her daughter. "Not yet. He sees the same need for secrecy, or he'd have found you himself. He always asks over you."

Darius scoffed. "Then I guess I'll die never knowing his face."

"They won't kill you. If Varro hasn't killed Nikolaos, then I'm sure he'll treat you more favourably." Their algus prisoner locked in the dungeons would have been tortured to death by now had he been in any other city, her own included. Yet not only had Varro let him live, but had fed and watered him, even conversed to glean insights into the Empire that Lex didn't have.

Lex had expected to have to plead with the Warlord to treat him mercifully.

"Nikolaos didn't drag Margalvia into a war…" Darius's voice softened as his eyes met hers again.

For a moment, she was lost for words. "If Varro is angry then lay the fault with me."

Darius exhaled and shook his head. "No. They won't respect a man that palms off the blame."

"Then what do you want me to do?"

"There's only one thing I want." His face darkened into a scowl. "Help me kill Hadrian."

"I'm not sure that will end the threat—"

"I don't care if it ends the war. I just want him *dead*."

It was as if the thought of running had never occurred to Darius, and suddenly she was ashamed for having contemplated it herself. She squeezed his hand. "Not just Hadrian. We'll destroy the entire Viridian Legion."

He paused, thoughts flickering behind those eyes which were all too easy to read—conflict. "All of them?"

"Have you seen any that didn't deserve death?"

After a few seconds thought, he shook his head. "Before last week, I'd thought I'd seen torment and anguish, yet what I saw in the eyes of those men, women and children won't leave my thoughts, even in slumber. The Viridians need to be stopped. But doesn't your God frown on revenge?"

She scowled. "This isn't revenge; it's retribution. The Goddess cries out for it." And even the God of Justice should take notice of his wife's plea.

Darius raised an eyebrow. "But does she cry out to *you*, or her husband, the God?"

Lex turned her head away, trying not to let her rising temper out again. Darius had a way of aggravating her when it came to her religion. "Do you want to show Hadrian justice or not?" she asked.

He murmured and put his hand on Lyra again. "I don't know if it's justice or right and wrong any more. I want revenge, for Lyra and all the others that have suffered at their hands."

She hadn't heard him speak like this for a long time. Her hip stabbed with pain again as she recalled the scoundrel Archimedes had turned him into, and how hard she'd worked to bring part of the old Darius back.

From the way he now talked, Lex wouldn't be surprised if he went straight after Hadrian, but to do so would be far too perilous. She'd been keeping eyes on the Warlord whenever she could, and his movements had defied her best efforts to predict. However, one thing was sure: the Warlord rarely travelled without hundreds of legionnaires, especially the Viridian Guardians, the select few warriors emblazoned with green tattoos, one for every blood sacrifice made to their warlord.

"I have a plan." Lex reached into her pocket and pulled out a small map.

As she unrolled it, Darius turned and flared ferven across his hand to cast light onto it.

"I heard," he said. "Varro said it's something to do with your father. What am I supposed to do? Kill him?"

Lex scowled. "Do you really think I'm so callous as to kill my own father?" She'd killed people she cared about before, but it was never for *her* benefit.

He looked at her for a while then shrugged. "I can't think of any other use I can be."

"I've been laying subtle foundations for the First Alliance for a while, but my problem is he still cannot believe a rakkan city would go to battle against another. Centuries of history show rakkans *always* band together against us." Humans knew little of rakkans and saw them as wild monsters with an innate hatred of humans, rather than people not all that different from themselves. But who could blame them, when all they saw were the Viridian Legion's invasions of their homes?

"Can't you just speak to him?" Darius asked. "Won't he believe you?"

"He believes nothing without proof. You don't know how stubborn he is. You need to help me prove to him you're now at war with Viridia."

"How do I do that?" Darius scratched his chin and looked down at the map. "Slaughter Viridian Legionnaires?"

"Sort of. You need to defeat the commander waging war on our western lands to show that this isn't just a ruse. Bring him the head of Hadrian's second-in-command."

"The one with the signet ring? Sounds easy enough." He shrugged.

She couldn't tell if he was being sarcastic. "You also need to gain my father's trust. He won't give a rakkan the time of day, let alone come to trust them, but you can pose as an algus first. Then, once he's impressed, has seen you lead men to victory, and has faith in you, we'll speak with him together and tell him the truth."

"Lead?" A low murmur came from Darius's throat. "This sounds like a lengthy process."

If it wasn't, she'd have achieved her ambitions long ago. "Go to Laltos and join our armies."

"Isn't that dangerous? Everyone in the city hunted me the last time I was there."

If only Darius knew the half of it, but the horror stories people told of him were too long and numerous to tell. Plus, most of them were true. "They know of your deeds, the slaughters, assassinations"—she avoided the word "massacre" though many

77

spoke of such—"and most fear your name so much it's uttered to scare children into obedience."

Darius's brow furrowed, and his cheeks flushed slightly.

"You must be careful," Lex continued, "prove to them you're not the wicked traitor the tales depict, and show them the real you." She pointed on the map. "My sister is leading the new push west, and she'll be the perfect witness. My father is very mistrusting, but he can hardly argue if two of his daughters have seen you defeat our enemies."

Darius sighed and rose to his feet, rubbing the back of his neck with one hand. "I guess I owe it to my old self to try. You're sure this will impress him enough to trust a rakkan?"

"No. You'll also have to be charming, funny, witty and loyal."

His face dropped. "Then we're in trouble… Would you settle for mildly amusing, when in a good mood?" The worried look on his face gave her little confidence, but she knew such a man was beneath the surly complaints. He had to be because they grew closer to losing the war by the week. Now she just had to hope the news of her engagement didn't cloud his mind further.

9

Darius – Royal Roads, North of Margalvia

It wasn't long before Darius and Lex set off on horseback from Margalvia, along with a caravan of half a dozen wagons tugged by brown oxen to haul the weapons Lex had traded. A few rakkans came along to assist, including Julius, much to Darius's distaste.

It was only a few hot days before Darius's ears tired of the rumble of wooden wheels. Yearning for the smoother Royal Roads once they reached Denehill, he resigned, for the moment, to trot as far ahead as possible, alongside Lex, whose gaze rarely stopped scouring the parched landscape.

The caravan's walk to Denehill took thrice as long as he was used to, and soon after they reached the Royal Roads, he realised their pace would last the whole journey.

Atop a swift refreshed every half-day, the route from Laltos to Margalvia passed by in only a few days, but now, with heavy goods in tow, Darius lost count of the days before they reached halfway.

At the end of another long day's ride, he pulled the reins of his tired horse to bring it to a halt beside Lex and her steed. Hooves scratched across the sandy dirt road and brought wisps of dust floating up while the caravan's monotonous rumble gradually eased. *Finally, a rest.*

He looked back at the rakkans sat at the front of the wagons.

At least this was the end of the road for them. Now in the Empire, the rakkans would leave for home while Darius and Lex awaited her contingent of humans to come and take over.

As they waited, Darius watched the road shimmer in the heat. The hardened surface cut across the dry landscape without a bend visible before disappearing over a hill. The King may have been an enemy, but Darius admired his efficient infrastructure. At either side of them was a backdrop of rolling hills coated with light brown dirt broken only by the odd patch of withering vegetation.

Next to him, Lex took a drink from her waterskin before splashing a little onto her face.

"I can't believe we're only halfway there." Darius groaned and wiped the sweat from his brow.

"Why are you surprised? I've seen swifts advance in an hour what takes an army two days."

"I'd hardly call our mangy bunch an army…"

Lex's horse nickered as she scanned the landscape while her falcon soared in the cloudless sky above.

"I don't know why you're always so paranoid," Darius said. "With Tiro around, who could surprise you?"

"He can't see everything."

Darius's thoughts drifted back to Lyra as they so often had. Despite the substantial distance between them, he felt her connection stronger than ever. It was as if she were sat next to him yet there was no soft fur to reach out and touch, no ear to scratch behind, no cheek to brush against his leg when he was blue. As hard as he'd tried though, he could never access her vision as other algus seemed to with their escorts.

"How clearly can you see what Tiro sees?" Darius asked.

Lex frowned and closed her eyes. "It's not clear at all, not like seeing with my own eyes. There's no image, yet I know what he sees, if that makes sense."

Darius grunted. "No. Clear as blood. I don't get that kind of feedback from Lyra." He worried it meant he didn't care for her enough.

"Perhaps Archimedes did something to your connection."

Sounds like an excuse. "I feel I'm getting closer to Lyra with every step I take away."

Lex's next words were notably softer. "Trauma has a way of bringing those we love closer to us."

Their conversation was interrupted by footsteps behind, followed by Julius's voice. "Darius?"

He turned to see the sweaty rakkan, nose red and peeling.

"Everything good?" Darius asked, thankful for a distraction from sadness. "Enjoying the sun?"

The rakkan glared at him.

"How are the oxen faring?" Lex asked.

"Well," Julius said. "They've handled the weight better than I thought they would, though I suppose the swords are only thinly layered with kuraminium so not as heavy as I'd feared."

"Well, they had to be light," Darius said. "How else could those feeble humans use them?"

Lex rolled her eyes and went back to scanning their surroundings.

"We'll be heading back," Julius said. "I'll tell Brutus and Sulla you're looking a little brighter in yourself."

Darius frowned. "Do I?"

The rakkan looked him up and down then studied his face for a few seconds. "No. Still look like a dog eating a nettle. But it'll stop them asking me about you."

"Fair enough." It was hard to believe Brutus and Sulla didn't think Darius was tough enough to make the journey this far, or why the sword-master of all people had volunteered to accompany him.

"Give them both my regards," Darius said.

Julius nodded. "There's one last thing. Brutus asked me to give you this." He pulled a rolled-up parchment from under his cloak and handed it to Darius.

"What is it?" Darius asked.

"It's a scroll. You unravel it and it has words that you can read—"

"Do I look that stupid?" Darius snapped.

Julius grinned and opened his mouth.

"Don't answer that," Darius interjected. "Just tell me what it is."

"It's a collection of rakkan wisdom."

"Shouldn't be long then," Lex added with a wry grin.

Julius shook his head. "I would have given it to you before, but I looked at it myself and couldn't help but keep reading it on the journey."

Darius inspected the brown roll of parchment, a dozen inches wide and just thick enough to wrap his hand around. The few times he'd tried reading, it hadn't been a fast process to say the least. "So, Brutus thinks I need more wisdom? Send him my thanks for the insult."

"Even the wisest of us still have things to learn," Julius replied.

It was rare that insightful words left the rakkan's mouth, but Darius noted them when they did.

"And the unwise…" Julius looked him up and down. "Well…they need all the help they can get."

"*Thanks*," Darius said.

"I think you'll find the story of Trogus and Arria interesting at least."

The last name stirred a nervousness Darius hadn't felt in a long time. "Arria as in the Staff of Arria?"

Julius nodded then returned to the other rakkans and headed towards the road home. *Lucky bastard.*

Meanwhile, Lex still looked around them as if expecting to get attacked at any moment.

"So…" Darius cleared his throat.

She half turned her head towards him. "Are the others out of earshot?"

"Yes."

Her shoulders sank a little. "We need to discuss something before my aides come."

There were several things that she could be referring to, but he got a strange feeling he wouldn't like whatever it was.

"Spit it out then," he said.

"I'm not coming with you to Laltos." She stared into the distance, failing to meet his eyes as she often did when it would have mattered most.

"Why?" Was he expected to be charming and witty without her help? *Does she not know me?*

"It's complicated, but I have something to tell you first."

Was this where she would plead for him to carry out another task for her, a task that would turn yet more against him? After the last time, he'd stick to being an obedient warrior.

"I'm to be married." Lex had stopped scanning their surroundings and held her head facing away, not giving him even a hint of emotion.

He paused, mouth hung open and not sure why he'd expected anything other than his feelings for her to lead to misery.

"Married?" he said.

"To the Regent of Xavala, the Silk City. My father suggested it to gain an ally, given the tax issues we've had with the King recently."

Who? Darius flicked the reins of his horse and led it directly into Lex's line of sight. The brilliant sun behind her now pained his eyes, but as he squinted, she still avoided his gaze.

"You're marrying someone? For politics? What happened to 'I'm done with men'?"

She finally met his stare. "Do you remember what I told you? Don't hold out for me."

"I thought…" He remembered all too well. He'd thought those words had hurt, but this was something else. He'd assumed she'd sworn off all men, not just him.

Just what I need… She'd taught him to care after Archimedes had drained his compassion, and this was his reward—pain from caring for someone that didn't return it? He wondered whether she really knew how he felt. Would telling her change anything, or would it make it all the more unbearable when she rejected him again?

"Lex, you can't marry him."

"Darius, please…don't." She winced, as if she'd been expecting him to protest.

84

"I…" Darius began, "I have to tell you something first. I—"

"Stop it." Her eyes widened, her body tensed so much her horse became unsettled.

"But you have to hear this. I—"

"Darius, stop!" Her shout was followed only by her quickened breaths and the hiss of dry dirt scraping across the road. "I know. I've told you, don't hold out for me. If you're lonely, then find a wife, or a whore. You won't hurt me again. I won't let you."

"When did I hurt you?"

"We tried. After only a few days together, the old you went from my bed to the bed of another. Accept it. We will *never* be together again!"

The shrill words took a second to register, "never" ringing over and over in his ears. Whatever she did next, whatever the look was on her face, he didn't see. The sun's glare filled his vision, yet his mind was left dark. His old self had failed her, wasn't worthy of her.

Only feelings of anger and emptiness surfaced. There was nothing else inside him. Why had he thought anyone would want to be with that? The only thing he was good for was killing, and he wasn't even always good for that.

"I'm sorry to be blunt." Lex's face came back into focus as she looked down at her horse's head and stroked it until her breathing slowed. "This marriage is for the best. We all have to do what's required of us, and sometimes more." Her voice had returned to its usual flatness. "Find someone else to be with."

It took a second, but the words finally sank in. "Who's your betrothed?" Darius asked, curiosity getting the better of him.

"He's a powerful regent named Aristippus. His city of Xavala is between Laltos and Toria. It's wealthy but a shadow of what it was before Toria strangled it. They're close enough to aid us in battle once I'm wed."

Any place close to the Empire's capital and the King's throne wasn't to be trusted in Darius's mind, especially ones near the war front that never sent their armies to aid Laltos in battle. Most regents he'd heard about or seen were fat oafs, carried around by the people they made treat them as gods.

"Aristippus…" Darius grimaced. "Stupid name. Sounds like the name of a malingerer. I'll bet he's so lazy he sits down to take a piss."

A sullen expression came upon Lex's face, darkened even in the bright light. "Not far off. He's a man who likes to indulge. I've only met him a few times."

"Yet you're marrying him?" Was it all women, or just Lex that made little sense to Darius?

"Like I said before, it's politics. Laltos needs allies. He's the only one willing."

Darius turned his head away, mind reeling, and cast his gaze in the direction of Laltos to give his eyes a rest from the sun. Caring about people caused so many issues he often wondered why he'd ever bothered, but the fact was he did.

"Couldn't one of your sisters marry him?" he asked.

"Apparently not. He asked for me."

No doubt this regent had been taken with Lex's beauty the same way Darius had. How could he compete with a regent, even a lazy one? It was all a game to these powerful people, and underlings like Darius, Lyra, and even children like his baby brother and Omid paid the dues.

More anguish filled Darius at the memory of the young boy Lex had killed in Laltos.

"Your mind is made up?" Darius asked.

"Yes." Her quick answer and stubborn nature shattered whatever smidgen of hope had remained in him.

"So, you're leaving me now to see him?"

"Yes. I need to take him these weapons and that tree in the wagon."

Darius started and whirled his head back around with a snarl twisting his face. "You're giving those weapons to another city?" Kuraminium edged swords had one main use—fighting rakkans—and only Laltos could be trusted with them. "Did my warlord agree to this?"

"I have to." Her stony face was as emotionless as ever. "They have something that we need far greater than weapons. And even though I'm marrying him, he still won't forge an alliance with Laltos without payment of a dowry."

Darius shook his head, feeling another betrayal on his shoulders if he didn't report this back to Varro or Brutus. "I suppose you want me to hide this from the others."

Lex's eyes widened. "You must! Those weapons are for Xavala to help fight the Viridians. Plus, without what they're giving us, we won't have what we need to attack Viridia. That city is a fortress—high walls reinforced with kuraminium bars that have *never* been breached."

The stories Darius had heard had been along the same lines, though he'd never seen the city himself. "What are you getting in return?"

"Sulphur."

"For?"

"When burned, its smell is intolerable, even for a rakkan. I think it will be of great use in battle against warriors with flaming armour."

Sounded like they were to be the first trial of this weapon from Lex's imagination. *How lucky we are...* "That makes sense, and I'm sure Varro would agree. Why lie?"

"I didn't lie. I just didn't tell him."

As Darius ruminated on it, he realised this was probably the least of his and Varro's worries when it came to Lex's secrets. Why risk the First Alliance crumbling? It wasn't like he'd see the Margalvians any time soon to report it to them. Only when he did see them would he ruminate on loyalties. "I won't say anything for now."

Her shoulders dropped as she exhaled, and he looked behind her to the wagons loaded with weapons and one other unusual item—a tree with its own tall cart and protected with cloth from both prying eyes and the blazing sun.

"What's the plant for?" he asked.

"It's a mulberry tree."

When she said nothing further, he raised his eyebrows at her.

"The King has forbidden anyone west of the River Toras from growing them," she finally said. "Tax disputes, nothing of interest. I'm curious to see what my future husband, the Silk Regent, does with the gift."

What an odd law. Just when Darius thought he understood the layers of her schemes... "And what if he doesn't react as you hope?"

She shrugged. "Then once Viridia is in ruins, I'll have no further use for him."

A smile almost formed on Darius's lips but was soon replaced with a hollow feeling, barren like the road ahead of him. Would she discard *him* completely once he was past use? If he'd never regained his rakkan powers, would they still be speaking? After all, his main use was as a warrior.

He cast his gaze out again to the empty road ahead where Laltos's white towers stood far away at the end, beyond the horizon.

"I assume if I don't see you soon, you'll keep in contact via Tiro," he muttered.

"Of course." She brought her horse alongside his. "Tiro will lead you to Selene, one of my adopted sisters." She prodded his side, and he looked to see a small piece of parchment in her hand. "This is a gift for you. I was going to take care of it myself, but thought you might like to."

He frowned and took it. When he unrolled it, the words "Bita, Trade Street, Dolthea" became visible. It was the town where he'd taken Lyra to see that strange priest, Aran, but he was damned if he knew where Trade Street was. "Is this supposed to mean something?"

"It's Omid's mother. I tracked her down."

Memories of the boy's chirpy face surfaced as Darius's fingers curled the parchment closed. What little the boy had said of his mother was too faded to remember. All that Darius recalled was the boy's wish to find and free her once he'd become an algus, and now only Darius and Lex were the ones aware of it.

Darius looked at Lex, her face apologetic and almost warm—though it might have been from the heat. If she really cared enough to do this for the dead boy, then perhaps he'd misjudged her.

"If you find yourself in Dolthea," Lex said, "perhaps you'll do this for us."

He nodded and slid the parchment deep into a pocket of his tunic. After a pause, he caught sight of clouds of dust approaching on the road ahead.

"Those will be my aides to take the wagons to Xavala." Her cue to leave.

Darius pulled the reins tight in his hands. "I guess I'll head to Laltos. Wouldn't want to impede your wedding plans." At least he could ride harder without the caravan and not take weeks to arrive.

"Don't forget"—she clutched the reins of his horse—"don't use your real name."

It had been a while since he'd had to use his alias, but it looked like "Philippos" was returning to Laltos. *Alone.* The thought of her leaving him stirred a little bitterness.

"I guess I won't be invited to the wedding," Darius said, "so good luck. I hope you don't get caught in one of the many lies you've told." He whipped the reins and set off along the road, leaving a cloud of dust behind him.

10

Brutus – Margalvia

Brutus slouched in the chair beside Varro with a sigh. There was so much he wanted to say but not when their prisoner was there. So instead, Brutus silently puffed his pipe.

His brother sat on the throne at the head of the table in the commanders' meeting room, grinding two stones in a circular motion in his hand. The lighting was dim, even by rakkan standards, so much so that shadows flickered across the Warlord's face with the movement of the flames from the two clay oil lamps in front.

Across the table, Nikolaos bit into a strip of salted pork, cheeks flushed as he savoured the rare taste of meat. Still, the algus ate better than many Margalvian citizens who suffered on rations, as Brutus had yelled at his brother many a time.

At either side, the human was chained to a guard and had been given a clean, scale-green tunic if only to save them all from a stink.

"The King must have had plans." Varro didn't blink as his gaze pierced Nikolaos's distracted figure.

"He's tight-lipped," Nikolaos said through a mouthful of food he didn't deserve. "I doubt he says much to anyone other than his closest advisors. And even then, he has an official mouthpiece to do his talking for him. But I can tell you one thing"—the algus took a gulp of water—"the quieter it seems, the more you should fear."

"If you give us nothing but empty phrases," Brutus growled, "then why should we feed you?"

"I, uh." Nikolaos cleared his throat. "I can tell you this. As head of the Laltos Guard, I was privy to more knowledge than Lex. There were whispers that the King and the Waif Magician have colluded for decades. How else would she evade capture for so long? I wouldn't be surprised if the Staff of Arria was back in the King's hands once the Magician's done with it."

Varro searched the algus's eyes for a few seconds longer then waved a hand. "Take him back."

"Wait!" Nikolaos stood, eyes wide and fearful. "Can you give me any news of Laltos?"

Brutus chuckled. "Give us something solid and we'll return the favour."

"I heard one of the rakkans muttering, the Viridian Legion—"

A guard put a hand across Nikolaos's mouth and wrestled him out of the room with minor effort, leaving the two brothers alone.

"You shouldn't give that human the time of night," Brutus said, "never mind waste good food on him while others go hungry. Can't trust a word he says."

"Mercy begets more truth than the rod. He's better than nothing."

Brutus scoffed. "Sometimes, nothing is better, especially with humans. What's to say he doesn't have an escort out there, communicating with him, somehow?"

"Alexandra was sure that's not the case. That's enough for me."

"I know most algus don't have them, but it would still be safest to assume he does."

The Warlord didn't respond, just continued to grind the stones in his palm.

Brutus took a long drag of his pipe and let the smoke linger on his tongue, trying to discern flavours from the confused mix of leaves he'd stuffed into the pipe in a hurry. It lacked the thick taste of ash that he craved most of all, the taste that the leaves his wife dried and mixed had. It always made him recall being home with her as he seldom was. There was no more satisfying taste to compliment a cup of peaty firewater.

He offered Varro a drag, but the Warlord shook his head.

"I remember when we were children," Brutus said. "I was always at the head of our imagined commander tables." Even though it was over a century ago, he recalled his brother's thoughtful stare as hard as it was now.

"You were the oldest. Don't read too much into it." Varro smiled wistfully.

Brutus cleared his throat. "So, are we going to talk about Viridia or ponder on the King's imagined plotting longer?"

"There's nothing more to say. I told you, my decision was final. You're the only one I trust to send there."

Brutus took in a few more lungfuls of smoke and eased them out, obscuring his vision. The taste didn't grow on him. Neither did the thought of trying to infiltrate Viridia. "Julius shared my concern that someone will recognise me."

"I don't see why they would."

Brutus waited a second for his brother to elaborate, but nothing further came. "You really know how to reassure a man. My old lady won't be happy to hear that I'm going away again." Though, after decades of war, she was used to the time apart.

Varro shrugged, face blank and pensive, then he ran a hand through his hair. Even though usually reserved, Varro's current muteness was abnormal.

"Something else on your mind?" Brutus asked.

After a moment's pause, Varro sighed and leaned in with a whisper. "I'm thinking about Darius."

In all the years they'd known the lad, Varro had never been one to worry over him.

"Why the concern?" Brutus asked.

"I fear the ethic you've instilled in him will die if his escort does. I see him listening to Lex more than us, and now he's done this. He says he was attacked, but I suspect she's played a part in this."

Brutus shared the concern. Every day over the last few months, he'd seen more glimpses of the old Darius he'd watched grow from a timid child into an honourable warrior. But now, that man had withdrawn to be replaced by darkness.

"I gave him something that might help," Brutus said. "The third scroll of the Creator." A finer collection of wisdom hadn't been written, even though Brutus struggled to read it as with most script. "I'm sure he'll follow orders while you decide his punishment."

"Yes…" Varro murmured while the shadows still stretched over his face.

Brutus bit on the end of his pipe. "How severe will you be?"

"The commanders don't have confidence in him. If he isn't to hang, they want him exiled. As for me, I haven't decided if I can trust him or not. I'm concerned Alexandra will always have sway over him."

What man isn't swayed by a beautiful woman? As soon as Brutus thought it, he realised Varro was an exception to the rule. The two women the Warlord had let into his life seemed to have little effect on his decisions.

"Do you really mistrust her," Brutus asked, "or are you bitter over your failed relationship?" Perhaps it had been his brother's resistance to her influences that had come between the pair, or the dirty looks of rakkans after he'd mated with a human. Of course, given it was Varro, no one dared utter a word to his face.

The Warlord shook his head and closed his eyes. "I'm not bitter. Alexandra, on the other hand…" The words trailed off as they so often did when Varro spoke of the few months he and Lex had been together. As curious as Brutus was, he knew not to press his younger brother on the matter.

"Don't come down too hard on Darius," Brutus said. "Perhaps people will be more forgiving when he comes through for us."

"*If* he comes through." Varro's face fell into darkness as one lamp ran out of oil. In his hand, the stones scratched against each other as he ground them faster.

For the last few years, Brutus had watched his brother's relationship with his adopted son strain, and not just because of both their affections for Lex. Recently, the Warlord had never forgot their brother's death. Felix died for Margalvia, and protecting one he cared for, but all Varro saw was a wasted life.

Not wanting to get further into the subject of loyalty, Brutus let silence linger for a moment before speaking. "You should concentrate on preparing the Legion for war."

"I do. It's all I think on. All I want is this city safe."

"As do I." The fate of the home of his wife and brother gave Brutus many a sleepless night. "If Sulla's correct—"

"Forget about Sulla. You heard Nikolaos; the King is as much a threat as ever."

As Brutus opened his mouth to interject how untrustworthy the algus was, Varro held up a hand and continued. "Just a few days ago, we caught a human spy watching over the city from the mountain top near the northern gate."

"Fine. Keep your eyes open, but the Viridian Legion must be dealt with."

Varro paused, slowly putting his grinding stones on the table. "I want you to get information before I make a move. I've yet to hear from the Branz and Azure Legions whether they'll support us or Hadrian. If they choose him—"

"They must back us. We aren't the ones that broke the mine's treaty."

"We'll see. Perhaps they won't take sides."

After Archimedes had fallen and the Staff of Arria was stolen, Brutus had thought the legions would let each other be. Too bad he was wrong, as always.

"Our miners say it will only take a few days for us to tunnel our way back in," Varro said.

"It never ceases to amaze me the speed at which rakkans mine."

"But now isn't the time. Hadrian will just attack us again."

"They must have been ready for war to attack so swiftly," Brutus said. "Hadrian is crazed but no fool." He took another drag of his pipe and grimaced at the mixed taste again. Giving up, he spat and tossed it onto the table, spilling smouldering leaves into the carvings on its surface.

"Find out what his next move will be," Varro said, "and how heavily defended the mine is so we can get it back. After making those weapons for Alexandra, our kuraminium reserves are low."

Brutus murmured and scratched the stubble on his chin. "I still don't like these trades. Maybe Hadrian knew of them and wanted to put a stop to it."

"I doubt it. Besides, would you rather starve?"

Guess not. With another murmur, Brutus pressed his palms into the table and stood. "I'll need a pigeon fancier to come with me and bring his homing birds. I'll have him send word when I find anything. Just do one thing while I'm away."

Varro raised an eyebrow. "What?"

"Stop listening to the lies of your algus prisoner."

11

Darius – Laltos

The first time Darius recalled entering Laltos he'd been a hunted man. And not much had changed since. He hoped his hair being several inches longer would make him unrecognisable.

The arched gateway into the city passed a deep shadow over his head as he entered. With a sigh, he closed his eyes, glad to at least be in the shade. Every time he focused on Lyra, he felt the heat of her fever, and it had only worsened.

Too late for his liking, the sun was setting and cast an orange haze across the sky. After a few days' contemplation, he was no less confused as to how he'd go about his task of winning over the Regent. Lyra clutching to life played on his mind too much to focus.

Rows of spear-wielding hoplites lined the dense city walls, still as statues but eyes tracking the movement of everyone below. Their iron helmets and skirts of leather strips were clean and monotone grey, in contrast to the filthy and torn clothes most of the people in the bustling street wore.

The smell of sweat clogged Darius's nostrils and mixed with the stench of disease and decay. Even the citizens in their clean though tired dress looked thin. It was the same malnutrition and sickness as in the other towns. The Viridians had overrun many of the farms, and even coins and gold weren't enough to feed everyone in the west now. There were too few to buy grain from in bulk.

The shadow of the gateway passed, leaving the sun to scorch his head again. He didn't know what was worse, the hotness on his tender forehead or the dazzling reflection from the white stone the city was built from. Although his black leather tunic helped him blend in as an algus, it only intensified the heat.

As he walked through the streets of the lower city, Tiro coasted from one rooftop to another. One benefit to the bland buildings was he spotted every algus and guard placed on the walls and roofs, though being without a kuraminium sword put him on edge at the sight of so many.

Soon, he needed to impress a man he knew little about. All he recalled from his conversations with Lex was the Regent had a passion for anything analytical and complex. *Great… Hope he likes strong drink otherwise we'll have nothing to discuss.* Lex had given him greater insights, but how was Darius supposed to retain information when all he dwelled on was Lyra…and now Lex's marriage?

Squeezed on either side of him in the road, mules pulled two carts, sparsely filled with potatoes and wheat but valuable enough to warrant a soldier escort. Slumped at each side of the street were sullen men and women holding out hands that remained empty.

One ragged boy caught Darius's eye, alone in a doorway. Wearing only rags around his waist, every rib showed under the thin skin on his chest. Who was Darius to complain of his problems when there were children like this in the Empire?

He dismounted and walked up to the slave who barely had the strength to look up. A few other beggars peered at him with hungry eyes while he palmed a silver crest and reached to take the boy's hand.

"Bless you, son," he said, playing his part as one of the Empire's "gods."

The boy weakly grasped his hand and frowned when he felt the metal. Thankfully smart enough to be discreet, the boy closed his fingers and brought his fist to his chest.

Tears welled in his eyes.

"Go. Eat," Darius said, uncomfortable in the beggar's continued stare. He waited as the boy feebly got to his feet and walked away while a few of the other beggars picked up on what had happened.

Darius's scowl chased away their thoughts of pursuing the lad. But who could blame them? They probably had children to feed too.

With a sigh, Darius climbed back atop his horse and carried on. The buildings in the lower city were tall by Margalvian standards, at three storeys, but nothing compared to the heights of the towers ahead in the walled-off upper city where the masters dwelled. Far to the back of Laltos, in front of the face of the short, flat mountains, the tallest towers rose as part of the Regent's palace, thin spikes forming a ring just as Lex had described.

Soon, he rode over the river, through another arched gateway into the upper city, then guided his horse into a large square with a fountain at the centre.

Darius froze, stirred by a bitter, haunted rush within.

Wings of water from the stone statue caught his eye, and he pulled his steed to a halt.

A figure of the Goddess Dianoia reached out to the heavens with an open, wailing mouth, a pained grimace on her face, and water trickling from her eyes. Art wasn't something he was familiar with, but even he saw how the intricate marble carvings brought the figure to life like a ghost from days long forgotten. The piece was so detailed and unworn it couldn't have been more than a few years old, a tribute to the Regent's adopted religion.

As Darius looked, a patch of stone near his horse's hooves stole his gaze. Was it still stained with blood, or was it his imagination?

He stared, memories replaying in his mind. That was the spot where Lex had ended Omid's life. Blankly, he stared, for seconds, perhaps minutes. Dianoia was right to cry out for justice…if there was such a thing.

Was that all Lex wanted now? As uncomfortable as her marriage was to him, he should have expected disappointment. He guessed he should heed her advice and try to move on. He still had Lyra. *For how long?*

Eager to forget the thoughts, he whipped the reins hard, and his horse started into a trot. Tiro continued guiding him until he passed through a final gateway in the third line of walls that protected the palace. Bear statues guarded the entrance along with lines of soldiers and considerably more hard-faced algus than in the lower city. The grand building farther up the hill was held up by stone pillars that looked as ancient as the cliff behind.

Stairs ascended at the front up to an entrance with a large device mounted above. As he got closer, markings became visible on a vertical scale, and a metal pointer was creeping upwards so slowly it was almost imperceptible.

When he reached the steps of the palace, he dismounted and breathed in the fresh mountain air no longer teeming with maladies.

Soon after, a boy slave approached and patted the horse's neck. "Hey, girl."

Glad someone recognises her. "Do you know where she stables?"

The boy nodded, so Darius let him lead the mare away for a well-earned rest while he surveyed the new class of people roaming around.

Atop the stairs, a slender, impeccably dressed man was pacing up and down whilst chatting with a woman a foot shorter than him that yawned frequently. Neither had armour or weapons, but the silver eagles carved into their belt buckles matched the one Darius wore.

Before Darius wondered whether the woman was Lex's sister, Tiro dove and landed at the side of the street, in front of an auburn-haired woman that had a cheeriness to her face he'd not seen before in the city.

She smiled and crouched. "I thought you'd never arrive. Where is he?"

Tiro turned to face Darius, and she looked up. When their eyes met, she gave him a warm smile that he'd only ever received from friends.

"Philippos?" She stood then strode towards him. From the outside, the only similarity she had to Lex was her height, for she lacked the slenderness, cold blue eyes and scowl of her sister. Selene's loose, green tunic melded her into the grass lawn behind while the slightest of bulges under her belt betrayed a concealed dagger.

"You must be Selene." Darius gave her the most authentic smile he could, given what he'd just seen. He hoped it didn't look as fake as it felt.

102

A slight redness surfaced on her cheeks. "Lex was right. You *are* handsome."

For a moment, Darius was lost for words. He'd believe Lex paid him a compliment only when he heard it from her own lips.

Selene pulled back her curls behind her ear, giving Darius a better glimpse of her freckled, olive skin and hazel eyes that gazed keenly at him. The cuteness of her face hadn't struck him until now.

He wiped the sweat from his forehead, suddenly remembering what a state he must have looked. "What else did Lex tell you of me? All good, I hope."

"That's for me to know…" Her mouth curled into a grin. In only a few sentences, she'd given him more compliments and warmth than Lex ever had.

A sweaty aroma still hung in the air, and it was only then he realised the smell hadn't all been because of the people of Laltos. Unsure how to avoid her noticing his stink, Darius smiled and regarded the palace and the odd device on the front.

"Admiring the clepsydra?" Selene asked.

With a harder look, it became clear the markings on the scale were times, and the hand tracked them much like the shadow on a sundial. Yet, it looked nothing like the water clocks Darius had seen, which had been a simple bowl of water with a hole in the bottom so the water level tracked time passing.

"How does that metal hand move upwards?" he asked. "Where's the water?"

"In clay tanks behind. Impressive, isn't it?" She proudly lifted her chin. "It moves at a constant speed and tracks the time on the markings, unlike a normal clepsydra which slows as the tank runs low."

"Did you create that?" he asked, captivated.

"No, but my father had the idea."

It was far beyond Darius's imagination how such a device worked, and the mind behind it suddenly made him sweat even more. If the Regent had such intellect, he'd be impressed by like-minded men, and Darius was out of luck in that regard.

"I can show you how it works later," Selene said.

"Thanks. I'd like that." Curiosity was getting the better of him, and he could use it to connect with Theodoros. "Will you be introducing me to your father tonight? I think I need to bathe first."

"I'll say." Selene shook her head, auburn curls bouncing and shining in the setting sun. "Not today. An envoy of the King is with him, overseeing the census and taxes."

It was heartening to hear the King was busying himself with human politics rather than mustering an army to attack Margalvia again. "Sounds expensive. I hope you hid all those treasures I hear you have in the Laltos Bank."

"As if we'd risk treason." She lowered her voice. "The King's Sword is here."

Although confused, Darius nodded along because she said the name as if everyone knew it.

As they gave a few more introductions, a man's voice from afar interrupted them. "Selene!"

Darius looked to the yell's source. At the top of the palace steps, the two algus he'd noticed earlier now scurried down.

A low groan escaped Selene's lips. "Great," she muttered under her breath while putting on a smile. "Gorgias."

"I didn't notice you down here." Gorgias returned Selene's phoney smile.

Human behaviour was so strange, sometimes it baffled Darius. If they hated each other, why bother to act nicely?

While they exchanged insincere pleasantries, Darius gave a quick smile to the woman behind Gorgias, but she only greeted him with a bored stare. *She's a cheery one.* The two algus wore grey leather tunics without a visible crease, and the man's slick black hair had so much oil Darius was surprised it wasn't dripping.

Now closer, Darius was struck by the man's young, almost juvenile face. The cheery woman was fair-skinned and quiet but stared in a way that unsettled Darius. He'd had enough of this couple already.

"And who's this?" Gorgias turned to Darius.

"Philippos," Selene said. "Lex's friend from the Silk City."

"Ah." Gorgias smirked and seemed to relax a little. "I thought for a moment you were one of the King's algus."

Darius raised an eyebrow. "Do I have the look of a man demanding coin?"

"Well, you have that discontented sulk that all tax collectors seem to bear…and the stench."

As charming as his companion. But it took more than that to anger Darius.

Gorgias paused and frowned. "Have we met before? You seem oddly familiar."

Darius's first instinct was to reach for the sword at his waist, but that might be an overreaction to the innocent question from an unarmed man.

"I don't think so," Darius said. "You'd remember me."

Gorgias's eyebrows lifted. "Arrogant one, aren't we?"

"No. Just a realist."

Selene rolled her eyes.

But as far as Darius knew, there weren't any other half-rakkan, half-humans in the Empire. "Who's your friend?"

Gorgias turned and ushered the slight woman forward with an arm around her shoulders. "This is my wife, Fourteen."

"You number your wives?" Darius raised an eyebrow.

Gorgias coughed and the orange sun reflected in his glaring eyes. "That's her name."

It took all Darius's restraint not to grin at his mistake. Thankfully, he maintained his polite demeanour, though it didn't lessen Gorgias's glower.

Looks like I'm making friends already. To Darius's credit, he'd never been introduced to one of the Numbered before and certainly had never heard of one being married. He'd given little thought to what they did now that Archimedes was dead, but it seemed they hadn't all fallen to the ground like puppets cut from their strings.

"You should choose a new name," Selene said, echoing Darius's next thought.

"I asked," Gorgias said, "but she—"

"I have a name," Fourteen said in a monotone voice, higher than Darius had expected. "I'm Fourteen. I have no shame in my past."

A proud smile spread across Gorgias's lips.

"Guess I've been put in my place." Selene lowered her gaze. "Are you both heading west once the census is complete?"

"No." Gorgias's expression fell as flat as his wife's. "My mother apparently has more urgent things for me to be doing than saving our towns from invaders."

"Mother telling you what to do?" Darius laughed. "Who's fourteen again?"

Selene chuckled, but Gorgias's laughs were forced and sarcastic. "One drawback of your mother being the wealthiest woman in Laltos. I can assure you I'm a *man*, not a boy."

"I'll take your word for it," Darius said. "You should grow the fluff on your chin; it might help avoid confusion."

Gorgias's face flushed.

"It seems I arrived at the perfect time." Darius slapped a hand on the hilt of his sword. "I'm ready to kill rakkans and have no mother to stop me." Whether his mother was even dead or alive, he didn't care. He still remembered her slap to his face while he retched, sick from his brother's blood.

After a few exhales, Gorgias said, "Selene, I had no idea you needed outside help now."

"I didn't invite him." Selene crossed her arms. "It's Lex that wants me to look after him."

"I'm an unwelcome guest then, am I?" Darius turned to face her as the warm smiles she'd given him before faded.

"I've met men like you before," she said. "Fetching and arrogant, but tame. I'm doing a favour for Lex by allowing you to accompany me. Maybe she thinks you'll learn a thing or two."

Darius didn't hear a word past "fetching," but ignored the unsettled feeling the compliment provoked. "I'm here for your benefit, not mine. Lex wants me to help take back the western lands. This city needs the farms and grain."

"What makes you think you can do what we can't?"

Why were some people so reluctant to accept help?

Darius folded his arms. "By the colour of your tunic, the small twigs caught within it, and the calluses on the fingers of your right hand, you're an archer that picks off an unsuspecting rakkan or two from the trees. But I can beat them on the ground and drive them out of a town."

Gorgias cleared his throat. "Looks like we have an algus as deadly as the King's Sword here. How lucky."

"You're of little use to me then, Philippos." Selene sighed. "Like you said, I don't have use for a swordsman. I hide in the trees. Go and save the towns yourself, hero."

Try as he might, Darius couldn't pinpoint where this conversation had taken a turn against him. In his known life, everyone seemed to want him for his warrior skills, yet these people wanted nothing to do with him when he offered aid. He must have been more of an irritating bastard than he realised.

He thought for a few seconds about his next words. "Maybe I'm arrogant. I don't intend to be. I can fight with a sword, but as you've seen, I need a little assistance overcoming my tendency to…act, or speak, without thinking."

Selene raised an eyebrow and looked him up and down before speaking again. "Are you a wagering man?"

"Depends on the bet."

"Beat me with a bow at two hundred yards, and I'll forgive your arrogance and allow you to accompany me."

Hell, not a bow. Rakkans rarely relied on archers given the men threw rocks farther than a catapult. Still, he doubted anyone shot accurately at such a distance.

"I sense I don't have a choice in the matter," Darius replied.

"See, my smarts are rubbing off on you already." She grinned, which was at least a start to her warming back up to him.

"You'll lose," Fourteen said. "She's the best archer in Laltos."

Just my luck.

"Thanks for ruining the surprise." Selene huffed.

"Let me know when this little contest will be," Gorgias said, face glowing. "I don't want to miss it."

"Shouldn't you ask your mother's permission first?" Darius muttered quietly, so only Selene heard.

Her smile widened while Gorgias stared.

Then suddenly, his skin paled, and the algus stepped back, reached for his wife's arm to clutch it tight.

Am I that fearsome?

Selene's face fell too, staring behind Darius as if she'd just seen a rakkan warlord.

Darius realised the sounds of people walking and talking in the street had quietened. He turned and immediately locked eyes with an old woman at the head of a group of algus walking down the steps from the palace. Scaly skin peeled on her bald scalp, and her slender face bore a slight grin along with greedy, satisfied eyes.

Following over her right shoulder, everyone in the group had a large black eagle sewn into the white fabric across their chests, making it easy for Darius to guess they were the King's envoy.

One man stood out among the rest, the only one with a hood up, who turned slightly towards Darius for a few seconds with a cloaked stare.

The orange haze in the sky darkened to a deep red as they watched the group walk down the street and disappear through the gate out of the palace grounds.

Selene, Gorgias and Fourteen fidgeted.

"I don't know who's worse," Selene said, some colour returning to her cheeks, "the King's Sword or Orator."

"By the looks on your faces," Darius said, "you'd think they just floated by."

"The King's Orator is worst," Gorgias said. "A silver tongue can doom a city with more ease than an algus with a sword, especially when it lies like a rakkan tongue."

"You've never seen the Sword fight, have you?" Fourteen said. "I'd rather face a legion of rakkans than him."

Only having seen a glance of either people, all Darius knew was he'd rather fight the old woman, who he guessed was the Orator.

"As much as I enjoy your gossip," Darius said, "I've had a long journey and need rest." *And a few stiff drinks.* But maybe he'd try some of Laltos's famous tarnflower tea instead. "Lex said I could stay in her home. Can you show me to it?" He turned to Selene expectantly.

"Well," she said, a smug look returning to her face, "I'm sure a man as capable as yourself doesn't need my help in finding it."

Usually, obstinacy annoyed him, but there was something about her attitude that he liked.

"Come on, Lyra. Let's find our own way." He looked down at his heel.

The empty space behind made his stomach drop. *Lyra*. How had he forgotten? He'd been chatting as if his escort weren't laid dying.

Selene raised an eyebrow. "Seeing things now? How long were you riding in the heat?"

Darius looked up with a face that wiped away her amusement. "I must retire," he said flatly. "Will you meet me tomorrow?"

"Sure… Here at noon… I'll introduce you to my father." She opened her mouth to say something else, but he quickly gave her and the other two algus a nod then turned and strode down the street. Any mood for conversation was now replaced with a longing for solitude, the state in which he felt Lyra's connection strongest.

"Tiro!" he called over his shoulder. The bird leapt into the air after him. "Take me to Lex's home." The falcon seemed to understand and soared to a nearby building.

Sorry, Lyra. I'll return soon. But first, he needed to beat Laltos's best archer at two hundred yards. And learn to talk to her without being an arse.

12

Lex – Xavala, the Silk City

With a dagger gripped behind her back, Lex eased the door open, wincing at the faint, high-pitched whine of the hinges. She stepped with soft footsteps into the blinding light of the cramped room, only taking a few paces before her mark slowly came into view around a corner.

The man sat with his back to her, hunched over a beech wood desk while scribbling on a parchment so erratically it had masked the sound of the door opening. Atop a lofty tower of the Xavalan palace, a draught from the window beside him ruffled his white silk robes. The note twitched, would have flown away if not for a gold weight on its corner. The shutters outside went bash, bash, bash in the wind.

She didn't know his name—and would keep it that way—but recognised he was no algus. A glance around the sandy-coloured walls was all it took to know they'd be difficult to clean if splattered with blood.

Her eyes scanned the legs of a pigeon waiting on the bottom of the window. *Nothing attached.* So with a swift kick, she slammed the door closed behind her.

The pigeon fluttered out to the sky as the man started. He looked over his shoulder, dark eyes widening when he did.

"You." He bolted up from the chair and backed up to the wall. Despite the draught, his expensive robes were stained with patches of sweat, and half his long fringe was stuck to his forehead.

I knew it. She hadn't been sure. Only the worry in the man's eyes when she'd first met him had made her suspicious. "Whom do you write to?"

He glanced out of the window, at the fall that would kill him. The sweat stains under his arms darkened. The shutters bashed.

"You're the one who killed my slave," she said, "snuck into my wagon and spied on my gift to the Regent. You know you leave me no choice."

"The Regent will know. I'm his friend." The man's fearful eyes bulged, his mouth twisted into a grimace of white teeth. "You wouldn't dare kill me."

The rich always talked before the end, tried to threaten or bargain. Lex squeezed her dagger. "I wouldn't dare let you live."

"I saw that tree. The King will find out, sooner or later."

"Then I choose later. Spies can't be left alive. If only you hadn't been writing a letter, I might have let you be." Though cutting her slave's throat made his chances slim.

"The note is to my family." The man's voice broke, and his eyes darted down to the parchment. "I'm no spy."

"Then you won't mind me reading that."

She burst forward, grabbed for the parchment as the man reached out first. *Liar.*

His hand took hold of it before hers, but her finger caught the edge, and she flared algor across it. The parchment froze in a heartbeat; a blue film spread to the man's fingers, and he cried out and dropped it.

A swift hand to his mouth silenced the scream, and a flare of algor seized his throat closed. Then she urged the cold deeper, driving it down his gullet and into his heart like thrusting a sword. As his neck stiffened, his legs folded, collapsing his body to the floor with a thud.

Lex picked up the frozen parchment, read the first few lines and confirmed her suspicions. Even in the Silk City, the least friendly with Toria in the Empire, the King's spies permeated.

She held the stiff parchment out of the window and crumbled it in her hands. The tiny fragments soared away with a gust of wind as Lex knelt to inspect the body.

Running her finger lightly across his neck, she verified that there were no breaks in the skin that would betray algor as the source of death. If everything thawed before discovery, it would look no different from a natural death. Better to cover it up than try to prove he was a spy to his friends.

As she tidied the scene, a bell disturbed her, announcing the noon hour in the city below. Lex tensed. She was supposed to be preparing to meet the Silk Regent.

With the speed of the wind howling outside, she bolted out of the door and down the spiral steps. Once down, she ran through a deserted corridor to a wider staircase where she slowed down given this area of the palace was busier.

Thankfully, no one saw her scurrying, and a few corridors later, she'd slipped back into her bed chamber.

She leant against the wall by the door, cooling her sweaty back as her deep breaths gradually eased. *Let's hope the Regent doesn't need silencing too.* If not trustworthy, an alliance was useless anyway.

She began undressing and walked towards the bed at the far side of the room.

"Where have you been, mistress?"

The voice made Lex start, and she whirled to face the dressing room door, dagger pointed.

The slave woman's eyes widened for a second but soon returned to a forced normality. Evidently, it wasn't the first time a blade had been pointed at her.

"Apologies. You startled me." Lex threw the dagger on the bed, then continued loosening her clothes and let them fall to the floor.

When there was no reply, Lex looked back to see the woman looking more shocked than when she'd pointed a knife.

Apologies from algus always surprised those treated as lesser their entire lives. The slave wore a white, finely stitched tunic, which—along with her high cheekbones and seductive brown eyes—let Lex guess the Regent liked to have her around. *I wonder how much he likes her...*

Lex held out her arms as the slave woman regained composure and came to drape a cream silk tunic over the algus's naked body. Even the warm evening breeze entering through the open balcony doors that tickled her skin was an unwelcome touch. She longed to feel hard chainmail again.

"Must I wear nothing underneath?" she asked.

"The Regent insists, mistress," came the reply over her shoulder.

Lecherous toad. While the woman dressed her, Lex looked around at the extravagant bed, a carved, gilded dressing table where she could make herself beautiful and proper for her future husband, and a six-foot balcony with a view overlooking the flat, sickeningly affluent city below.

The slave moved to Lex's front and wound the second piece of silk over her left shoulder, briefly meeting her eyes before quickly looking away as if she'd committed a heinous act.

While Lex waited, two white moths flew in from the balcony, so large each wing was almost the size of her palm. They fluttered together in the room for a while until the slave caught sight of them.

She waved her hands. "Shoo. Apologies, mistress. They're forever escaping and flying about the city." Her cheeks reddened.

"You need not be nervous around me," Lex said. "I'm not so pathetic as to take out my frustrations on workers."

The woman grinned slightly but otherwise ignored the comment.

"You have a delightful smile," Lex said.

At that, the girl froze for a second before returning to tying the clothes in place. "Thank you, mistress."

It was all too easy for an algus to lower the guard of a slave by being kind. None were used to it. Then, when relaxed, they couldn't hide their reaction to an intrusive question.

"Has Regent Aristippus ever laid with you?" Lex asked.

The woman's smile dropped, then she gave Lex a nervous look and pressed her lips shut, telling Lex all she needed to know.

The slave quickly stepped back with a nervous flush to her cheeks again and looked over the tunic flowing down to Lex's ankles. "You look stunning, mistress."

If she didn't, she wouldn't be there. "Will my betrothed be long?"

The slave's eyes fixed on Lex's chest and she gasped. "Oh, mistress! I forgot to say, you must remove that." The woman reached out to the pendant hanging around Lex's neck, but she took a step back.

"No. I never remove it."

"But, mistress, the Regent dislikes religion, especially the Order."

"I'm well aware. But if he can't bear the sight of a mere figurine of the God of Justice, what will he do on the day of judgement?"

"I won't need to do anything," a deep, smooth voice called from the door, "for such fantastical nonsense will never happen."

Lex turned as the slave's face dropped like she suddenly needed to visit the latrine.

Dressed in cream silk with golden jewellery weighing him down, the dark-eyed, youthful Aristippus swaggered into the room. Two concubines followed behind in dresses so thin they could barely be called clothes.

The slave bowed deeply while Lex bent a knee and gave the Silk Regent an enticing smile, so well-rehearsed it required little thought.

"It's nice to see you again, Regent," Lex said.

"You know," the Silk Regent said, "I might object to that superstitious symbol if it weren't suspended on such a beautiful figure." His voice lowered to a seductive growl as he stepped forward and took her hand to give it a kiss.

Don't make me vomit.

The smell of cedar from his perfume assaulted her nose. She blinked to quell the sting and tried to steady her face enough to grin and meet his eyes, taking in his smooth skin and cleanly shaven, square jaw. If she didn't know the man, she'd think him attractive. "Did you receive our gift?"

"Of course." He stepped back and beamed, showing gold teeth. "The weapons will be of great use."

116

"I hope you'll put them to use at once. Laltos needs your cavalry to defend against the invasion." Even Viridians respected the nimble horsemen.

The Silk Regent shrugged. "Who knows? Our alliance has other conditions, as you know." His eyes widened and dropped to her chest, this time not focused on the necklace.

She turned away, afraid he'd read the grimace threatening to break out on her face, and instead let him admire her posterior as she strutted out onto the balcony and leaned against the parapet.

The city she gazed over below was half the size of Laltos, but the wide streets and large houses with ornate amphorae and exotic plants decorating them wouldn't be paraded there. As the only major city in the Empire without a river, the Silk City survived from the riches of trade rather than working the land themselves.

"You'll never believe this," Aristippus slid in next to her, "but I almost joined your religion a few years ago."

He was right; she didn't believe it, and at this rate, the Silk Regent seemed bent on testing her temper even more than she'd expected.

"I went to the Chief Priest and asked for one of those escorts he gives to the adherents."

Probably just wanted a new plaything. "I take it you were unsuccessful."

"Yes. He didn't seem to think I was sincere in my belief."

"Pity."

"So, I said to him," the Silk Regent's voice rose, "he was right. I'm not foolish enough to believe in superstitious nonsense. You'd have to be as stupid as a rakkan to live by it. Agathos and Dianoia…a married god and goddess forming one makes no sense. Besides, who has need for a divine tyrant when we can enjoy ourselves instead?"

Judging by his slightly protruding belly, he certainly seemed to be doing that.

"You don't like the idea of good and evil then?" Lex asked.

A guffaw burst from the Regent. "They aren't real, only men trying to label such things. Do you know what good and evil are here?" He leaned in close to her and whispered, his breath itching her ear. "Whatever I say they are. The algus are the gods here."

Again, she resisted a grimace, but at least he was consistent. Without the God of Justice, morality was nothing more than the will of the most ruthless and powerful. "I commend your coherence. You wouldn't believe how many decry the acts of others as immoral whilst denying the arbiter of such things."

The Silk Regent turned to his concubines. "I think we have a philosopher among us." He chuckled. "Yes, I've met a few like that—empty-headed fools. They denounce what I do as if it had some objective meaning rather than expressing their own personal disapproval. They say we shouldn't cheat and kill, but why? Why should I listen to them? I'm more powerful than they. Why should I follow the rules of society rather than feather my nest? Pursue life's pleasures—that's my philosophy."

It was obvious to Lex why others denounced acts in the same breath as denying the Arbiter's existence. The pull of moral instincts was inescapable in most, difficult to throw off, so it left the person with baseless intuitions they never thought deeply enough about.

The Silk Regent took her hand. "Here in Xavala you can indulge in your fantasies."

She smiled and forced colour to her cheeks, feeling the touch of his soft palms that had never fought a day in their lives.

Give me a warrior's calluses any day. "I'm not a slave that can't say no to you. This is one fantasy you can't have until you've earned it."

She withdrew her hand and strutted back inside to the bed chamber where the slave stood awaiting orders.

Aristippus followed, running a hand down her backside. "You won't get my cavalry until I get what's mine."

Lex spun around to meet his hungry eyes, resisting the urge to strangle him. "I have another gift for you."

"You spoil me."

"A mulberry tree."

The amusement vanished from the Silk Regent's face. "It's here?"

"With my caravan." Her eyes searched his and saw the pangs of fear she'd expected. Now she hoped they'd turn hungry once again.

Instead, his eyebrows forked. "You dare bring that here? What if the King has seen it?"

She shrugged. "Perhaps it's time we stopped caring what the King thinks."

"I don't care what he thinks." His voice sharpened to a bark. "The swine can rot in his capital for all I care, but as long as every other regent is loyal, I have no choice. You know what he does to those that break the law."

"It's a law only designed to control you. Aren't you tired of it?"

Aristippus glared. "Of course I am! The mulberry leaves we used to grow to feed our silkworms were thrice the quality of the dross the King sells us now, not to mention his prices are a drain on our coffers."

Before the War of the Two, when Xavala's mulberry forest gained the name the "Scorched Forest," the Silk City had been the wealthiest in the Empire. Lex knew men envied what history told of their forefathers' wealth and glory.

"Grow your own trees again," Lex said. "My father isn't best pleased with the King himself. It isn't just rakkans we can help each other with."

Finally, the Silk Regent's scowl softened, and his brow furrowed. "We'd be foolish to defy the King."

Lex stepped forward, into the cloud of perfume around him, and ran her hand across his cheek. His angry eyes melted as was always the way with her touch.

"Send Laltos the cavalry," she said, "and we'll help you in many ways." A king that ignored Laltos's plight deserved revolt. "One day we may even replant the mulberry trees over the whole Scorched Forest."

The Silk Regent smirked. "I get the impression that being married to you will never be boring." His hand slipped down the small of her back.

"That I can guarantee. So, am I to get nothing in return for the weapons I gave?"

He smirked and took a step back. "No. I'll give you the sulphur you requested. I'll have it loaded into your wagons. As for the tree, I'll keep it, make sure it's safe."

This time Lex's wide smile was genuine. Sulphur was better than nothing for the war. "What about food? We need it." Especially since she'd traded with the hungry Margalvians.

"I'm sorry. Our harvest has been poor this year too."

She cursed and moved towards the door, eager to forget all she had on her shoulders. "Well then…someone mentioned that I had to visit your farms and see where the finest silk in the Empire is made."

The Silk Regent puffed up his chest. "I can guarantee you'll never see a fatter silkworm than here. Better than anything from the east."

"I don't doubt it."

She took his hand, but before she led him outside, a frazzled old man with deep frown lines burst into the room.

"Regent…" He paused to catch a breath.

"I'm busy," Aristippus replied.

"But it's important. Isidore has been murdered, here in the palace!"

Lex suppressed a curse.

13

Darius – Laltos

Heat thrust Darius from his sleep. He gasped. Drenched blankets stuck to his body. *Not again.* He sat up in bed and threw them off. Lyra's fever was only worsening since he'd left.

Thin streaks of light ran across the wall from the shuttered window, announcing dawn had arrived, which gave an end to his torturous attempt at respite.

Getting up, he wiped himself with the few dry parts of the sheet then paused and waited for the air coursing through the shutters to cool him. With every movement, Tiro's eyes followed him from a perch in the corner of Lex's guest bedroom.

Thankful for at least some company, Darius walked across the wide room and stroked the falcon's breast, finding blood stains that hadn't been there the evening before. "What did you eat this time? Pigeon or duck?"

Tiro gazed up at him.

Can Lex sense me through him? He was still glad to have an escort there, even if it wasn't his own. Loneliness was a curse, ironically more so in a busy city such as Laltos.

He pushed open the shutters to reveal the view of the upper city and nearby palace. The towers cast long shadows over the town and fell across the clepsydra's marker on the palace front, which had fallen to the bottom of the scale sometime in the night. Despite regarding it many times, he still couldn't fathom how such a device moved up at regular intervals. Every water clock he'd seen had irregular markings as the water slowed its trickle out as the bowl emptied. He'd considered an oddly shaped tank to keep the flow constant but concluded it wouldn't work.

How was he to impress a man whose invention was beyond his comprehension? The only ideas that had surfaced were flattery, bribery, praise of his daughters, and presenting the head of Hadrian or his second-in-command. *I need better.*

And that wasn't his only problem. He wouldn't beat Selene with a bow. His best plan was to win over the Regent enough to make *him* be the one to convince Selene to take Philippos with her, but that led him back to the first problem.

Darius clasped his temples to calm his spiralling mind. When he closed his eyes, the heat surfaced again and beads of sweat formed. *Lyra.* He let her feel his connection for a few minutes before wiping his brow. He had until noon, and rather than wallow, he'd spend it practising with a bow.

After putting on his algus costume, he left the room to search Lex's home, locating a bow and quiver with relative ease and grabbing some cooked eggs from the kitchen staff. Once outside, he set off in search of a quiet place for target practise.

While wandering the streets of the upper city, he walked past the courthouse he'd once been taken to, only recognising it by the axe-wielding God carved atop the entrance. In the otherwise quiet street, shouts and cries rang out from one of the shuttered windows facing the road. He hoped it was a captured Viridian being tortured for information. Still, the screams stirred him to imagine the man's agony, so he picked up his pace to get away.

In the next street, he swiped an empty wooden crate as a makeshift target and wandered back up to the palace. Despite the earlier deserted roads, groups of well-dressed citizens marched up and down the steps, leaving no suitable place to shoot. To the side of the building, he spotted a quiet grass lawn with no pathway, so he made his way across and to the back of the palace.

Evenly cut grass stretched out for at least a couple of hundred yards until it stopped at a vertical cliff face.

A few guards stationed at the rear doors moved in front of the pillars to monitor him, but if they'd recognised him, the horns and bells of alarm would already have sounded.

He stood the crate on its side and counted two hundred paces away. When he turned, it took him a second to locate the small target.

Here goes nothing. He nocked an arrow, aimed, and loosed it, unsurprised when it struck wide beyond the mark. At least he was strong enough to make the distance. His next try was no better, and arrow after arrow failed to threaten to strike.

He loosed again and swore as it missed the target.

"Aren't we keen," a voice called from one of the palace doors.

Darius turned to see Selene, now dressed with sleeves of chainmail visible under her leaf-green tunic while curls of her hair fluttered loose in the wind in an unnervingly seductive dance.

"I needed the practise," Darius said. "What say we duel with swords instead?"

Selene laughed. "You know, women like confidence in a man."

Darius nocked another arrow, praying this one hit its mark. He loosed it and watched it soar past its intended target. *Damn.* He resisted the urge to snap the bow. "I'd better hope you prefer honesty."

"Then tell me, honest man, why do you wish to accompany me so desperately?"

Darius looked to the ground, wondering how much of the truth was wise to share. "I've seen the towns, out in the far west."

"You're telling me you're moved by the blood of our people?"

At least he could give a truthful answer to that. "The spilled blood bothers me more than you can know."

"Then why do I get the impression that you're hiding something?"

"You caught me," Darius said sarcastically. "Truth is, I've fallen for you, can't bear to be parted from you."

Selene clutched her chest and spoke in a mockingly high voice. "I thought it was just me."

Darius laughed, surprised at the sudden amusement after his mood of late. It had to be a special woman that elicited laughter from a surly clod like him.

Taking off the bow slung across her back, Selene stepped beside Darius then nocked an arrow. "Three shots. Closest to the centre of the crate wins."

"We're doing this now? You're supposed to be taking me to see your father."

"All in good time, handsome."

The comment on his looks made him uneasy, much like the times before. Words of reply left his mind momentarily.

As they prepared for the contest, another algus emerged from between the pillars of the palace and strode across the grass towards them. Darius's intrigue turned into annoyance when he recognised Gorgias's black hair.

"You're going through with this then?" the algus asked as he approached.

Selene's face paled at the sound of Gorgias's voice while Darius stared. He noted the algus's unshaven chin and guessed his mockery of the day before had struck a nerve.

"I thought we'd discussed this last night, Selene," Gorgias said. "It's best outsiders don't get involved in our affairs, especially ones so crass they make rakkans look appealing."

"I'll travel with whom I please," Selene shot back.

Darius clenched his jaw lest he speak his mind and instead nocked an arrow while the pair of algus squabbled. He slowed his breathing, trying to relax and keep the bow steady, but his pounding heart repeatedly nudged his aim wide.

When finally still, he loosed the arrow, and it arced up and down before piercing the bottom of the crate. After a moment of disbelief, he laughed. *Perfect time for luck.*

"Not bad." Selene turned back to face him.

Darius shrugged, reining in his glee. "Not bad. About a foot shy of the centre."

Selene drew back her bowstring, paused for a second while the breeze wafted her hair before she loosed the arrow. It darted through the air, straighter and swifter than Darius's had, and skewered the middle of the target.

She looked at Darius with a smirk, but it lacked the smugness of the smile spreading on Gorgias's face.

"How's that possible?" Darius stared at the crate.

Before she or Gorgias came out with a witty retort, Darius readied another arrow and took a shot. But this one missed the target, causing Gorgias to laugh so hard that his slick hair lost its shape and fell across his forehead.

The high-pitched chortle grated Darius's ears. He suspected breaking Gorgias's jaw would win him favour with Selene, but decided against it.

Selene didn't bother to take another shot, and Darius nocked his last arrow. If he missed, then he didn't know where he'd begin proving his loyalty to Regent Theodoros without her as a witness to the hell he planned to unleash. All he wanted was to go out and slay the invading Viridians, not play games, but Lex's plan had merit.

However, it would be foolish to leave the First Alliance's fate to his skill with a bow.

"I have a proposition," he said.

Selene raised an eyebrow.

"Rather than testing my skills as an archer, why not test yours? I'll wager you can't hit the target with another arrow."

Selene laughed. "Did you not see my last shot?"

"Let's make it easier—at a quarter of the distance. If you can't, I go with you. If you do, I'll leave Laltos on my own."

She frowned and shrugged. "Fine. Your loss."

Across the short, spiky grass, the three of them walked forwards, Selene eyeing him as if expecting a con. When she and Gorgias stopped at the agreed distance, Darius kept striding directly into her line of sight.

"What are you doing?" she asked.

"I never said I'd make it easy for you." He stopped six feet short of the target and turned to face her. Withdrawing his sword from his scabbard, he moved slightly to one side, giving her a view of the crate, then readied for the incoming shot.

"You're insane," she yelled. "Your chainmail won't block an arrow, and I can barely see the crate past you. I could pierce your heart. You'd risk death just to accompany me?"

"You said you're the best shot in Laltos." Darius had dodged plenty of arrows in his arduous training. Sparring with Brutus and Julius blindfolded had attuned his rakkan senses well, though it had given him many bruises along the way. But this time, the iron heads of Selene's arrows would do more than bruise. She was right about his chainmail.

He shifted and readied his sword, suddenly questioning his positioning.

After a bewildered shake of her head, she nocked an arrow and drew back the string.

Darius closed his eyes, needing only a second to sense the background movements of the air until able to perceive any changes. He was as ready as he could be.

Then Selene loosed the arrow.

It sliced through the air, sending ricochets to Darius's skin. Without time to think, he shifted to the side, out of the arrow's path but giving himself space to swing.

The ricochets grew in strength.

The arrow neared.

Intuition mapped its path in his mind.

With only a split-second to spare, he swung his sword, felt a shudder and clang from the flat steel reach his hand that told him he'd struck the arrow before he opened his eyes to see it bounce into the dirt.

The two algus stood in silence while a few of the guards by the palace pointed and exchanged words. As they stared, Darius strode back towards the pair with a grin.

"Lucky." Selene's eyes opened wide with a newfound awe that only broadened his smile.

"It's funny," Darius said, "the more I train with a sword, the luckier I get."

"Enough of this nonsense," Gorgias said. "You lost the original wager."

Selene looked ready to argue but paused under the weight of Gorgias's glare. The juvenile man wasn't much to look at, and it surprised Darius a woman like Selene indulged his presence.

"Why do you listen to this dullard?" Darius asked.

Gorgias stepped up to him, nose to nose. "This 'dullard' is the son of Hera."

"Selene. Let's see your father while this nobleman goes to tell his mother about the mean Xavalan man."

Gorgias's frown morphed into a smug look. "You haven't heard? The Regent's still in discussions with the King's Orator. They're demanding a new tax per head in exchange for aid."

Selene groaned. "Tell me the census has at least finished."

"It has. Regent Theodoros is furious at the extortion but has given our armies permission to leave."

"Finally."

"I have better news. My mother has agreed I can leave with you."

Selene's face froze. "You've never fought a day in your life."

"And that changes now."

After a long pause, Selene turned to Darius. "Philippos. You're to come with us."

"What?" Gorgias shrieked.

Darius bowed his head to her. "Thank you. But do we have to go with this boy?"

"Man!" Gorgias snapped.

"Enough, you two," Selene said. "We leave this afternoon."

"But your father…" Darius said. That was the reason he'd come, and it'd be hard to build trust with the Regent if he'd never spoken to the man. "And you promised to show me how the water clock functions."

"We've been stuck in this city long enough." Selene flicked her hair over her shoulder. "Our armies have left the west under-protected for the sake of the King's damned survey, not to mention we need food and to protect the roads. My soldiers and algus will leave when the clepsydra hits the highest mark."

That barely left time for Darius to gather supplies, but it seemed he had little choice. The Regent would have to be impressed by his skills as a warrior alone, and he prayed fate gave him the greatest opportunity for it on his travels—to meet Hadrian or his second again and slay them.

Just the thought brought to the surface a dark hunger inside. Whatever Viridian warriors they came across, soon Darius would get to release the anger that had festered within him since Lyra's wounding.

His reprisal would match the name they called him—Darius the Dreaded.

14

Nikolaos – Margalvia

Nikolaos wished he could see the looks on the rakkans' faces when he escaped, when they knew he'd fooled them, the authors of lies themselves.

Gnawing a stale crust of bread fit only for a rakkan, his head chilled from the metal bars of his prison cell pressed against him, long past caring about the congealed sweat and grime coating them. *My face must look a horrid state.*

He glanced back at the doorway in the dingy passage outside, where the guards came and went when changing shifts. Their irregular patterns were designed to be impenetrable, but he'd solved the formula after months of careful watching. But it wasn't guards he now looked for…

Why, after so long, did Lex still tread through those doors to check in on him, as if being imprisoned wasn't her doing? At first, he'd resolved to spit in her face if she visited, but then thought it best to feign interest in working with the rakkans alongside her. He'd never trust the scum, though.

Was she the only traitor, or was his beloved Laltos and its riches now in the hands of a treasonous regent? He hoped so, because it would make his own ascendency to regent all the ' easier.

Nikolaos allowed his gaze to fall to the iron shackles and chains on his wrists where the metal had been welded closed. He conjured a thin film of algor across them, just enough to hear the crack of metal freezing, then banished it quickly.

He tugged, observing the hairline fractures. They didn't visibly widen but were spreading over time, and time was all he had. Repeated cooling made the metal ever more brittle, and his hope was they'd soon break.

On the floor by his hands, he slid his fingers across to collect more specks of the powdered munlock he'd been handling and placed them back into a pouch he'd fashioned. His dormouse escort, Xenia, had needed to venture far and wide in the contemptible city to secure so much of the poisonous herb, and carrying it without risk to herself wasn't easy.

Never one to pay attention to herbalism, Nikolaos was unsure of the dosage required to kill a grown man, but he'd soon find out. The delicate plant and its tiny blue flowers was extremely potent.

His mind shifted to Xenia, who was already clinging onto the side of an amphora deep in the storage cellar with a tiny pouch of poison between her teeth.

Drop it in. Hurry, before I feed you to a snake.

She obliged. Now he had to wait and follow the first person that drank from it. If fatal, he knew the dose required.

As Nikolaos collected the remnant specks of munlock from the floor, a figure rounded a darkened corner outside his cell and strode out of the shadows.

Nikolaos started, grabbed the pouch, and slid it under his leg before spreading a few bits of straw across the floor.

As the person neared, a lamp in their hand cast flickers of light over a stern face.

"Nikolaos," Varro said in a firm voice. "I have something to ask you."

"Happy to help." Nikolaos gave what he hoped to be a confident smile. He didn't know what was most satisfying, that the Warlord believed his lies or that they gave him food and potent drink. Paralysing the uncertain leader into inaction was easier than making an underling dance for coins—such was the intellect of rakkans, though. The Margalvians thought themselves better than the Viridians, but they were no different in Nikolaos's eyes. A rakkan was a rakkan.

"Lex said you've visited Xavala frequently," Varro said. "What do you know about the city?"

A lot. Nikolaos considered the Silk Regent as one of the most fun to entertain. But his escort had overheard Lex's planned alliance, and he'd do his best to frustrate it. "Not much, only that Xavala is loyal to the King and would join any assault on Margalvia."

Varro's frown deepened, his obsidian eyes piercing Nikolaos so deeply he worried the Warlord saw his plan for escape.

"Can Regent Aristippus be trusted?" Varro asked.

To feather his own nest, perhaps. Little else. "I'd trust him with my life." Nikolaos cast his gaze down and shifted his leg when he realised the pouch was half-visible. He held his breath.

"Give me something useful and I'll have the guards feed you meat," Varro said.

With his mind distracted, Nikolaos struggled to concoct an adequate lie. The truth was all his mind mustered. "The Silk Regent despises rakkans as much as the people of Laltos."

Varro murmured.

"May I ask you a question?" Nikolaos asked.

The Warlord's silence was all Nikolaos needed to know he was granted permission.

"Has Lex been in allegiance with you since the war began? When we were children? When she stayed with me after a rakkan killed her husband? When I made sure she ate?"

Varro scoffed and turned to walk away.

Typical rakkan. "Did I earn my meat?" Nikolaos called after him.

"Not even close." The Warlord's cloak disappeared around the corner, leaving Nikolaos in darkness again, never knowing who was watching.

When he finally escaped, he was in two minds whether to go to the King or Xavala. Laltos couldn't be allowed to ally with Margalvia. Only a foolish city trusted rakkans. In all of history, rakkans had sided with their own in the end. The Battle on the Mount and War of the Uncharted were two of many where rakkan enemies had put aside rivalries to fight alongside one another.

No. It wouldn't happen. He'd escape and expose Lex, no matter what it took.

With a grunt, Nikolaos flopped to the straw bed and swallowed his hatred, ignoring the strands of wheat already itching his skin.

While lying on the mattress in search of slumber, a tingle in his stomach told him his escort had seen something. He closed his eyes to block out the filthy rakkan cell and immersed himself in feeble Xenia.

A servant runt of a boy wrapped two arms around the poisoned amphora and waddled down an underground corridor. Xenia followed by flitting from one crack in the black stonework of the wall to the next, until the boy entered a kitchen.

He placed the amphora on a table-top and wiped sweat from his brow while Xenia darted behind the leg of a cupboard.

"Is that the water?" came a woman's harsh voice.

"Yes," the boy replied in a timid tone.

"You look beat, lad. Have a cup and sit down."

The boy obliged and poured himself a generous helping into a cup then downed it as Nikolaos murmured in frustration. A child was useless in testing potency on grown men, for he already knew what would happen. After half an hour, paralysis would set in, particularly of the upper abdomen and chest, and the wheezing mimicked the onset of an aggressive bug. With time, the boy would deteriorate until finally unable to breathe at all.

Don't follow him, Xenia. Wait for the next. The boy left and Nikolaos's escort waited as instructed.

While doing so, she made it known to him that her hunger pains were becoming even more agonising. *Stay put!*

Many rakkans came and went without consequence, but after a while, a large warrior finally poured himself a cup in passing and drank.

Perfect. It wasn't more than a few seconds before he slammed the empty cup down and marched out of the room.

Xenia moved without instruction after the heels of the man while Nikolaos returned to his own senses with a smile. If all went well, he'd treat himself to a little of the salted beef he'd saved in celebration. Not that he could relax completely, for there was still one thing left to do—ensure escape from his cell. The kuraminium bars were too strong to crack with his algor trick, which left the key as his only option.

Luckily, he already had a plan for that, as well as for what he'd do once free.

Laltos would end up better off under his command. He'd see its riches spent wisely. They'd defeat the Viridian Legion by allying with the King, finding the Staff of Arria, and wiping out the rakkans once and for all. Compared to that, Lex's First Alliance with the demons themselves was unthinkable.

I'll expose you soon, Lex. Laltos will be freed from traitors.

15

Brutus – Viridian Camp

Brutus carefully spread the branches of the bush across the pigeons' cage, interlocking them with the metal until the only clue the birds were there was the occasional coo.

"They don't like being so enclosed," the pigeon fancier mumbled. His flowing blond hair was tied behind his head to show his overly large ears, which matched his flat, wide nose. The look of concern in his eyes while he glanced at the birds was like that of a parent looking on his children.

"Next time we meet, don't bring the pigeons," Brutus said. "Otherwise I may as well carve 'spy' into my forehead if someone sees us."

With a nod, the pigeon fancier took the lone bird he'd removed and pushed through the tangles of the bush towards the overcast night sky. Attached to the bird's leg was a note he'd scrawled, detailing the locations of Viridian troops Brutus had scouted so far.

Brutus followed, and once they were in a more open part of the shrub, the fancier lifted his arms and let the pigeon fly. With erratic flaps of its wings, it broke free of the branches and went on its way, climbing at first before soaring away from the Viridian camp in the valley below.

"See you in a few days." Brutus pushed his way out of the bush.

Now trudging back down the slope to the camp, Brutus made use of his high vantage point to better study the troops packing up. Defences were loose, being far outside human lands in the famishing mountains. "Uncharted," the humans called them, because rakkan charts weren't worth the price of the parchment and no human had mapped them.

Along his travels, Brutus had gained Viridian colours and armour from a scout, but still swallowed down vomit at having to wear them every day. He'd covered the proud "M" tattoo on his arm with bandages, but as always, he had to pick the opportune moment to join the couple of hundred warriors at the site.

Half the pine trees this side of the mountains had been reduced to stumps. The Viridian tents clung to the mountainside as the white-headed peaks loomed behind, telling him they were about halfway to their home city and too far from Margalvia for his comfort, too far from his beloved.

At the centre stood the tallest tent, pointed like the head of a spear, with a nearby fire that set the fabric aglow in the night. Brutus hoped a Viridian Commander resided there, but he hadn't happened across one so far.

He cursed at the memory of the last time he'd been on a task such as this, when he'd sworn never again. *If Varro weren't my brother…* Give him the battlefield any day, where his skills with his trusty hammer were the difference between life and death, rather than fortune.

As Brutus neared, a bunch of soldiers towards the edge of the camp shouted at one another. The centurion hardly kept track of his men coming and going, forgot their names and referred to them as "you over there" and "long-shanks". They were an ideal group for Brutus to slip amongst and act as another layabout pressed into the army.

A few legionnaires walking along a path Brutus was soon to join glanced at him. Walking with false confidence, all Brutus received were a few raised eyebrows as he slowed his pace and joined the back.

One slim but athletic legionnaire at the rear glanced over his shoulder and gave Brutus a deep frown. The Margalvian stared back for a few seconds, not breaking his gaze and clenching his hammer.

The rakkan narrowed his eyes but turned around without a word.

Brutus watched the back of the rakkan's head as they lumbered, noting the thick scar cutting through the short black hair from the back of his neck all the way to his forehead.

It wasn't long before they entered the camp, which relieved Brutus. He slinked away from the frowning legionnaire between the haphazard arrangement of tents.

The steam and smell of overcooked food soon filled his nose, and he moved towards the tall, crackling fire. A grubby chef dished out bowls of what looked like blood chowder. Seeing the grimaces of those eating it, Brutus had no urge to join them. The taste usually left a lot to be desired, but nutritionally, it gave a warrior everything he needed.

The Viridian Legion fed its warriors well, while the rest of their people lived on scraps—except for the high-powered women. To be a woman of stature in Viridia was like a blessing from the Creator. They enjoyed fine clothes and wine whilst the men fought for spoils, all for the price of producing more soldiers like queen bees.

Thinking it best to blend in, Brutus walked up to the chef, took a bowl of chowder, then sat in front of the fire to feel its warmth on his legs. Several legionnaires and younger teens also huddled near the heat while supping the meal and muttering to one another.

A young adolescent passed by Brutus, nose bloody and scratches across his shins and arms. He sat beside an older centurion who put his arm around the boy.

"How did the trial go?" the centurion asked.

"Seven of us passed, two died," the boy replied sulkily.

"Don't mourn them. They were weak. Only a couple more trials to pass before you become a legionnaire."

After a while, the old centurion retired to his tent, which left the boy to sup soup next to Brutus.

They exchanged a glance. *Poor lad.* When Brutus had seen the Viridian trials, it made him appreciate his home all the more. They hunted human and rakkan slaves for sport and were underfed to encourage them to steal food, yet punished harshly if caught doing so.

Only the strong and smart thrived. The Viridian Legion were born and forged for war.

It was hard for Brutus to see young ones suffer. When a man couldn't have children of his own, it made him view them in a fresh light.

His wife's tears after years of trying played on his mind again, and how the weeping had lessened the day he'd brought home a half-human lad. They'd both known he'd be trouble, but maternal and paternal instincts soon took over.

Turning his attention back to the Viridian boy, Brutus opened his mouth to speak but was interrupted by a rakkan barging between him and the lad.

"You look hurt, boy," the legionnaire said without a trace of genuine concern in his tone. "How about I tend to your wounds?"

Brutus recognised the scar across the rakkan's head at once.

"I have a sponsor," the boy mumbled.

"I won't tell." The legionnaire smiled to show a set of half-rotten teeth. "It can be our—"

"You heard the lad," Brutus said with a glower. "Push off."

The legionnaire turned to him with narrowed eyes. "You… It isn't often I see an unfamiliar face."

The words quickened Brutus's heart, the ever-present anxiety of a spy he loathed. "It isn't often I like to speak to an unfamiliar face, so beat it."

The scarred rakkan looked down to the bandage on Brutus's arm. "Injured? Funny that it covers your colours." The rakkan reached out.

But Brutus jumped up and grabbed the rakkan's outstretched hand. A few of the legionnaires whirled around as Brutus then took hold of the rakkan's fingers and clenched his fist, feeling two snap backwards.

The scarred rakkan grunted in pain, stifled a yell.

"If you don't get out of my sight, I'll break the rest." Brutus shoved the rakkan away.

The warriors around scowled. Arguments and fisticuffs within the Viridian ranks were hardly uncommon. Still, he eyed them all with a hand on his hammer and waited for the first to dare intervene.

Thankfully, none moved.

Cradling his hand, the scarred rakkan backed away while smiling with a look in his eye that made Brutus even more nervous. *Should have broken his neck instead.* Brutus fixed his glare on the rakkan as he slowly walked away and disappeared between the tents.

Sitting back down, he gave the callow lad a nod, which was met with a glare.

"Don't get any ideas," the lad said.

With a roll of his eyes, Brutus went back to watching the flames in front of him ripple and flare in chaotic waves. As he did, he listened to the inane chatter for so long he was forced to get more chowder to feign a reason to stay.

When the sky lightened to announce the impending sunrise, Brutus was ready to call it a night.

But something caught his eye. A wiry, tattooed warrior with thick red hair walked along with a hunched back and a hand pressed to his heavily bandaged waist. Across his bicep were two viridian bands, and he talked as he moved with another short, stout rakkan sporting the same bands.

A Viridian Guardian. Must be fate. Brutus stood and walked towards the commanders as casually as possible, his hand still curled around his hammer. Only when he was closer did he see the black signet ring on the guardian.

"Another raid and only one new prisoner," the guardian said. "We had to kill the others."

"You're lucky," the other commander replied in a nasal voice. "Only the Numbered seem easy enough to capture, and bringing them back to Viridia is becoming a hassle. My centuries are restless. They miss the spoils from the raids and are eager to stay in human lands, to pay back those wretches for our dead brothers."

Brutus slowed his paces and walked beside a tent close by, pretending to be searching for something lost in the mud. He'd heard of them capturing algus before, and the mounting number of prisoners struck him as odd. What use would the Viridians have for so many?

"Keep your men in line." The guardian grimaced and came to a halt, grabbing his abdomen. "I've found breaking the algus before taking them back makes it easier."

Brutus moved to the side of the nearest tent and paused once out of sight of the pair. A fleeting glance around confirmed no one was there. He strained to process why Hadrian was so focused on taking algus prisoners.

The commander sighed. "I'd rather be on the war front. I want to see the humans starving, see them suffer the same pains of hunger they've inflicted on us for so long."

"I need a break from it, after catching a sword from that fiend. Those damned Margalvians have forced us to accelerate our plans."

It was only then that Brutus realised who the "fiend" was and who the guardian was—Hadrian's son Cordus. He might lead Brutus to the Viridian Warlord himself.

"The attacks will continue as planned," Cordus said, "assuming no more Margalvian ruses. How spineless do you need to be to resort to assassination over open battle?"

As Brutus willed them to speak more of the planned attacks, a rakkan came up behind him and growled. "I knew you'd be up to no good."

Brutus whirled around to see the scarred rakkan, sword in his unbroken hand and bloody resentment in his eyes.

Squeezing the handle of his hammer, Brutus took in the peripherals of his vision to see nobody else within sight. *Time to end this one for good.*

16

Darius – West of Laltos

Darius slugged the cup of burnt wine while he caved in walnuts with his other hand, imagining them to be Hadrian's head. *Wait. Wait. Wait. That's all we seem to do.* How wrong he'd been to expect war when he'd left Laltos with Selene. At this rate, he might as well have been a pacifist.

Lex had asked him to lead men against the Viridian Legion, not to give them a stroll in the woods. He'd never been so uneasy in such a heavily padded chair as the one under his backside.

It felt odd considering he was in a tent on the outskirts of a small raided village amidst one of the many recently-charred forests between Laltos and Viridia. Tomorrow, that village would belong to Laltos once again, as had the last four.

This time, would Darius's sword finally hack the Viridian fiends that had injured his escort? Or would they be retaking empty husks again? All they saw of Hadrian's second-in-command was the carnage left from his footprints. Even Tiro had tired of the non-events and had returned to Lex, or so Darius presumed because the bird had vanished one day.

Patters from the drizzle outside filled the monotonous green tent. Its contents were fit for a god—thick, feather-stuffed mattress large enough for four, cow-hide floor covering and amphorae of strong, burnt wine—had been carried for miles on wagons and had been accompanied by hundreds of soldiers and dozens of algus. *Pity the food isn't so luxurious.*

Selene had led the caravan, and Darius was happy to silently follow, taking the time to make idle chat to gain favour with her and the other algus. His quips seemed to resonate with a few of the well-off nobles, though they drew unamused scowls from the rest, especially Gorgias, who'd been as insufferable as a blister on his heel.

He cast his eyes to the scroll on his lap, seeing if this time his focus lasted more than a few seconds. As he read, he heard the words in his head as if Brutus spoke them, imparting insight like he so often did—or at least tried to.

Wisdom of the Creator

1. My child, keep my words and store them up within you.

2. Keep my commands and you will live; protect them as a mother does her cub.

3. Say to wisdom, "You are my sister," and to knowledge, "Stand with me, brother."

4. Bind them on your fingers; write them onto your heart.

Darius paused, the words echoing what Lex often said to him of listening to his heart over his head when making decisions. *Look how that worked out for Lyra.* He unrolled the parchment a little further and skipped a few lines.

17. The prospect of the righteous is joy, but the hopes of the wicked come to nothing.

18. A city is glorified through the blessing of the honest, but it is destroyed by the tongue of the wicked.

That reminded Darius of something Gorgias had said about the dangers of a silver tongue. Didn't this scroll have more to offer than the words of a pompous man-child?

Darius unrolled further until a larger block of text came into view with a name that seized his attention.

The tale of Trogus and Arria

Never has a tale been told of such sorrow than that which befell Arria and her beloved Trogus. As if it weren't enough for a wife to curse a son, a son to murder his parents, but their pain is nothing when compared to the countless that have since suffered because of the iniquities of one.

He cast his eyes quickly across the text to get to the part of most interest to him.

…and so it was that the Staff of Arria and Twin Blades of Trogus entered the world, to coronate kings, queens and overlords for millennia to follow.

"Am I interrupting?" Selene's face peeked through the flap of his tent.

He rolled up the scroll and leaned back in his chair, propping his feet up on a stool in front. "Yes. You are. But I forgive you."

She raised an eyebrow with a smirk threatening to form on her lips.

Does she mean to make that seductive? He returned the grin. "You coming here meets the definition of the word 'interrupt', doesn't it?"

"I never took you for a reader, let alone a pedant over words."

"Then perhaps you've underestimated my smarts."

"Oh really?" She stepped into the tent and stood with a hand on her hip. "Then tell me, genius, how does my father's clepsydra work?"

Had his asking over it on the road made him look idiotic? "As it happens, I figured it out. I could explain…but I'm not sure you'd understand."

A laugh had already left his lips when she kicked the stool from under his feet, which made him chuckle even more.

"Why must you always tease me, Philippos?"

Drawing a smile out from Selene had become as easy to him as handling a sword, and he still took pleasure at the one now across her face and the rouge it brought to her cheeks.

"The real question is"—Darius stood and slowly moved towards her—"why do you seek my company if I tease you?"

The flush in her cheeks deepened. "I'd rather be teased than fraternise with Gorgias." Her eyes fell to his lips, which unnerved him more than if she'd drawn a sword. "I kind of wish it was just the two of us."

"I see…" He moved a step closer. "Is there anything else you wish for?"

She raised an eyebrow. "Winning the war would be pretty high on the list, and… How about you? If everyone was given three wishes, what would yours be?"

He halted his approach and frowned. "First, I'd wish away Gorgias's wishes."

Selene chuckled and eyed his lips again.

There were many things he'd wish for, but none that he'd like to divulge to her.

"So, to what do I owe this visit?" he asked.

As if snapping out of a daydream, Selene blinked and shook her head. "The scouts have returned, confirming what my escort saw."

"And? Have the Viridians left behind only corpses again?"

"I'm meeting with Gorgias and the other algus to discuss. Are you coming?"

"Of course." He tossed the scroll onto his stool and was soon out of the tent and feeling the hard soil of the clearing under his boots.

"You're in a rush." She followed him out as he made his way over to her larger tent, stained the perfect shade of green to meld into the surrounding foliage. Its billowing sides formed a circle, and it was littered around with the iron-cased bodies of soldiers tucking into supper or packing supplies into bags.

One man caught his eye, struggling while trying to drag a black metal chain towards an open crate.

Kuraminium restraints.

It wasn't like they needed them, having never caught a rakkan yet, but it seemed Selene always liked to be prepared. There was much he tried but failed to decipher about her—like her sister Lex, who also dwelled on his mind. But, unlike Lex, Selene was willing to answer his questions.

"So, you have an escort?" he asked.

"Yes. I'll bet you two crests you can't guess what animal I chose."

Wonder when her games will become tiresome? She seemed the type to have something large and blatant as an escort, and perhaps the conversation would distract him from the reminder of Lyra. "There are too many possibilities."

148

"It flies."

He opened his mouth but shut it when feeling the urge to play along. *A bird?* It wouldn't have been his choice, but he guessed he could narrow it down to a bird of prey, and a large one at that.

The old Darius had chosen a panther. Their stealth and raw power made them ideal for tracking and hunting, which his old self had taken full advantage of, so he'd been told.

"Alright," he said. "A bird of prey like a peregrine would be most useful, but as your sister has one, I get the impression you'd differentiate yourself."

"Is peregrine your guess?"

"No." He delved into the recesses of his knowledge, and to his surprise, found he knew more than a regular warrior should about birds. "I'm thinking something big, and given I haven't seen it so far, it probably likes to spend its time in the sky."

She tried to suppress a grin, but he caught sight of the dimples in her cheeks.

"My guess is a kite."

Her smile stretched wide in a way he knew meant he was wrong.

She flicked her hair over her shoulder. "Oh, Philippos. Looks like you lose this wager as well."

"So, what is it?"

Her pause made him more certain that she enjoyed torturing him, but finally she spoke. "*He* is a pteron, named Paris, for future reference."

"Interesting." Somehow, it made sense. Not a bird, but a winged reptile the size of a hand with the teeth of a shark. "They're good over long distances, and—"

"The best."

He snorted. "I stand corrected. The *best*, and useful for giving people who tease you a nip. I find it no surprise you had to one-up Lex's escort. Do I sense jealousy?"

They reached the entrance to her tent, and she paused in front of the slack cloth, the golden trimming reflecting in her eyes. "You may find it a surprise that I chose Paris before her, and flight distance wasn't the reason she chose a falcon."

He didn't know about "surprising," but it was definitely interesting. "So, why did she?"

"They're the fastest. And what do falcons hunt?" With a raise of her eyebrow, Selene disappeared inside, leaving Darius's slow mind to catch up.

Ducks? Pigeons? Realisation hit him so fast he felt a buffoon for not seeing it before. He'd seen rakkans and humans use a few carrier pigeons but had thought nothing of it. Now he did, it had always been for something urgent, something an enemy would love to intercept. Lex was even more cunning than he'd thought, hard as that was to believe.

He followed Selene into the tent to join her, Gorgias, and half a dozen others Darius had trouble recalling the names of. They all sat on uncomfortably tall wooden stools around a blocky table. A few oil lamps tried but failed to light the parchments scattered across it given the dark green canvas obscured too much light from the sun. Apart from the table, the tent was bare, with only sealed crates piled in places. *Packed up, ready to march to battle?* Darius's sword arm yearned for exercise.

"Philippos," Gorgias called with a smile so sneering he may as well have spat the word.

Darius walked around, wiped the rain from his brow and gave the algus a pat on the shoulder to dry his hand, noting the lack of chainmail underneath his black tunic. *Guess we aren't to see battle after all.* Of the other algus, most of the men gave him a nod but the three women had faces so sour he didn't dare say more than "good evening" to them. But what woman wouldn't be tired after traipsing through a forest with over a thousand sweaty men?

Darius took the last empty seat as one of the three slaves standing at the side moved to pour him some wine.

He waved the man away, wanting to keep his head clear. "So, how many Viridians are there, and when do we attack?"

Selene cleared her throat. "I'll make this quick. Scouts say the grain stores appear to have been looted, and there's little sign of anything of use there. We've seen no humans left alive, but some rakkans are holed up in the stone tower at the centre of the village. It's doubtful any loot remains there." Her head sank as low as Darius's mood, and she glanced around at a few of the algus before speaking again. "I don't see the use in fighting here."

"There's always a use," Darius said. "Even one dead warrior is one that won't kill tomorrow. What if a commander is there?"

"There isn't. There are other towns that need our help more." Selene's voice became sharp. "We'll move onto the next place where we can actually save someone and get supplies."

"Why not kill them first?"

"You think I don't want to?" Selene's nostrils flared. "You don't think I want every rakkan I see to feel the sting of my arrows? Believe me, if we had time, I'd already be raining death on those fiends."

It was the first time Darius had seen Selene so fierce, more like Lex with every passing moment.

But he couldn't contain his frustration. He scoffed, threw his head back and put his hands into his tunic's pockets lest they see his balled fists, which drew a few disgruntled looks from the algus.

One woman scowled, her thick black monobrow forming a "v" on her head as it always seemed to around him.

"Philippos doesn't know about Dolthea," Gorgias said. "Perhaps if he did, he'd see our need to move on with haste."

That was the first time the algus had referred to Darius without an implicit insult.

As Darius leaned forward, his fingers suddenly caught the tiny parchment in his pocket, the one with a name and address in Dolthea on it that he was loath to forget.

"Are you going to tell me about Dolthea?" Darius looked at Selene. "Or should I guess again?"

She sighed. "Apologies, but you're not the only one. Only Gorgias knows because it's his escort that brought the news." She took a deep gulp of wine before continuing. "Dolthea's Guard spotted two rakkan scouts near the city walls last night—legionnaires rather than thieves. They've also seen a commander who we think is Hadrian's second-in-command."

Darius tried to keep a blank face but willed her to say more about his intended target.

"We think an attack is impending," she continued, "and we can't afford for their grain stores to be taken. Laltos needs them."

Darius stood and leaned on the table. "Then what are we wasting time chin-wagging for? Let's get on the road to Dolthea."

"Are all Xavalans so impatient?" the algus with the monobrow muttered through the side of her mouth.

"Only the good ones."

"Enough." Selene's hard stare lacked any amusement at his comments. "We'll move to Dolthea when we're ready. There are already a few Numbered there scouting the area."

Monobrow scoffed. "As if we can trust those air-heads. It seems most had their intellect sucked out by Archimedes along with their memories."

Gorgias scowled and opened his mouth to speak, but Darius spouted first as the insult cut him deep. "And what's your excuse for being a fool? I'd trust a Numbered over you any day."

Monobrow blew a furious snort from her nose. "Why are you here? We could do without a weak, petulant fool with less restraint than a two-month-old dog."

Darius grimaced. "I am not *weak*."

Whoever spoke next, Darius didn't note as words flew at him from all directions. He regretted beginning the insults soon after saying them.

As he avoided Selene's frustrated gaze, his attention was drawn to Gorgias and the confused frown on the algus's face.

Darius gazed back in an uncomfortable exchange that gave him the urge to sit, which he did and took the excuse to break eye contact. When he looked back, the algus smiled at him.

Meanwhile, Monobrow cursed loudly. "I'll bet such short tempers are why the Chief Priest rarely gives Xavalans escorts."

Darius grunted, wondering how much provocation made it justifiable to slap a woman. "I have an escort, Lyra, if you must know."

"Lyra." The algus scoffed. "A name as dull as her master. And where is she? I'll bet even *she* can't stand to be in your company."

Darius stood so quickly he almost knocked the table over, then towered over the algus. "Watch your tongue!"

She flinched away, lips sealed.

After a pause, his rage dampened, and he noticed his outburst had forced silence on the tent. He sat back down, slowed his rising breaths, and fought back curses. *So much for making allies.* They weren't the ones he should be angry at. Judging by the ease with which he aggravated people, he'd have been best to leave the algus right away before he said something else untoward.

"That was uncalled for, Philippos," Selene said.

Yet, if he left without a word, they'd think him just an ill-tempered knucklehead. Selene seemed well-liked, and the more he pondered on it, the more he realised they all respected her integrity and honesty. Should *he* try to be more like that?

He tapped his fingers on the table for a few seconds, then gave a tired sigh that brought out an exhaustion in him he hadn't noticed before. "I…apologise. I'm a little snappy about my escort." The next words felt harder to say than the apology. "She was injured a few weeks ago."

Selene's frown softened into a more familiar sympathetic gaze. "How bad is it?"

"I don't know if she'll live." His voice was barely above a whisper. It hadn't been long since he'd last connected with her, but sometimes even an hour felt too long.

"You could always beg the Chief Priest for a new one," Monobrow said.

Gorgias huffed. "What a thing to say to the man!"

Of all the algus to sympathise, Darius had never expected it to be Gorgias. Darius stared for a second at the once insufferable man who now looked at him with a trace of pity.

But he didn't deserve any. It was his own fault Lyra was injured.

"Ignore her, Philippos." Selene stood and walked around to him, then placed a hand on his shoulder and grazed his neck with her thumb.

The touch sent gooseflesh up his skin, and he turned to brush her hand away lest she notice. "It was them—the Viridians. That's why I may seem such a surly bastard. Well…more of one."

154

Their eyes locked, and the tenderness in Selene's sorrowful gaze almost eased his pain and made him forget the others were in the tent watching.

"Chin up, man." Gorgias grimaced like it pained him to be nice. The algus stood as well and came to his side. Thankfully, he didn't stroke Darius's neck too. "You'll get your fight, eventually."

"When?" Darius asked.

"The men will pack up the camp through the night, and we'll leave tomorrow at dawn. It will only take a few days to march to Dolthea."

One night. Who knew whether the Viridians in the nearby town would join the assault on Dolthea. Then, more would end up like Lyra, like the corpses of civilians and slaves that lay in the blood and ashes of the human villages.

His mind slipped back to the slaughters he'd seen. Would his hunger for vengeance be assuaged for a few nights? The longer he dwelled on it, the more furious the village full of Viridians made him.

While pondering, it suddenly dawned on him that a night would give him enough time to sneak in and slaughter the invaders with no one being the wiser. Not even the thought of the blood put him off.

With nothing else to say and eager to escape the conversation, he made to leave. "I'll see you all in the morn, then." He gave a nod to the algus around the table, patted Gorgias on the arm and threw a genuine smile of gratitude to Selene, which she returned.

Then he left the tent with a sense of relief. *Look at that. They don't hate you as much now.* It was a far cry from winning trust, but it was a start.

On his way back to his tent, he thought more about whether attacking the Viridians in the village was a foolish thing to do. This time there was no Lex, Brutus or Varro to instruct him—not even Lyra to help.

What would Brutus do? The months he'd spent in Margalvia listening to the mentor's advice urged him to action, but he wished the rakkan were here to ask directly.

Still, Brutus was far away and possibly in danger from the Viridian's himself, which agitated Darius more.

It seemed he'd have to decide for himself. The consequences of the last choice he'd made wouldn't be pushed from his mind, but even with a cooled temper, the choice became clearer when he imagined the fate of the next settlement those Viridians would attack. They might end up fighting under Hadrian's second.

No. He couldn't allow it. It wasn't what Lex had in mind when she'd asked him to lead men against the Viridian Legion, but to hell with it. Leading himself would have to do for now.

It was only a few hours until nightfall. That's when he'd enforce grisly justice.

17

Darius – Village, West of Laltos

The wind swept through the trees and carried the chortles of rakkan warriors all too relaxed in their surroundings. The rain swelled from faint patters to a prolonged hiss.

Darius stalked forward. Water trickled around his boots. The rare rainfall failed to sink into the parched soil.

Through the leaves, he glimpsed the crenellated top of the stone tower a few hundred yards away. Ruined huts were scattered across his vision, the hardened clay mostly smashed to rubble. But the sight was so commonplace in his travels that he only noticed the blood sprayed across the waste now. Legionnaires crossed the streets in the village ahead, trawling around for loot, but the tower was all he focused on, his rakkan eyes tracing for any weakness in the round stonework that sloped into the ground like a thorn flattened at its peak.

Whatever the structure had been used for before, now it provided a refuge for the bulk of the warriors that prepared to move onto the next settlement.

The warm leather hilt in his hand felt more comfortable than an instrument of death should, and how he wished the sword were made of kuraminium. Steel would have to do, with only a thin black metal centre and edging to withstand the rakkan blows.

He was glad the other algus weren't there. Now he didn't have to hold back.

Although he didn't know how many were inside the tower, it didn't matter. There weren't enough to stop him. The only obstacle to the slaughter was the solid wall, barricaded door, and the lookout stood atop. He hadn't seen them, but he was in no doubt they watched all below. It would be a greater feat to evade rakkan watchers than it had Selene's human sentries.

Darius shortened his paces, shins carefully brushing aside branches and leaves. Columns of pine trunks blocked his movements from view for a while before the soil turned to hard road underfoot as he reached the edge of the village. He ducked behind a demolished wall at the sight of a prowling legionnaire and slid across.

He peered around the side at the tightly packed fragments of huts jutting upwards across the street.

Slowly, carefully, he made his way from one hiding place to the next, stepping over the bodies that the heavy rain had failed to wash clean.

Only holding his breath spared him the stench of decay that lingered in the air. Whenever a rakkan crossed the path ahead, he froze, slipped down out of sight, then waited for them to leave before continuing onwards.

Halfway into the village, footsteps suddenly splashed in puddles to his right.

He ducked by two bodies standing chained by the wrists to wooden posts. Deep lacerations cut across the women's backs and made Darius wince. The wet, torn auburn hair of one had too much resemblance to Selene's for comfort.

Soon, the sound of more footsteps came, and he hid beside the woman's body, avoiding looking at her pained face. To his surprise, a slow breath escaped her mouth. She twitched.

Darius looked up, caught the eyes of the auburn-haired girl to see the mix of rain and tears falling from them. *Who was it that said none were alive?*

"Kill me," the woman rasped through split lips.

As uneasy as the thought made him, how could he refuse?

He slowly raised his sword.

The woman closed her eyes with relief spreading across her face.

But he paused. "Do you want death now, or would you like to see it first?"

She opened her eyes. "See what?"

Darius grimaced and let his eyes burn. "Revenge."

After a rasping exhale and a pause, she nodded weakly.

He returned the nod and turned his attention back to the footsteps still splashing. He traced their source with only his ears and counted two pairs, heading from north to south at the other side of the building to his right.

Then the footsteps stopped, followed by grunts and muttering.

Darius crept around, watched the stone tower disappear behind a hut, and only stopped when he was at the corner around which the mumbles had last echoed.

Another two guards stood a few streets away.

Unless he wanted to keep circling around all night, he'd have to start killing. Just the thought of the fight brought a greedy anticipation to the surface.

Ready to burst around the corner and surprise the two closest, he instead paused. Killing two rakkans was no challenge ordinarily, but to do so silently when they wore armour was a stretch even for him.

Crouching low, he considered his options. *I'm not that fast.* Creative ideas came to him with as much abundance as they usually did—not at all. *To hell with it. Do it the Darius way.* Why be silent when a ruckus would draw to him the fight he so desperately craved?

He slowly stood and let a glowing blue film of algor creep down his sword to coat it for death, then he strode around the corner.

Only a few feet from the reach of his weapon stood two warriors facing one another, cuirasses covered in old blood the rain had made flow again and helmets jutting low over the chin in a manner that only the Viridian Legion's did. Each had a green stripe atop their helmets, and neither had a shield, only a sheathed sword at their waists for protection.

The pair's heads turned towards him and he glowered as they froze and stared mutely at him, unaware how close they were to the afterlife.

"You two are terrible guards." Darius lifted his flaring sword, waiting for one to move, or make a sound, but the eyes through the sockets widened as if they recognised him even in algus attire.

"Is one of you going to shout in alarm," Darius said, "or do I need to make you scream in pain?"

The warrior on the left let out a yell while the other went for his sword. As they moved, Darius swiped from behind to behead the legionnaire before he withdrew his weapon, and let the other's cry echo from the shards of walls for a few seconds before ending him with a stab through the collar.

"That's for Lyra, you swine."

The legionnaire yelled for another beat before dropping in a pool of filth. Darius tensed, forehead burning; the two deaths only enraged him further, like they'd unleashed a caged fiend.

More shouts came from the direction of the tower and the streets around. Meanwhile, Darius pulled his sword free and wiped it on the wet skirt of one warrior, shuddering as he did. Once clean enough, he slid it back into his scabbard and took a fallen gladius, enjoying the cold kuraminium in his palm.

That's more like it. Now he could burn the blood away.

He turned and stomped down the road towards the tower. Heavy boots thudded through puddles from every direction.

After only a few strides, he was within the sight of the auburn-haired woman. She looked at him with eyes filled with pain and lust for revenge.

The first of the legionnaires emerged from one of the adjacent streets holding a shield and spear.

Darius sent tongues of fire down his blade, giving the warriors no doubt who was to send them to their deaths.

With a fearless roar, the legionnaire charged. After a dodge and one savage blow from Darius's sword, he fell bleeding on the road while the next two came forward.

Darius grabbed the fallen rakkan's shield from the ground. *Let hell come forth.*

Throwing all his weight into every stab of his sword and bash of his shield, they all hit with a satisfying crash. Whether on sword, shield or flesh, Darius didn't track, feeling only the anger released with each fierce blow.

Five took him on at once and he summoned all his speed. He dropped with a raised shield to block their blows and swept across the exposed thighs of each with his gladius. The flurry sent them all falling to the dirt with howls of pain.

As the fight went on, more bodies fell, joining those of the butchered humans.

Blood gushed.

Darius kept moving forwards, eager to escape the mess in his wake and keep it from his vision.

Ten, twenty, fifty… Darius didn't care as the numbers mounted, only adding to humans that wouldn't die in the invaders' next assault.

Minutes passed, but it didn't feel long enough. His anger soon had none left to vent upon.

When the last legionnaire fell with a gladius in his armpit and a cry of anguish, Darius stood and let the rain wash his tunic and boots.

Heavy breaths of wet air spewed from his mouth from the exertion while he stared at the stone tower now directly ahead.

Judging by the dead, only a few Viridians could be left alive. But that was a few too many. All they'd managed to score against him were two slashes to the forearm and thigh.

Ferven still seethed on his sword as he lifted it then tossed it spinning towards the door. The metal speared the wood, and it ignited, thick black smoke bursting forth after only a second.

Darius kicked up another fallen gladius and snatched it before marching to the now deathly silent tower.

No one came out to meet him, and by the time he'd reached the entrance, the door was nothing more than wet ash.

He stepped inside, the circular room bare except for his bloody footprints and a spiralling stone staircase.

Without hesitating, he began climbing. His bitter disappointment grew until he got to the top to greet a single centurion sat with his back to a stone merlon.

A sword lay in his lap. The warrior's green-striped helmet was on the floor to his side, and half his face hung down with sagging, aged skin.

"Get it over with." The centurion spat at Darius's feet.

Darius extinguished his blade, feeling the rising urge to stab and twist it inside the brute's stomach but frustrated by the cuirass blocking his strike. "Not going to die fighting like a man?"

The centurion scoffed. "I just watched you cut through my century. What's the point?"

It was hard to argue with the logic. "I take it you know who I am."

"Darius the Dreaded." The centurion's nostrils flared.

Darius ran his finger along the blade in his hand. Now that he recalled the moniker, something about it intrigued him and had done ever since meeting the Viridian Legionnaires weeks ago.

"Answer me something, and I'll let you live," Darius said.

By the twisted look of disgust on the rakkan's face, anyone would think Darius hadn't offered him the chance of life.

Darius continued. "Why do you Viridians call me by that name?"

The centurion grinned to show his empty gums. "It's a compliment. Be flattered."

Darius wasn't, and he waited while the raindrops trickled from his hair.

"The Denehill massacre," the rakkan said, as if it meant something to him.

"I'd keep speaking," Darius said slowly, quietly, "because my patience is almost spent."

"So, it's true?" The centurion's face wobbled as he chuckled. "Archimedes took your memories?"

Darius took a step forward, raised his sword and pointed it between the rakkan's eyes.

"Wait!" The centurion held out both palms. "I'll speak. We heard only the rumours, so I can't say for sure. Years ago, a swathe of the Empire's algus convened at Denehill to lead an assault against Margalvia and then the other four legions after it. On the day they were due to march for battle, less than a hundred algus reported in. When they checked on the rest, they were found either poisoned or strangled in their beds." A deep snigger rasped from the rakkan's throat. "You could smell the humans' dread from Viridia. They didn't dare attack any of us for an age. If not for Archimedes, it would have won us the war. You were a hero for a time, until you turned on your own kind." The rakkan's face contorted with the last words.

Darius let the story sink in for a moment, not finding any reason the rakkan would fabricate it. But he struggled to understand why Lex would never mention it. All he recalled her saying was there were stories about him.

Was this one of those human tales that children used to scare one another? It was hard to feel pity for algus that sought to exterminate his friends, but the thought of being a hero to these man-eating rakkans only deepened his unease at his former self.

How many algus had he killed? Perhaps he'd been no better than the Viridian Warlord…

"I want you to give Hadrian a message from me." Darius crouched down until their eyes were level, both hot with ferven, disgust and loathing. "Tell him and everyone in your foul legion that I'm in these lands, and I'll slaughter every last one of you I see."

The rakkan's scowl deepened, but Darius saw the trembling in his lips on the sagging side of his face.

"It's time for your warlord to live in fear," Darius continued, "to wonder when the day will be that I come for him."

Darius stood, inhaled until his chest pushed against the chainmail around it. "And let Hadrian know that I'll *never* stop until I've seen the life fade from his eyes."

The centurion swallowed, a new fear in his gaze that even the prospect of death hadn't elicited. "So be it, but he won't stop. He wants revenge, we all do, for the years of starvation, torture, massacres."

Much to Darius's disgruntlement, feelings of pity surfaced as the rakkan spoke. But before he could acknowledge or resist them, a winged reptile landed on the top of the merlon behind the rakkan.

The creature stood only the size of a hand and its sharp teeth protruded as its head flicked from side to side and surveyed the pair.

It was Darius's turn to feel dread. *Selene's escort.*

18

Sulla – Margalvia

Sulla marched along the front of the impenetrable shield wall of the Black Legion, his boots crumbling the dry mud below. Unlike the round human shields that left openings for spears, rakkan scuta were oblong and curved like a half-cylinder, melding together into a kuraminium wall as strong as thick basalt. In the slight gaps poked spears, usually headed with kuraminium spikes but now only blunt wood.

Opposite them on the open training field was another shield wall, the Red Militia, equally fierce in Sulla's eyes and ready to drive forward.

"Chief," the Militia warriors said and gave him a nod that he returned with an unease he didn't display. He still wished he trained alongside them instead of receiving respect and tribute from those he led. *Wish Claudius was still here.*

"Show them what the Militia are made of," Sulla shouted to his men. "First one to break their line will get as much firewater as his stomach can hold."

A few chuckled. The prize would cost him that week's half-pay, but who cared?

How he'd love to roar and fill the cloudless, crisp night sky with rage alongside them. But there wasn't the time. There was only one rakkan he was looking for, one that had been busy for days.

Finally, he glimpsed Varro's horned helmet at the side of the shield wall. The Warlord stood on a small hill along with a group of other commanders and their servants who made sure each warrior had the equipment they needed. The servants themselves wore clothes so ragged even Sulla could have afforded better in his days on the streets, not to mention the thin frames underneath them from sacrificing food to keep the legionnaires fed and strong. *Hope their sacrifice pays off one day.*

"Warlord!" Sulla yelled, eager to stop dwelling on the downtrodden.

Varro's eyes met his, and the Warlord waited until Sulla was out of the tense space between the two shield walls.

"Forward!" Varro yelled.

Hundreds of footsteps rumbled behind Sulla, followed by a mighty crack like thunder. The clash sent a tidal gust of air that even a human would have felt.

The servants winced at the ear-splitting noise while the commanders stood unmoved.

Sulla looked back as the grunting legionnaires met shield to shield, rammed, dug in their heels to thrust. Prodding spears hit helmets, shoulders and necks, many a killing blow under normal circumstances. At last, Varro was preparing to face the Viridians.

After a few moments watching over his men's performance, Varro turned. "Sulla. Where have you been? I haven't seen you in—"

"Too long," Sulla interjected. "I've been busy, making sure Lyra is taken care of amongst other things."

"How is she?"

"Doing a little better. Her fever is breaking and the wound's smelling less. The ointments seem to be helping." He wasn't sure why, but he'd been drawn to caring for Lyra more and more. Sometimes those were the only moments he got to dwell, to figure out whether he'd forgiven Darius, whether saving Sulla from a life of pilfering crumbs outweighed one rash act. "Have you decided on Darius's punishment yet?"

The Warlord either didn't hear or feigned he hadn't, because he just surveyed his screaming warriors.

Sulla waited a few seconds for the deafening noise behind to quieten enough for him to think. It didn't, and after a while, Varro ushered Sulla farther away up the field of grass as light as the Warlord's hair.

"So Lyra's through the worst of it." Varro's mouth gave a hint of a smile. "That's a relief...but you can't spend all your time with her."

"Far from it. I've checked on her now and again. Mostly I've been speaking with my commanders, getting ready for your order to retake the mine, and we've found—"

"What order?" Varro's voice went quiet.

"I assumed that you'd give the order soon."

"Assumptions are dangerous. I told you, I won't attack until we have a strategy and know how many warriors we can spare without opening ourselves up to an attack by the King."

Sulla bit his lip and used all his willpower to keep his next words calm. "Hadrian may mistake our hesitation for weakness."

168

At first Varro gave no reaction, then he exhaled slowly. "Let's talk farther away." He looked around then led them off until the clashes of shields were only a murmur in the night air.

"What's wrong?" Sulla asked, knowing the Warlord well enough to know that nothing fazed him but the direst news.

"Brutus has sent word."

"That was fast."

"It wasn't much, but it's puzzling. Hadrian is capturing as many algus as he can find."

"That's strange," Sulla said. "Is he trying to get information?" That was the only reason Margalvia took captives.

Varro took off his helmet to reveal a face paler than usual. "I don't understand why Hadrian's doing it, and that worries me."

Since becoming warlord, worry was all Varro did.

"Why hesitate?" Sulla asked. "Let's do what you do best—go to battle. You were the Black Commander that won the Battle of Uxon, and the Battle in the Mists with only a century of men."

Varro sighed. "Things are much simpler in the field."

"Then let's fight."

Varro shook his head, hair falling across his beleaguered eyes. "I won't risk leaving Margalvia until I know Hadrian's plans and what the King is up to. My scouts are assessing where the humans' armies are."

"I'm tired of you listening to that rat Nikolaos. Archimedes is dead. The King is no threat. If we don't act against Hadrian soon, I'll be forced to take it upon myself."

Varro glared, lifting his chin with only the slightest of movements, but one that forced a silence that almost broke Sulla's resolve. Almost.

The Warlord's next words were so low and tense they betrayed the lethal thoughts behind them. "The scouting will take at most a week. Then we'll move for the mine when *I* say so."

Sulla pressed his lips together again, but this time his frustration only grew until the effort pained his mouth. "Every day we wait, they get stronger."

"If our alliance with Laltos is impending, then we'd be best waiting to launch an assault with them."

"Laltos? We can't wait for Lex's First Alliance dream. Act now!"

Varro lifted his head, breathed in deep and made Sulla feel small by comparison. "No," the Warlord growled.

"Damn it, Varro, when will you be a leader?" He shoved his head towards Varro but stopped an inch short of butting him.

At the move, the Warlord's eyes erupted with white-hot ferven. "I've had enough of your insolence, Sulla. I don't care if you question me, but I refuse to be threatened. I'm your warlord and you *will* obey."

"Then give us orders to fight Hadrian!"

"I won't give orders unless I'm sure it won't bring the death of every man, woman and child in our city!" The Warlord breathed heavily, beads of sweat forming on his arms. "It wasn't too long ago that the King's army stood poised to raze our home, as they did Gerunda."

"I can't back you on this," Sulla said. "Claudius ordered me to—"

"Claudius is dead," the Warlord said flatly, "and even if he lived, I am the Warlord of Margalvia, and I command the Red Militia."

"I'm the Chief. The Militia take orders from *me*!"

"Render to me"—Varro's voice had never been so icy—"or surrender your position."

Silence followed. Sulla glanced over his shoulder to see all the commanders staring at them. He wanted nothing more than to drive his fist into Varro's jaw, but knew from experience that his blow would never land, and he'd instead be left nursing far worse injuries in front of the Black Legion.

"Fine," Sulla said through gritted teeth. "We'll do it your way, Warlord. But know this, my men—*your* loyal subjects—feel the same as me. We won't wait forever."

19

Darius – West of Laltos

The pouring rain eased to a haze of drizzle as Darius walked. Water dripped from the needles of the forest canopy onto his head. At any moment, he prepared to see Selene appear with a stony face like Lex's when he'd done something untoward.

How much had her escort seen? His blade ignited with ferven?

Surely not… That had only been when he was on the ground. Hopefully she'd just think he'd gone rogue.

She can't complain. I'm not her slave. So what if he went to slaughter her enemies? Hopefully the Regent would hear of it. It was better than slaughtering algus as his former self apparently had.

After Selene's reptilian escort had flapped away, Darius had let the Viridian Centurion leave and made his way back to the camp. Darius didn't bother to tread lightly now, but soon regretted his sloppy footsteps when water and mud seeped into his boots.

The first he saw of Selene was her wet auburn hair flapping behind a tree trunk ahead, and she didn't move until he entered her line of vision.

The sudden tension of his muscles once under her gaze surprised him, ready for her to draw her weapon at any second. But she remained still. Instead of the hateful stare he'd expected, her heavy eyes looked on him with something far worse than contempt—disappointment.

Rain droplets fell down her cheeks and onto her tunic, which almost gave the impression she wept, although she hadn't.

She met his gaze, but after a few seconds, he couldn't bear the sad look, so he bowed his head and surveyed his feet.

"Damned mud," he muttered. "Going to be a pain to clean."

Her only response was a tense breath.

For a few more moments, he waited for her to speak, waited for the tirade to start as Lex's, or Brutus's, would already have, but instead she picked at the dirt underneath her fingernails. It was too much to bear.

"What did you see?" he asked.

Her expression remained flat. "Dead rakkans, one of whom you no doubt taunted before killing."

At least she hadn't seen him conjure ferven.

"I hope you didn't speak with him," she continued. "They're all liars."

If you only knew… "Why do you say that?"

"They say gomans never lie, and rakkans never tell the truth. I can vouch for that." The look of repugnance he'd seen only once before returned to her face.

Not for the first time, their conversation made him want to fidget, yet this time it wasn't because of them growing closer, but because of *his* lie on the verge of being revealed.

"I showed mercy to one once," she said with a shake of her head, "after he pleaded with me to let him return home. He said he'd never fight again. I was young and stupid. A few days later, that same rakkan was part of a horde that killed five algus."

Whilst the same might happen with the rakkan Darius had spared, he hadn't let the warrior go out of mercy. The warning he wanted to impart would hopefully put off more invaders.

"I'm sorry," he said. "I know I shouldn't have gone behind your back, but I knew I'd return before the end of the night, and it's no problem for you or anyone else if I slaughter your enemies."

"It's no problem." Her voice was soft and...almost apologetic.

It threw him; the arguments he'd been rehearsing not once played out like this.

"You're not angry?" he asked.

"Why would I be angry?"

"I guess...it's like...I disobeyed your orders."

She shook her head with a look of pity. "I'm not your mistress, Philippos. I don't give you orders. We're all algus here and we work together."

She made it sound like she valued his opinions, which, outside of Lyra, felt a fresh concept to him.

"What if you'd died out there?" she added.

"There are still dozens of you and hundreds of men. It's enough to defend Dolthea if I were to fall."

She stepped towards him, rested her hands on his cheeks and squeezed, hard. "You...are an idiot."

He frowned, even more uneasy now she was touching his skin. "I'm sure you're right, but I don't understand why you aren't angry."

A wistful smile came to her face, and she looked up at him with the same pity one did a child. "We haven't known each other long, but long enough that I don't want you to die."

"I get that. The battles won't all be so easy, and you'll need me to—"

"It's not about battles." She shook her head with a look of bewilderment.

"Then what do you need me for?"

"Do I look like I *need* you for anything?" She raised an eyebrow. Hunger came upon her eyes, which set a nervous feeling in his stomach, a feeling he'd not felt about anyone except Lex. *And this is her sister.*

"If you don't need me," Darius said, "then why do you care if I die?"

Her eyes widened in confusion, and a gasp escaped her lips. She paused for a few seconds before speaking again. "Would you not care if *I* died?"

The time he'd spent with her recently replayed in his mind, the laughter, the charm, the warmth it brought him to induce a smile on her face. When he thought on her question, he imagined a rakkan plunging a sword into her heart, imagined her whipped and strung up like the woman in the village and realised the fury it would set alight in him—almost as livid as when Hadrian had forced a dagger into Lyra.

Upon reflection, so obvious was his care for Selene he wasn't sure how he hadn't noticed before, and she apparently felt the same. No one had ever looked at him with the same gentle gaze as she had, as though he was more than a warrior.

She pushed him away with a force that knocked him into the tree behind. "I can't believe you have to think so long about that." She marched off towards the camp.

"Wait." He grabbed her arm, turned her back around. "It's not that I have to think whether I care, I was more thinking about…why you would care about me."

The slight shaking of her head made her hair sway and drip rain almost hypnotically. "You are perhaps the strangest man I've ever met. Let me guess, you're an orphan?"

He frowned, suddenly irritated by the intrusive question. "Why do you ask that?"

"Clearly no one has ever cared about you."

His frown deepened. "Many do. I have allies, and my escort would die for me." She almost had many times, for no benefit to herself.

But could he really say the same of the rest? Brutus, Sulla, Lex—of course they'd saved his life, but was that for his benefit, or because they needed him?

"Philippos…" She kissed her thumb then touched it lightly on his cheek, making his heart race. "I care if you die, and that's why"—she moved her thumb down to his throat and pressed it in until he felt the pressure in his breaths—"you're *never* to do this again. I know what it's like to lose an escort, so I'm giving you one pass, and one pass only."

"Or what? You'll kill me?"

"No! Why do you… I'll just be forced to part ways with you."

"Even after you saw what I did? You've seen how strong a fighter I am."

She scoffed. "I don't put up with your grumpy backside because I like how you handle a sword. Which reminds me—how in hell did you defeat so many Viridians single-handed?"

176

He shrugged, glad she had to ask the question as it meant she hadn't witnessed his rakkan powers. The lies brought pangs of guilt. "I picked them off a few at a time. They didn't know what was happening, and…there was a woman clinging to life in the village. Her pain lit a fire in me. She saw revenge before I ended her suffering."

Selene shook her head. "Die fighting for something worth fighting for, not gratifying a lust for revenge."

Too bad that revenge was all he had for the moment, though from what she'd said, he was beginning to wonder whether there was something missing in his life, a connection to someone perhaps.

"You said you knew what it was like to lose an escort." Darius moved his body an inch closer to her, reading her eyes carefully as sorrow filled them at his words. "It happened to you?"

She swallowed, and her lips twitched before she spoke. "My father had the Chief Priest bond me to a brown bear cub when I was six. I had him until he died…ambushed by a rakkan while digging roots to eat." Her round cheeks flushed. Her face strained as if she was forcing herself not to shed a tear. "That was the fiend that I let live."

No wonder she doesn't trust rakkans. Darius couldn't imagine showing anyone such mercy. Was it noble, or foolish? Seeing the sadness on her face, he judged it best not to inquire. "Do you know how this bonding works?" He chose his words carefully so as not to ask something he, as an algus, should have known.

"I don't think anyone does besides the Chief Priest. He's the only man to have ever done it, invoking the Goddess, Dianoia. Who else but the mind behind everything that exists can link two into one…much like a marriage in a way."

Darius had never heard of any wife that knew her husband's thoughts as he knew Lyra's. "Can't be like that, otherwise marriages wouldn't last very long."

"I wouldn't know. But I care for my escorts more than any pet, or friend, so I understand what it's like to watch something you love die."

Unsure what to say or do, Darius moved his hand from her arm to her shoulder, then onto her cheek to wipe away the rain from her soft, warm skin. How he wanted to hold her, take her into his arms to ease his own feeling of helplessness if nothing else, but he was too hesitant to act.

"What was his name?" Darius asked softly.

A wistful smile spread across her face, a welcome relief from the sorrow. "It was Philippos, if you can believe it."

Darius mirrored her grin. He wondered if it was coincidence but then remembered it was Lex who had given him the name back when Archimedes had chased them, and she had to get it from somewhere.

"A fine name," he said. "Strong. Brave. Valiant. Sounds like he was a fighter."

"He was." Selene twisted her hips and ran a hand across her scabbard, grasping a curved claw that hung from it on a strip of leather. "It was his. He's still always with me."

The black claw was twice as long as Darius's finger, and as he poked it, the point felt sharp enough to tear through his skin. "I'm glad I was never on the receiving end of it."

"I wish I could say the same." She snorted. "Try growing up with a bear that wants to wrestle all the time." Rolling up the sleeve of her chainmail, she showed Darius an old scar six inches across her forearm.

"That's nothing. Try lying next to a panther that thrashes in her sleep."

178

"Men…" She rolled her hazel eyes with a grin. "Always trying to outdo you."

"I'm glad we amuse you. At least we're good for something."

Her gaze slipped down to his lips. "I can think of a couple of other uses."

Before he asked her what, she lifted her eyebrows then turned and strode between the trees back towards the camp.

He stood and collected himself, wishing she wasn't wearing a cloak while he watched her walk away. But his heated pondering soon turned to confusion over their earlier conversation.

What would she do when she found out the truth about him?

The guilt over lying sat uncomfortably with him, but he wouldn't jeopardise his mission for the sake of her. Deciding things for himself had got Lyra sliced open.

Oh, Darius. Don't let yourself care for her too much. He should distance himself now because she'd only do it for him when she learned the truth.

20

Lex – Xavala, the Silk City

Lex leaned over the wall of her balcony and watched the march in the street below, put on only to exude dominance. Lines of hoplites with spears and shields marched, carrying the white-eagle banner of the King.

Curses. The sun beat down on her burnt neck, but she didn't shift her gaze from every passing algus, fearing one in particular was among them. So far, there was no sign of him, but soon…

The Silk Regent was already on edge about his dead friend, and this would only upsurge the pressure. There was no chance the Xavalan Cavalry would ride to Laltos if the King's soldiers were here.

Damn. She'd been relying on them to push west as the Margalvians hopefully hammered the Viridians from the south, but neither had happened.

Most would call her a fool for trying to ally a rakkan together with a human city, but she knew they could be trusted.

Usually, the sight of Darius's slaughter of Viridians through her escort's eyes would have brought her morbid satisfaction. A few more repeats of that and it made her efforts with her father that much easier. So why did Darius and Selene working so closely linger in her thoughts?

Pain stabbed at her hip from the bent position, but she didn't cease scanning the street below, didn't even take a drop of the weeping plant's tears she required to numb it. Despite visiting countless surgeons, mystics, and self-professed healers, she'd never found a way to stop it other than blocking out the pain. It only acted as a constant reminder to stay focused on the here and now.

Better than wallowing in the past, I suppose. She had too much experience of that.

Disturbing her thoughts, she sensed her falcon reach out to her, growing restless at being away for so long. Now perched on a top branch above Selene's camp, his wings were poised to set him back on course to the Silk City.

Not yet. She still needed to watch over Darius. She'd reward her escort with a feast of gulls, pigeons and songbirds when he finally returned, but for now, she wouldn't leave Darius alone.

Lex still struggled to discern her feelings over how close her sister and Darius had become. At first, she couldn't bear to hear the chatter and sent Tiro away to keep at a distance. Yet, she was the one that had pushed Darius away. She didn't want a relationship but couldn't demand the same of him.

That didn't stop her imagining the two of them locked in each other's arms again, their bodies hot and sweaty pressed into each other... *Even when I keep them at arm's length, men give me grief.*

"Watching our honoured guests?"

Lex started and whirled around to see the Silk Regent's disgruntled gaze. Unusually for him, not a single gold chain or jewel glistened from his figure other than the sheen of his silver tunic.

"Don't sneak up on me like that." She turned back to the road without her usual seduction.

"Don't worry. Your mulberry tree is safely hidden."

"It's your tree now." She gave him an icy stare that brought more fear to his eyes than she'd hoped. "What is the King's envoy doing here?"

"More tax demands." The Silk Regent grimaced. "Must be serious this time because the King has sent Ophelia."

Lex ripped her gaze from the street, read the Silk Regent's face in the hope he jested or tested, but the worry had only amplified. Ophelia, the King's Orator, never brought pleasant news to a city. No wonder the Silk Regent wasn't showing off his wealth.

"Are you sure that tree is hidden?" Lex whispered.

The Silk Regent swallowed. "As good as can be. Don't fret. I heard that the King's Sword isn't with her at least. Now, come. Let's greet her."

While it brought relief, the King's Sword being apart from the Orator was so unusual it brought a new concern too, and that wasn't the only thing whirling in Lex's thoughts. She'd killed one man that had tried to get word to the King. If there was another she'd missed, then the King's Orator wasn't here to discuss tax.

***

Lex gave a bow of her head to the King's Orator as she sauntered through the grand doorway into the palace. The entrance was large enough for an elephant to fit through, but now all it let in were ranks of Torian soldiers that provoked unease with every thud of their feet.

After first observing the woman's bald, patchy head, Lex soon did everything to avoid staring at it, casting her eyes across

Ophelia's snowy silk cloak instead. While it lacked the lavish decoration and colour one saw in the likes of Xavala, it displayed a wealth and intricate needlework that told Lex the woman cared more for her appearance than she liked to reveal. By contrast, the blotchy leather belt fastening her tunic was well-worn and clashed.

"Alexandra of Laltos," Ophelia said with a voice meant to sound as soft as her cloak. But it was transparently forced to one that often acted too. "Such a pleasure to finally meet you." Her smile caused skin to flake from her cheek and fall to rest on her shoulders.

Now I see why she wears white. Lex swallowed her urge to retch and put on a smile with a rare feeling of self-consciousness, unsure for once whether the one receiving it would be convinced as to its authenticity.

If Ophelia wasn't convinced, she didn't show it and instead turned her smile to the Silk Regent. "I'd express my pleasure at seeing you again, Regent, as I'm sure would you, but we both know that I'm here with, shall we say, undesirable negotiations to conduct."

The Silk Regent, who hadn't bothered to smile in the first place, let his dark eyes narrow. "Where's the King's Sword? I was told he'd be accompanying you."

"He will be. Jason's collecting something for me."

"Fine. I won't waste your time any further. I'll leave my slaves to show you to your room. Meanwhile, I'll help myself to the Torian sea bream you brought."

With that, he turned with a waft of his tunic and marched out of the entrance hall as Lex recalled his earlier boasts of feeding any of the King's gifts to his hounds.

"Men." The King's Orator rolled her grey eyes. "If we aren't attractive, they don't even care for politeness."

"Not all." Lex saw the advantages to an off-putting physical appearance. She didn't know whether to fear or admire the woman for having got so far without looks.

"The only men I trust are the King and the Sword." Ophelia grinned. "The last man who I allowed to trick me soon learned his folly. His skin made for a sturdy belt."

Lex held her gaze up while swallowing down sickness. She knew the story to be true from the wicked satisfaction in Ophelia's eyes.

"I wouldn't take Aristippus too seriously," Lex said. "His motives are rarely hidden, and his distaste is for the King, not his representatives."

"While in this city, I am the King." Ophelia's lips tightened into a thin line. "Tell me, who is *your* distaste for?"

The sudden question caught Lex off guard, having expected the King's Orator, or the "silver-tongued snake" as Laltos called her, to maintain a deceptively pleasant demeanour.

"Want the truth?" Lex asked.

"Always." A peckish grin spread across Ophelia's face.

Lex lowered her voice to a whisper as she leaned in while trying to avoid touching the woman. "I have little time for most Xavalans." *Best not to let her think our alliance is too close.*

The King's Orator raised an eyebrow. "I see. Do you always give gifts to people you dislike?"

Lex's blood ran cold, and she cursed for letting the Silk Regent bar her from wearing a sword belt. "What gifts?"

Surely Ophelia couldn't know of the tree…unless one of Aristippus's men betrayed him.

"The weapons," Ophelia whispered while her grey eyes mined Lex's, almost lulling her into a trance.

Lex quickly composed herself, hoping her face wasn't as flushed as it felt. "They weren't a gift. We want the Xavalans to use them to aid Laltos."

"Why? If you want aid fighting rakkans, you need only ask Toria."

It took all Lex's restraint not to break the woman's nose, wishing the King's Orator had hair just so she could rip it out. *Like we haven't asked for your help.*

"Every part of our empire is important to us," Ophelia continued, "including the cities west of the River Toras."

Forget scales for skin, Lex was surprised the King's Orator didn't have a forked tongue. *And they call rakkans liars…*

"I find that a little hard to believe," Lex said. "Toria's armies are still hiding at the other side of the Great Bridge."

The King's Orator shifted her gaze down for a second before smirking. "There. Didn't take long to see your true feelings towards me."

Lex looked down at her white knuckles until she unclenched her fingers with an unspoken curse.

"Never mind, dear. I'm sure next time your temper will be better controlled. Meet me this evening for supper with the Silk Regent."

Before Lex could think of an excuse, the King's Orator whisked away, leaving a waft of flaking skin to float in the air behind her.

Lex held her breath and turned away with another curse as she was left to focus on her hip pain once again.

It wasn't often she felt outsmarted, which only deepened her worry over the Silk Regent's ability to keep a secret.

21

Nikolaos – Margalvia

Today was the day. At least, Nikolaos had planned it to be. But even the best-laid plans of the most genius minds were sometimes foiled by nothing other than chance.

Slumped on the floor of his cell, he gazed at the metal chains on his wrists that mocked him with their thin but unbreakable strength. The guards had changed them the day before. Weakening them with algor had worked in part, but the rakkans had noticed the cracks, and his escort hadn't been able to carry the key to release him.

So much preparation wasted. Over the last few weeks, Nikolaos had devised memory techniques to retain all the information he'd gleaned. On the floor of his cell were scratchings from pictorial representations of the military outposts the commanders had mentioned, memorised by seeing animal heads emerge from lines. For the names of various people, he'd found rhymes to suit their importance.

His thoughts returned to his grimy cell. If his memory was right, the hour was noon, but he wasn't certain for he'd been kept deep underground for too long. If midday, most of the city would be snoozing.

Sensing his wandering mind, Xenia crawled up his thigh. He took her into his hand and ran his finger across her soft brown head.

Outside his cell, the desperate wheezes of the prone guard farther down the corridor continued. Why hadn't he died yet? Surely it wouldn't be long now. Any second, the munlock would paralyse his lungs. The waiting was almost as arduous as torture.

If only he could break his chains. If only he could warn the Empire.

The rakkans would know the poisoning was him. Only a few days ago, Xenia had dropped pouches of munlock into water jars in the garrison.

She fidgeted, as restless as him, but there was nothing else to do but wait. And so, he did, until he heard noises above the rasping of the guard, soft boot-steps that used each exhale to mask them.

A faint light grew in the corridor, flickers bouncing from the black bars of the door.

Nikolaos sat up and pushed himself backwards across the floor of his cell until his back hit the wall. *Is this it? Have they come to execute me?*

The rasping man outside suddenly choked in pain with a few splutters before falling silent for good.

Then the footsteps began again.

Before Nikolaos had time to fear, a hooded man moved in front of the door and turned to him. The only light shone from a wisp of algor on the hilt of the figure's drawn sword. It didn't reach far enough to pierce the darkness shrouding the man's face but did show the unusual length of his sword, which was already wet with blood. More stains splattered his trousers and grey tunic, and Nikolaos's eyes were drawn to the silver eagle emblazoned on his belt.

"Yes?" Nikolaos asked nervously, far past the point of hope.

The man froze, statuesque in his fixation on Nikolaos before drawing a hand across his belt buckle to wipe the drops of blood and coat it with a shine of algor.

Nikolaos gasped, seeing now in the brighter light that the eagle's wings were raised, not lowered as worn by a common algus. *A King's man… That long blade…* Dare he think it? Not only a servant of the King, but the King's Sword himself?

"Jason?" Nikolaos whispered.

The man nodded beneath his hood then brought a finger to his lips to command silence.

How did he know Nikolaos was here? *What does he want of me?*

As the questions circled, the King's Sword withdrew a key from his pocket and unlocked the door.

Nikolaos took in the algus properly for the first time. The man was rumoured to never wear armour, but Nikolaos had dismissed that as exaggerated tales. Yet, the slim-fitting cotton showed the algus's wiry figure and no chainmail or cuirass underneath. Standing only at average height, he betrayed nothing of the dread his name brought.

Jason strode into the cell and unlocked the restraints on Nikolaos's wrists while the two shared a silence that Nikolaos figured was more uncomfortable for him than the King's Sword, who angled his head down to continue obscuring his face.

Nikolaos considered breaking the quiet by telling the algus everything about Lex and the rakkans, but Jason's muteness brought a dumbness to his own lips.

The time for telling will soon come. Then, the city he'd grown up in would be liberated from the traitors.

At the thought, the fantasies of his youth came to the forefront of his mind. Played correctly, Nikolaos could emerge a war hero and be given the regency of Laltos himself. *That's if there's any justice in the world.*

Once he'd released Nikolaos's chains, the King's Sword stood and offered him a gloved hand.

Nikolaos hesitated, worried that what lay in wait at the end of this journey was worse than the hangman's noose. But he soon shook it off. He had to stop Lex.

After Jason helped him to his feet, the pair left the cell and made their way through the hallway.

That was the simple part. His captor fools should have broken his legs, as the humans did with their captives. No chance of escape, and when done carefully, it bore little risk of infection and premature death.

The Margalvians had spared him torture, but his rations had been paltry compared to the feasts he was accustomed to, which had left his tattered grey tunic sagging from his frame.

Hunger knotted his stomach, so powerfully he'd have eaten the escort still in his hand would she have satiated his appetite for more than an hour.

Nikolaos had to feel his way by running a hand along the wall of the black corridor. A few yards later, he almost tripped over a body lying prone on the shadowed floor. He stepped over before pausing.

"Wait," he said, wincing as the King's Sword skidded to a halt with a growl.

Nikolaos crouched and felt around the guard's waist until he found the sheathed sword and a wet patch that made him shudder.

Nikolaos tried to withdraw the gladius, but it weighed a ton. *Curses.* He'd forgotten they made the damned things out of kuraminium. He'd have to escape weaponless.

More importantly, he set himself to stealing the corpse's boots. The sheepskin insides were damp with sweat—at least what he hoped was sweat—as he pulled them on. They'd do.

After a few moments of staring into the blackness in every direction, he dared another whisper. "Ready."

A spark of algor ignited from Jason's front, but all Nikolaos saw was the back of his head. As curious as he was, he stayed behind the algus as they crept through the hallways.

Now weakly lit, the corridor was twice as tall as him but so narrow only one could pass without brushing against the black hardened lava that made the walls.

More dead guards met their feet, lying in pools of blood impossible to avoid.

On they crept. Nikolaos's escort had mapped out the corridors and exits to the underground garrison passages well, but he had no idea how Jason navigated, nor how he'd already cut the throat of every guard along the way thus far.

Each of their steps were careful and light. The corridor's walls had a green moss covering them in places as if contaminated with an infectious disease. How anyone lived in such filth was beyond Nikolaos.

Then again, as the old saying went—rakkans were nothing more than rats on two legs.

No matter how many blind turns they passed, Nikolaos's heart picked up when approaching each. At one, he spied a hint of sunlight, which turned into bright rays as they rounded a corner. Lots of enclaves and doors dotted the corridor on their left and right, but only one door was ringed by a halo of light. *Oh sunlight, I'd forgotten the joy you bring.*

As they approached the door, murmurings from outside grew and made the King's Sword stop and grunt. Two lines of shadow swept beneath the exit before Jason thrust Nikolaos into a recess to the left while he darted into one opposite, then banished the little algor he'd been using to light their way.

The metallic snap of a lock opening echoed in the corridor.

Hinges groaned as a muttering voice entered, followed by a crash as the door slammed shut.

Nikolaos pressed himself so hard into the wall he almost sank in. Thankfully, the lip of the recess was enough to shield him from view, but it also blinded him.

His escort froze in his hand while Nikolaos slowed his breathing and made sure each exhale was aimed away from the passage.

The approaching footsteps made it harder and harder for him to keep his breaths slow. His pounding heart demanded more air.

"Always me…damned sunlight," a deep voice muttered.

Nikolaos readied himself mentally without moving an inch, urged Xenia on as she climbed down his arm and leg then onto the floor.

The mutters grew louder.

Now or never. Xenia, go!

His dormouse bolted across the corridor.

"Huh? Little rascal—"

Jason burst from the recess. In a blinding flash of algor that lasted less than a heartbeat, he cut his sword through the rakkan's neck then plunged them into darkness again.

The thud and gushing that followed echoed from the walls, and only Nikolaos's imagination saw the dead guard fall.

Xenia scurried back up his leg, and, wasting no time, Nikolaos stepped over the corpse and began towards the exit.

The thought of sleeping on a mattress and silk again brought the first joy he'd felt in months.

He took careful steps to the outside door and slowly tested the handle, but the King's Sword nudged him away.

"Wait," Jason muttered.

The sudden guttural voice gave Nikolaos more of a shock than when he'd first laid eyes on the algus.

Jason waited a few seconds, breath held as if listening for the faintest of sounds outside, before he opened the door with confidence that no one lurked on the other side.

After a nervous pause, where Nikolaos tried but failed to understand the algus's behaviour, he followed Jason and squinted at the sudden bright light that engulfed him.

Ouch. His eyes would barely open. A few seconds went by while he waited for his vision to adjust, but it didn't. So many weeks had passed in darkness that it could take minutes—time he didn't have.

After he felt he'd aged a year, his eyes finally allowed him a glimpse of the outdoors. Blackened stone-brick buildings came into focus, down streets so narrow a horse and cart wouldn't fit.

How grateful he was for the city's dark stones now. Heaven help him had he had to deal with the glare of Laltos.

The King's Sword was already halfway up the street, gazing back beneath his hooded tunic, now showing all the blood that covered it. Not needing instruction, Nikolaos bolted after him but soon tired after so long without testing his muscles.

Jason kept a slow pace for him. Tall snow-capped mountains poked above the shuttered buildings. Only a few roads to take and they'd be at the gate.

Suddenly, the thudding of footsteps grew, bouncing from so many of the walls around them it was impossible to pinpoint their source.

But the King's Sword seemed to be in no doubt, pushing Nikolaos with a force that knocked him onto his backside. The algus's gaze never wavered from an adjacent street ahead.

Before Nikolaos could clamber back to his feet, dozens of legionnaires wearing long black cloaks rounded the corner.

"There!" The blare of a rakkan horn followed the shout.

Nikolaos's bowels loosened at the sight of the storming black armour. *Only a god can save us now.*

The King's Sword drew back his long blade then pounced. Legionnaires' heads moved from side to side to keep track of the algus's swift, zig-zagging approach that even Nikolaos struggled to follow.

A flash of steel was all he saw before blood gushed from the thighs of two legionnaires at the front, followed by a haze of sparks and the falling head of another.

It took a few moments for Nikolaos to snap out of the awe-struck stupor that had overcome him, and he scrambled to his feet.

While the King's Sword cut a hole through the legionnaires' defence, Nikolaos bolted after him, dodging through the leaden swipes of those left at the side of the street with enough life to still swing.

The two algus pushed on—rakkan legs, arms, necks, all cut in a blur one after another without the King's Sword taking a wound. As impressive as Nikolaos found Darius, this algus was something else, possessing an elegance that the half-rakkan brute never displayed.

They turned a corner and entered even narrower streets that the mountain fogs hadn't escaped.

But it wasn't long until the city's northern wall came into view, three times the size of a man and without a foothold.

They approached with haste as Jason's sword found the smallest of gaps in defence that each legionnaire left when they tried to parry his strikes. The long blade let him stab the point from a distance their weapons couldn't reach—not that it would have mattered.

More bodies fell, and the stone wall was soon all that stood between them and freedom. Nikolaos's eyes were drawn to a spot in a dark corner where a rope hung down that the King's Sword was cutting and slashing his way towards.

As soon as they reached it, Nikolaos leapt and grabbed hold of one of the knots that allowed even his feeble muscles to climb.

Meanwhile, Jason protected his ascent.

As Nikolaos finally slung a leg over the top of the wall, he spied the mists swirling at the far end of the street. He trained his eyes to make out a horned figure tearing towards them.

"The Warlord's coming!" In a panic, he let go too soon and fell. Jason leapt as Nikolaos slammed into the ground outside, feeling the stones strike both his hip and Xenia's soft body in his pocket.

Blinding pain consumed his thoughts, his sight, his body. He cried out as he felt as if all his bones were crushed and snapped—his escort's pain.

But it lasted only a second before leaving as quickly as it had come, as quickly as Xenia's life faded. *Curses. It's such a pain to get a new one.*

While Nikolaos scrambled back to his feet, the King's Sword landed beside him. Then the pair took off out of the city, chased by only the Warlord's furious roar that pierced the wall and Nikolaos's nerve.

They sprinted up the rock-strewn slope at a pace no rakkan could match, but it took an age for the terror to ease, for his hands to stop trembling.

"Where are we heading?" Nikolaos huffed as they ran.

"Xavala." Even on the run, Jason didn't sound out of breath.

Thank the Goddess. "Why did you rescue me? How did you know where I was?"

His questions were met with a silence that he assumed would last until the Silk City.

Not that he'd complain. He couldn't have chosen a better place to spread the word about Lex. He prayed to every god and goddess that she was there and he could watch them throw her into a cell to rot.

The Empire would soon know what he'd been dying to say for so long, but the thought wouldn't bring him any joy until his words finally reached someone with the power to act.

22

Darius – Road to Dolthea

Darius's horse rocked him back and forth as it ambled, which made the trees and marching soldiers ahead swing in his vision. Taking his hand from his pocket, he glanced down at the piece of parchment and read the words "Bita, Trade Street, Dolthea." They weren't far.

The first thing he intended on doing on arrival was this favour for Omid. *I can do something useful for once.*

The clear blue skies peeking through the canopy overhead lifted his spirits, gave him hope they'd arrive in time, because a Viridian Legion attack on Dolthea would have undoubtedly left columns of black smoke.

However, the relief soon turned to discomfort at the thought of Selene. While she rode at the head of their army, Darius traipsed behind, watching the rears of the soldiers as their skirts of leather strips swayed with the thuds of footsteps.

At least he didn't have to lie to her further while apart.

He withdrew into his own thoughts and felt out for Lyra as he so often did on the journey. Their connection was instantaneous, and relief swept over him as he sensed her cool presence, so different to the hot and fevered state she'd been in shortly before. Although not yet recovered, her quiet mind told him she slumbered, so he quietly returned to his surroundings.

Instead, he took the scroll Brutus had sent to him from a bag attached to his horse's saddle. Riding atop a stallion was hardly the easiest place to read, but he needed some nuggets of wisdom. Ever since the revelation of the Viridians' admiration of him, questions troubled him over his former self's decisions.

But one hope lingered. If an upstanding rakkan like Brutus had liked the man, he couldn't have been all bad.

Guiding the horse with only his thighs, he unrolled to where he'd last left off.

33. There is a way that at first seems right to a man, but that will ultimately lead to death.

34. A wise son brings joy to his father, but a foolish son hates his mother.

Darius wondered what that made a man that did both, conscious he had no fond feelings towards his own mother. *A wise fool?* Had he once brought joy to his father? No one in Margalvia seemed to know much of the rakkan that had died long ago. It seemed only tales of men that did great deeds survived in the stories, which reminded him… He quickly unrolled to further down, surprised he'd forgotten about the story until now—Trogus and Arria.

The human-rakkan war stretches back to the beginning of history, to Trogus and Arria.

But in the beginning, there was peace. Two tribes were created to rule over the world, one made for the other just as a man was made for a woman. Their dominion stretched from coast to coast, and they were imbued with sharp minds and skills that no animal shared.

The tribe of the south was led by the patriarch Trogus, sculpted from clay by the Creator and given people to follow him. To survive the cold of the mountain ranges, Trogus was given a gift that no other shared—ferven. Warmth, comfort, life. These were the sacred duties entrusted to the patriarch.

The tribe of the north was led by the matriarch Arria, sculpted from ice and also given people to follow her. To counter the burning sun of summer and fires fuelled by ferven, Arria was given the gift of algor.

"Doesn't it make you queasy to read on a horse?" Selene's shout carried over the thumping footsteps, causing Darius to look up.

At first, he was surprised that the trees had grown more thickset, but then the walls behind Selene's mounted figure caught his attention. They stood twice the height of a man, just as he'd noted only weeks ago, when carrying a bleeding panther in his arms.

The perimeter outside the walls had been cleared of trees, which at least gave no attackers a free route in. *Guess they don't believe in tree-gods here like Omid did.* Above the walls, tall wooden buildings poked up, the dark, pointed frames making it seem more ominous than he knew it was. Dolthea still stood, not burning, not drenched in blood.

He quickly rolled the scroll back up as his horse trotted towards Selene who patiently waited for him. She'd removed her green tunic and now her hair fell on bare chainmail.

"Avoiding me?" she teased.

"No, no…" *I'm a lousy liar.* "Just catching up on a bit of reading, watching your rear—I mean the rears of your soldiers—their backs, I mean." He probably should have stopped at "reading."

She smirked. "Do I make you nervous, brave hero?"

Whatever he felt, it was so rare for him that he had trouble identifying what it was. Only Lex had ever made him so…edgy. "Considering you could take off my head at two hundred yards with a bow, perhaps I *should* be unsettled."

His horse reached hers, and she turned to trot alongside him towards the town, so close their legs occasionally brushed against each other, which he suspected was deliberate on her part.

"I don't think it's my bow that scares you," she said. "It's my sharp intellect."

He forced a laugh. "I enjoy your jests."

"You know very well I wasn't jesting." She narrowed her eyes but couldn't prevent the smile growing on her face. "What were you reading?"

"Something…not sure if it's legend or history. A story of Trogus and Arria."

"I can't say whether it's true, but the legend says they were the original pair. Arria was the first queen."

"Of Toria?"

She shrugged. "Of all humans. Toria wasn't established that long ago. She came before we splintered and started quarrelling amongst ourselves."

"And who was Trogus?"

"The first rakkan. His lineage was said to stretch far. It's claimed that overlords of the past wielded the Twin Blades, imbued with the fire of Trogus himself. Imagine weapons as deadly to us as the Staff of Arria is to rakkans."

Darius hoped the nervousness in him wasn't apparent. "Where are they now?"

"Lost, fortunately for us. Or maybe they're just legend, but…have you ever seen the Staff of Arria?"

"Yes." *Unfortunately.* "Why?"

"It's blackened as if it will crumble to ash, and the Twin Blades of Trogus are said to be the weapons that burned it."

Sound useful. Making a note to ask Brutus more on them later, Darius continued through the wooden gateway.

He was unable to take comfort in the refuge of the walls when he spotted how thin the gates were and the frail soldiers with drooped faces that stood by them.

If the guards were solemn, the people of the town looked far worse, many snoozing in the gutters as in Laltos, probably sheltering from surrounding villages burned to ash.

Each man, woman and child had the same haunted fear embedded in their eyes, and the festering smell of human waste grew with every step.

"It's a good thing we arrived," Darius said to Selene, wondering how far his threat to Hadrian had spread. Would the Warlord be hesitant or angry?

Regardless, now inside the town, his mind turned from legends of heroes of old and instead dwelled on the note Lex had given him—Omid's mother. He'd only just arrived, but if he didn't take advantage of the peaceful air, he may not get another chance to free her before the Viridians attacked.

"Do you know where Trade Street is?" he asked Selene.

She shrugged. "Why do you ask?"

"There's someone I'm looking for."

"Who?"

"Just someone."

"A man of many mysteries. Who exactly are you, Philippos?" Her tone was still playful, but her lingering stare made him suspect it was a genuine question.

"I'm no one important—simply a warrior following his orders, a man trying to find his place in the world." He hadn't given the words much forethought but surprised himself at how true they sounded once said out loud.

A scruffy old beggar staggered towards them at the far side of the main road, one hand supporting himself against the wooden facades of the buildings lining it, the other with a cup in his hand. His dirty cap, torn sleeves and slow steps made Darius suspect he was a drunk.

"You there!" Darius called. The man continued stumbling for a moment, then looked up with a furrowed brow and pointed to himself.

"Yes, you!" Darius shouted, pulling a coin from his pocket.

"What are you doing?" Selene asked.

The man's eyes widened at the glint of silver and he wobbled towards Darius's horse, taking off his cap to release greasy grey hair that spilled across his shoulders in clumps.

"Can you show me to Trade Street?" Darius asked.

The man's gaze didn't waver from the coin. "Of course, Algus." He made no movement until Darius tossed him the crest.

As soon as he did, the man began hobbling, swerving from side to side. When at a safe distance, Darius manoeuvred his horse after the man.

"You know that will house him for a week?" Selene asked, following at his side. "This isn't the affluent Silk City. He'd have done it for a bite of a stale loaf."

It wasn't like Darius had to worry over money because Lex was happy to supply more whenever he ran low. "What can I say? I'm a generous man."

A quizzical frown followed by a smile came on her face like she was both shocked and impressed. *Guess riches* are *the way to a girl's heart.*

It was only a couple of long, wearisome streets before the man stopped and pointed. "Trade Street."

Darius surveyed the flat wooden buildings at each side of the street. "I don't suppose you know where I can find a woman by the name of Bita?"

The man's lips curled into an impish grin. "Third door on the left is the one you're after." With that, he began hobbling back to the main road, leaving Darius with Selene, who now had a sombre expression on her face.

"What's wrong?" he asked.

"Nothing." She sighed. "I think I know what you want this 'Bita' for though. Perhaps I should leave you to it."

"No. Stay. This won't take long." He wondered what she thought he was doing because it was highly unlikely that she knew the truth.

He climbed down from his horse, thankful to use his legs and let the blood flow freely. Leading his stallion by the reins, he walked towards the third building, which had a double door of dark, polished wood with an unlit clay lamp perched above.

Selene followed him, hanging back and now eyeing him with suspicion.

Approaching the doors, he noted the iron knocker on the right-hand side and a small hatch at eye level that was closed.

He knocked with two loud bangs and listened for movement, but the only sounds within were muffled moans and pants from the second floor.

Either someone was in discomfort or was thoroughly enjoying themselves. How could they do that when their town was threatened with invasion?

After not hearing any footsteps, Darius lifted the knocker to bang on the door again when the hatch slid open.

The eyes staring through were murky green and as threatening as the gruff male voice that followed. "Yes?"

"I'm searching for Bita," Darius said.

"She's reserved for the rest of the day."

"Then un-reserve her."

The man paused for a few seconds with a murmur. "That'll cost extra."

A price was expected, but Darius hadn't reckoned on paying just to see her. But now he'd guessed what she was reserved for, and why Selene's mood had changed.

There were several ways Darius could attempt to see Bita, either peaceful or violent. Given Selene was watching over his shoulder, he guessed peacefully was worth a try. "I'll pay four crests."

A loud guffaw rumbled through the door and the eyes momentarily disappeared. "She's no youngster, but she's worth more than that for the afternoon."

If that were the case, then the twenty-nine crests in his pocket were definitely not going to be enough to free her. *So much for the peaceful option.*

"Open this door. Now." His voice turned as cold as the algor now flaring from his eyes.

"You don't scare me." The green eyes narrowed. "We're Torian citizens, and this house is owned by one of you algus."

With a curse, Darius turned to Selene and lowered his voice. "I don't suppose this town's under martial law?"

She grimaced. "No. If you want her, you'll have to pay."

"Fine!" he shouted back at the door. "Ten crests if you bring her out here now."

The hatch snapped shut, which Darius took to be acceptance of his terms. Now he just had the problem of freeing the woman.

He glanced at Selene, who stood watching him silently. Despite her and Darius getting on well, he doubted she'd overlook him murdering citizens. "Can you lend me money?"

"You want me to pay for you to see a whore?" she snapped.

"I won't lie with her. I want to buy her."

"Oh! Even better. I'm to buy you a concubine?"

Darius laughed, which sent Selene's cheeks deep red as her scowl darkened.

"No," he said. "I owe a debt to a relative of hers. This is my repayment of it."

"Oh." Her expression softened, though from the sulky tone of her voice, it seemed reluctantly so. "What debt?"

"That's for me to know. Do you have money or not?"

"I do if you'll tell me why you're doing this." A hint of the usual playfulness returned to her tone.

"You…" He shook his head, thinking of who it was she reminded him of, when it suddenly became obvious. "You're just like your sister. So curious, hate to be left out."

"I'm not inquisitive of everyone." She stepped towards him then leaned in to whisper in his ear. "Just the fascinating ones."

The tickle of her breath sent gooseflesh down his neck, and the raised eyebrow she gave him after pulling away told him it was deliberate.

Before he thought of a reply, two snaps sounded from the latches on the door, and it opened with a groan. Stepping outside was a tall, slender woman with dark olive skin that bore some wrinkles of age. They took nothing from her beauty. Straight brown hair flowed almost down to her waist, and her simple, sleek clothes highlighted all the slim parts of her body.

"You requested me?" She gave him a seductive smile and a subtle lick of her lips.

"You can drop the act." Darius pulled the door closed behind her with the iron knocker to ensure the man didn't hear. "I'm not here for that."

The woman frowned. "Then what—"

"Do you have a son?" Darius's deep voice came out curter than he'd intended, but he didn't want this to drag on.

"I… I don't know, I—"

"You would have been separated years ago. Did you have a son?"

She swallowed. "Yes."

"What was his name?"

"Omid," she said weakly.

Darius sighed and took a moment to consider what his next words should be. He hadn't planned what he'd say beforehand and now regretted the fact. To tell a mother that her son was dead would probably require more comfortable surroundings. "I'm here to free you."

The air of confusion that overcame her face took him aback, hardly the reaction he'd expected.

"Why?" she asked.

Is no one grateful for my help? "Because I'm a generous man."

More moans escaped from the second floor, which would normally have made him feel uncomfortable, but that was nothing compared to the stare Bita gave him, so intense that he almost turned and left it at that.

"You're too old to be my son," she said after a while.

"I never claimed to be. I just had to be sure it was you."

"Where is he?"

Darius cleared his throat, coughed, and feigned any excuse to delay the next words out of his mouth while he considered them. "He's not here."

Selene frowned at the pair, focusing her attention on Darius, which made him wonder exactly what was going through her mind at this bizarre conversation. Social skills and politeness weren't something he'd trained to master, or even grasp.

"Where will I go?" Bita asked, the pitch of her voice suddenly rising as the moans upstairs grew more rapid. "Without a master I can't eat, I have no shelter. What am I to do?"

The fear in her welling eyes left Darius without the words to comfort her. "I thought a slave would be glad to be freed…"

"I've been a slave all my life. I have no family, no one to help me." She panted, and Darius soon regretted doing what he'd thought would be a kindness.

"Just relax." Darius stepped towards her and took her firmly by the shoulders, dipped his head to her level and tried to think of any words that would placate her. "I was a friend of your son, which means I won't leave you to starve in the gutter."

"*Was* a friend?" Tears pooled in the corner of her eyes as a look of knowing spread across her face. "He's dead, isn't he?"

Darius lowered his head and stared at his boots, at the rakkan bloodstains he now found more preferable to the woman's despair. He opened his mouth to speak but there were no words to utter, so he nodded instead.

Howls, cries, screams—all the things Darius braced to hear next were nothing compared to the pain of the silence that followed. The room upstairs fell quiet and left only the sound of Bita's tears falling onto the ground.

Selene stepped forward and placed an arm around the woman while looking at Darius as if asking what the hell his plan had been and why they were in the street doing this.

As hard as Omid's death had been to witness, as hard as it had been to feel Lyra bleeding in his arms, or his baby brother dying, he knew what Bita now bore was worse.

As always in times of emotion, a question repeated in his mind. *Why should I care?* The more he saw in the world, the quicker he dismissed it with the simple resolve that he clearly did care.

"You should know…" he said, trying to speak softly, "I got the wretch responsible, blinded him and watched his throat get slit."

Bita closed her eyes and leaned into Selene, who stared at him with a bewildered grimace.

"What?" he mouthed. Knowing justice had been done would have helped ease *his* pain.

"Take her to my workers," Selene said to him. "I'm in need of a new servant. I'll treat her well and pay her a fair wage."

Darius smiled, could have kissed her, but instead gave the algus a nod of thanks. "You're not coming?"

"Someone has to settle the debts with her master."

"Thank you for the loan. I'm good for the money." Or rather, Lex was.

Selene eased Bita from her shoulder into his grasp, and he began walking her back towards the main street. The booms on the door echoed behind, and Darius thanked fate that he had Selene to aid him. Such kindness had never impressed him before, but in her, it just magnified his guilt at lying to her. Lex's First Alliance couldn't come soon enough.

He cursed in his mind, debating whether or not to tell Selene the truth, but always remembering what going against his commander's instructions had resulted in before.

But the temptation wouldn't leave him, and those giving orders were nowhere around. At some point, perhaps he'd be tempted to act on his own authority again.

23

Darius – Dolthea

Later that evening, after he'd introduced Bita to Selene's workers, Darius made his way to the lodge he and the other algus had been assigned for the duration of their stay in Dolthea. As he wandered from one street to the next, he soon lost his way and wondered how many he'd turned down. *Great. I'm hopeless without Lyra navigating.*

He'd stopped to look around at the buildings and roads when he spotted Selene striding towards him. All he wanted was some quiet time to spend connected to Lyra, and had it been anyone but Selene, he'd have pretended not to see them. But for her, he waited, although an unease grew in him with every step closer she took.

"You'll be pleased to know Bita's paid for in full," Selene said.

"That's good news," Darius said.

"I won't tell you how much you owe me just yet."

That wasn't what made him edgy. "Let me know the damage tomorrow."

"Don't worry. I will." She exhaled and ran a hand through her hair. Darius watched every strand slip through her fingers while wondering how soft it felt.

"Feel like a drink?" he asked. "I could use a bottle or two of firewater." If only to calm his nerves.

"What if the rakkans attack?"

"Then I'll fight drunk. Perhaps it's only fair I give them a chance for once."

She grinned. "My heavens. It's so tragic when the handsome ones are so conceited."

Every time she gave him a compliment, it made his entire body heat. "I jest. Haven't you learned by now that a serious remark never leaves my mouth?"

"Haven't you learned I'm the same?"

"Ah." Darius nodded, ran his hand across the stubble on his chin. "I guess I'm not handsome then."

They shared a look for a moment, Darius waiting for her to correct him, but the smirk on her face soon dashed his hopes.

"So…" he said. "Drink? Or are you still afraid the rakkans will come?"

"I get the impression you aren't fazed by them."

It wasn't like he needed to be, apart from those that knew his weaknesses… "They'd need great numbers to beat us."

"You give them less respect than they deserve."

"You think the Viridian Legion deserve respect?"

"Respect as warriors. They're dangerous, especially if you speak with them as you did. You can't trust a word from their mouths."

He raised an eyebrow. "There might be some that can be trusted, out there somewhere."

"Nonsense." Her voice dropped low. "I showed mercy once but never again."

As much as he hoped for a hint of openness in her, labouring the issue might do more harm than good. "I need that drink."

She nodded, and the pair walked to the lodge, meeting some of their soldiers on the way but too busy chatting to notice. The growing ease with which Darius talked with her was always coupled with a foreboding of something painful soon to ensue. So far, the only two women in his life he cared about—Lex and Lyra—had brought him hurt, whether deliberately or through no fault of their own.

Selene and Darius reached the lodge, which was nothing but a plain wooden building like the others on the outside, but as they stepped inside, Darius's eyes were assaulted by flamboyant bright colours of tapestries hanging from the walls. Squinting with his nose turned up, he followed Selene directly upstairs to a high-ceilinged corridor with doors to each room illuminated by rows of lamps flickering on shelves overhead.

Selene paused outside the first door, her eyes glistening with the reflection of the dancing flames. "This is me. I have firewater inside."

"Can I ask you a serious question?" he asked.

"Of course. Whether or not you get a serious answer is another thing…"

"Your sister Lex…"

At the words, the smirk on Selene's face flattened and she pressed her lips tightly together.

Darius continued. "I've seen her toy with more men than I can count, seen her seductive gazes, her flattery. Men are easily fooled—"

"That depends. Lex can do it with ease because she's sickeningly beautiful. The rest of us have no such luck."

210

Darius scoffed. "As if you can't do the same."

"Why do you say that?"

"Look at you…"

Her cheeks flushed, and her gaze fell to his lips. "Philippos…I have a question for you too."

It took him a second to recall that "Philippos" was him. The other thoughts racing through his head set his heart pounding. "Yes?"

"Why did you help a slave?"

In two minds whether to tell the truth or lie, he decided on a half-truth. "Like I told Bita, I owed her son. He helped me." As the first person Darius recalled caring about after his memories were stolen, the boy was never far from his mind.

"You're not like any algus I've ever met."

More true than you know. "You said that before. Why am I different?"

"You don't see people by status or wealth. You spoke to Bita with more respect than Gorgias."

Darius scoffed. "Because she deserved more." Selene's compliment wasn't the cause of the lump in his throat. It was the way she stared, pupils wide, to take in every detail of his face. It was like she was the first person to see him—not as a warrior, but as a man.

Selene's mouth lost its grin, eyes now bored into his while she inched forward and made his heart rush all the more.

He wanted her in his arms. Who couldn't adore the way her button nose twitched every time she made a quip, or the loyalty and care she showed by wearing her former escort's claw attached to her scabbard?

"You impress me, Philippos," she said finally, "but I still know little about you."

211

"Not much to know. You know *me*. My history isn't important."

"That's true." She moved her body closer to his and placed a hand on his hip. "Do you want to come inside?"

"Sure… I could use that drink."

"…I didn't mean for a drink." The heated look in her eye told Darius exactly what she wanted. His face burned. Since kissing Lex all that time ago, he hadn't kissed another, let alone gone any further.

At last, his own feelings became clear as he imagined running a hand through Selene's hair, which now shone auburn in the lamplight. For a moment, he wondered whether to see this as a betrayal to Lex, but after recalling her urging him to find another woman, she couldn't be mad at him inadvertently being drawn to someone else.

He brushed his nose against Selene's ever so slightly. "You aren't using me like your sister, are you?"

Her lips grazed his. "Do you want a slap?"

"…No."

Their lips locked as Darius wrapped an arm around her waist, pulling her body into his. Her kiss was soft, her tongue gentle while it glided across his.

After a time far too short for Darius's liking, she broke away and stared like she wanted to devour him whole, a look he returned.

She took his hand, pushed open the door behind her and began leading him into her room.

His stomach lurched. He didn't recall being with a woman before. Old Darius had liked whores, but *he'd* never ventured there.

Worries of not knowing what to do scared him more than the entire Viridian Legion, but he was damned if he would let fear get in his way.

Before another doubt crossed his mind, he followed her into the room and kicked the door shut.

24

Darius – Dolthea

Darius awoke with Selene's head resting on his chest, rising and falling slowly with every breath. Her hair tickled his neck. Half in slumber, she hugged him tightly, and with every beat of her heart, her warm body pulsed over his sensitive skin.

One of her legs folded over his, and he savoured the memories of them wrapped around him last night. Why had he been so afraid, so hesitant before? Now he understood why most men seemed obsessed with it, but he doubted just any woman would have made him feel this way, like Lex…

He shook his head. Lex had turned him away. Selene had accepted him.

The cotton sheets ran across his sticky skin as he stretched and sank further into the woollen mattress. He inhaled the warm air deeply, taking in the soft floral scent of Selene's hair.

The nervousness was gone. The more of her he saw, the more beautiful she became. Why he hadn't realised it sooner he didn't know, but those brown eyes now had a pull stronger than any he'd seen. He hadn't even woken in the night in a cold sweat thinking of Lyra.

Selene stirred and wrapped an arm over his shoulder.

"You awake?" she asked.

For a moment he considered staying silent, just to enjoy her embrace longer, but eventually relented. "Yes."

"What hour is it?"

"Don't know. Don't care."

She chuckled. "You enjoyed my company last night?"

I'd have thought that was obvious. "More than you know."

"Oh, Philippos." She breathed a deep sigh and moved to get up, but he held her wrist in place, drawing out a giggle from her again.

"We need to go," she said. "The town needs to prepare for an attack."

"Just a few moments longer."

She tugged against his grasp, and though he could have held her with ease, he let her slip free.

"Rumours may spread if we're up here together into the late morning." She emerged from the sheets, giving him another chance to ogle her naked body while she gathered her chainmail and tunic from the floor. "I'd rather my father didn't hear of this."

"Perhaps you shouldn't make a habit of inviting men to bed with you then." Darius raised an eyebrow.

She threw her tunic at his face. "I'll have you know I never invite men to my bed."

"I'm flattered then." Darius took great pleasure in the revelation, and the irritation on her face told him she wasn't lying. "So, what's the issue with your father? You think he wouldn't approve?"

"To put it mildly."

Best make sure he never finds out then. "I won't take that personally considering he's never met me. I hope you'll still introduce me when we return to Laltos."

"We'll see. Depends how quickly you repay me for freeing the slave." She gave him a smirk before pulling on her undershirt and chainmail. He watched, enjoying his view of her back, and recalled running his hands across it while her fingernails dug into his shoulders.

"I thought after last night my debts might be forgiven," he said. "Wasn't I worth a few crests?"

She snorted a laugh. "If I were generous, I'd knock off a couple."

"Ouch." He sat up with a deep sigh and searched for his clothes on the floorboards. "Never took you for a miser."

"Maybe I'm generous, and you were only worth one." Her laugh was muffled as she pulled her tunic over her head.

But Darius couldn't bring himself to laugh at that quip, wondering if it were a truth that was veiled in humour.

Deciding he'd best rouse too, he slid across the bed, knocking Selene's pillow aside as he did, and he saw the hilt of a dagger poke out underneath.

What the…? With a quick glance to check her head was still covered, he shifted the pillow to hide the weapon again, wondering whether she always kept it there or if there was something particular about him she was wary of.

"Can I ask you a question?" She turned towards him.

Darius had a feeling he wasn't going to like it. "It's a little late to be getting to know me."

"What's with the 'M' tattoo on your stomach?"

He'd hoped her human eyes weren't sensitive enough to see that in the dark. Only when naked had he remembered it. "It's a long story." He snatched his trousers from the floor and began pulling them on. But the deepening of her frown made him suspect he was drawing too much attention to it by avoiding her question. "Tell you what," he said, "I'll regale you with the story when you tell me why there's a blade in your bed…"

Her eyebrows rose, lips parted slightly as if to speak, but it took her a moment to find the words. "You can't be too careful."

"I hope you're not afraid of me."

"It's not about you."

He should have been relieved at the fact, but his curiosity got the better of him. "Then what? I can keep a secret. You can trust me."

She paced over and slowly sat beside him, tense and rigid as if freezing, despite the stuffy air in the room. "Swear you won't tell anyone else."

Darius was all too familiar with hiding things. "I swear it."

She sighed and angled her head down until her hair obscured her face. "It's because of Gorgias. We have a history, and I'm worried he'll seek to silence me."

"Why would he?" *And why does she fear a juvenile mother's-boy?*

"I know his secret. He's a eunuch."

Darius's thighs tensed and pressed inward at the sudden images coming to mind. "I won't ask how you discovered that."

"Ugh." She lifted her head and grimaced. "Don't even think it. I was in the wrong place at the wrong time. He doesn't want word to spread that he's less of a man, and I've used it against him one too many times." Her hands clenched the corners of the mattress. "I used to be a slave once. He's no idea what that's like, thinks his infirmity is the end of the world… Folks like us know better. There are people suffering real trials out there." She closed her eyes.

217

Darius brought his hand to cover hers, which still clasped the mattress.

"If you fear for your life," he said, "why not just kill Gorgias, put an end to your worries?"

"His mother would find out it was me, even if it cost her entire fortune."

"I'm not afraid of his family. Say the word and I'll kill him for you."

Her eyes flew open. "Don't joke about this."

"Who's joking?"

She regarded him for a moment then smiled weakly when she saw the lethal determination in his stare.

"I can't ask that of you," she said. "If you aren't scared of his mother, you should be." She slipped her free hand underneath the pillow and pulled out the blade, handing it to Darius.

He took it and held it up. Knives were one weapon he didn't often use. The cold blade reminded him of the time he'd wielded one to try to save his baby brother from an algus bent on murder. He'd failed.

"So, what's your secret?" Selene asked.

"How long do you have?"

She laughed. "Long enough. Tell me about the tattoo."

The dagger weighed heavy in his hand, despite being made of steel. Now, the tattoo hardly seemed important. "It's a boring story. I have a better one."

"It best be good then."

He let the knife fall from his palm and sink into a floorboard. "I first fought with a dagger when I was a child, six years old."

She turned her body towards him. "Why's that?"

"An algus came for me when I was young, to take me away from my family. I managed to snatch a knife from a soldier, but he took my brother and stabbed a sword through his gut."

"Oh…" She gasped.

"I tried to save him, but I couldn't."

He'd never told anyone that story before, the one memory Archimedes had left in his mind. He still wasn't sure whether the details of that day were true, but that didn't stop them from haunting him.

"Did you ever find the algus that did it?" she asked.

"I didn't need to. I killed him with that very knife."

Selene blinked. "You killed an algus when you were six years old?"

"Yes."

"How?"

Because I'm stronger than ten men and faster than most. "He was a cripple, could barely walk without a cane. Wasn't much of a challenge, but fast enough to gut my brother."

Selene stroked his cheek and gave him a long kiss on the forehead that stayed with him after her lips left his skin. "You're not alone. Something similar happened to a man we were hunting last year."

Darius's heart picked up. He'd said too much. *Damn my loose tongue.* "Well, I guess it's common."

"Not really. Before Archimedes, most people welcomed being taken away to become an algus. My parents were freed and enriched when I was adopted into the Regent's family."

"Then I'm one of the few unlucky ones."

"I guess. It says a lot about you that you didn't turn out like this other man." Her face twisted in disgust, hardening her usually soft features. "He's worse than the Viridians, a murderer. Children tell stories about him like he's a prince of darkness, enjoying watching the pain the rakkan invasions cause us before disappearing into the shadows. Some call him the Slayer of Gods."

Darius's mouth suddenly dried. *What is it with people and nicknames?* From what the rakkans had told him, his old self was far from perfect but wasn't sadistic. If all of Laltos and Viridia had heard tall tales of him, then he had no idea how he'd explain himself to her and the Regent. *Hope Lex has a good plan.*

Selene took him in a long embrace before parting with a sigh. "I'm glad you told me your story. I know you better."

"Me too." Darius gave a sigh, glad she wouldn't press him further on the tattoo. "What's for breakfast? I'm starved."

"I don't have time." Selene fastened the buckle of her sword belt and stepped towards the door. "I'll be surveying the town's defences if you want to find me when you're ready. The Viridians could attack at any moment. Our scouts can't see far this close to the forest."

She opened the door and left while Darius put on the rest of his clothes, longing for the attack to come. The sooner he severed the head of Hadrian's second-in-command, the sooner he could tell Selene the truth and brace for the aftermath.

25

Brutus – Viridian Camp

Brutus pulled the helmet from the dead Viridian Legionnaire. A heap of swords, axes, cuirasses and more filled the tiny hovel from floor to roof, the collections from dead humans all thrown on without order or care by the looters.

Space was tighter still since Brutus had added two strangled Viridian warriors to the room. He'd turned them face down, so they didn't stare back at him with their blue lips and ringed necks. It was a risk to kill them, but worth it to get close to the rakkan Brutus had finally found—Hadrian.

He ran a finger along the green stripe atop the helmet to clear the mud. While Brutus didn't know the origins of this century's marking, he knew that these recent arrivals in the camp were tasked with guarding the Viridian Warlord's chosen dwelling. Brutus had snuck up on two of them under the setting sun while most of the other rakkans slept. He'd yet to find another way to get close enough to Hadrian.

Brutus slipped the helmet onto his head. For weeks he'd eavesdropped on commanders, bribed centurions and legionnaires, which had yielded interesting information but nothing of Viridia's plans for Margalvia. The sooner he found something crucial, the sooner he could return home to his wife, brother and comrades.

Brutus shuffled to the door and pressed his ear to it, conscious that the change of guard should have happened by now, and the dead rakkans would be missed if he wasn't swift.

Once satisfied no one was around, he cracked open the door and left. The small, boxy dwellings in the village were so crammed together the streets only had space for two people—or one if their shoulders were as wide as Brutus's. He wouldn't complain at the good cover it gave him though.

He ran a hand across the clay buildings as he walked quietly but confidently in the manner he'd learned yielded the least questions.

It was only a few turns before he reached the heart of the village and approached the entrance to the main hall, double doors beneath a bell tower where Hadrian had settled himself.

Only two fatigued guards stood outside, sheltering from the sun under a flap of cloth suspended with sticks above. The Viridian marks on their head matched Brutus's own and weren't common. He suspected they were on punishment duty because they were the only centuries to guard the Warlord.

Walking towards the guards, Brutus made sure his chin was lifted, as relaxed as the two rakkans he'd killed would have been.

"You're late," one hissed. "Where's the other guard?"

"Relieving himself." Brutus lowered his head to obscure his eyes a little more. "It's fine. You can go. He'll be back in a minute."

The guards sighed but did as he suggested, leaving Brutus to take up position in their place. After a few minutes leant against the wall, when the entire town settled into a tense silence, Brutus peered through the keyhole. He was relieved the only thing he saw was an empty entrance hall with closed doors on each of its three sides.

He carefully eased the door open and crept inside. Immediately, he sensed mutterings from another room ricocheting from the walls. *Damn. He's awake.*

After pushing the main entrance closed, he pressed his ear to each of the interior doors, stopping on the third when the murmurs became louder, though still unintelligible.

It only took a few seconds before one voice boomed so forcefully the door vibrated. "Why didn't you tell me before?"

A muffled voice replied.

"It changes everything!" Hadrian bellowed.

Upon recognising the voice, sweat beaded on Brutus's head, back, arms—places he hadn't realised produced sweat—as he imagined the Warlord finding him there.

"They won't listen, Father," a voice replied that Brutus recognised as Cordus's.

"I've had enough of people keeping things from me," Hadrian barked. "How can I lead if the lessers won't keep me informed? No wonder they're afraid to venture out."

"I didn't intend to keep it from you, Warlord. I thought you'd already heard—"

"Don't make excuses, Cordus, unless you want to find yourself on my sacrificial altar. You're supposed to be leading these men. How will you ever fill my boots as I filled your great-grandfather's?"

Cordus didn't utter another word.

Brutus shifted his head and peered through the crack of the door, just able to make out a seated shadow of a figure, as tall sitting as Brutus was standing. Another man stood with a bowed head to the left, the only other in the sparsely furnished hall.

The only details Brutus made out were the two bands on the commander's arm and bandages wrapping his waist.

"Tell me exactly what the Dreaded one said again," Hadrian demanded.

Darius? Brutus had thought Darius was patting his own ego when, years ago, he'd claimed the Viridians called him "Dreaded."

"He'll…slaughter everyone in the lands to Laltos's west…" Cordus said.

"And?"

"And…" Cordus's voice grew ever more hesitant, "he won't rest until you're dead."

Guffaws burst from the room, followed a few seconds later by Cordus's own laughs, which sounded forced even from Brutus's distance.

"Let him try," Hadrian said. "I'm tired of these Margalvians acting as if we're the ones in the wrong. They side with humans against us…" Hadrian spat. "It's a disgrace, a betrayal to rakkankind. The other legions won't stand for this."

Every time Viridians complained of how beaten down they were, Brutus had to swallow the rising bile in his throat. He wiped the sweat from his brow and peered inside again.

Hadrian stood and paced from left to right, floorboards groaning with each step and eyes glowing amber. Despite the sizeable room, the Warlord's armoured body seemed to fill the space as if his shadow stretched from wall to wall.

"And those humans," the Warlord muttered. "They act as if we're the aggressors, as if Archimedes and their armies hadn't driven us back, deep into the mountains." Hadrian's voice rose to a roar. "As if *they* were the ones that had starved for decades. No. I take back what is ours, and I feel the weight of my grandfather's gaze from the stars in every battle, feel his strength course through me."

Brutus was no student of history, but even he had heard of Hadrianus the Great, the rakkan the current Viridian Warlord had changed his name to emulate. Brutus supposed it was an effortless way to steal the worship of a fallen hero for oneself.

A brief pause followed before Cordus dared speak again, though his voice remained shaken. "Have your plans changed?"

"No. We get the grain from Dolthea before we attempt the siege."

"But the Margalvians might—"

"They won't have time to react. Finally, revenge will be ours."

Suddenly dripping sweat, Brutus rifled through potential targets in his mind to guess where they were talking of. Apart from the mine, only Margalvia itself had military significance to them. Like the Viridians, Archimedes had forced them all the way back into the walls of their city.

"Finally," Cordus said in a low, greedy tone, "that city will fall."

By the Creator… Brutus had only two pigeons left. He'd planned to save them for something substantial, and this definitely fit that.

After another long pause, Cordus spoke. "We need to discipline those that won't fall in line, Father."

"Once I'm through with your men, they'll lick the dirt from my feet, should I command it. I don't care if they're afraid of Darius. They'll go at dusk, take Dolthea and kill the Dreaded one. After all, they're two centuries against one man. They'll succeed

225

if they stay in formation. It's not like he has an army. The Black Legion wouldn't be so far from Margalvia."

"Does that mean…" Cordus said, "you agree with what I suggested before?"

"No. It's not tough enough." Hadrian moved in front of his son and bore down on him. "They need to fear me more than Darius, and you too. They'll prove they're worthy of the Viridian mark on their helmets."

Brutus heart suddenly picked up, feeling the green stripe atop his head like a target the Warlord was about to ram a fist into. Every instinct told Brutus to run now, but there were so many questions left unanswered that might be vital for Margalvia's survival.

"But Father, it will thin out numbers."

Hadrian's amber eyes flared white, lighting the room, and drove Cordus back a step. "How else should I address desertion?" Hadrian picked up the wooden chair he'd previously sat on and smashed it on the ground so hard it splintered into dust.

Brutus wrenched his eyes from the gap and stepped back himself.

"They didn't desert," Cordus said. "They're still here."

"They didn't carry out my orders!" Hadrian yelled, followed by another crash. "I've had it with those centuries. They're scared by a mongrel, then lie to me about it. There's only one way they'll learn, and I'll make it a lesson for all the other centuries. Decimate them!"

Brutus turned and started towards the exit. He ripped the helmet from his head with a force that almost pulled off his ear. Anything was better than being caught in a decimation.

The clank of metal footsteps sounded inside the hall behind him. Then a bash, but he didn't look back.

Faster than he'd moved in his life, he was out of the door. He pulled it closed and was several yards up the street when a sonorous voice boomed from behind. "Stop where you are!"

Without thinking, Brutus skidded to a halt. He turned, saw Hadrian's towering figure striding towards him with murderous fire in his eyes.

Hadrian grabbed the collar of Brutus's cuirass and pulled him with such a force that all thought of defiance fled from Brutus's mind.

"Where are *you* going?" Hadrian's deep voice whispered as he bared his teeth. "Trying to flee and desert before the decimation?" Short red hair mixed with streaks of grey covered both Hadrian's head and cheeks along with an oily grime of dirt and sweat.

Brutus could try to fight his way out, but the Warlord seemed to take him for a regular soldier rather than a spy. He reckoned his odds of surviving a fight with Hadrian were lower than surviving a decimation, so he bowed his head. "No, Warlord."

Hadrian grunted then pushed him forwards.

"All warriors report to the northern field!" Hadrian bellowed. Despite the dense village, the shout paining Brutus's ear would reach the outskirts.

It wasn't long before roused warriors were running through the narrow streets, collecting weapons and making their way north where none yet knew the fate they were in for.

Hadrian shoved Brutus forwards, and he took the hint to follow the rest. Every corner he passed, every open door, Brutus considered trying to slip away, but the Warlord stayed within range to grab him and break his neck. At least in a decimation his chance of death was only one in ten, though that was hardly comforting. Margalvia hadn't used the practise for decades, but it was effective for forcing unruly soldiers into obedience.

When Brutus reached the edge of the village, there were no walls or markers. The buildings simply stopped, cobble road turned to dirt, and they were in a field already trampled by hundreds of heavy boots.

"Commanders! Round up the sixth and seventh centuries here!" Hadrian stamped his foot. "Get sticks for them to draw lots."

Brutus looked around; every path away was now rammed with encircling soldiers, tightening the noose on the condemned at the centre.

Fear gripped the faces of those centuries at the sudden realisation of what was happening. Soon, they mirrored Brutus's rapid, heavy breaths.

A tall commander walked past and scowled. "Surrender your helmets, weapons and armour." He ripped off one legionnaire's green-striped helmet to reveal sweaty black hair underneath.

More from the condemned centuries were pushed into the centre, leaving a ring of space between the punished and the rest. Many of those watching wore anxious faces too, as if they knew it could be their group suffering the same fate next if they angered the Warlord. Such was the wider intention of decimation.

Brutus stripped the rest of his armour—first the cuirass, then greaves and arm-guards—then stood in the undressed pack so dense he barely felt the evening's chill.

"Lesser mortals," Hadrian yelled, stepping out into the ring as all heads turned to him. "You've been called here to witness the penalty for dereliction and cowardice. The sixth and seventh centuries have let one man scare them away from their mission, then lied to their warlord and god about it. For that, they'll be decimated."

A commander came forward with a bunch of sticks in his hand and offered them to the condemned.

Each man took one gingerly.

The first few breathed a sigh of relief once they realised they'd chosen a long one, but the next was a younger man whose eyes widened in panic.

The lad clutched his hair and began panting as he gaped at the short stick in his hand. He tried to bolt into the crowds encircling, but the armoured Viridians pushed him back in with curses.

It wasn't the first time Brutus's life had lain in the fate of chance. But that brought no consolation.

As the commander turned to him and offered a hand, one in ten didn't offer him any comfort.

Fear gripped him; his mind turned to his wife, his brother, his adopted lad—the ones that had made his long life that much more bearable. *Keep them safe, Creator.*

He swallowed and took a stick with a meaty fist, covering it from view.

He held it low along with his head and slowly opened his hand to reveal a stick twice the length of his thumb—a long one. *Thank the Creator.*

Beneath his foot, he spied a stone the size of a man's head sunken into the mud. That might come in useful should someone try to take his stick.

Clubs and thick bones were thrown to the ground around the condemned, the tools those with long sticks would use to start the execution.

"No!" The young legionnaire with the short stick now knelt in the dirt with a red graze across his cheek.

A scream broke out behind Brutus, followed by rhythmic thuds and cheers from the encircling warriors.

Then a rakkan next to the young one swung a club for his knee.

The boy leapt over the weapon and kicked the rakkan's chest. Bone crunched. The warrior fell away, but another three behind grabbed the lad before he'd landed.

Brutus watched the boy in front of him. The long-sticks that didn't partake in a decimation suffered the same fate as the short-sticks. It was a punishment for all. Yet Brutus couldn't stomach beating to death unarmed, unshielded men.

Someone struck the young rakkan across the belly with a club that Brutus knew from experience would make the boy want to throw up his guts and then some.

He cried out all the air in his lungs, bent over in pain as a fist hammered his thigh.

Brutus grabbed the sunken stone he'd noticed earlier, finally willing to act, only to watch a rakkan snap the boy's forearm.

Brutus grimaced, strode over to the lad and stood over his head.

Another legionnaire kicked the boy in the groin, and he rolled over. By now, half a dozen other rakkans surrounded him, kicking, clubbing, punching. On his pale skin, patches of red and purple already covered most of his broken body.

There was only one decent thing Brutus could do. He raised the stone high while the boy turned and met his eye.

Seeing Brutus, the boy relaxed and closed his eyes.

With a yell of anger, Brutus brought the stone down, felt the heavy weight jerk as it hit the boy's skull.

The body went limp, dead, spared the intolerable slow beating.

The surrounding rakkans soon lost interest and turned to find another poor target of the decimation, while Brutus dropped the stone at his feet, wiped the gore from his legs.

He glanced at Hadrian, who stood overlooking the horrors with folded arms and a stern face. Next to him, Cordus scowled at the condemned while clutching his bandaged crotch.

If only Brutus had the strength, he'd kill the Viridian Warlord himself. For now, all he could do was send word to Varro of the impending assault on Margalvia.

26

Darius – Dolthea

Darius awoke to a gentle peck on his cheek. The grin was already spreading on his face by the time he opened his heavy eyes to Selene's arresting face, so close he counted the freckles on her nose. After a week, he still hadn't tired of waking next to her.

"Hey, handsome." She gave him another kiss as she lay atop his chest.

"Hey." It took him a few seconds to realise her bedroom was as dark as night, with no hint of sunshine through the shutters. "Are we rousing early today?"

"No, I've just had something on my mind for days," she said in a voice too firm for the hour. Her fingers slid through his hair. "I was thinking that when we go back to Laltos, I'll introduce you to my father."

Darius smiled, realising that having Selene introduce him would make winning the Regent over much easier. "Thanks. I'd like that, but did you have to wake me for it?"

She slapped him on the chest, playfully but with enough force to chase away the slumber that had been creeping back in. "This is serious," she said. "I want us to see him together."

Darius frowned. "I'm struggling to see how you'd introduce me when we *weren't* together."

"Oh, Philippos, you fool. I mean, I'll introduce *us*. Together."

All sleepiness bolted from Darius's mind. *Like a suitor?* He'd wanted the introduction, but she'd been so careful to keep their relationship a secret that he'd never suspected such a thing crossed her mind. The sudden thought made him clammy.

"I…er…is that what you want?" Darius stammered.

"Ah. I see. So, that's what this is to you…" She swallowed painfully. The fact it had been him to cause it only brought him more guilt than usual.

"No, it's not that." Darius fumbled with his words. "Definitely not that. I'm just shocked. That's all. I thought your father wouldn't approve."

"Wouldn't approve of you sharing my bed…"

Darius was sure there were many other things the Regent wouldn't like, including his half-rakkan blood.

And what would Selene do when she discovered his secret? He'd be ashamed at the embarrassment it would cause her when the truth came out.

Yet, her morose face made it hard to disagree. After all, it was what he wanted, and not just for his mission.

"Alright. I'd be glad of it, but can we let him be the first to know?"

Her wide smile brought him a mixture of joy and remorse. She snuggled her head into his chest, filling his nose with the scent of her hair. His lies would wipe the grin from her soon enough, and he prayed she would forgive him for them.

Selene quickly fell back asleep, but Darius lay wide awake, scenarios of her reacting to his rakkan blood playing on his mind. None ended well, especially if she found out from someone else.

Perhaps I should tell her everything now. He'd wanted to many times over the last few days, when they'd assisted the town in bolstering its defences and helped the well-off in the city to flee east.

As Darius ruminated, the chimes of bells sounded outside. At first, Darius found it odd, wondering if his sleep-deprived mind was playing tricks on him.

Selene bolted upright. "The bells." She launched herself out of bed and grabbed her chainmail. "The Viridians…"

Darius sat up. *Finally.* He'd waited for so long he'd almost forgotten the reason he was there.

But now his opportunity had come for them all to see for themselves that he fought in Laltos's interests. It just worried him that Selene had to be in danger for him to do it.

A nervousness he seldom got before a fight swept over him, and this time it wasn't the thought of blood that provoked it but of Selene taking a dagger to the gut. The temperature in the room seemed to rise despite his nakedness and the hour.

Ignoring his worries, he threw on his undershirt, chainmail and tunic and was busy fastening his sword belt while Selene tied the leather strap holding her bear claw.

"Follow me down when you're ready." She picked up her bow and quiver, which rested beside the door as they ever did. "Stay by the stables and wait for me to call for you."

"To hell with that." Darius darted towards her, trousers almost falling from his waist. "I'm not letting you out of my sight."

"The last time I saw you fight you had little care for your own life or any of ours. I'll send you where you're needed and where you won't be such a worry."

"No." His voice came out as a growl.

She opened her mouth to protest, but Darius took another step towards her, eyes wide. There was no way in hell he'd risk her getting hurt.

"Fine. If you were any other man…" She turned and bolted so fast it was clear she was trying to lose him, but Darius followed her down the hall and stairs, past a few citizens huddled in the reception room, and out of the front door.

The night air was dry with stiff winds that didn't bring the smell of ash and charred wood Darius expected—yet. The Viridians couldn't have reached the town.

Gorgias sprinted down the street along with Monobrow, and they skidded to a halt when they spotted the pair. "Selene!"

Darius and Selene stopped and tried to hear Gorgias's voice between his heavy breaths and over the still clanging bells. "They're heading for the northern wall!"

"What?" Darius turned but saw no smoke with his rakkan sight. "No fires?"

"They must be after the grain," Selene said. "They won't risk the place burning until they have it."

That was one benefit to a town made of wood that Darius hadn't considered, whose design had struck him as foolish, even if they'd lacked the funds to build from stone.

"Early sightings suggest they have the advantage in number," Monobrow said. "They're in two groups. One century is in the south and some algus are already there. The rest are to the north."

"Go south and ensure they don't break through. As for you"—Selene turned to Gorgias—"come north with us."

235

Monobrow set off at a sprint while Selene, Darius and Gorgias ran the opposite way with a swelling mass of soldiers following at a slower pace. The street was broad enough to fit dozens of invaders abreast and was hard underfoot with dust spiralling around in the gusts of wind. Ahead, the tall bell tower chimed louder and louder.

Darius drew his sword. He was tempted to storm outside the walls but was unwilling to contend with the trenches, spikes and traps they'd added.

As they approached the wooden tower, it suddenly burst apart. A black mass of figures exploded from its foundations. A second later the crash pained Darius's ears, and the armoured rakkans stampeded down the street towards them.

The collapsing tower fell. Shattered wood rained down from above, whipped by the wind.

The invaders charged behind a thick wall of black scuta that would repel any algus blows.

What the… How did they get inside?

"Tunnels!" Selene cried as if answering his question.

They must have started deep in the surrounding woods to avoid the scouts.

As he prepared to charge to aid the defence, the ground ahead burst open. Molten stone and dirt flew into the air.

Fiery pickaxe heads rose from the hole, dug into the sides like claws and were soon followed by Viridian helmets rising, spitting ferven.

Selene and Gorgias drew their bows and unleashed arrows.

Darius braced for the incoming rakkans, unwilling to leave Selene's side. A few soldiers and archers joined them but not enough to calm Darius's worries.

From the bell tower's ruins, legionnaires still charged. The soldiers in the marauders' path fled to the sides of the street, wise to not resist with a phalanx.

The only one left in defence was a brave algus whose flowing hair and slightly hunched back Darius recognised from sharing a few firewaters with along their travels. *Wish I remembered his name.*

The algus stood isolated with only a glowing sword in his hand and a brown bear escort to his left. As the warriors approached, the beast reared on its hind legs then crashed down onto a legionnaire, taking his helmet in its jaws.

Even at a distance, the mauling and cries filled the street while the algus protected his bear's flank.

Avoiding the beast, the legionnaires fanned out. They cut down soldiers rushing to defend, while Selene and Gorgias continued loosing arrows.

Gorgias's hand trembled more by the second, and soon he loosed at half the speed of his companion.

Darius's urge to fight grew, but even he couldn't stop a charge of such momentum. Gorgias was right to fear.

A few seconds after the thought, a legionnaire speared the bear deep through the side while another three slashed the algus to pieces.

All Darius imagined was Selene in the man's place.

"We need the high ground," he growled, moving closer to Selene.

"To the roofs!" she yelled.

Thankfully, a few algus archers already stood atop the buildings closest to the Viridian shield wall and sent barrages while escorts soared above. Eager to join, Darius nudged Selene, and they ran to the closest door.

She tried the handle, but it didn't budge.

"Move over," Darius said. With his shoulder, he smashed the door from its hinges, and it slammed flat onto the floor.

Stepping over the wooden slab, he ignored the gaping stares of the half a dozen slaves huddled together in the corner, and he tore up the staircase in front.

"Follow us or die," he called out to them as he ran up, not as a threat but as simple fact. Thick wooden beams whisked overhead at a height a human couldn't jump to reach. He took the steep stairs two at a time, wishing there were a rail to grip.

Selene and Gorgias followed him through to the back bedroom. Darius shoved the closed shutters from the window and clambered out of it. After only a few seconds, he hauled himself up onto the roof, glad for once at the light human armour he wore.

The rooftop was flat and exposed him to the gusts sweeping across the tops of the trees surrounding the town. Every movement triggered an unnerving creak from the clay roof tiles, but he took hold of a sturdy ridge at the edge and extended a hand down.

First, he pulled Selene up, while soldiers clambered up from the next-door window. Next, Darius helped Gorgias, then the six slaves with so much speed he practically tossed the skinny men and women onto the roof.

With the last of them up, he turned to see Selene frowning at him.

"Yes, I'm strong," he said, not quite regretting his show of strength if it saved all their lives. He stepped past her and the slaves now huddled together in the centre and looked out at the rampaging warriors below.

The main charge had passed them but had dispersed to hack at every door, man or woman they happened across, living or not.

A few legionnaires leapt high and grabbed the roofs before hoisting themselves up. Meanwhile, in the street, one stood over a beheaded woman. Another burst through a door followed by piercing shrieks that hurt Darius's ears more than the bells had. This time there was no rain to wash the red from his vision.

He glanced away, seeing Selene first, who had one foot resting on the ankle-high ridge at the edge of the roof while firing an algor-headed arrow at the street.

Gorgias hesitantly followed her lead with his bow at the other side, leaving Darius standing with only a sword in hand, like a tool without a use and wishing the ridge didn't extend so far as to block his view directly below.

Crashes from the rooms underneath sent vibrations through the roof tiles. Tempted as he was to jump down, he took pause at the sight of the already bloody, cratered road. Just the thought of his boots touching it gave him a shiver.

Get over it. Now was his chance to show them whose side he was on.

He stepped to the edge.

"Don't even think of it," Selene called out.

Acting as if he hadn't heard, he stood ready to leap into the fight when a pale hand appeared and grabbed the roof a few feet away from Gorgias.

The algus continued loosing arrows obliviously.

Cursing the jumping power of rakkans, Darius rushed towards the man, flaring algor across his sword. A helmet rose, followed by a hand with a gladius ready to kill.

Gorgias started at the growl of the rakkan, jumped back and tried to nock an arrow, but violent shakes overtook him.

As the rakkan drew back his sword to strike, Darius closed the distance and slashed at the legionnaire's neck. Still hanging by one arm, Darius's sword ripped through the rakkan's spine.

239

The body fell, and Gorgias's rapid breaths didn't ease while Darius glared at him.

"Pull it together, man," Darius said.

No sooner had the first hand slipped away than a second appeared and clasped the roof near Selene's foot.

Darius started back towards her. "Selene!"

She caught sight of the hand too late as another arm swung over and grabbed the ridge an inch from her boot.

Dropping her bow, Selene took the hilt of her sword and pulled, only for the blade to get stuck in its sheath.

She tugged her belt while the attached bear claw flailed.

The legionnaire's snarling head rose above the ridge. He reached out and seized the sheath and weapon.

Without a thought, Darius tossed his sword towards the fiend's arm. The rakkan jerked out of the spinning blade's path, ripping Selene's sword belt free. As Darius's sword spiked into the wooden roof, the legionnaire let Selene's weapon fall to the street below, scabbard and bear claw in tow.

"No!" Selene shrieked with an outstretched hand that failed to grasp her falling items.

Before Darius reached her, an arrow from Gorgias's bow pierced the legionnaire's neck.

After the body fell out of sight, Darius glanced back and exchanged a look of gratitude with Gorgias, whose face was now hard and resolute.

Meanwhile, Selene was transfixed on the street below. She ripped Darius's sword from the roof and leapt off the edge with a cry.

"Selene!" It was Darius's turn to shriek. Why would she be so foolish?

He reached the edge just in time to see her land and grab a thin leather strap from the dirt.

"Damn her," he growled but immediately had the same foolish urge to jump. In only minutes, the Viridians' numbers had swollen threefold, and the coursing wind seemed to bring more and more. At the rear, Darius spied one warrior walking with laboured steps and two viridian bands across his arm.

Hadrian's second? The fiend was too far away to spot a signet ring.

Below, Selene's shout dragged Darius's gaze back. Over a dozen legionnaires stared at her. Another dozen joined them in turning with glowing eyes as algor burst from her sword in a blinding light that made her hair flash purple.

How he wished he could jump and slay them all, use his rakkan strength as in the last village, but now wasn't the time to reveal himself.

"Sword," Darius barked at Gorgias with an outstretched hand.

The algus took seconds to shakily withdraw the blade, seconds Selene didn't have.

More rakkans approached her on the blood-stained street, scuta in front of them, forming a wave of metal. Each legionnaire held a ferven-coated gladius tucked at their side.

Darius had never seen such trained warriors outside the Black Legion, a sight that made the wind bite his sweaty skin. *Where the hell are the other algus?*

Selene disappeared through the door beneath him, and her harried footsteps echoed through the building before suddenly stopping.

"Philippos!" Her voice came through muffled but unmistakable. "The stairs are destroyed!"

Gorgias finally offered the hilt of his sword but too late. Darius leapt from the roof and landed hard on the street, almost twisting an ankle.

Knees still reeling from the touchdown, he scrambled back inside to the front room now littered with shattered tables, chairs, broken floorboards, and a pile of jagged planks where the staircase had been.

Selene ripped her sword from the body of a legionnaire she'd just slain to leave them alone in the room.

A rumble of running warriors grew outside. Darius ran to her, quickly scanning their surroundings but finding no way of escape. He eyed the scutum and gladius of the dead rakkan by their feet while avoiding the blood. A flash of ferven would boil it away, but then he'd be left with the stench and Selene to deal with.

The drumming of feet on floorboards told him how outnumbered they were before he turned to look. As he did, the door frame and walls burst apart as warriors behind shields charged towards them, seconds away from crushing them to blood and bone.

Think, Darius! As per usual, ideas didn't surface. There was no other choice.

"I hope your damned bear claw was worth it," Darius growled as he stooped to pick up the scutum.

Selene took her eyes off the attackers. "It's kuramin—" Her breaths stopped, shock suddenly overtaking her face as Darius straightened with the shield and turned to face the back wall.

With a yell, he charged for the wooden barrier, grabbing Selene by the waist as he did and throwing all his weight behind his shoulder.

It hit the wall. A shock wave pushed the air from his lungs and made his arm go dead. But the wood yielded, and the pair toppled through the hole, tripping over a jagged lip of wood untouched by the shield.

Free but reeling, Darius skidded along the dirt atop the scutum while praying they'd found an empty street.

He stopped a yard short of two pairs of running legs that came to a halt.

"Selene?" Monobrow's tone was high but instantly recognisable.

Forcing air back into his lungs, Darius got up to one knee, lifted the shield and swivelled to face where he and Selene had come from.

She'd got back to her feet and stood ready a few yards away, repeatedly glancing towards him as if he'd charge for her next.

Darius hadn't the time to worry about her reaction now.

Black metal shields grew larger through the hole in the wall until they burst through with legionnaires behind.

Darius caught the hungry eyes of one that snarled.

The rakkan's glare fell to the shield in Darius's hand. Then, the hate-filled eyes widened.

Suddenly, the legionnaire slowed and tried to stop, but the bodies behind drove him further on.

Darius stamped his heel with rakkan strength, which sank it inches into the dirt road. He bent a knee, braced, and watched the charging mass until only a split-second from him.

Then, he flared algor. The cold burst from his body, enveloping his arms and scutum.

The shield wall hit, many times the force of when he'd barged into the wall, but the bodies folded as they touched the icy scutum and couldn't conjure ferven in time to save themselves.

Only a few heartbeats later, the charge overcame Darius's strength, and he fell backwards, breaking his fall with an elbow and relying on the dead bodies piling on him to block any incoming strikes.

Arcs of blue light filled his vision, followed soon after by streaks of fiery orange. The algus slashed and cleaved, spurting blood and gore that Darius had to close his eyes to ignore. With every laboured breath the stench choked him more.

He retched, pushing off the heavy bodies from atop him and rolled away while the algus bought him time.

When the nausea didn't cease, he flared ferven across his torso and stood, opening his eyes to see a dispersed group of rakkans that all stared at him.

Their once hateful eyes now filled with fear.

Joining them in hesitation, the algus likewise gaped with more dread than the rakkans.

No more secrets. No reason to hold back.

One rakkan turned and ran. A second later the rest followed, sprinting in all directions away from him, shields and swords bashing into one another in the panic.

Finally, Darius's time to prove his allegiance had come. Justice would be done.

Snatching a gladius in each hand from the fallen, he chased the fleeing warriors down with ease. First, he cut the back of the thighs of one, then hacked the rakkan's neck to the spine. The next died by the same strikes, too slow and panicked to anticipate his attacks.

One after another, they fell. At first the algus joined him in mercilessly driving away the attackers, but soon after, even they stopped the fight.

They froze, watching every gladius he blocked with rakkan strength, every limb he hacked off, every shout of pain he silenced, every pool of blood he avoided before it revolted him.

Amidst the few routing invaders left, one stood bloody in the street with his helmet askew, making no move to follow the rest. With two bands across one bicep now stained red, the commander was finally close enough for Darius to make out the black signet ring on his right hand and the familiar face and bandaged waist.

Although yards away, the rakkan's deep breaths filled the air in the deathly silent town. Even the gusts of winds settled.

"Not going to run?" Darius asked.

Cordus shook his head. "I'd rather face you than my father."

"Hadrian's your father?"

The rakkan didn't reply, and while at first it surprised Darius that the Warlord would send his own son to battle him, upon reflection, it wasn't surprising at all. Neither was the commander's preference to die by him rather than Hadrian. At least he'd make death swift, far quicker than Cordus deserved.

But, unlike the rakkan, he longed for the day he faced Hadrian again.

With a grimace, he sprinted up to the commander who tried to thrust out a shield. Instead, Darius's sword stabbed up and under the cuirass into the rakkan's belly, so deep his hand hit bandage and flesh.

This time the blood flowed hot and heavy, fizzled as the ferven of his blade burned it away. It bothered him far less than that of the innocents.

Cordus yelled as Darius twisted the blade.

The screams echoed. Everyone in the west of the Empire would hear justice served, hear the pain of a man that had inflicted far worse. The howls pained Darius's ears more as he dragged the sword up to the ribs before they weakened into feeble moans.

After the sounds had died, he let the rakkan fall, ferven still raging on his arms, which had burned most of the clothes on his upper body. Even the chainmail had melted away at the touch, leaving only rags hanging.

With a turn of his head, he regarded not only the algus staring but soldiers behind them and even more whispering to each other. Judging by a rough count, Darius assumed the other side of the town was safe, for almost all the algus now stood gaping with weapons, ready for a fight.

Letting the ferven still heat his one remaining gladius, Darius walked towards Selene.

Gorgias was close by, but at the first movement, he stepped backwards, along with most of the soldiers around.

But Selene stood firm, as any fit leader did. Her brow furrowed and cheeks flushed while one hand tightly gripped her flaring sword.

The iciness of her glare rivalled her sister's and made him all the more desperate to explain himself, but every step brought a greater gnawing in his stomach, fearing the words about to leave her mouth more than the puddles of blood he now stepped around. *I pray she's ready for the truth.*

27

Sulla – Margalvia

Sulla paced along the cobble road, eyes tracing the bloodstains that still darkened the cracks beneath his feet. So many dead, from a single algus? And why?

The Warlord strode alongside him in a dense cloak that billowed in the breeze, so black it melded him into the night.

A few ordinary folks walked the streets too with worried faces and sometimes children in tow, always keeping a sensible distance from the armoured rakkans. Sulla watched the servants, merchants and the like who had been wise to keep away from past warlords and militia chiefs, so he didn't take it personally.

"It's strange." Sulla again recalled the count of warriors lost in the jailbreak. "Nikolaos was an algus, but the wretch never struck me as important to the King."

Varro's gaze swept across the stained road as well. "I told you the King was watching the city."

Sulla cursed. They'd never attack Viridia now. The night's air had unusually blown away the mist and granted them the bright light of the full moon to see the remnants of the carnage. *At least this time it's not Darius's doing.*

In the weeks that had passed since Sulla had last seen the half-rakkan, it had become easier to forgive, easier to see that his intentions hadn't been foul. He'd just acted like the old Darius Sulla was loath to cease clinging to. If only the commanders and Warlord shared his view, but they still debated punishment for the disobedience.

"Let's rest," Sulla said, tired of pacing as the Warlord seemed to do when brooding.

Varro nodded, and the two strode to the garrison. As frustrated as Sulla was at the Warlord's inaction towards the Viridians, even he couldn't argue that now was the time for it. Soon it would be, however. They owed it to Brutus to act on his warning. *I owe it to Claudius.*

As they strolled, a helmet to the side of the street caught Sulla's eye. Thankfully, it didn't have a severed head inside, but the heavy bloodstains suggested its owner had died, regardless.

Varro walked towards it and bent down; his eyes narrowed. "No other could have done this." He picked it up, ran a finger across a grim scratch next to the eye socket. "Nikolaos must be important for the King to send his own bodyguard."

"You should be careful, Blondie. Don't trust a word Nikolaos said."

The Warlord's angry stare fixed on Sulla, who knew right away the nickname was the reason for it.

"Old habits…" Sulla shrugged.

Varro rolled his eyes and stood again. "What was said was said, and what's done is done. Send warning to Alexandra."

"Can't." Sulla frowned. "She said she was going to the Silk City. We have no pigeons that home there."

Varro cursed. "Then send a cryptic message to Laltos for when she returns."

"Will do."

As they continued down the street towards the garrison, Sulla saw the Warlord's gaze noting every bloodstain on the road, each one bringing a deeper shadow to cross his face.

"Was easier before, wasn't it?" Sulla asked.

"What?"

"Before we were in charge, when the deaths of men didn't stain our conscience."

"Give me a sword over a crown any day." Varro's voice was so soft Sulla wondered if he were meant to hear it.

"Do you regret becoming warlord?"

Varro stopped and glared at him again.

"Don't look at me like that. I'm not foolish enough to challenge you."

"That wasn't what I was thinking."

"Then what?"

Varro began striding again at pace, watching each footstep and only breaking concentration to gaze at the stained cobbles.

"Nikolaos was head of the Laltos Guard," Varro finally said. "Perhaps he'd met the King."

"If you ask me, it's a good thing you lost your new algus friend."

Sulla didn't wait for the Warlord's reaction and instead turned his gaze to the stars above.

"In any case," Varro continued, "the King is obviously as big a threat as ever."

Sulla's spirits sank at the words. "As is Viridia."

"I haven't forgotten." Varro's face hardened with determination, the resolve Sulla had been longing for. "We need to increase our defences in Denehill while we prepare for battle."

"Battle?" All trace of sorrow fled Sulla for a moment as the fight to avenge his former Chief beckoned. "Against Viridia?"

Varro turned up his nose. "That remains to be seen, but one thing is certain: the Black Legion will strike."

28

Darius – Dolthea

Darius stopped a few feet away from Selene and let the ferven on his sword fizzle out. "Is the town safe?"

Her eyes traced his figure up and down. "That depends."

"On what?"

"What your intentions are…Darius."

He wasn't surprised she guessed who he was. What did shock him was the contempt with which she spat the name and how it hurt more than when the shield wall had hit him.

"You've seen my intentions." Darius pointed his gladius to all the rakkan corpses strewn across the street. "To end the Viridian Legion. To kill Hadrian's second-in-command and next, the Warlord himself." His tone grew higher and more desperate.

"Do you think us stupid?" Gorgias finally summoned the courage to step closer, but his slender face shone with sweat. "Why would you want that?"

Selene's narrowed eyes revealed she was of similar scepticism.

I need Lex. She was supposed to do this with me. "What I told you was true," Darius said. "Hadrian and his legion almost killed my escort. My city is at war with Viridia. Blood needs to be repaid with blood."

Selene stared with a mixture of hurt and rage in her eyes that only betrayal provoked.

"I came here to show you something." Darius raised his voice to address all listening. "Not all rakkans are your enemy. We can be your allies and drive your enemies back to the gates of Viridia. Look at me, half-rakkan, proof that both races can work together."

He paused as Selene continued glowering.

"*I* am not a foe," Darius said. "What I've done here today I will do again and again. I have no reasons for doing this other than those I've given."

Gorgias and the other algus looked to Selene, who took a deep breath. "Disperse!" she yelled, shriller than usual. "Check every street and dwelling in the town. Those that were on guard duty should return to the gates and ensure no more are coming." She took a few steps closer to Darius and lowered her voice. "You. Come with me."

Darius obliged, keeping the kuraminium gladius in his hand. It was only a few minutes before they reached quieter streets with less scattered bodies, but they weren't heading towards their lodging, the room where he and Selene had spent most nights.

To quieten the struggles in his mind, he reached out to Lyra and connected at once. She was awake and alert to the danger he'd been in, but otherwise the fevers had lessened further. The fact should have made him elated, but even he sensed the fear in her, not because of the battle, but because she mirrored his own angst at the impending conflict with the one he cared for.

His lies had caused the rift, and if he ever wanted her to care for him again, he had to tell her the truth.

More oil lamps than usual hung in the streets. The patches of light illuminated a stable ahead of them, where restless nickering and stomping echoed out. It seemed not only humans had been disturbed by the thunderous crashes of the invaders.

Next to the stables were their wagons. Selene led him up to one cart and pointed for him to sit on the wooden lip at the rear, his back facing the canvas flapping violently in the night's breeze.

With a frown, Darius silently obeyed and sat to take the weight from his legs, only then seeing Gorgias, whose flushed face was behind him. *Am I that distracted?*

"Darius…" Selene said.

"The one the south calls the Slayer of Gods?" Gorgias asked, tone full of disapproval. "The one who killed Archimedes?"

"It wasn't I that killed him." Darius considered whether to give them the full story and decided the truth was best. "But my gouging out his eyes probably sealed his fate."

"You speak with no remorse," Selene said, exasperated.

"I won't lie and say I regret it," Darius said. "It was either me or the goman. But I do regret the consequences for Laltos. It was never my intention."

Gorgias scoffed. "More rakkan lies. And to think I defended you to the other algus…"

"It wasn't just you fooled by his lies," Selene added.

Darius took a pause to calm his frustration. "I'm sorry I lied to you both. If I believed any of you would hear me out had I been open from the start, I wouldn't have lied."

Selene stepped forward until close enough to strike him had she wanted. "What do you want?"

You, was the first answer to his mind, and he was a little surprised it was. Lyra had to be his priority, as did his mission for those still ruminating on his punishment.

"The Warlord of Margalvia seeks an alliance with Laltos," he said. "I'm here to prove our willingness to fight our own kind. Now that I have, I'll go to your father and plead the case."

Her eyes searched his for an age but gave him no clue what she was thinking.

"My father won't listen to you," she said. "You'll never get into the city."

"That's why I need your help, your trust—"

"You're Darius, the traitor algus that slaughters defenders like me. You're the enemy." She grimaced.

"I'm not—"

"Last year you killed our algus on our own streets. Before, you were responsible for the massacre at Denehill."

"I've never killed an algus in Laltos. As for the rest, Archimedes took any memories of those deeds from me. I'm not the same man I once was. If I wanted to hurt either of you, or anyone in this town, I would have slaughtered you all long ago."

After another pause of intense concentration, she turned to Gorgias. "Do you believe him?"

The algus scoffed and wiped the sweat from his brow. "He's a rakkan."

"What more can I do?" Darius stood, moving closer to Selene only for her to flinch away.

"And what did you want from me?" she whispered, gazing at him with a trace of the vulnerability she once had. "Why get close to me?"

"That wasn't my intention," he whispered, though once he'd spoken the words, he braced for a knee to the groin or a slap across the cheek. "However close we grew was genuine, not a scheme."

"And I suppose seducing my sister 'just happened' as well?" Selene scowled.

"What?" Darius muttered. "I didn't seduce her—"

"She was quite taken with you, the new man from Xavala, better than any fighter she'd ever seen. Was I a Plan B when she wouldn't accompany you to Laltos?"

"No!" As frustrated as Darius was at the accusation, he was at least glad Selene didn't suspect her sister of any part in it. Lex's part and story were hers to tell, but that left him alone to convince the Regent of Laltos. "I already slaughtered your enemies. What the hell do I have to do to prove it to you—go to Laltos in chains?"

Gorgias's expression lifted, like a boy being offered honey. "We have restraints in the wagon."

At the words, Darius scoffed but felt himself sink into the hole he'd dug when Selene lifted her gaze.

"That would do it," she said. "I can't think of a greater proof that you don't mean us harm. How can I trust you if you don't trust me?"

She had a point.

Darius tried to formulate a rebuttal to her but failed. "How do I know I'll be safe?"

"There are algus here whose families you've killed," Selene said. "It might be safer for you to be in chains and appear less of a threat."

"Algus won't kill a prisoner of the Regent," Gorgias added.

As hard as he tried, Darius couldn't think of a better way to seem unthreatening or get an audience with the Regent. And without her trust, whatever they'd shared would be lost. The only one that had ever seen him as more than a warrior would forever view him as less, as a murderer.

"Fine." He tossed his gladius to the ground, turned, and clambered into the wagon. It took only a few moments to spot kuraminium chains and shackles.

He grabbed a set already attached to the heavy base of the cart and gave them a tug to test their strength. When the links didn't give a fraction, he concluded they'd hold even Hadrian himself, a thought which made him hesitate.

I have to. She had to see him for who he was, not the Slayer of Gods.

After grabbing a padlock and key, he brushed aside the cloth to trudge.

"You're really doing this?" Selene asked.

If she wasn't there, he'd laugh at the suggestion. "I'm doing this for you, not for your father." He closed the shackles around his wrists, along with the chains, then hooked the padlock ready to close. "You'll have to do it."

Gorgias stepped forward, but Darius drove him back with a snarl. "Not you."

Selene paused, Darius praying she'd seen enough for him to prove his loyalty.

Just tell me to take off the restraints.

But his hope changed to nerves when she walked forward.

"Say you'll vouch for me," he said. "Promise me you'll take me to your father." That seemed the only way he'd get out of the chains.

With an almost reluctant grimace she muttered, "Fine," then snapped the lock shut and snatched the key.

"Satisfied?" Darius asked.

"Not even close." Selene's face hardened, which brought a gnawing doubt to Darius's belly.

"Selene. You have to believe me."

She took a step back from him.

"I'm not going to hurt you," Darius said.

"You already have," she whispered.

Gorgias raised an eyebrow.

"I'm too close to separate the truth from lies," she continued. "My father will know what to do."

"Let's do this without an audience," Darius growled with a stiff look at Gorgias.

Selene sighed and turned to the algus. "Tell the men we leave for Laltos with the grain tomorrow."

With a scowl, Gorgias backed away, leaving just the two of them by the stables.

More drumming of hooves sounded inside that mirrored Darius's pounding heart.

"Please, Selene. You know the real me. I wasn't lying about everything. I lied about my name, not who I am. What I told you about myself is true. How I feel is true."

"I don't believe you." Her alluring eyes stared at him as one would a reprobate, even less than a mere grunt. "As the saying goes," she continued, "gomans never lie, rakkans never tell the truth." With that, she strode away, cloak billowing behind her.

What now? The fact she didn't trust him stung more than the shackles. His palms became sweaty, and he tugged at the chains again, skin peeling from his wrist at the ineffective force that proved he'd never break free.

Desperately, he inspected the link that attached him to the wagon. It had been welded correctly. *Damn.*

29

Nikolaos – Xavala

After many hard days and nights of travel atop swifts and sleeping under the night sky, Nikolaos grew tired of the King's Sword, especially his fondness of staying mute.

Only a day had passed before Nikolaos told the King's Sword everything of Lex and the rakkans, but he may as well have spoken to a pet because all he received in return were silent stares from beneath a hood.

At least the man had spared him some coin in the closest human town to buy clothes and proper food, but Nikolaos longed to enter the Silk City if only to speak with a long-time friend again.

One day, under the setting sun, Nikolaos finally spotted the city in the plains on the horizon. He sighed, gave a kick to his swift, which urged it on all the faster behind Jason's grey steed.

Soon the pair were in Xavala, where Nikolaos expected the King's Sword to take him immediately to the envoy in the city, but instead found himself escorted to the Silk Regent's palace, as if lulling him into a false sense of familiarity.

Inside, he took no time to rest or waste the opportunity to get a witness to whatever the King wanted of him, so he ordered slaves to fetch the Silk Regent while he paced up and down, his new boots wearing away at the carpet on the floor, much like his patience.

Jason stood watching, in no apparent eagerness to take Nikolaos to the fate for which the algus had rescued him. *Suits me.* Still…it was concerning.

Breathing into his hands, Nikolaos smelled his breath. *Pleasant enough after the mint leaves.* He didn't recall ever having felt this nervous before, but months of bitter resentment would now be remedied with one conversation. All he needed was to tell someone of Lex's treason, and they'd depose her father at once. *My time is near.*

Being in the hallway with so many silent guards and spears at regular intervals disturbed him enough that his best efforts to draft a pitch for the Silk Regent were subpar at best.

"I heard the Regent had a visitor."

Nikolaos whirled around to the voice that had appeared from nowhere. Behind him stood the King's Orator. Usually she made him recoil, but today he took great pleasure at the sight of her peeling head.

"I didn't expect to see you." Nikolaos smiled, the first genuine one he'd ever given the hag. "I was waiting for Aristippus."

"He'll be a moment." Ophelia returned the smile. "He's just seeing to more pressing guests."

Nikolaos's anger was too great to cloak this time. "Is one of those Alexandra of Laltos?"

Ophelia cleared her throat. "Jason. Make sure he doesn't go anywhere."

Nikolaos's body tensed, wilted a little as the King's Sword walked forward a few paces, as if to remind Nikolaos he was within range to kill. The algus froze in a statuesque manner while Ophelia returned through the doorway.

Wish they'd just tell me what they want.

Nikolaos twitched, eager to return to pacing but unwilling to turn his back on Jason now. Instead, he cast his eyes about the paintings on the high ceilings of the hallway.

The next few minutes passed slower than those in his prison cell, but Ophelia finally returned.

"Is Aristippus ready?" Nikolaos straightened his tunic and belt.

"I'm afraid not." Ophelia stopped at Jason's side and clasped her hands together. "The Regent is still busy, but I'll be happy to speak with you in the meantime."

Nikolaos clenched his jaw. "I'd prefer him to be here too. I heard of his marriage and—"

"What the Silk Regent is doing is not your concern, but I can assure you *I'm* most interested in what you have to say."

Nikolaos walked forward and craned his head to see past the King's Orator, at which point Jason raised a hand to the hilt of his sword.

Eyes now firmly on the algus, Nikolaos stepped back with a gulp. He supposed it didn't matter who he informed first.

"If it must be so," he said. "I need to report treason and warn the King of an alliance plotted between Laltos and Margalvia. I heard it whilst captive in the rakkan city and can provide detailed information to aid in the overthrowing of Laltos's regent and his allies. You'll need a scribe to note all this."

Ophelia looked him up and down. "How *did* you end up in a rakkan prison? Rakkans don't take captives and you don't seem to be starved."

"The traitor convinced them to spare my life because I was once close to her. As for the food, I used my wits to get decent rations."

"How do I know you're not the traitor, spinning me a tale right now?" A suspicious look crossed Ophelia's eye, but it wasn't half as frightening as Jason's hand still resting on his sword. Ophelia may have been many things, but a fool wasn't one of them. Considering she wasn't an algus, the woman had surpassed any ordinary woman or man in history.

But Nikolaos was tired of skirting around the facts. "You know I'm not. Why else would you free me? Come to think of it, why did you?" It wasn't a stretch to assume the King's Orator gave the order.

Ophelia scratched her bald scalp, causing skin to flake off onto the red rug. "I'm sure we'll get to that at some point. But what you say intrigues me. We've been having issues with Regent Theodoros of late. I was there only a few weeks ago and found myself questioning where his loyalties really lie."

Nikolaos let the woman stare aimlessly at the ceilings for a while, hoping the images of algus there, portrayed as immortal gods, gave some of their wisdom to her. Before Nikolaos's time, Ophelia was an advisor to the current king's father, King Medus I, and scribes attributed Ophelia as the influential force behind Toria's conquest of all the human cities. Nikolaos's mother had profited handsomely, taking over most of the farms surrounding Laltos in her twenties. Regent Theodoros had also done well once the Queen of Laltos had been executed and he was installed as leader.

But that was then. When King Medus II took the throne, tensions between cities grew, with rebellion often whispered of but never attempted.

"Fear not, young man," Ophelia said, dragging Nikolaos back from his pondering. "Come. Let's discuss this in my room."

Nikolaos sighed deeply. Ophelia turned and walked away, and he followed, checking over his shoulder every so often to see how close Jason was behind the pair, who unsurprisingly tailed them all the way.

Tall wooden doors were pushed open by slaves dressed in fine red tunics of a similar shade to the rugs, almost making them disappear in a way that Nikolaos made a note to imitate in his own halls one day. Inside, the ceiling was twice as high still, and a fire kindled within a stone fireplace carved into an orgy of women that heated the room more than the embers.

In the centre stood a mahogany conference table with carved legs in the shape of serpents and at least twenty seats around. Only one wooden chair had white cushioning, with the rest plain and curved inwards at the back.

Wasn't this the Silk Regent's office? But it hadn't had the table and chairs before. The intricate carvings and shade of wood seemed Torian, like Ophelia had brought them with her.

The King's Orator took her seat and sighed with a smile.

Nikolaos sat opposite, feeling a lump in the chair in the small of his back, as if it had been deliberately designed to be uncomfortable. *Bet her negotiations last half the time.*

Meanwhile, Jason walked over and stood over Ophelia's left shoulder, hands finally off his sword and held behind him.

"Send for a scribe," Ophelia called to a slave, "and bring food and drink for my guest."

Just the mention of food made Nikolaos's mouth water with thoughts of salted sea bream, a Torian speciality. "Thank you, Ophelia."

"It's nothing. Now tell me exactly who is plotting this conspiracy?"

"Alexandra, daughter of Theodoros." The words came out faster than Nikolaos could articulate them, having wanted to say it for so long, but they were intelligible enough to elicit a frown from the King's Orator.

"Are you sure? How do you know this?"

"I saw it with my own eyes. She tried to kill Archimedes. She fought our algus and conspired with the rakkans to have me imprisoned in Margalvia." Often, when alone in his dark cell, Nikolaos had wished Lex hadn't stopped them from killing him. She'd obviously wanted him to suffer and watch the betrayal of Laltos, to watch the plundering of riches in the Laltos Bank that he'd worked for so many years to control. *Shrew.*

"You saw what happened with Archimedes?" Ophelia leaned forward.

"I did." Nikolaos took a deep breath, then proceeded to tell the details of what he'd seen in the cave, how the Waif Magician had stolen the Staff of Arria, how Darius had blinded the goman, and most importantly, Lex's part in every treacherous act.

Ophelia's face turned from pleasant and inquisitive to a harsh frown as Nikolaos spoke, especially when he told her of the planned First Alliance. The conversation was so long and thorough that the slaves brought a selection of fish, vegetables, fruits and white wine, which neither of them touched until Nikolaos uttered his last word.

"If what you say is true," Ophelia said, "it poses more of a threat than any of us imagined."

Finally, someone else saw the urgency of these matters. After bearing this burden on his shoulders for so long, Nikolaos sighed and helped himself to some well-deserved wine and sea bream. "Is she here? Will you arrest her?"

"No," Ophelia said. "She left a few days ago, but I'll notify the King at once. I'd never have thought her capable of such a thing. We've been watching her for the last few months, ever since she became promised to Aristippus."

Nikolaos cursed that he'd missed her. If only Jason had rescued him a couple of days earlier… "Well, that marriage won't happen once I've finished speaking with the Silk Regent."

Ophelia murmured. "We'll see. He's a most troublesome governor to deal with. If he had half a brain, he'd command an army that would make the King tremble, but fortunately for us, he thinks only with his genitals."

Nikolaos smirked, recalling his past wild exploits with the Silk Regent. The city had more brothels than food stores, and together, he reckoned they'd visited at least half. He couldn't think of a less suitable mate for Lex. "I take it Theodoros arranged the marriage."

Ophelia nodded. "So my informants tell me, and that she's already gifted her betrothed a mulberry tree."

It took Nikolaos a moment to make a connection between the Silk City and what he'd always considered a rather arbitrary forbidden tree. Now he felt a fool for never realising the King's intention was to control Xavala's supply of food for its silkworms. As fond as Nikolaos was of Aristippus, he understood the King's frustrations with the Regent's imprudent nature. "At least the Xavalans are predictable."

"That they are. Did you know I was brought up here?"

"No." Nikolaos knew little of the most powerful woman in the Empire beyond fantastical legends. "You were born here?"

264

"As good as, but no." Ophelia leaned back in her chair and sipped her wine. "My mother moved here shortly after my birth. My skin reacted to most clothes, and she'd heard there was nothing softer than Xavalan silk."

The thought of Ophelia young and weak was so alien to Nikolaos that he wondered whether the woman was being truthful. "Did it help?" he asked.

"Does it look like it?"

Ophelia stared, as if waiting for an answer, but Nikolaos felt safest treating it as a rhetorical question. "She must have been wealthy to afford to dress a baby in silk."

"Not wealthy, just quick-fingered. You had to be. Xavalans care only for themselves."

Too true. "It sounds as if we'd be better off if both Laltos and Xavala were brought to heel."

A toothy smile spread across Ophelia's face, as if the Orator had been waiting too long for Nikolaos to utter the words. "Quite." She picked up a plate of grapes and offered them. "Perhaps you can help me with that."

Nikolaos fidgeted in his chair, trying to shift the point at which the lump dug into his back. He took a few grapes, poured himself a deep cup of wine, and swallowed a few big gulps. The longer the conversation went on, the more it struck him as curious why the King's Orator had asked nothing more of Lex's treachery.

"You're the Silk Regent's friend, correct?" Ophelia's voice was now silky and smooth, yet Nikolaos had no recollection of when it had turned so coaxing.

"That's right. How do you know that?"

"I know many things," Ophelia said. "Now, will you help me address this treason?"

"That depends on how. I'm not in fighting shape—"

"Oh, my friend, no. You misunderstand me if you think I mean to quarrel with the Regent." Ophelia chuckled, but her eyes showed no hint of amusement. "I just want you to withhold your information on Alexandra for now."

"Why? Why not send Jason to kill Lex and Regent Theodoros? It would solve all your problems."

Ophelia broke her gaze to pick a few grapes from the platter on the table. "Killing a regent has consequences, and I'm reasonably sure that Regent Theodoros will not take fondly to us killing the only heir from his genos. As for Aristippus…I don't trust him. Let's wait and decide how to deal with Laltos as a whole."

"So, she'll be allowed to walk free?" Nikolaos leaned forward and clutched his sore back.

"Rest assured, anyone opposed to the King will be dealt with in good time." Ophelia slipped another grape into her mouth and chewed. "We have our plans for Laltos."

Did she mean to choose a new regent? It wouldn't have been a stretch to assume the King already had someone in mind, but outside Theodoros's kin, there were only a few others, including Nikolaos, with enough wealth, algus and leadership experience to hold the regency.

Is that why they rescued me? Despite his full belly, a new hunger re-awakened that wanted satisfying.

"Very well," Nikolaos said with a stiff nod. "I'll keep this to myself."

"Excellent." Ophelia leaned forward, resting her elbows on the table. "Now, let's get you into a more comfortable chair, for I need the names of Theodoros's family and associates. My spies have a lot of work ahead of them."

Nikolaos smiled. "My pleasure."

30

Darius – Road to Laltos

Darius had never put so much trust in another as when he'd shackled himself, and he soon regretted it. The last he spoke with Selene was at the stables. Not long after, the soldiers were left to prepare him for their journey to Laltos.

When they asked him to surrender the algus attire he wasn't ordained to wear, he complied with a clenched jaw and knew any aggression now would only harm his cause in Laltos.

Only when without his eagle belt buckle did the soldiers' taunts begin, the jeers, the spits that he conjured ferven to fizzle away.

"Murderer!"

"Rakkan scum."

The wagon was soon packed with so many goods there was barely room for him to sit, then the caravan of wagons loaded with grain set off.

Facing backwards on the rickety frame, Darius saw nothing of Selene as she presumably rode with the algus at the head of the company. It took four oxen to pull the wagon he was attached to, and still it moved at a sloth's pace.

Despite the slowness, the journey was a struggle given he couldn't stretch his legs, and sleep eluded him most nights.

All the way, uneven stones in the road produced a deafening rattle of wooden wheels. The gusts of wind that swept across the deforested hillsides brought dust and grit through the tree stumps. With that, and the blazing sun, he could barely see.

After many days, nights and miles, the shackles chafed his wrists so much that he wondered whether putting them on had been a mistake. At least the pain took his mind off Selene, off the hurt of her leaving him alone on a voyage that might well be his last if events were to turn sour.

The jeers from a few soldiers continued no matter how much he tried to block them out, the threats to break his legs, the animal impressions meant to impersonate rakkans.

Following behind Darius's wagon, a skinny soldier with a fluffy moustache tossed a rock at him, not for the first time.

The small stone sent light ripples of air at his head. Bracing his neck, he let it glance off his forehead, grunting in pain to give the impression it hurt far more than it had. Taking the easy hits seemed to spare him follow-ups.

The hoplite chortled as Darius gritted his teeth. *After I just saved their hides…*

He didn't blame them for their anger. After reportedly slaughtering so many algus then Archimedes, he should have been counting himself lucky they hadn't followed through with the threats to break his legs.

The road arced to the right, and Darius continued wondering how much Selene would speak up for him with her father.

He sighed and shook his head. Lex might be the only human that would aid him, but did she even know where he was? He hadn't seen Tiro for weeks.

The wagon came to a halt as the caravan stopped. Darius groaned and stepped out to give his numb legs a little exercise.

The soldiers gave him a wide berth, not as stupid as they looked.

Thoughts of what lay in wait in Laltos soon brought Darius images of torture and death. At least Lyra was with him in a way. She'd live on, even though he'd failed her.

While he stretched his legs under the sun's blaze, the soldiers began moving away to clear a wide space about him.

He glanced around in confusion, and a figure walked from behind the wagon and blocked the light from his eyes. Once his vision had adjusted, he saw Selene approaching.

"Darius…" Her mouth hung open for a moment as her narrowed eyes scanned the scratches on his forehead.

He turned away with a low growl. "The cuts are the least of it." His voice rose. "I've been berated by your men while you didn't so much as come and speak with me."

She shot her soldiers a disgruntled look. "I didn't tell them to—"

"You didn't stop them."

All the soldiers quickly left under the weight of her glare, off to join the others farther up the caravan.

Darius clenched his fist and gazed into her hazel eyes.

"You should be grateful I'm taking you at all," she said, "after what you've done to us over the years."

"I've had many chances to hurt you, but I didn't. I wouldn't. The time we spent together wasn't a lie. I saved your life from the Viridians. You'd be dead if I were just another algus."

"You only did that to save your own life," Selene said.

"I jumped down to save you!" Darius tensed his arms, rattling the chains as he pulled against them. The wagon groaned, slid a fraction. "I could have left you to die."

Selene frowned and searched his eyes, deep in thought as her curls blew back in the wind, away from her sun-kissed cheeks.

Shaking his head, Darius turned to survey the plains of tree stumps that reminded him only of death. "Please, Selene. I fe—"

"It doesn't matter what you say. I can't believe anything from your mouth."

"Then believe what you saw with your eyes, what you felt with your hands." Why wasn't it obvious to her? Her stubbornness only frustrated him further as she walked away.

"Just tell the Regent what I did," he called after her, "let me plead my case. If I meant anything to you…"

Her determined strides only lengthened at his words, leaving him alone with just the oxen and dead trees. Even after being snubbed, he couldn't drag his gaze from her.

He hoped he'd done enough to get through to her, but decided it was time to formulate another plan. If all else failed, he'd need to save himself.

31

Lex – Laltos

The half-ton brown bear reared on its hind legs. It towered over Lex in a manner that never ceased to give her pangs of fear.

"You've made your point." Lex didn't budge an inch.

Her father chuckled, green eyes frosty and unblinking, the only specks of colour against his straight white beard and hair that fell thin over grey robes.

At full stretch, the bear's head reached higher than even the nine statues around the edge of the marble throne room. One for each battle won by the greatest Queen of Laltos, they now seemed distant, stained, and aged, like memories of those times. Since defeated in the Torian Conquest, Laltos had little history of success.

Her father waved a wrinkled hand at his escort. The bear sank back down onto all fours and moved closer to her with a tilted head as if offering an apology.

She patted her gently.

"You see?" Theodoros said. "Why must you be the only one in the family to never choose a bear? Even the rakkans cower before her. The miscreants deny it, but it shows in their eyes."

"She didn't help you much against the King's Orator from what I hear."

Her father's face twisted. "Ophelia seems indifferent to the war but I'm not." He paced the marble floor around the large circular room, between the white pillars while casting his gaze over each statue and his own throne in the centre. "The King won't send troops unless we pay. Heaven knows what he's planning because he knows I won't. He'll watch while the rakkan scourge devour us."

Every insult to the rakkans grated on Lex's nerves, as if each pushed her one step further from the First Alliance. "Don't you mean Viridians? Not all rakkans are eating us."

Her father scoffed so hard he spat.

Sensing she wasn't getting anywhere, she'd try to brighten his mood before pressing the issue. "The Xavalans have agreed to support us with their cavalry. They've also sent us supplies of sulphur, so there is good news."

"That's good indeed." Theodoros ran his fingers through his long beard. "When will the cavalry be here?"

"I don't know. I must wed the Silk Regent first."

Her father stopped his pacing, switched his hand from his beard to the fur of his escort. "If there were any other way to win this war without letting that reprobate into our house…"

"Anything?" Lex asked. She knew hyperbole when she heard it, but she'd latch onto anything at this point. Darius might arrive back victorious at any moment.

As bitter as her father was for accepting an unpleasant regent into his treasured family, he wasn't half as bitter as Lex. *She's* the one that had to sleep with the man.

"But who else will aid us?" her father asked with a sigh. "I've tried. You've tried. I don't think they'll care until one of our cities is burned to ash and they see the threat the rakkans pose. The false sense of security Archimedes gave them still twinkles in their confident eyes."

"I saw something curious on my travels," Lex said. "I was near the southern mountains, not too far from Denehill when—"

"Why were you there?" her father asked, raising a grey eyebrow. "I heard the rakkans hold it now."

"They do," Lex said, continuing the lie. "I didn't go close enough to be noticed, but I saw a group of rakkans attacking from outside the city walls."

Theodoros scoffed. "Probably fighting over hunks of meat. Nothing but animals they are."

"It was certainly not over scraps of meat." Lex lifted her chin. "The attackers wore viridian bands yet the ones in the city wore black."

"Margalvians?" he said quietly, as if to himself. "Perhaps there was a disagreement."

"Hardly. There were at least two centuries involved. This was a coordinated attack."

"Are you suggesting that the Viridians and Margalvians have some internal conflict?"

She shrugged. "I'm just reporting what I saw. I know little of what happens within the world of the rakkans."

"No." Her father's voice softened. "They hold up well under torture. It seems we understand little about them."

Thank Agathos I've got him to realise that much at least. "If they are involved in a conflict, it can only help our attack on Viridia."

Theodoros grimaced. "I don't see why. Once we attack, the rakkans will band together, as they always have. You're not old enough to remember, but I am."

273

"Perhaps…but it's uncertain. Rakkans have been known to not always side with their own kind."

Theodoros rolled his eyes, to which Lex clenched her jaw. When it came to war, the records of human history were clear that rakkans always fought as one, but their history was written from the human perspective. Lex knew the tales of the other side, and they showed a more nuanced picture.

"Now you come to mention it," Theodoros said, "I recall hearing of a rakkan who once saved a human girl's life from a Viridian Centurion set on killing her."

On the outside, Lex nodded with a fascinated look, but inside she smiled ear to ear. He'd forgotten that it was her who told him the story. So much effort had gone into even opening his brilliant yet stubborn mind to these simple ideas.

She let him be in silent contemplation for a few moments, disturbed only by the bear's claws scratching against the marble floor.

The silence stretched out until her father grimaced and shook his head. "No. What am I thinking? As if rakkans would ever help a human. I've fought them all my life and never seen an ounce of pity in them. On the contrary, I've witnessed so much blood, slaughter and cruelty at rakkan hands that I'd rather share this world with demons."

Lex cursed under her breath. As she opened her mouth to respond, they were interrupted by the creaking of the main doors opening. A stern-faced algus strode in with hurried steps and headed straight to the Regent.

Gorgias? As the newcomer leant to whisper in her father's ear, Lex subtly took a step closer but was still unable to hear. The discomfort in her hip grew as she tried to read lips, but even that failed. After almost a minute of murmurs, frowns and shocked eyes, the algus stepped away.

The Regent's face had turned as white as the marble pillars, a shade of fury Lex knew all too well. He cleared his throat and began speaking in a strained voice. "It seems Selene's on her way back from a successful campaign. She's not only secured vital grain supplies and killed Hadrian's second-in-command, but has the assassin Darius in chains."

For a split-second, Lex's mouth fell open. The pain in her hip surged as if a spear had been driven to the bone, but she quickly gathered her composure and forced her lips together.

How did this happen? Where was he?

She should never have recalled Tiro and taken her eyes from Darius. She didn't need her escort that badly once back in Laltos. *Fool.* As soon as she found out where Darius was, she'd be on a swift to find him.

How this affected their plans for the alliance was too confusing to contemplate. A ring of pressure tightened around her head.

"Where is she?" Lex asked, trying to make her voice casual, but her desperation made it high pitched.

"She'll be back today," Theodoros answered. "Her scouts just arrived."

Damn. Too close. "So, how have we only just heard?"

"She sent word she was returning days ago but never mentioned that reprobate Darius before now. I'm sure you've heard why that might be…"

Did he know they became close? Lex didn't dare raise it unless he spoke of something else. Besides, Selene was the least of her worries. Lex's first instinct was to free Darius, but it would be virtually impossible on her own. The constant presence of guards, and every algus in the city knowing he was there, would cut off any chance of using her position.

No, the only way to save Darius was to secure the alliance she wanted. But there was too much more she needed to do before her father would accept it, especially now Darius was exposed.

Had he proved his allegiance before being captured? She prayed so but could hardly rely on it.

"Is something troubling you?" Theodoros asked in a quiet voice, green eyes suddenly piercing hers. "You need not fear Darius. I'll make sure he doesn't get the chance to hurt any of us."

Lex couldn't tell whether the concern on his face was suspicion or worry.

"Just pondering the implications," Lex said. As soon as her father turned away, she sauntered towards the door. "I'll leave you to it. Sounds like you'll have a lot on your hands."

Time was scant. Who knew what her father would do and how long Darius had. She had to make sure of the alliance, otherwise Darius would soon meet the God of Justice.

32

Darius – Laltos

Darius bowed his head, fixed his gaze to the stone road and away from the hundreds of eyes that glowered at him. The shadow of the gates of Laltos passed under his feet. If only it shielded him from those watching, as it did with the sun.

It wasn't the first time he'd entered a city to stares of hate and disgust; it had been the same when he'd first arrived in Margalvia, when rakkans spat in his face and shouted "hang him." This time there were no yells, just a prolonged murmur as masses of people gathered.

Lines of soldiers with spears stood to attention and guarded each side of his path as far as he saw. He knew the road led to the jail and then the palace, even if currently out of sight.

Surely Selene wouldn't take him to prison. If things turned awry, escaping would be difficult, but Darius would die fighting, no matter what. He owed it to Lyra, to Sulla and Brutus.

His one friend in this city, Lex, was powerful and well connected. Surely, she'd ensure his safety. He had to keep telling himself that or the worry threatened to overwhelm him.

The soldiers at the head of their party filed off into different streets as they walked, leaving Selene and a small detachment of guards in front of Darius, now walking behind the wagon at Selene's insistence. She'd told him walking would look better. His legs thanked him for the movement to relieve his stiff and tired muscles.

After a long trudge through what seemed like endless lines of gawking citizens and slaves, they approached the courthouse with its familiar symbol of Agathos engraved across the entrance.

Darius scoffed. The only justice he'd see in his lifetime was whatever he enacted himself. Whether it existed in the next life, as Lex believed with her married gods, or whether a next life existed at all, Darius didn't relish finding out.

The wagon stopped outside the entrance.

Selene and her men approached him and began wrestling with his chains in the carriage.

He scoffed as they struggled with the heavy links. "Need a hand?"

The remark received only pokes in the back with spearheads.

"Don't think of running," a thickset soldier mumbled. "We'll break your kneecaps."

If he'd wanted to run, he would have, but the words brought a growing unease as the situation sank in.

"Enough of that," Selene muttered to her soldiers.

At mulling over what may follow, Darius felt more pangs of fear from Lyra's lingering presence. *Don't worry, girl. I'll make it back to you.*

His unease deepened when Gorgias emerged from the doorway of the courthouse with a smug grin on his oily face.

Behind him, men came wheeling out a new set of kuraminium restraints.

Darius had seen them before. For the arms, the "crossbar," a straight rod with shackles fixed to each end, which limited movement. For the legs, two shackles connected by only six inches of chain.

"What's happening?" Darius asked.

Frown lines creased Selene's brow. "I don't know."

Gorgias stopped a few feet away and shook his head. "I'm to restrain you."

"He already is," Selene said.

"Then we're to take him to the dungeons."

Darius tensed, pulled against the chains again as if they'd suddenly weakened. It was his turn to feel dread. He looked to his left, then his right, at the rows of soldiers and hateful glares on their twisted faces.

I'm a fool for doing this to myself. Decisions like that were why he was a grunt and not a warlord.

"Who ordered this?" Selene asked. "We're supposed to be seeing my father."

Gorgias spoke next in a voice calm yet forceful for once. "It's the Regent that has ordered this."

Selene's eyes narrowed, jaw clenched as she looked first at Gorgias, then to Darius for a second before turning away as if she couldn't bear the sight of him.

"Fine," she said. "*I'll* speak with my father." She turned towards the palace.

"Wait," Darius said before thinking, his voice soft and in a tone that he only used with her. "Don't leave me." He'd dared to trust her, and she was the only one he trusted when so vulnerable.

She glanced back at him, angry eyes piercing his. "My father knows best. I must speak with him first." With that, she stormed up the winding road.

Darius wondered how far she'd go to argue for him but didn't dare hope in case it ended in disappointment.

"Arms out," a thickset soldier growled as he moved from behind Gorgias.

For a second, Darius considered keeping his arms down, knowing no one had the strength to force them up. He reckoned he could kill three of them when they tried to secure the new restraints, but the thought of broken knees made him oblige with a scowl.

"I don't suppose I'm to see the Regent later?" he asked. "To plead my case?"

As if Darius hadn't uttered a word, Gorgias watched on as four burly men lifted the bar and placed it across his shoulders, while another two snapped the shackles shut.

The cold metal bit into his wrists next to his current restraints. With the outstretched position of his arms, each breath became more laboured than the last.

Then, the short chain was secured to his ankles. The soldiers finally unlocked the chains attaching him to the wagon then dug spearheads into the small of his back.

"Move!"

While Darius made his baby steps towards the doorway, Gorgias walked beside him with a slight grin that gave Darius the urge to thump him.

The algus ran a hand to tidy his slick hair. "The Regent wishes you to pay for the bloodshed you've caused."

The pleasure and lack of anger in his voice sent chills through Darius's body. That confidence only came from a man that had complete control.

Still, if word of Darius's capture had reached the Regent, hopefully that meant word had reached Lex too. Yet, she was nowhere to be seen, and despite checking the sky and every window ledge of the surrounding buildings, the spotted breast of her peregrine was notably absent too.

"What's the plan?" Darius asked. "Let me rot in a cell?"

"At first," Gorgias muttered.

"And after I saved your hide… Perhaps I should have let that rakkan gut you."

"Perhaps."

"But I didn't."

Gorgias stared at him with the same trace of pity he'd shown when Darius shared Lyra's story, but his face soon twisted into a grimace. "What did you expect? That we'd have mercy on you? That coming here in chains would make a difference?"

"I expected nothing." If only it was true, he'd have been spared the regret.

"Liar. Never mind. It won't be long until we get the truth from you."

Darius needed no clarification to know what that meant, to recall the screams he'd heard coming from below the courthouse on his last visit.

"Better hope I don't spill too many secrets," Darius muttered, "for your sake."

Gorgias frowned. "What?"

Darius leaned in close enough to smell the algus's musty odour and whispered, "Maybe I know some… *emasculating* secrets some would prefer went unsaid."

Gorgias's face flushed as his gaze contorted from shock to fury in a split-second. He'd realise it was Selene that told Darius about his little secret, but at this point Darius wasn't too bothered about getting her into trouble.

"She wouldn't tell you," Gorgias spat.

"How about I kick you in the groin and test if she spoke the truth?"

Gorgias grabbed him by the collar and pulled him sideways, leaning into his ear. "Get inside. You know nothing."

"I know enough." Darius shuffled his feet hastily to keep up while Gorgias shoved him into the courthouse. "Maybe my silence can be bought."

"What use is gold or crests to you now?"

"Not gold, you fool. My freedom."

Gorgias pushed Darius through the doorway then spun him around and thrust him against a wall until the pair were nose to nose.

The algus looked from side to side, checking the soldiers were out of earshot, no doubt. "You ask the impossible. Too many have seen you restrained, and I'd let you yell my secret from the highest tower before I become the traitor that released the Slayer."

If only Darius had been so loyal to the Margalvians, perhaps he wouldn't be in this mess. "Then don't free me, just spare me the worst of whatever it is you're planning. Get me tears of the weeping plant."

Gorgias frowned and stared for a few seconds, thoughts whirling in the algus's mind that only seemed to enrage him more.

"No one will know," Darius whispered.

Frowns and grimaces continued to flicker across Gorgias's face until he shuddered and cursed. "Damn you. I'll see what I can do."

Darius gave a hesitant sigh of relief.

"I won't go easy," Gorgias said. "They'll know if I do."

"I don't expect miracles."

Gorgias bit his lips together and gave a stiff nod. It was as much as Darius could hope for, but he wasn't done pushing his luck.

Once inside, he shuffled through the maze of corridors, which began regal and ornate near the entrance but darkened with the stench of rot and blood once in the underbelly.

Some doorways were so narrow Darius had to go through sideways with the crossbar. Soon, he was thrust into a cell in the basement, and Gorgias slammed the gate shut.

"Not taking off the restraints?" Darius asked.

"No. Regent's orders. You're too dangerous."

Looks like I'm not getting any sleep tonight. The torture was starting earlier than he'd feared and sleep deprivation was one of the nicer things to expect over the next few days.

He cast his gaze around the cramped cell, which wasn't long enough either way to lie flat, and the walls were plated with cold kuraminium. Blackened marks scarred the walls and floor where the last inhabitants had tried in vain to use ferven to escape.

"I'll be back tomorrow," Gorgias said. "I'll have them bring food and water."

"Don't spoil me… It's not like you owe me your life." Darius wiggled his outstretched hands and watched the algus retreat up the corridor and nearby stairs.

Who knew whether Gorgias would really help him? If possible, the algus would merely ensure there were no unfriendly witnesses to the torture that might overhear something. But with a secret so delicate, Gorgias might not risk even a random soldier overhearing, no matter how easily they were controlled. Rumours spread faster than disease in cities like Laltos.

But Gorgias wasn't his key to freedom. Selene would talk to her father, and where was Lex? What about the alliance? If he could just speak to Theodoros, maybe he could convince the

Regent. He'd be willing to forgive and forget the misunderstanding if it meant severing Hadrian's head.

Surely the Regent would want a fighter like Darius on his side. Deep down, all the powerful wanted the cold-blooded slayer at their command.

He carefully dropped to his knees and sat against the damp metal wall, the hardness already chilling his backside. He closed his eyes and reached out to Lyra; her anxiety raced through him once connected again. She was doing better to be so worried. At least he could take solace in that, and that he wasn't alone. *I won't give up, Lyra, and I won't forget why I'm here. If you can, let the others know I'm in trouble.*

33

Selene – Laltos

Selene eased the door open, her sweaty fingers slipping on the varnished wood. After so long trekking through villages and dry dirt, some smoothness should have been nice to touch. But it wasn't while anger, hurt and dread filled her stomach. *Does he know?*

Within the room, the white hair on her father's head poked above the back of a chair. Sat quietly in conversation with Lex, not even a slave or guard had been allowed in to overhear.

His private chambers were dim, with only strips of light glaring through the closed shutters. The rays cast shadows over the portraits adorning the wall, Selene's own watching over the room along with her adopted brothers, sisters, nephews and nieces. Hot, stuffy air hung in the space and made her sweat even more.

She took a deep breath, the stone in her stomach only alleviated a little by her sister's presence. Even Lex had been fooled by Darius's lies. She'd suffered heartache and betrayal more than most, and Selene direly needed council in such things.

Selene's light footsteps across the carpet were enough to turn her father's head, his piercing stare even less friendly than she'd feared.

"Selene." Lex got up and gave her a weak smile as she embraced her. "He knows."

A chill ran through Selene's body, sweat suddenly cold on her skin.

Lex kissed her cheek and whispered again, "Someone told him. I've softened him as best I could."

As Lex moved away, she left Selene in the gaze of her father's narrowed eyes. "It's worse than I thought." He sighed and finished a deep cup of burwine in one gulp.

Lex took Selene by the hand and led her to sit on the padded bench by her father. On a small table just in front of them lay an assortment of fruits and a cup of wine already ready for her. At least he didn't appear to want to disown her. *Yet.*

"Let's be candid with one another, shall we?" Her father ran a hand up and down the golden stitching of his tunic. "I know about you and Darius, but so far I'm not aware of anyone important outside our family that knows."

If only that were true... "How did you find out?" Selene asked.

Theodoros lowered his gaze to the amphora of wine. "Slaves can tell when a bed has been shared by two."

"Then it's only a matter of time until more hear of it," Selene muttered. They'd all know how foolish she was, how she'd been taken in by a charming liar, how she'd been befouled with rakkan taint.

"It's likely others already know," Lex said, "but they're keeping it close to their chests for now. It's not your fault. How were any of us supposed to see through his lies?" Lex gazed at Selene without a trace of anger or resentment, as if trying to read her reaction to the words. Why wasn't Lex more hurt after entrusting Darius with her own escort?

"It's not just that," Theodoros snapped. "Yes, the thought of Selene sharing a bed with a rakkan makes me vomit, but I'd prefer my daughters didn't do that with any man, whether half-rakkan or not."

Lex's eyes narrowed. "Remind me, were you married when my mother fell pregnant with me?"

Selene's ears perked up, never having heard such a thing before.

The Regent's flushed cheeks gave the answer to Lex's question that his mouth refused to. When he finally spoke, his voice had lost its sharp edge. "You're too bright for your own good."

As interesting as the conversation was, Selene's mind refused to focus and instead dwelled on the moments she and Darius had spent in bed. The man had been so convincing.

Looking back to her father, she didn't dare so much as breathe or touch the wine and food that made her salivate after the interminable journey home.

Theodoros caught her eyeing the food. "Eat. Don't think because I'm angry I'll see you starve."

Under her father's watching eyes, she helped herself to segments of orange and a cup of red wine, but no sooner had she started eating when her mind slipped from worry over her father to worry over the man now heading to the cells.

"What will happen to him?" she asked. Despite the frown it put back on her father's face, she continued staring, demanding an answer. "Will you speak with him?"

287

"He'll get the same treatment as any other captured rakkan," Theodoros said. "We'll make him talk and separate the lies from the snippets of truth."

Lex shifted uncomfortably, deep worry lines on her brow that her father didn't seem to notice. As furious as Selene was with Darius, the thought of him being tortured brought her no pleasure either.

"I urge you to hear his story with you own ears, Father," Selene said. "I only trust you to discern the truth."

"Tell me," Lex said, "is it true he saved your life in Dolthea? And that he liberated a village all on his own?"

Theodoros raised an eyebrow.

"Yes…" Selene said. "He risked himself to save me. It's also true he freed a village, though I'm not sure the human corpses and burnt huts appreciated it much."

Lex's jaw clenched and Selene swore she seemed frustrated at the answer. There was something she wasn't saying, but it was best not highlighted in front of their father.

"Have you any insight into what he was up to?" Theodoros asked. "Why hide amongst us?"

"He claimed that Margalvia and Viridia are at war," Selene said, praying for her father's insight, "and that his city wants an alliance with Laltos."

Lex opened her mouth to speak, but the Regent burst out laughing, which turned into a fit of coughs. "An alliance. As if we'd believe such nonsense, but the thought of it is amusing I must admit."

"What if he speaks the truth?" Lex asked. She always had to spark debate, but this time Selene shared her doubts.

"It's possible," Selene said. "Trouble is, I have no idea what he really wants. Perhaps to kill you, Father. He was always keen on meeting you, but if he wanted to assassinate you then why travel with me?"

"We'll find out soon enough." Theodoros's face darkened as the sun's rays weakened through the shutters. "The interrogators will get it out of him."

Selene brushed her hair back, using it as an excuse to partially shield her face and the conflict it surely exposed. "I don't think that's wise. Please speak with him. If you harm him, we may never find out the truth." Torture only brought more lies to rakkans' mouths than usual.

Her father's eyes widened with a flash of anger but soon after lowered in silent, tense contemplation. "All my life I've watched rakkans show no mercy or pity. At first, I tried to be the better man, but when faced with such evil every night and day, it seeps into a man, gives him a longing for justice so strong it consumes him. And consumed I am. Darius has seen that same evil too, yet he fights for those fiends. No. I won't release him."

The thoughts echoed the doubts in Selene's mind, but she'd hoped for a less emotive response than her own. "Maybe I can be there when you both speak. I can ensure he tells the truth about our travels in the west."

"Out of the question," Theodoros snapped.

Lex sat forward. "Then perhaps I—"

"Even more ludicrous. He's infected one of my daughters, so why should I allow him to do it to another?"

Lex scowled. "I'm not some—"

"Not another word." The Regent sat upright. "I may be many things, but I'm a father first. I won't allow my children to be spoiled by this affair any further. Both of you are forbidden from speaking to this half-rakkan again, do I make myself clear?"

Both Selene and Lex argued but were silenced immediately by a burst of algor from their father's eyes. "Not. Another. Word!

I'll die before I see this family suffer any more than it has to." Theodoros's voice and stare chilled the room. "If I hear of either of you seeing or so much as asking about that half-rakkan, I'll have you taken in chains from this city. Then I'll execute him! Better that than let him get inside your heads. Selene, your misplaced feelings for this man are plain, and you'll be confined to your quarters."

Selene started. "I'm not a child—"

"Yes you are! And you're mine!"

Selene glanced to Lex, who raised her eyebrows. They knew better than to argue.

"As you wish, Father." Lex stood and turned to Selene. "Let's retire. You must be weary after your trip."

When the Regent gave her only a final look of disappointment, Selene stood and walked with Lex out of the room.

As Lex closed the doors, a bell rang loud from inside, no doubt summoning the guards that would ensure Selene didn't venture out.

Lex glanced from left to right in the long, empty hallway before speaking. "What did Darius say to you?" The stare she gave Selene was even firmer than their father's.

"Only what I said."

"Did he ever do anything that makes you think he's different to the man of the stories?"

Many things, but they may have all been part of the ruse. "I've no idea what he wants. Doesn't matter, anyway. We can't do anything."

Lex lowered her voice. "What if it's true? Can you imagine Laltos being allied with a rakkan legion?"

290

The thought had barely crossed Selene's mind, striking her as absurd as soon as she'd heard it, but the look on Lex's face wasn't of fear or hurt, but zeal.

Selene fidgeted. Was there something Lex saw that she was missing? After all, her sister was one of the sharpest algus she knew.

Contemplating whether Darius told the truth all along brought a lump to her throat. But it didn't mean he'd been honest about his feelings for her.

"Do *you* believe him?" Selene asked.

Lex's jaw tensed. "Yes. I trust him."

34

Nikolaos – Xavala, the Silk City

Nikolaos doubled over as the guffaws stole the air from his lungs. Wine dribbled from his lips and stained the white clothes as he desperately tried to swallow. Too late.

The Silk Regent patted him on the back and wiped the tears from his eyes. "And then the whore had the cheek to act surprised, as if she hadn't done it."

Finally able to breathe in once again, Nikolaos swallowed and leant back against the plush chair in the Regent's private quarters. On the other seats around, Aristippus's scantily dressed concubines smiled with fake amusement, but the Regent either didn't notice their falsity or didn't care.

Thankfully it was just them as the King's Sword had been called away. The summer hours were cool but humid, and the stuffiness was only worsened by the thick scents from both the Silk Regent's body and the burning incense in the room.

Nikolaos placed down his cup of wine, knowing as soon as he took another gulp the Silk Regent would do his best to deliver a further punchline and stain his tunic more. It had been so long since Nikolaos laughed, he was tempted to bait the algus into it.

But that would further distract the conversation from where he wanted it to lead. The King's Orator may have forbidden him from revealing Lex's secret alliance for now, but Nikolaos would do his best to ensure none of Lex's plans came to fruition.

"I spoke with the King's Orator recently," Nikolaos said.

The Silk Regent raised an eyebrow. "Did she finally tell you why they rescued you?"

"No. She was evasive, but it must be for my knowledge. She brought me up to date on how your talks are going, the disputes and tax demands." That last part was a lie, but Nikolaos knew by the narrowing of the Silk Regent's eyes that he'd hit the right mark.

"It seems talks in Laltos were even more sour," Nikolaos added.

"I can believe that."

"Regent Theodoros is barely clinging to power. The King may soon depose him and install a new regent." Nikolaos puffed out his chest in a manner that brought a grin to the Silk Regent's face.

"I see where you're going with this." Aristippus leant back in his chair with a chuckle. "But my word doesn't count for much with the King, so I don't see how I can guide him to…the right man to replace Theodoros."

Nikolaos pretended to take a gulp of wine. For now, his head needed to remain clear. "You misunderstand. Let me worry about the King. I just want our relationship to begin right away, to ensure a strong allegiance between Laltos and Xavala."

"Why do I sense you're about to ask a great favour of me?"

"Because I am. Though I'd hardly call it 'great'. All I need is for you not to marry Lex."

The Silk Regent's frown was one of a man struggling to string thoughts together after too many drinks. "Why do you want that? Aren't you two friends?"

The word "friend" only brought painful memories. They'd been close, but now that he looked back, he'd always seen there was something off about Lex—the way she used to speak to and treat slaves, calling them by name and letting them rest when tired. *What's wrong with her?*

"We were," Nikolaos said, "but I'd recommend a whore any day. Far more worth the money."

"I don't pay for whores." Aristippus smirked. "I'm the Regent. This city and everyone in it belong to me." He brushed back the fringe of dark hair from his eyes and gazed at one of the women at the side of the room.

Nikolaos glanced over to see a tall, slender woman with raven hair and most of her curves exposed by her silk dress. "She looks expensive. You must save a fortune."

"Remind you of anyone?" Aristippus chuckled, gulped down the rest of his wine and held the empty cup out while a slave scurried over to refill it.

His stomach is more bottomless than I remember.

The thin, dark eyebrows on the concubine's face arced into a permanent scowl, just like another woman Nikolaos knew.

"Not as alluring as her but will have to do until I get the genuine thing." The Regent's tone turned from conversational to low and bitter. "I can't recall the last time I had to wait so long for a woman. This marriage can't happen soon enough."

Typical Aristippus. Luckily for Nikolaos, he knew how quickly the Silk Regent lost interest. "Forbidden fruit always tastes sweeter," Nikolaos replied. "But I can assure you she's not worth the wait."

Aristippus's mouth fell ajar. "You mean…you?"

"We were young. She might be more experienced now. I hope she's more interesting for you than she was for me."

The lie was enough to turn the Silk Regent's face from amused and hungry to a grimace of resentment. "More interesting? You mean she's a poor lay?"

"Well…" Nikolaos began, "the word 'starfish' comes to mind. But maybe she's improved."

The Silk Regent pulled open his tunic and wafted his hairy, sweaty chest with a disgruntled growl. Then he downed another two cups of wine. "All this wait for an unmoving starfish?"

Nikolaos grinned. "I thought you wanted the alliance with Laltos more than her. You'll still have that, especially if I become regent. Put in a friendly word from me with the King's Orator and I'll make it most profitable for you. After all, I'll have control of the Laltos Bank."

The words weren't enough to wipe the sulk from the Silk Regent's face. "Sounds tempting, but I don't want to join you as the King's lapdog. Lex is the only one with the stones to stand up to him."

Nikolaos pretended to drink again, instead swallowing down his anger at the insult. "I can assure you that's not true."

"Oh really? Prove it."

The thought of telling the Silk Regent the truth of Lex was tempting but brought to mind the King's Sword often watching over his shoulder. Ophelia wasn't a woman he expected to escape from should he cross her.

"You'll have to take my word for it," Nikolaos finally replied.

Aristippus stared, unblinking, hunger back in his eyes. "I won't."

Standing, Nikolaos let the false amusement fall from his demeanour and began pacing around the room, past the concubines, still like living statues. It had taken all his energy not to shout the truth about Lex in the streets ever since he'd arrived.

Perhaps I should let go. "Everyone get out," he barked.

All the slaves and women looked to the Silk Regent, who gave a nod without taking his eyes from Nikolaos. While they left, Nikolaos pondered how much he trusted the Silk Regent to not reveal the truth when in future talks with the King's envoy. *He's a lecher but not an idiot.*

After the door closed behind the last of the slaves, Nikolaos sat beside the Silk Regent, leaned in close enough that the algus's perfume stung his eyes. "I'll tell you something the King's Orator would rather you didn't know. You can't tell anyone I told you. Keep up appearances for now."

"Obviously."

With a deep breath, Nikolaos began. "Alexandra is planning an alliance between Laltos and Margalvia."

The Silk Regent gaped. "With rakkans?"

"Yes, and she's been planning it for some time. She's responsible for Archimedes's death." Nikolaos went on to explain everything he'd seen and the full depths of her betrayal, which made the Silk Regent grimace and sweat all the more.

"I knew I couldn't trust her entirely," Aristippus said, "but I never suspected…"

Nikolaos allowed the Silk Regent a few moments of pondering before breaking the silence. "What will you do? Call off the marriage?"

"I'm not sure." Aristippus ran a hand across his jaw. "Act like nothing is awry for now, but this demands action. We could lure her here, kill her, and… Do you think Regent Theodoros knows of this?"

"Most certainly. But fear not. He won't be regent for much longer."

35

Darius – Laltos

A whip lashed Darius's back. He grunted at the sharp pain. Shackles tugged at his wrists, his arms still stretched apart by the crossbar but now suspended from the ceiling. With trembling knees, his weak legs struggled to take the load from his arms and chest while he sucked in heavy, laboured breaths, much like a crucified man. With each breath came the smell of his own sweat and filth.

The last few days had been hell. The room he was in was bright for a torture chamber, with thin windows glaring at the top of the stone walls. Located half above ground, it stood next to the street, so the city's residents heard his cries.

Another lash erased all thought for a moment before the pain lessened and joined the dozens of other scores. Each one hurt more as the skin softened like a bruised fruit. His back may as well have been on fire, he wouldn't have been able to tell the difference.

How could Selene let this happen to him? She'd seen who he really was, heard the story of his baby brother that he'd never told before. After all that, he'd foolishly hoped she'd help, or at least visit him.

Whipping was usually reserved for punishment, and despite their questions and demands for answers, he knew that's what this was about. But it could have been worse. He saw the instruments hanging from the walls—the rack that ripped apart limbs, the vice that crushed bone—all smeared with dried blood from the last victims.

Engulfing his back in ferven would burn the whip in an instant, but then they'd get the rods again, or more malevolent tools. *Hell no.* This was best, despite the pain growing to the point of passing out, despite lasting for days after.

Thank the heavens for the tears. At least the whips left his limbs intact, unlike the rods of the soldiers that visited him in the night.

"That's enough," a man's voice ordered from behind.

The whip-wielding soldier stepped away as another man came forward to face Darius. His stare was as bald as his head, with no shred of empathy. "Tell us the truth, or you get another thirty lashes."

Darius squeezed his eyes shut. Thirty more would kill him. "Alright." He'd always known he'd talk—everyone did—but had to make it appear they'd coerced it out of him or they'd never believe him. But he'd only give them whatever wasn't harmful to Margalvia. "My mission was to drive the Viridian Legion from Laltos's lands and kill the commander of the invading armies. Margalvia seeks an alliance with you."

The bald man's blond eyebrows narrowed, and he stepped across the room to a table where a thick parchment lay unwound. He ran his finger methodically down a page. "Which algus aided you when you were last in Laltos?"

Darius grunted and shot a steely gaze at the man. They'd never whip Lex's name out of him.

"It says here you were close to Algus Selene," the bald man continued, "accompanying her for a while."

"True."

"Why the interest in her?" the bald man asked.

No matter how angry Darius was with her, deep down he still hadn't been able to stop caring. Hurting her wouldn't make his situation any better.

"She's a skilled fighter," he said, "and has the ear of the Regent. It made my task easier." It was doubtful they'd believe him. *Damn my slow wits.* He needed someone with brains in situations like this.

"I don't buy it. Ready for another thirty?"

Just the words brought phantom lashes of pain to his back. "If I tell you more, let us be done for the day."

The bald man raised his eyebrows. "I'm sorry, are you trying to negotiate with me?"

"It would appear so."

"I don't bargain with—"

"Oh, let him have it." Gorgias's voice rang around the walls from behind Darius for the first time. How long had he been standing there?

The bald man stepped back, and his mouth hung open for a second. "But, Algus…"

"Another thirty may harm him too much. We want him alive."

"Then why not blind him first as we usually—"

"The Regent wants him intact. No blinding, no broken limbs."

With a creased brow, the bald man turned again to Darius. "Then tell us about Algus Selene, and you may return to your cell."

Darius coughed, grimacing at the pain it caused on his back. "She's no traitor. I just got close to her because she has a nice arse."

The bald man scowled. "Another thirty—"

"Calm yourself," Gorgias said. "Selene isn't of noteworthy rank in the military and is of no strategic significance."

"She's the Regent's daughter!"

"Exactly. He wanted to get closer to the Regent. There's your answer."

The bald man went back to his parchment and began scribbling extra notes with a reed pen.

Gorgias finally came around to face Darius, who shot him an exasperated look.

The algus raised his eyebrows, as if asking why he should help more.

The kuraminium bar made it impossible to breathe. Darius trained his eyes on it before giving Gorgias a knowing stare.

"I'm concerned with his breathing," Gorgias said.

The bald man glanced up from the page. "Why?"

"It seems… strained. I fear he may not make it through the night unless we free him from the crossbar."

An incredulous stare came upon the bald man's face. "All we've done is whip him."

Gorgias turned and cleared his throat with an exuding authority.

"Fine." The bald man turned to the soldier beside him. "Chain his ankle to the kuraminium ball when he's back in his cell and release him from the bar."

Thank the Creator. Darius could lie on his front and avoid any contact with his mutilated back. *Finally, some sleep.*

"Before you take him back," Gorgias said, "I'd like a word with him."

The bald man gave the pair a quizzical look but exited silently along with the other soldier as ordered.

As soon as the door slammed shut behind them, Darius let out a groan. "I can't take much more."

"Please. I'm already risking my neck by getting you tears. Do you have to make my work harder with your sarcasm?"

"Forgive me for amusing myself, trying to keep myself sane. You think taking dozens of lashes is easy?"

"If you'd prefer something different, then speak up."

"Save your excuses." Darius grunted and looked away. "It's not just lashes. I *know* you're aware of the soldiers that come to my cell at night to thrash me."

Gorgias remained silent, confirming Darius's suspicions, but he was too exhausted to press the point. "Do you think they suspect Selene of being a traitor?"

"I doubt it, but then…the Regent has had her locked in the palace. You could save all this by just telling us why you're here, and who the real traitor was."

For Lex, he'd let them flay him before he'd talk. "I've told you why I'm here. I don't know how long I can hold my tongue about other things… You saw how easily I talked today."

Gorgias narrowed his eyes. "Maybe I should just kill you now, say it was an accident."

Surprised he hasn't already tried it. "I wonder what the Regent or King would do if they learnt I died under your watch before revealing anything of significance."

The frown on Gorgias's face deepened.

"As I thought." Unfortunately, that got Darius no closer to escaping this hell, and it seemed only one person could spare him the pain. "I want to speak with Regent Theodoros."

"Why?"

"To make my case, tell him why I did what I did. To say I'll fight with his armies again."

Gorgias clicked his tongue and walked to the table where the parchment was still laid out with the torturer's scribbles. "Will you give him a different excuse than the one you've already given? Because I can assure you, he's heard it and doesn't trust a word."

Darius gritted his teeth. "It's the truth. Why else would I fight the Viridians?"

"To kill Regent Theodoros?"

"I would have already done it."

"Maybe you just want to learn Laltos's weaknesses. Or perhaps an assault on the city is coming and you wanted to hide among us until the right time."

Darius murmured and rattled the chains attached to his wrists. "Let me down. The tears will wear off soon, and I'd rather be alone in my cell when they do." Only withdrawing to connect with Lyra made the pain tolerable when the tears' relief waned.

"Very well." The algus left the room while Darius ruminated over his options. He didn't know what was worse, the agony or the constant confusion in his head over what to do. It was almost easier to give up hope, but he wasn't through fighting yet. *Where are you, Selene, Lex, Brutus, Sulla...? I need you.*

36

Sulla – Margalvia

Sulla thrust his fists into the thick wooden door. He barged it open with such a force it crashed into the wall behind and split in two. He stepped through into the Warlord's office, a sizeable room carved from stone, deep underground with four supporting pillars and an assortment of stone chairs.

At the far side, Varro stood alongside Julius, both topless with a sword in each hand and sweat dripping from them. The only others in the room were two thin servants, a cleric and a blacksmith who stared at the sudden crash.

"Sulla." The Warlord's chest rose and fell rapidly as he glowered at the interruption. "What the hell are you doing?"

By the door, Sulla eyed a rack of swords running along the wall, droplets of water hanging on the side of each blade. If he had to use them, he was sure he'd come out worst, but it might come to that.

He stepped forward. "Darius has been captured."

Varro's eyes glowed orange and he cursed. "That's why they say Lyra's been agitated. How was he caught?"

"We don't know. A racing pigeon just arrived, and the letter was brief. Unsigned, so probably from Lex. The humans have him chained up in Laltos."

"That doesn't excuse you bursting in here." Varro flared ferven across a sword before driving it down into the stone floor. "Give me the message."

Sulla took a few hesitant steps forward and handed over the slip of parchment while they both continued glaring. *He won't take action, same as after the jailbreak. I know it.*

The Warlord looked over the note, reading the plea for immediate assistance through non-violent means. Sulla couldn't care less about the last part, for he knew Darius's world would now be nothing but blood and cruelty.

When finished, Varro tossed the parchment onto a chair and began pacing. "First an algus sends this city into a panic and now this. Alexandra's alliance is looking more fantastical by the day. We'd be better planning as if facing our enemies alone. Call our armies to arms so we can defend—"

"Defend?" Sulla's yell sent a deafening echo. "We should focus on Darius, not turtling!"

Varro stopped his pacing. "The King had an algus go on a rampage, freed our prisoner. On top of that, Brutus has reported that Hadrian is planning to attack Margalvia."

"And you're only telling me this now? How long have you known?"

"A while."

Sulla clenched his fists. If the Warlord didn't trust him enough to tell him of such a threat, then what use was a Militia Chief? "Darius needs us, alliance or no alliance."

"Can we afford to lose Darius from the Legion?" Julius asked calmly.

"I'm not sure we have much of a choice," Varro replied. "Whatever Alexandra expects us to do eludes me."

"She wants us to free him, boss." Sulla marched forward until only a foot away from the Warlord, close enough to smell the sweat dripping down his body. "She wants the alliance so we can destroy the Viridian Legion," Sulla said, "like we should have been working towards weeks ago. If we'd been focused on these things all along, then we wouldn't be in this quandary."

"What does that mean?" The Warlord's voice quietened to a menacing whisper. "Are you saying this is my fault?"

"If the boot fits… We're still ready for the order to retake the mine, instead of waiting for word from Brutus."

Varro squeezed the hilt of the sword in his hand and stepped forward a few inches, staring down his nose.

Sulla braced.

"Let's not quarrel," Julius said, trying to push Sulla back. "We all want the same thing, don't we?"

"What would you have us do, Sulla," Varro asked, "march the Black Legion for countless miles across hostile territory, past human cities, until we reach Laltos, then besiege it?"

"Yes!" Sulla took a step back, knowing better than to take Varro on, but didn't relax his grimace. "There are routes we can take that avoid the busy human paths. We need to save Darius. Come on. He's our friend."

"A friend that has let us down many times, a friend that repaid our care and protection with actions that flattened his mind, a friend whose boldness led to my brother's death." The Warlord paused while the cleric dipped his head with what appeared to be a silent prayer. "Regardless," Varro continued.

306

"I'm warlord. I can't make decisions based on friendship. How would we defend Margalvia when our armies are away?"

Sulla lowered his gaze and ran a hand across his forehead, feeling the deep scars that he'd taken because of rash decisions in the past. "I didn't mean we send the Legion. Send a smaller group of us."

"What can a small band do against an entire city?"

Julius gave Sulla a shrug as if in agreement with the Warlord.

Sulla exhaled with a slight shake of his head. He couldn't leave Darius to rot. "We can sneak into the city. We can at least try."

The Warlord froze, seeming to ponder the suggestion for a while before murmuring and beginning his pacing again. It seemed to be how he ruminated, with his heavy boots wearing their leather against the ground.

Reflecting, Sulla remembered the contrasting ways of his old Militia Chief, who always sat still whilst thinking. Recent events had pushed the pain of loss to the back of his mind, but once Darius was safe, Sulla would still be out for revenge.

"Suppose we tried this," Julius said. "If the alliance isn't in place by the time we arrive, then we may not have any other option than to fight."

"I care more about Darius than the alliance," Sulla said. "I'll spare the men if need be."

"No. I don't see there's anything we can do," Varro replied. "And you're right. We've waited for too long to retake the mine. It's time we acted."

Why did the Warlord wait until *now* to commit warriors? "I don't believe it. You're just going to leave Darius?"

"I'll let Lex handle it. Don't forget it's partly his own fault that we're even involved in this war in the first place, a fact I'm still determined to seek punishment for. But do you think I like this? You think I want to see my greatest warrior executed?"

"You think I want to see my *friend* executed? You think I'll stand by while it happens?"

"Don't take that tone with me, Sulla." The Warlord's voice dropped again. "Darius is my friend too, but I have thousands of civilians relying on me as well."

"Being a leader doesn't mean you need to be heartless and dithering."

"It doesn't? How many enemies do we have lined up at our gates wanting to raze our city? The humans attacked Denehill yesterday. They raided a food caravan the day before. The Viridian Legion is ready to march on us. You don't see. You're Red Militia, but this is what I have to deal with, the wolves biting at our heels. If I make *one* mistake, this whole city becomes a bloodbath as all our friends are slaughtered. The fate of Margalvia lies on my shoulders. I can't have friends."

Sulla sighed. "If the yoke is burdensome, let someone else—"

"Need I remind you, that it wasn't so long ago that your mouth was to my ear encouraging me to kill the last warlord and succeed him. I'm here because you talked me into it, because you were too weak to defeat Warlord Catonius yourself."

"Weak? I might be Militia, but you know I could have been promoted to Black Legion if I'd wanted to be."

"But you aren't. The Militia, and you, answer to me. Your job is to relay my commands. Darius followed his orders to go to Laltos, so why can't you follow yours?"

"I'm sorry I won't blindly follow as Darius did. To think you won't aid a man that showed such loyalty to you—"

"Think you can do better? Then challenge me." The beads of sweat trickled down Varro's hard chest.

What could Sulla do? He didn't fear the Warlord but lacked Varro's fighting prowess. If he ended up dead in the sands of the arena, that wouldn't help Darius.

"I thought as much," the Warlord said. "Now get back to preparing the Militia."

"Oh, I'll prepare them. We're heading to rescue Darius."

"Sulla, I swear if you disobey me, I'll—"

"What? Kill me? Because that's what it'll take to stop me."

The Warlord stared, chest rising and falling with his deep breaths, but the sword in his hand didn't flinch. Varro may have been fearsome, but he didn't kill lightly and had a temperament that Sulla respected on the battlefield.

"That's what I thought," Sulla said.

"If you won't obey, then get out of my city."

"Don't worry. I'm leaving. And I'm taking the Militia with me."

"You're not taking them anywhere."

"They'll follow me." The truth was he had no idea how many of the Militia would back him, but whether it was two or two thousand, Sulla would free Darius or die trying.

Varro gave a long exhale. "Do you know how many rakkans have been captured since I became warlord? I do."

"And how many are dead?"

"Every one. But I can name all of them. So don't say I don't care. How many of your men are you willing to lose to get Darius back?"

"I'm not sacrificing anyone. They'll come with me willingly."

"Sulla, if you leave with your men, you're not welcome back."

The Warlord wasn't one to make an empty threat, and it wasn't that Sulla took any pleasure in disobedience. As hard as it was to remember in their heated moments, he respected Varro.

Sulla took three deep breaths before replying, wanting to be sure he could live with his decision. "Then let it be so. I hope one day you'll see sense and learn that if we don't have loyalty to one another, then what we're fighting for isn't worth anything. Just know that if it were you in Darius's boots, I'd do the same thing. Margalvians defend their brothers."

Varro's eyes widened, and his scowl softened into a regretful frown.

"Margalvians defend their brothers," Sulla repeated.

When Varro's gaze fell away, Sulla took his cue to leave. As angry as he'd been when he entered, a sadness grew with every step towards the door. Without Margalvia, what was his life worth?

***

Sulla turned slowly around, two dozen commanders surrounding him with eyes and faces as hard as the volcanic rock of the surrounding walls. The whirling made his vision hard to focus, made ruminations become muddled, but he wouldn't show any disrespect by facing away.

"Is everyone here?" Sulla asked.

Atticus, Sulla's most trusted commander, and softest spoken of the lot, stepped forward, his beady obsidian eyes focusing on each commander in turn. "We're here. What's the crisis?"

Sulla had said nothing, but why else would a chief call them to an urgent meeting? He knew they suspected because they all wore armour and sword belts.

"Many of you won't like what I have to say," Sulla began, turning slowly as he spoke, "but this is a request, not an order."

A few furrowed brows and grumbles were all he received, so he continued, "All I ask is you relay this to your men whether you're with me or not."

Most nodded, but the nervousness in their eyes was plain.

310

"I'm going into exile"—Sulla hurried his voice to overlay the gasps—"and I'm going to Laltos to save Darius from the humans."

Another commander, the broad-jawed Horatius, stepped forward. "Then I'm with you."

Sulla snorted a laugh. "Hold on, I haven't finished, haven't even told you my plan yet." To have so many act on a simple command had never sat well with Sulla. He'd rather they use their own minds. "You might be a fool to follow me."

"Then fools we'll be," Atticus said with a large inhale, "but fools loyal to our chief."

More than a few scowls and grimaces from the other commanders told Sulla that all weren't with him, but that was fine. Even the former chief wasn't liked by everyone, despite being one of the most brilliant leaders on record.

"Don't decide now," Sulla said. "Take a few hours to dwell once I've told you everything." With a deep sigh, he told them the whole story, why he was going, the kindness Darius had shown to him more than once—like the debtors from Sulla's street days that the half-rakkan had chased away.

Sulla owed Darius more than his measly life. One day, he hoped Varro forgave him for leaving. But for now, Darius's life demanded he act.

37

Darius – Laltos

For Darius, the whippings were only the beginning. When the skin on his back flayed, they began with other tools, from sharp metal to blunt and forceful blows. His stints in the torture chamber weren't the end, because once alone in his cell, the pain continued as his body healed before they went at it again.

Days passed. How many, he didn't keep track, but he knew it would need many fingers to count. His hopes Selene would help faded, leaving only hurt and rage.

Damn Selene. He'd trusted himself to her.

One day he woke with no stamina to summon, despite a few days of rest. Still, they took him through to the room and went to work.

Darius gasped, his desperate pants growing more and more rapid as the spike pressed under his fingernail. Ferven crackled in his throat as he roared and shot Gorgias a heated stare for the tenth time.

Finally, the algus reacted. "That's enough." The sheen of sweat on his forehead made it shine almost as much as his hair.

The bald torturer pulled away and left Darius to collapse onto the wooden chair beneath him. His tired muscles had little strength or energy left, but still tensed so tightly they cramped.

At least he wasn't in the crossbar… The stench of sweat filled his nostrils, and only now the pain had receded did he notice it again.

"We need to break bones." The bald man walked over to his table of instruments. "You're being too soft."

Darius had heard the man's name days ago but refused to think of him by it. He was nothing but an animal.

Gorgias stepped forward from the wall he'd been leaning against. "Say I'm soft again and I'll show you how *soft* I am."

The bald man didn't look up and just smiled to himself, which only made Gorgias's glare more venomous.

"Get the guards to take him back to his cell," the algus spat.

As calm as if asked to fetch a pot of tea, the man dabbed the splatters of blood from his tunic with a cloth then sauntered to the door behind Darius.

The squeak of the hinges was the only thing that told Darius he'd left.

"I…" Darius paused for breath, his voice now nothing more than a weak rasp. "I can't take much more. Make it stop. Please."

Gorgias's young eyes surveyed him up and down with pity. "You probably feel worse than you look, and that isn't a good thing. Some already think I'm not punishing you enough."

Darius coughed. "And you? Have I been punished enough for killing Hadrian's son, for saving your life, for—?"

"For threatening me?"

Though Darius had hoped for the man's mercy, all he received after was a sombre quietness. Perhaps he had made his situation worse in blackmailing him. "You should do something about that bald man. He's insolent."

"You're one to talk."

"Just kill him." Sometimes the thought of the man's death was all that kept Darius going through the painful, sleepless nights.

Gorgias sucked in his cheeks. "Can't say I'm not tempted."

"Loosen one of my restraints next time I'm to be with him. I may be weak, but I can still break his neck like a twig."

"Unfortunately, I can't just murder people. Humans have rules. Neither would it do your cause good." With a shake of his head, Gorgias strode towards the exit and out of the room.

Darius stared at the stones of the wall opposite, at the instruments hanging that he was all too familiar with.

After a couple of minutes, the latch on the door behind clicked and it eased open.

"Changed your mind about the bald one?" Darius expected to see Gorgias walk back in front of him.

But after the door closed, only silence remained.

"Darius?"

His stomach turned. The voice whispered as soft and familiar as it had been in bed in Dolthea. *Selene?* After so long, Darius wasn't sure he wanted to see her.

A light hand touched his shoulder, far too close to his tender back for comfort. "Get off me!"

The hand retracted, and he heard slow footsteps before seeing Selene approach from his right, her hair flat and baggy eyes heavy.

He turned his head away, rising pain repeating the sting of every lash on his back and causing ferven to heat his throat like heartburn.

"I had to see you," she said, "to get the truth."

Darius tried to make his voice forceful, but again it rasped. "You've already had it, as have my tormenters."

Selene grimaced as she looked his body up and down, at the bruises and scars. "Has my father spoken to you?"

"Only through lashes, fists and knives, but I guess you already knew that."

The offence on her face at the suggestion was as insulting as it was laughable. "Of course not. I've been locked in my quarters, and this is the first chance I've had to sneak out. I didn't want any of this."

Darius roared, the ferven in his throat spewing out. "You're the one that brought me here!"

"You put yourself here. I had no choice."

"You damn well did. Just like I had a choice whether to leave you to die at the hands of the Viridians. Foolishly, I thought spending my nights with you had meant something. I thought you saw me for who I was, not my reputation."

Selene flushed. "It meant something to me, as much as I've tried to purge it from my mind. But why should I believe you? I want to, but I need you to give me a reason to."

If only he had his hands free to wring her neck… "I didn't lie when it mattered. I'm the man that freed a slave, slaughtered your enemies, killed Hadrian's second-in-command—his own son—and saved your life. Well, now it's my life, and you've decided to leave me to the vultures. If you want certainty that I fight for you, then I can't give it to you—no one can. You'll have to take a risk, have faith like the rest of us." And how he regretted placing his trust in her now.

Selene walked over to the table and collapsed onto the chair, eyes spearing his as if it would reveal more truth. The only thing he hadn't told the torturers about was Lex's involvement.

The thought reminded him, where was she? Why wasn't she helping?

"What did you want with Bita?" Selene asked.

Darius frowned, almost ashamed at the reminder that he'd neglected to so much as think about Omid's mother. "How is she? Where is she?"

"She came back with me. She's working in my home."

Darius closed his eyes and took what brief pleasure he could from her words.

"So, why did you free her?" she asked again.

"If you want your money back, you can go to hell."

She huffed, nostrils flared.

"The reason you're confused is because I have no interest in killing her, you, your father or anyone in this city." Well…he hadn't started with such, but in the hours of agony, he admitted to dark thoughts of his captors' city perishing in rakkan fire.

Selene sighed, put a hand on her forehead and grimaced. "I can't sleep, and now that I've seen you it will haunt me all the more."

"I'm sorry you have a conscience."

She paused, eyes full of sorrow but still narrowed in suspicion as if seeing a lying murderer, not a man that had cared for her, shared with her.

But, had he been in her position, he'd be conflicted too. But he'd have done anything to save her, and that was the difference.

"You asked after her," she said softly.

"Who?"

"Bita…the only reason you would is if…" Over the next few seconds her eyes seemed to drain of sorrow and instead fill with a steely resolve. "I believe you," she said. "I'll fix this."

The tension in Darius's muscles increased until cramps set in again as he tried to resist the urge to feel any more hope.

"I won't hold my breath," he said.

She shook her head and walked behind him to the exit, not daring to touch him but giving him a smile.

If it was meant to reassure, it failed.

The door opened and shut, the sound bouncing off the walls.

Darius let his head hang low, dragged in deep breaths, and fought the pain that came with each inhale. Perhaps Selene would at least get him a chance to plead with the Regent, promise himself as a warrior. That's what everyone saw him as, a weapon.

During the hours of agony, he'd begun to question why he let them treat him as such, whether he'd be best making his own decisions and accept the consequences, but he'd rather be a weapon than dead.

Finally, he allowed himself to cling to the slim hope.

38

Brutus – Viridian Camp

Thick mud squelched under Brutus's boots with each step. Crowds nudged him from all sides as they marched towards the open mountainside where the legionnaires had been commanded to amass.

A thin sheet of drizzle gradually drenched Brutus's body, sending rain trickling down his cuirass to soak his greaves. By now, he was used to it, but it still soured his mood further. It beat the scorching sun, but only just. He longed for a clear night to see the stars again.

He'd ducked out of the centuries called to attack Dolthea, but this time his luck had run out. It should have relieved him that the warriors had been ordered to fall back to the mountains, but dread filled him instead.

All centuries had been called. *Thousands ready to march.* The assault on Margalvia wasn't far away.

The whispers had started, but Brutus hadn't been able to find out much. Getting close to Hadrian again had been impossible. All the Warlord was interested in were the captured Numbered, and he'd shut himself away for weeks.

Brutus bumped into the back of a burly rakkan as the hordes ahead halted. His short frame didn't allow him to see very far, but he made out a series of crates through the gaps in the armoured bodies.

It wasn't long before a commander jumped atop them and reduced the crowd to silence with his mere presence.

"Legionnaires!" the commander shouted. "Today, you will learn of the destiny which lies ahead. Silence your tongues for your warlord."

The commander moved aside, opening his hand to a new figure stepping up to the crates.

The bull-horned helmet of the Warlord gave the silhouette of a gigantic frame. Brutus didn't need to crane his neck to see this time.

"My warriors," the Warlord boomed, "I stand before you today to announce the end."

The rakkans looked to one another with frowns as Hadrian surveyed them in silence.

"The end of our exile," Hadrian continued. "For too long we've been driven back to hide behind the walls of Viridia. For too long we've been forced to feed on scraps and remnants, been forced to watch our people starve…our women…our children."

Brutus shared the Viridians' pain, even though he didn't like to admit it, but it didn't excuse their actions by half. The relief after Archimedes's defeat should have led to less desperate measures rather than more savagery.

"My son was taken from me," Hadrian shouted, "much like many of your sons and brothers have been. Well, no more. The spirit of Hadrianus the Great stirs inside me. Today is the day our vengeance begins. Are you prepared?"

The crowd roared and swords bashed into shields in disarray before all falling into a unified, booming drumbeat.

"For many months we've been waiting," the Warlord yelled, "biding our time, preparing the way, until we were ready. Well, I tell you now. We. Are. Ready!"

Drums of metal continued. *This is it.* He was going to announce the attack on Margalvia. If so, Brutus would use the last remaining pigeon with the fancier to confirm the date.

"Watching you now," Hadrian roared, "I see the same hunger that burns in my belly. Hunger to avenge. Hunger to take back the lands and riches stolen, the lands my grandfather won. Hunger to make the humans rue the day they dared cross the might of Hadrian and the Viridian Legion. So, my friends, ready your swords, unleash your roars, and let the humans tremble with fear at the incoming tidal wave about to be unleashed upon them. A new god will declare his dominance over them."

Relief passed over Brutus at the mention of "humans" rather than Margalvia, though he hated himself for it.

"We'll hit them hard and swiftly," Hadrian yelled. "We'll march across the lands. We'll push until our vanguard reaches the walls of Laltos."

The relief that had come over Brutus quickly turned to panic. Perhaps he was naïve, but Lex had almost convinced him that a pact between Margalvia and Laltos was the solution to their problems. Yet now…

"Not for decades," Hadrian continued, "has the Legion taken the fight to the heart of a major human city. They've grown complacent, and we will catch them napping. Fill your bellies and gather your strength. Now we begin our march to glory.

"Have no fear in your hearts," Hadrian shouted above the thunder, raising his fists, "for I will stand amongst you on the frontline. I will lead our armies into war. My swords will taste first blood."

Thousands more fists shot up in the air, and boots pounded the mud underfoot in unison.

Brutus knew all too well Laltos's stone walls wouldn't survive long against such rakkan strength and ferven.

"This is the beginning," Hadrian continued. "One by one their cities will fall. First Laltos, then the rest of the Empire. And when we're done with the humans, we'll lay waste to those Margalvian scum in the south." Hadrian lowered his helmet. "History will tell of my glory, for I will write it."

The crowds erupted in roars as the Warlord breathed deep and soaked in the noise as if it imbued his spirit with ever more strength.

Possibilities ran through Brutus's head. If the Black Legion came to the aid of Laltos, it might be the thing that brought the First Alliance to fruition. *Time's short.* Even if the Black Legion set off today, they'd arrive after the Viridians.

Brutus prayed Margalvia would assist, but the decision wasn't his; it was Varro's.

He turned and pushed his way through the crowd. The dense huddle of bodies was tough to wade through, and his shoving earned him a few elbows to the face, but after what felt like an age, he broke free and far enough away that the cheers were no longer deafening.

His last pigeon wasn't a racer, but it would have to do. After he'd sent the message, he'd get as close to Hadrian as possible.

The time had come for him to put the fate of many over himself. If the chance arose, he'd slay the Viridian Warlord, even if it got him crucified.

39

Darius – Laltos

At first, Darius allowed himself to hope that Selene would aid him. But as the solitary days passed in his cell, hope turned to worry, then to frustration, then to anger.

When the time came to be taken to the room of hell again, he doubted he'd make it through because the weeping plant's tears had long gone from his system. So he reached out to Lyra for her comfort as they took him in and laid him prone on a wooden table in the centre.

Darius squeezed his eyes shut as if it would help him escape the pain from past whippings, where the skin had somewhat healed, but the throbbing hadn't.

He pressed his nose into a knot in the table. Now, a simple touch to his back was unbearable. He just had to hold on until…what?

Even if seconds away from relief, it was too long. *Make it stop. Agathos, Creator, anyone, make it stop.*

At first, he'd told lies during questioning. Then at times he'd told the truth. The beatings and lashing still came, week after week. Despite being held indoors, he'd noticed the temperatures drop as the last of the summer sun made way for the cool autumn. Pain was all he now remembered, and it didn't allow him to fully connect with Lyra without distraction.

The lashings began, first one then another. His damned mind wouldn't pass out from the agony.

He couldn't take it. *It's too much.* With a cry, he flared ferven over his back and heard the whip sizzle to ash in an instant. The three overseeing soldiers dropped back, shielding their eyes and faces from the flames that quickly heated the small chamber.

It was only a few moments before Darius's stamina ran dry, and the ferven fizzled out. He was now too weak to even pray that he hadn't made his situation worse.

He twisted his head to see the frown on the bald man's face that told him all he needed to know.

"Which algus helped you in Laltos?" the man asked.

Darius sighed. *As if they'll listen.* "Nikolaos."

The bald torturer scoffed, then moved to the other side of the room and began inspecting a set of chains protruding from a rack at the top and bottom, opening them up ready to secure Darius's ankles and wrists.

Sweat dripped down Darius's temples. *Where's Gorgias?*

"It's ready." The bald man waved over the soldiers.

One placed a key in one of the shackles around Darius's wrist to unfasten it. His heart pounded. *No.* He wouldn't let this go any further.

"The second you release my hand," Darius said weakly, "I'm going to crush your neck. And don't think you have the strength to restrain me."

The soldier stepped back with sheepish eyes.

323

The bald man regarded Darius, blond eyebrows forked. "You'll only make it worse for yourself in the long run if you don't co-operate."

"I'm not letting you rip me limb from limb."

"It's what you deserve," the bald man said.

Perhaps I do. At this stage he'd given enough named collaborators to keep the executioners busy for months—all false—but they'd seen through his lies. Even if he were to give them a real name, like Lex, it wouldn't change anything.

"Let's proceed." The bald man's face was as flat as a Numbered's, which was curious considering the man obviously wasn't one of them. "Get the stool."

A soldier scurried away while Darius watched him nervously. "Stool?"

"Yes. You'll wish you'd chosen the rack."

Darius suspected the man spoke the truth. He should have kept his mouth shut.

The soldier returned wheeling in a small stool with a pyramid shaped seat pointing upwards.

Darius needed no further clarification. "You'll never get me to sit on that."

The bald man raised an eyebrow. "You think you'll be able to stand once I drive daggers through the back of your knees?"

Darius frowned. "I've changed my mind about the rack."

"Too late."

"Didn't Gorgias want me kept in one piece?"

The bald man smiled for the first time. "Gorgias isn't here. You're mine."

"Perseus!"

The bald man flinched.

"What the hell is this?" Gorgias stormed into the room, his black cloak billowing behind him.

"Algus, I can explain—"

Gorgias strode up to the man and grabbed a fistful of his tunic. "Did I instruct you to interrogate the prisoner without me? And why aren't you using the whip?"

"He burned it. We had to change."

"Then you should have come to me. Did I authorise any other methods?"

"No, but I was given orders—"

"The only orders you should worry about are my own." Gorgias's eyes bulged. "Get out of here, all of you, before I have you all flogged!"

The soldiers exited so fast they could have passed for algus, followed closely behind by the released bald man.

Gorgias sighed as the door banged shut. "What did you say?"

"Water," Darius rasped.

Gorgias fetched a cup with a roll of his eyes and reluctantly held it to Darius's mouth. He gulped it down as best he could while lying prone.

"Don't worry," Darius croaked when he was finished. "Your secret's safe, though not for much longer had I been sat down on that."

Gorgias kicked the stool across the room and out of sight. "The Regent's orders are to keep you in one piece, despite the algus and people wanting to crucify you. Who knows what he's planning…"

It brought little comfort to hear of the Regent's oversight. Only Selene or Lex would aid him, the latter only a slim hope who Darius was yet to greet.

Surely, she knew he was chained up here by now. Why hadn't she come? Even Selene had managed a visit.

"I take it the Regent still refuses to see me," Darius said.

325

Gorgias stared down at him with hard eyes. "Yes… I think the time has come to start considering how you want to die."

"What?" This wasn't what Darius needed to hear. It took all his strength not to submit to death as it was.

"The best I can do is ease your suffering, a reckless accident resulting in your untimely demise."

Shaking his head, Darius looked around the room at the various sharp and blunt objects, none of which he preferred. He wasn't giving up that easily. "That's not good enough."

The algus approached him and crouched to meet him eye to eye. "I'm the only aide you have left. All those you befriended before have either left the city or have shut themselves away."

"What's that supposed to mean?"

"The only ones you were in good standing with before, as far as I've been able to ascertain, were Selene and Lex. Selene has made pleas to the Regent, but Theodoros found out she came to see you. She's been taken in chains from the city. As for Lex…she couldn't care less what happened to you."

A chilly draught suddenly swept through the room. Selene couldn't be gone… And if Lex knew he was here, why didn't she help him? Darius strained to keep his face flat and emotionless at the mention of her.

"If you're all I've got, then I guess I'm doomed." Darius willed Gorgias to say more, and not just because it gave his agonised back a respite.

"You'd do well to stay on my good side, or I may join Lex in leaving Laltos altogether."

Darius failed to prevent a gasp escape him. Why had Lex left? If she was trying to help him, surely, she'd make contact and let him know. But who would she go to for aid? Margalvia was too far away to go there and back with a force large enough to help.

"Don't worry." Gorgias smiled weakly. "I'm not planning to leave yet. But keep pushing me and…"

Darius paid no more attention to Gorgias's words. How could Lex abandon him? The pain of Selene's rejection was great, but at least part of him understood it. He'd lied. When it came to Lex, his one true ally since before he remembered, the thought she'd left him to die not only made him numb, but like…he couldn't even identify the feeling.

What's the point? Everyone he cared for either died or suffered. Maybe he was better off dead. Lex seemed to think so. He'd imagined nothing could be worse than watching Lyra's brush with death, but this was damn close.

"Nothing to say?" Gorgias asked with a raised brow.

"I…" No words came to his mind, not even to persuade the algus to help him. Suddenly everything was so…hopeless. "I…" *Lyra, I'm sorry. I tried.*

Gorgias stood back up and walked across the room. He ran his eyes over the various instruments hanging on the wall. "I think if I were in your position, I'd prefer my back broken. I can make it appear you fell down the stairs to your cell."

A broken back suddenly sounded appealing, a way to stop the pain lancing it, and to end the hopelessness of his situation. But it wasn't the way a warrior should meet his end.

He couldn't believe he was considering it, that it had come to this, but all escape roads now seemed out of reach.

"No," Darius whispered.

"Finally found your tongue, have you?"

"I want to die as a warrior. Do it with a sword."

"I can arrange that."

"Through the heart." It seemed the most apt way to die, and the way he felt, it couldn't come soon enough. "Do it before sunrise tomorrow when they bring me here again."

Gorgias nodded. "Very well."

40

Varro – Margalvia

Varro shifted the roll of parchment a few inches on the table. The coastal lines on the map met up with those on another sheet to form a continuous land mass. As he slid it, a parchment on the right fell out of line. He moved his hand over and shifted that too, but then one marked city disappeared underneath the one he touched.

He cursed. "More light!" The commanders' meeting room had only a few lamps, but they lit the room with an orange hue which bounced from the clouds of smoke puffing from the mouths of the six commanders huddled together.

It wasn't lack of light that led to Varro's frustration, it was the countless moving pieces strewn across the stone table that never seemed to line up with one another. Each commander sat around wore dark linen clothes, and the only weapon in the room was the gladius at Varro's side.

"Maybe we should leave off Toria." Julius stood and placed his meaty hands on a few pieces. "It's falling from the edge of the table."

Varro only wished he could stop thinking of the King's capital. "No. I want to span all the way from Viridia to Toria. Sort it out." He sat as the others began arranging the individual maps.

Underneath the parchments, the table's carved map of Margalvia and the surrounding mountains lay hidden. Its borders didn't stretch far enough for the conflict now ensuing. When the first warlords had engraved it, they'd never envisaged being embroiled in multiple wars stretching far across the land. *How fortunate they were.*

Varro locked his fingers together and watched as the pieces slowly came together, Laltos in the middle, Margalvia at the bottom, then to Laltos's left and right were Viridia and Toria. In between the four were roads, forests and mountains—obstacles that would affect the speed of an army's march.

Varro stiffened. "Mark on the map where Brutus said the Viridian Legion is amassed."

A commander walked forward, picked up some triangular stones and placed them near the mountains east of Viridia, almost a third of the way to Laltos.

Julius sat closest to the marks and let out a low murmur. "They could almost be in Laltos by now."

A few of the other commanders grunted in disagreement, but Varro remained expressionless. Between the markers and Laltos were thick forests, hills and other towns. In Hadrian's situation, Varro wouldn't rush—but Hadrian wasn't him.

"Surely we'd have heard something from Lex if so," Iuba said, the youngest at only seventy years old, yet often the wisest at Varro's table.

The fastest pigeon they had was already on its way to Laltos, but was now their chance to prove to Regent Theodoros whose side Margalvia was on?

Varro stared at the map, at the large dot reading Laltos that would put the Black Legion too far away from Margalvia to defend it, away from the roads to the King's capital that so worried Varro.

"If we were to assist Laltos, Hadrian's ahead of us," the Warlord said, "and without Dolthea's grain, he won't besiege. He'll assault. Time's short."

"We could march double time," Iuba said. "Use the Royal Roads and travel during the daylight hours as well. Hadrian won't."

"That'll be gruelling," Julius said. "Only the hardened warriors will make it, and we might meet other resistance."

The hush in the room and stink of old smoke only clouded Varro's mind further. "Carry on. Talk. All of you."

Julius thrust his arm forward so quickly it was like he'd been waiting for his moment. He picked up a black marker then slammed it down on the Urukan Mine. "Take it. The Viridians can't hold it while they're off fighting Laltos."

That had been Varro's first thought. He and Julius had fought together for almost a century, and the man was one of the few rakkans he would die for, but often the commander just echoed his thoughts and shed no fresh light.

"It's the obvious move," Varro said. "Predictable."

"Hadrian is a gambler," Iuba added. "He may think it possible but—if you don't mind my saying, Warlord—perhaps he's betting on your continued hesitation."

Varro stiffened, ensuring his face didn't tell of the self-doubt the commander's criticism had stirred.

"Hadrian underestimates me." Varro stared at each of the commanders and checked for any hint of scepticism in their eyes. Thankfully, he found none. "I'm patient, not hesitant. Our first strike will be sudden and devastating."

Julius cleared his throat. "Does that mean we'll focus all our efforts on Hadrian instead of the King?"

"It does." Worrying had achieved nothing so far.

"So, do we go for the mine, or assist Laltos?"

All eyes locked on Varro, a fervour in them at the thought of retaliation. He too hungered to stand on the battlefield again and focus on the moment, rather than the ones under his stewardship. Taking the mine was the most obvious choice, not gambling on an alliance with Laltos. That's what a good leader would choose.

41

Darius – Laltos

Darius ran his hand against a rough groove on the floor of his cell, where the kuraminium plates had been fused together. The cold metal stole the warmth from his hands, but all he thought of was the dark earth that lay beneath. Would he be fortunate enough to be buried within it, or would his body be hung in front of the crowds of Laltos, and left for crows to feast upon?

In the past, he'd tried his best to recover during the periods in which they released him from the crossbar, ensuring he didn't suffocate prematurely. But now he hadn't even the will to sleep, and it wasn't because he'd soon be dead—he'd experienced worse than death in the last few weeks—rather it was because he had no idea what would happen to Lyra after he was gone.

He reached out to her in his mind but pulled back when an almost overwhelming fear in her gripped him. She knew his pain, his state of mind. *Poor girl.*

The more he reflected on his friends and allies, the more he realised only Lyra had stood by him no matter what. The others always seemed to want him for something—his power, his knowledge, his ability to blend in with humans—but not Lyra. She accepted him in strength and weakness. He'd dared to believe Selene had looked at him in the same way, but still felt the marks of chains around his wrists that she'd done nothing to remove.

During the long hours of being trapped in this cell, hurt had turned to anger in his belly. How could she do this to him? How could *Gorgias* have ended up the only one aiding him, of all people?

All the suffering on him and Lyra of late was because he'd simply obeyed the wishes of others, first Lex, then Varro and the rakkans. They saw him only as a warrior, but he began to wonder whether he needed to be his own man. *Too late.*

Following orders may have been the right thing, but he saw the mistakes leaders made, no matter how much he wished they were infallible.

His thoughts drifted to Lex. Maybe her leaving was the only sensible thing to do—if she was in danger, he would have insisted on it anyway—but what hurt most was that she hadn't even said goodbye.

Would Darius see Omid or Amid in the afterlife? Was there even an afterlife? Many had spoken of it, but he'd never decided whether to feel anticipation or terror at the thought. If ultimate justice existed, Darius the Dreaded was in trouble.

At the far side of his cell lay the rolled-up parchment Brutus had given him. Gorgias had brought it to him days ago, but now, before he died, Darius was tired of the wisdom of a Creator that hadn't responded to his desperate pleas for help. The story of Trogus and Arria and their powerful weapons would remain unknown to him.

He was about to ease his body onto the floor to give his tired muscles rest when a loud thump sounded in the corridor.

He frowned as he heard a key turning in the lock to his cell. Was it morning already? The hours must have flown because he swore it was still the night.

Guess it's time to die. It was surprising and depressing how little fear the thought elicited in him.

He clambered to his feet stiffly, every movement paining his back and limbs that cried out for respite. Facing the entry, he hoped to see Gorgias wielding a sharp blade.

As the door opened, Darius winced at the lamplight bursting through. He waited for his rakkan eyes to adjust and bring the figure standing in front of him into focus.

A beautiful woman stood with two swords in hand.

Darius blinked, convinced his weakened mind had been driven to hallucination. "Selene?"

"Can you run?" She stepped into the cell. Her tired eyes scanned up and down his body as the dimples in her cheeks deepened with a grimace.

"I can barely walk," Darius said. Weeks with little movement did that to someone. "I thought you'd left Laltos."

"No. I've been confined to a room."

"Gorgias said—"

"You believe everything Gorgias says?" She flared algor in her eyes to get a better look at him and seemed to instantly regret it. Judging by the pain he was in, the sight of his battered body would have made even the hardest gladiators wince.

"There's only one way," she said. "My father's mind is elsewhere, so I'm doing the most foolish thing I've ever done. We're breaking out."

A laugh almost escaped him. Weeks ago, these words were all he wanted to hear from her. Now they were hollow. "Too late."

The lack of reaction to his words told him she knew it was true. "I moved as quickly as I could. Do you know how long it's taken me to plan this escape? It isn't easy from inside a room, bribing half the guards in the city, getting most of the algus out of the way on the same night. We're doing this. I'll carry you if I have to." She stepped closer until their noses touched and her warm breath touched his lips.

Even after weeks of pain, he couldn't help but imagine kissing her.

Stop it. You should hate her. "Really?" he said.

"Yes, because I love you," she whispered.

Darius sighed, the words no one had ever uttered to him brought only confusion to his exhausted mind. "I did…I don't know what I feel now. In the state I'm in, I only want death, not running."

Selene thrust a sword flat to his chest with the hilt pressing against what was left of the muscle. "Then die fighting."

As he took the leather hilt, the sensation of a sword in hand awakened him.

Before he could react, Selene ran her hand across the back of his head and pulled him into a kiss which he didn't return but didn't resist either. Those soft lips were just as warm and inviting as they had been weeks ago. His own probably tasted of congealed blood.

As they parted, she gazed deep into his eyes without a trace of the fear and upset he'd seen on her in the torture room.

"I'll go with you to the end," she whispered. Blinking out the algor shining from her eyes, she backed up to the door.

"Here." She tossed a vial to him. "Take some tears and fight through the pain."

Darius didn't hesitate in dropping a couple of the black tears onto his tongue, never so glad for the vile, bitter taste. *Lyra, I'll fight to the end to get back to you.*

Selene unhooked the black cloak from her neck and draped it over his back. The fabric felt like steel grating against his lashed skin, and he muffled a yell of pain into a grunt. "Couldn't you have chosen something softer? Even sackcloth would be better."

"I'm sorry but you're too conspicuous without it." Pulling the hood over his head, she tried to give him another kiss, but he turned away.

"This doesn't make us even," he said. "Not even close."

"I don't care about getting even. I just want you safe." She tossed him a pair of grey boots, which he slipped on, thankfully lined with wool and a lot more comfortable than the cloak.

"So, what's the plan?" he asked.

"My father has an escape passageway that leads out of the city. I've planned a route to the entrance to the palace. From there we play by ear because the guards can't be bribed. You'll need a new name to go by."

Darius pulled the cloak around him, the warmth and protection so unfamiliar it was as if he'd never worn clothes before. He'd forgotten what it was like to not feel every movement of the air on his sensitive rakkan skin, to not feel icy stone underfoot.

"This cloak is only fit for a slave," he said, "so the name should fit. Call me Amid." Just saying his brother's name made gushing crimson fill his mind. He shook off the memory and the urge to heave.

"Alright, Amid. Agathos be with us." She turned and exited the cell as Darius took a few deep breaths. The cuts and grazes on his back had finally grown accustomed to the touch of fabric when numbness from the tears began to set in. Still, this would hurt like hell.

Taking the first few steps out of his cell, he summoned the little energy he had left to come to the surface.

Whatever happened, he'd never let them bring him back to this cell alive.

42

Darius – Laltos

Darius's feet hit an unconscious guard as he left the cell. The bleeding man forced him to avert his eyes. Apparently not all guards could be bribed.

At the sight of the incapacitated man, Darius was a little surprised. Selene was committed.

She waited for him at the base of the staircase. While approaching, Darius ran his eyes up her athletic frame, which only weeks ago had been wrapped around him, yet now brought a confused mix of emotion to the surface—longing and betrayal. It took more energy to focus his mind than to move his pained limbs.

He held his sword out ready.

"I'm glad you can walk," she said.

"Tears doing their job."

"Can you fight?"

"My back is on fire, only three of my ribs aren't cracked, and my knees could buckle at any moment. But hell, that just gives them all a fighting chance."

She grinned, like she admired his valour. Little did she know that a few minutes ago he'd been ready to crawl into his own grave.

Setting off up the spiral staircase, she set a brisk pace that had him uttering curses with every step. The corridors at ground level were as dark as the night outside. Passages stretched off in every direction, seemingly endless and wide. It was less than ideal for sneaking, but Selene seemed to have ensured no guards were around. In the weak blue light of her algor, the coloured marble making up the walls and columns glowed odd shades of brown and purple.

Fresh air greeted his nostrils as they crept through the halls, a foreign smell now that he'd grown accustomed to sweat and blood.

"We'll take the back exit," Selene said, her own sword drawn, and algor-coated eyes narrowed and focused.

They crept down one of the corridors, its floor and interior unhelpfully magnifying the pad of every footstep. Countless doors went by that probably led to meeting rooms, courtrooms—who knew—but all were thankfully bolted shut with only darkness lurking behind.

As they neared a corner leading to the rear side, Darius looked back to check no one was watching from behind. *All clear.*

He turned back to see Selene's blade burst with a brilliant blue flash. It stabbed towards a man that had just rounded the corner.

The man ducked as the sword swept overhead, and suddenly Gorgias's shocked face was illuminated, his ever-preened hair now dishevelled.

Darius lunged forward before a thought crossed his mind, his fighting instincts not dampened one bit. His ribs thanked him for the rapid movement while Selene slashed again at the now hunched algus.

Darius thrust his sword between Selene's blade and Gorgias's neck. Sparks of algor sprayed as the swords clashed.

With a scowl at Darius, she stepped back while Gorgias scurried backwards across the floor until his back hit the wall. His dark eyes searched underneath Darius's hood.

"What're you doing?" Selene asked.

"I reckon I owe him." Darius let his eyes glow with ferven.

Gorgias's face first lifted in apprehension before his black eyebrows forked.

"Owe him for what?" Selene asked.

"I don't know, helping me when everyone else had deserted me?" This time she received his hateful ferven stare.

"You're helping him escape?" Gorgias turned his gaze to her.

"Be grateful," Darius said. "If I'm free, then your secret's safe."

Selene's face paled as Gorgias's nostrils flared. "Yes, I know you told him. You're lucky I didn't gut you."

Darius stepped forwards and pushed the point of his sword into the algus's throat. "Do you *want* us to kill you?"

Gorgias's lip trembled, but he lifted his chin proudly. "No."

Withdrawing his weapon, Darius walked onwards to the corner and checked how much farther they had to go. He was relieved to see the broad double doors at the end of the passage.

Selene still eyed Gorgias, sword ready.

As far as Darius was concerned, he'd paid his debt to the man in saving him once. Anything Selene wanted to do next was fair game, as long as it was swift.

"Sound the bells and I'll make sure they know you've been aiding our captive," Selene said.

Gorgias's eyes dropped. Darius's word wouldn't be believed, but the Regent's daughter would be.

"Leave now and I'll imagine I never saw you," Gorgias said. "Beware the side street on the east side. They called extra guards to a disturbance."

Darius waited for Selene to pass then followed her towards the exit.

While they left, Gorgias hobbled to his feet and ran away—as courageous as ever.

When they neared the door, Darius slipped his sword inside the cloak and beside his leg. "Would be easier if I had a belt to hold this thing."

"You'll have to make do." She eased the door open and peered out.

A chilly draught swept inside Darius's cloak, and he pulled it tighter around him, gooseflesh appearing on his arms. Weeks of meagre scraps for food had left him thin and chilly even on an autumn night. He'd have to hope he had enough muscle left to swing a sword more than a couple of times.

Selene stepped outside, and he followed her into the narrow space between the buildings, tall walls of stone on each side. He kept his head low and left enough distance trailing her that a slave would to his mistress.

They reached the end of the walkway and stepped out onto a main road. Darius was relieved only a few soldiers appeared to be about. Oil lamps hung in the street but left plenty of shadow, which they used to take cover in as they passed, the naked flames too weak to create more than small light patches in the enveloping darkness.

After a few minutes undisturbed walking, the thin white towers from the palace loomed ahead. Up to the residence, Darius had barely noticed the incline before, but now he felt every inch of it in his tired legs.

The farther they made it towards the palace, the more he allowed his hopes to build. What if he really escaped the city? He wasn't sure whether he'd continue with Selene or go back to Margalvia, whether he could forgive and forget.

"How do we get into the passageway?" he asked.

"There's only one way. The main gate to the palace then down to the cellars."

Less than ideal, but not surprising given the palace's outer walls would be the last line of defence in a siege.

A few wandering guards passed them in the street but paid no attention when they saw Selene's belt buckle.

The pair rounded a corner and suddenly the palace gates stood ahead, a sheer white stone wall with a rounded hole at the centre barred with thick iron. At least ten soldiers in glinting helmets walked in a group from the entrance, with two in algus tunics at the rear.

One couldn't have been older than fifteen, and he was thin as a rake—probably a former slave. The other was a brown-haired man, handsome some might say, who seemed lost in thought, counting the seconds until sunrise by tapping his finger as they sauntered.

Under normal circumstances two algus wouldn't give Darius a fleeting worry, but now…

Selene glanced around. With only one street leading up the hill, it wasn't like they had options. She continued her strides towards the entrance as the soldiers passed by on the other side of the street.

Darius hung back, ensuring his face remained hidden, without looking too much like an escaped prisoner trying to conceal himself.

The wandering eyes of the youngest algus swept to Selene, who flicked her hair to cover her face.

But the thin boy frowned at her. "Algus Selene?"

Darius cursed under his breath and swore Selene did the same, though she masked it well.

"Yes?" she barked while continuing her strides.

The group of soldiers stopped and turned to look.

"Aren't you supposed to be in your chambers?" the boy asked.

The handsome algus glanced at them with a wince. "Don't harass the woman, lad." He put on a smile and straightened his shoulder-length hair. "Algus Selene, how are you?"

She finally halted, took a second to transform her face from frosty to warm before turning to the man. "I'm in a bit of a hurry, if you must know."

"Fair enough." The algus's smile continued for a few seconds before it weakened. "But he does have a point. Why are you outside and who is your companion?"

Darius tightened his grip on the sword resting flat against his leg.

"My slave." Selene's voice was sharp. "My father allowed me into the lower city on business."

The young algus raised an eyebrow. "So late?"

Selene huffed. "Don't test my patience, boy."

"Now, now," the older algus said with raised hands as he moved closer. "I think it best we see you back to the palace and ensure everything is as it should be."

Selene scowled and placed her body between Darius and the group of men. "I'm as insulted as if you intended to take me there in chains."

Darius readied his sword underneath the cloak. The best he could do was to block should any of the soldiers try to take a swing.

He watched them all, trying to recall whether any of them were the ones that had paid him visits in the night.

"Then I must insist." The algus's cynical eyes narrowed in on Darius while his hands moved ever closer to the sword at his waist. "Who's the slave?"

The boy algus frowned and backed up a step, seeming to sense the sour turn the encounter had taken. If only Darius had energy...

A few of the soldiers looked to their algus leader nervously, torn over who held the authority here.

Darius was damned if he knew, but every minute that passed sapped a little more energy from his dwindling supply.

"Leave me be." Algor flared in Selene's eyes, and Darius took a step to the side, aware that the six soldiers' eyes were fixed on him. He pulled the cloak tighter around him.

"Enough," the older algus said. "Selene, you're coming with us." He turned to his soldiers. "Seize the slave."

One soldier marched forward and reached out a hand to grab Darius's shoulder.

Instinct took over, and he moved aside, catching hold of the man's outstretched arm. As soon as he'd done it, he cursed and retracted his hand. But too late. They'd seen his bloody and bruised wrists.

"What is this?" the algus barked at Selene.

The moment Selene's hand went for her sword, Darius whipped his cloak apart and thrust his weapon from hiding. Blue light burst into life as he wreathed it in algor before slashing through the nearest soldier's breast, as easy as cutting through a weed.

Two bright bursts of blue appeared to his side as Selene clashed with the algus.

Before Darius caught a proper sight, the soldiers rushed towards him, shouts ringing out into the night. *Hell.* They'd carry far.

One took a swing at his head, but he ducked just in time. The fabric of his cloak grated across his flayed back, causing him to cry out. *Damn it.* He flared ferven on his shoulders until the cloak caught fire and incinerated around him.

Within seconds, only ashes remained, leaving him free to move, but also leaving its withered, battered inhabitant for all eyes to see.

The soldiers paused at the sight for a second before leaping forward.

Darius tried to roll away, but he stumbled to one knee. The algor ebbed into nothing as his energy dwindled, until even consciousness seemed a struggle to cling to.

The glint of metal caught his eye just in time to bring his sword to parry a blow from a soldier as another grabbed him by the neck from behind.

A blunt blow to his stomach forced the wind from his lungs, and he collapsed to the cobbles, a forearm still crushing his windpipe.

Bells rang in his ears, whether real or from the countless blows to his head, he couldn't discern. All it would take was conjuring ferven, or algor, to stop the hands restraining him, but his last energy was spent.

Ringing bells continued, and the shouts increased. Darkness encompassed his vision. His mind faded in and out of black as his chokes failed to bring in air.

Selene swung her sword side to side, blocking blows from three algus. The young boy lay clutching a bleeding arm at the side of the road, and his handsome friend was still locked in combat, a vicious grimace on his face.

The arm around Darius's neck eased a fraction, allowing him thin breaths as they likely realised he'd ceased resisting.

Selene's cry was the last thing to hit his ears before a boot filled his vision and all went dark.

43

Darius – Laltos

Darius awoke being dragged along the stone street with two men supporting him under his arms. The pounding in his head was barely noticeable above the searing pain from the arms that clung to his flogged back. It took all his willpower not to yell and alert the men that he was awake.

Both soldiers were without helmets and had thick beards. Their hoarse breaths carried the smell of ale—likely the pair were embroiled from a nearby drinking house. What Darius wouldn't give for a gallon of firewater right now.

Up ahead, the palace stood in plain view, illuminated in parts by lamplight through the shutters, a white dome and white towers stretching and vanishing into the night's sky. He struggled to understand why they'd taken him into the palace grounds rather than the prison. Whatever the reason, it couldn't be good.

Muttering voices behind him were too quiet to discern anything but odd words.

"…choice…wants them…"

Darius closed his eyes and searched for any fathomable way out of this hell. Every muscle in his body begged him to give in and die, but he refused. He owed it to Lyra to fight to his dying breath.

"The ball and chain's here," someone called behind.

A horde of footsteps approached, followed by a thud that shook the ground.

Darius dared open his eyes to glimpse what lay in stock for him.

An algus peered at him, and the man's wrinkled face contorted in a grimace. "He's awake!"

The two carrying him dropped him at once. His elbows met the hard ground and saved his face with only an inch to spare. A trickle of blood dripped from the tip of his nose, staining the clean stones.

Something snapped onto his ankle, and the cold touch soon told him it was a kuraminium shackle. The soldiers and algus around all moved back a few steps, as if they might catch an infectious disease from him. Given his stench, he didn't blame them.

"Get up!" the wrinkled algus shouted.

Darius tried to push himself up, but his arms trembled under the weight.

"He's too weak," someone said.

"Maybe it's a ruse." The wrinkled algus narrowed his beady eyes and blew his grey fringe from his view.

Darius looked him in the eye, pleading for the man to find a shred of humanity and help him up. To his shock, the man's expression softened.

"Then again, he's been beaten enough over the last few weeks."

"Look how thin his legs are…"

Maybe Darius should have welcomed their understanding, but instead all he felt was disgust at himself. He'd never die prostrated like this.

Darius brought his knee under him and rolled back into a half crouched, half seated position. The chains dug into his ankle, and he followed them back to a kuraminium ball resting on a cracked cobblestone. It wasn't large, but it didn't need to be.

"I don't need your stares," he growled. "If you're going to execute me, get on with it."

"Execute?" The wrinkled algus smirked. "The Regent wants to see you personally, to discover how you corrupted his daughter."

That sounded like a conversation worth avoiding.

A few of the soldiers behind the algus shuffled around and from amongst them emerged Gorgias, his face a shade paler than usual. Darius stared for a few seconds before averting his gaze, not wanting to highlight the one who could be his last remaining hope.

"Just kill me." Darius looked at the old algus but knew Gorgias would understand it was him he spoke to. Hopefully, Lyra would forgive him.

"In time." The old algus waved at a few soldiers to help Darius up, but no one moved. "Hurry, or you'll end up alongside him!"

A dozen soldiers moved towards him from all sides, some with swords, others with crossbows loaded and aimed. Two grabbed his arms and helped him to his feet, while the rest took hold of the chain attached to his ankle and hauled the metal ball along.

Once moving again, Darius scanned his surroundings, but there was no sight of Selene. He wasn't sure whether to be relieved or concerned.

The large wooden doors of the palace stood in a gap between the outer pillars and were at least three times as tall as they needed to be. Slaves pushed them open as the soldiers bustled him inside.

White flagstones were replaced by hard marble under Darius's feet. Just as with everything in Laltos, the polished, clean exterior told nothing of the horrors committed within.

They continued thrusting him through the hallways, every guard stationed there turning to him with a grimace. Eventually, Darius and the mob entered a hall at the centre of the palace.

Tall cylindrical pillars spread throughout the vast circular space, along with a series of statues of sword-wielding women guarding the edges of the room, like a dozen goddesses convened to witness the final judgement. Their faces were stern yet worn, with marks that betrayed their age. *At least my blood will spoil these pretentious halls.*

At the far side, covered overhead with a royal blue tapestry, was a throne on which sat a man who Darius guessed was Lex's father, every bit as stern-faced as his daughter.

The Regent's green eyes were livid and unblinking as they burned into Darius. His white beard and hair fell over a blue scarf that matched the fine linen overhead, and the golden crown on his head glinted in the lamplight. To the Regent's right, a huge brown bear stood on all fours with its black eyes trained on Darius.

Dragging his feet, Darius focused on a woman that stood to the side, wrists chained together and head drooped with auburn hair spilling across her shoulders. Axe-wielding soldiers flanked her on each side; or were they executioners?

Despite the night's chills, Darius's brow was covered with sweat.

Selene lifted her head and he cursed. Blood dripped from her lips and chin from a crooked nose, and black bruising ringed her left eye.

But as he and the accompanying soldiers approached, she met his gaze and smiled. It gave him more strength than a week's rest would have.

The group came to a halt a few yards short of the throne, and the soldiers left him on his feet before backing away to a safe distance, just out of reach should he take a lunge at them.

The iron heads of their crossbow bolts still pointed at him, dozens in the room with algus and more.

"Regent Theodoros, I presume." Darius bowed.

The Regent scrunched his nose. "You presume correctly."

Darius stayed mute. He had to choose his words carefully, but there was a slim hope. Lex must have seen a possibility for her father to trust a rakkan.

Theodoros cleared his throat. "What have you to say for yourself?"

Hanging his head, Darius prayed for wise words. "I regret we had to meet under these circumstances. This wasn't how it was meant to be."

"What was the plan? Perhaps you'd prefer to see me asleep in my quarters to cut my throat."

"No, Regent. My task was not to kill you. It was to—"

"Poison my daughter's mind? Turn her against me?"

At least the Regent still referred to Selene as his daughter.

"I'm not against you, Father," Selene said.

The soldier to her left raised his hand to smack her.

The bear growled.

"Don't you dare strike her again." Theodoros shifted his furious gaze to the soldier. "I won't forgive you for striking a member of my family a second time."

Darius breathed deeply, fell to one knee, and panted; the little strength he'd reserved was spent. Only when he looked up did he realise the Regent was frowning deeply.

"It's true," Darius croaked. "She isn't against you. Neither am I."

"Then why has she injured two of the city's algus and even more of my hoplites?"

Damn. That didn't look good. "Why did she deliver me here to be tortured?"

Theodoros tapped his fingers against the thick armrests of the throne while allowing his eyes to scan Darius's feeble frame. Darius swore he saw a trace of pity in those eyes.

"Let's return to why you came here," the Regent said.

"Let's." Slightly recovered, Darius rose to his feet once again. "I was here to help you fight the Viridian Legion, to kill Hadrian or his second-in-command."

"Yes, so I've heard, and of your supposed alliance with Margalvia. But I don't see why I should believe you."

"Because no other reason for my actions makes sense."

Theodoros ran a hand slowly through his beard. "I at least have witnesses to you saving Dolthea. But why save Selene?"

Darius gazed at her, at the broken nose that made him seethe at the one who did it, at the curls he remembered falling across his face as they kissed. What else could he do but tell the truth? "Because I cared for her."

A few of the algus behind scoffed, reminding Darius that they were still there. For a moment he'd imagined this as a private audience. Others began chuckling amongst themselves.

Selene closed her eyes, a tear running down her cheek.

"Let's say I'm of a charitable mood and I believe you," the Regent said, which silenced the snickering. "It does nothing to excuse her betrayal of this city, or your status as Laltos's enemy."

Darius scoffed again. "Regent, if I were your enemy, my sword would have pierced your heart long ago."

Jeers rang behind him and echoed from the tall room. Weapons screeched as they were drawn from sheaths, ready to cut into his flesh.

He braced for the strikes across a back now accustomed to them, but Theodoros raised a hand before they whipped themselves into a frenzy.

As the shouts subdued to whispers, Darius couldn't help but marvel at a man that quelled a crowd with only a raise of the hand. In Margalvia, one only quieted men with a show of physical dominance.

"It's unwise to threaten me," the Regent said.

"It was not a threat, merely a statement of fact. This city is easier to get inside than a drunken whore. And your algus would never stand a chance against me."

"Yet here you are in chains."

"I'm not here through lack of strength, but for the lapse in judgement of trusting another." Darius bowed his head and sighed.

"That I can believe." Theodoros's glare slightly calmed of the rage it had first bore. "So, answer me this: why would Margalvia help Laltos against Viridia?"

Darius swallowed, certain Lex would be much better placed to make an argument. "They attacked us, and we have no more love for them than we have for the King. What sense is there in fighting them alone?"

Whispers circled him like a creeping ghoul, but the Regent's steely gaze didn't waver.

"Why would we ally with you?" Theodoros asked. "We've been at war with your race for hundreds of years."

"You've been at war with Viridia."

"As far as I'm concerned, Margalvia and Viridia are the same. History tells us such."

"Lies." Darius spat. "I'd sooner die than be associated with that city."

After a pause, Theodoros scratched his brow. "And what was to be the result of this alliance?"

"To destroy the Viridian Legion once and for all and see its warlord's head on a spike." Darius couldn't contain the ferven raging in his eyes at the mere thought of Hadrian.

"Darius slaughtered an entire town of legionnaires," Selene said, with a glance at the guard to her side as if expecting a strike. But the soldier didn't move, and she continued. "He didn't even know I was watching."

Theodoros's face was flat and unreadable. The fact he pondered gave Darius a slither of hope that the Regent wasn't completely averse to the idea Darius was telling the truth; surely, he would have balked or laughed if not. Even the Regent's escort gave away nothing, the only movement coming from the fur on its expanding chest as the beast breathed.

If only Lyra were here to offer Darius some comfort. How he longed to run his hands down her neck one last time.

"You put yourself in a lot of danger," Theodoros uttered. "Seems a colossal risk for you alone to bear."

Unfortunately, Darius had only thought about it once it was too late. "I'm a warrior, not a leader. I follow orders. I don't make them."

"I admire loyalty," Theodoros said. "For that I commend you. In another life, I may have even come to like you, Darius."

The words rang hollow, as Darius wasn't so much a fool to be oblivious to the impending "but."

The Regent sighed. "But what choice do I have when the most dangerous assassin in the Empire infiltrates my city?"

"People always have a choice, Father," Selene said. "They just often lack the courage to admit it."

A wistful smile broke on Theodoros's lips but soon faded, much like Darius's hopes. "Very well. My choice is to punish the half-rakkan that has killed so many of our kind."

There was nothing left for Darius to do except beg. His stomach turned at the mere thought, but Lyra meant more to him than his pride.

"It wasn't me that massacred the algus," Darius said. "Archimedes made me a different man from the one I was."

Laughs murmured behind him, as if they recognised he was virtually on his knees. Who knew, in a few seconds maybe it wouldn't just be virtual? He had little to offer, only one thing which everyone seemed to desire—himself. If that's what they all saw in him, then why not play on it?

"Let me fight for *you*," Darius said. "Isn't that why you kept me in one piece? I'll obey your orders. I'll see the Viridian Legion destroyed and its warlord lying dead at my feet. I'll be yours to command."

The chuckles continued, but Darius saw the flicker in Theodoros's eye as soon as he'd uttered the words. It was the same look they all had; they all wanted to use him as a tool in their war games.

Theodoros waved over a couple of the older algus watching, and they moved to join him. The elderly group fell into a hushed conversation, leaving Darius to watch the back of their grey heads. A ruler needed their advisors, but judging by the disgust in the expressions of the algus, Darius would rather the Regent decided on his own.

After what felt like an eternity of back and forth, Theodoros finally dismissed his confidantes and regarded Darius once more. "It's a tempting offer, but—"

"You don't trust me…"

"There's nothing you can say, Darius. You're a rakkan. How can you expect me to believe you'd keep your word?"

Darius clenched his fists. "A rakkan's word is worth no less than a human's."

"I don't trust your human half either, if you must know."

If what Darius had done so far didn't convince Theodoros, there was nothing more that would.

Darius tugged at his chains, the clank ringing in his ears, as the Regent waved to one soldier by Selene.

The man stepped forward, fist tight on his weapon.

"Father, you shouldn't do this!" Selene shouted. "He's on our side."

"Darius has shown he's far too dangerous to contain." A flicker of regret came over the Regent's expression. "The threat ends here."

Every instinct told Darius to fight, but his tired muscles longed for surrender. Why should he resist? This was what he'd prayed for in his metal coffin of a cell. *At least I'm not being crucified.*

"If I don't resist," Darius said, "will you return my body to Margalvia?" All he wanted now was to return to Lyra, even if it was only his body. He'd lie in rest in the calm, misty mountains.

"You can't give up!" Selene shouted.

A few grumbles emanated from the crowd, but the Regent ignored them. "Given you saved my daughter's life, I'll allow it if you don't resist."

357

Darius eyed the glinting steel axe as the soldier stepped beside him. It looked sharp enough to slice a hair in two, so at least death would come swiftly.

After giving Selene one last glance—half apologetic, half disappointed in her for turning him over in the first place—he bowed to avoid her horrified stare.

The man raised the weapon.

The eager anticipation was plain from the hushed noise in the room. Roars of triumph would likely erupt before his head hit the ground; he was glad he wouldn't be alive to hear them.

"Darius, I'm sorry," Selene said. "I love you."

He continued staring at the floor, still unsure what he wanted to say to her, unable to forget the anger at her actions leading to this very moment.

The air shifted above him as the executioner raised his axe.

Darius braced, waiting for the incoming cold bite of death.

When the axe paused at height and prepared to fall, a bang sounded from the entrance to the hall.

A sea of heads turned as a shout echoed out from the doors. "Stop!"

That voice… The gasps and mutterings buzzed around while Darius looked up and saw the shock painted on Theodoros's face. It confirmed what he suspected. *Lex?*

44

Nikolaos – Xavala, the Silk City

Nikolaos knelt in the doorway to his chambers, one eye on his sandals, the other outside to check the palatial hallways were still clear. Once sure the King's Sword had finally left him for whatever respite the silent algus required, Nikolaos slipped off his sandals and felt the hot, sandy floor on the soles of his sweaty feet.

He slipped a little whilst standing, and longed for the chillier Laltos floors to ease the heat, something he never thought he would. Although autumn endowed them with milder weather, even had it been the depths of winter, it would have been too hot for Nikolaos. Cloaking nervousness was easy for him in all ways except perspiration, and nothing made him more anxious than eavesdropping.

Spying got a man crucified, algus or not. Even the dagger at his waist was no consolation. *Wish Xenia hadn't got herself crushed.*

He had to see the Chief Priest of the Order and get a new escort when he was done.

After another quick glance in both directions, Nikolaos set off. Only a few doors away was the room of the King's Orator, and he was tired of being shut out of Ophelia's many talks with the Silk Regent. With every step closer, more sweat beaded on his forehead, and it was dripping once he reached the light, beech wood double doors.

A glance over his shoulder confirmed the hall was clear, and he pressed his ear to the gap in the doors. Mumbles and muttering were all he made out, so he tried a few different angles until he heard Ophelia's voice.

"This is too good to be true," the King's Orator said. "It's happening even faster than expected. I can't…" The voice became too muffled as the woman must have turned away.

Nikolaos shifted his ear again and risked peering through the crack to see the woman's figure pacing around the wide room.

But soon after looking, icy steel touched his neck.

He froze, chills suddenly running through his sweaty body as blood dribbled from the point of the blade. After a few seconds of the metal unmoving and hearing nothing, he slowly turned to see the King's Sword, face so close he finally stole a glimpse.

Jason's hard, glowing blue eyes were narrowed, creating wrinkled crow's feet in the corners, which joined the many folds of skin on his face.

"J-Jason," Nikolaos stammered, mind frantically searching for a lie. "I was just coming to see Ophelia. I knocked but there was no answer."

Jason's silk hood swayed as he shook his head, glanced down at Nikolaos's bare feet, then pressed the sword a little harder.

"I know what it looks like." Nikolaos usually would have bribed a man or algus in this situation but was smart enough to know not to try it with the King's most loyal guard. "The truth is I wanted to see if Alexandra had returned and she was keeping it from me." The only idea that came to Nikolaos's mind was to fight—he was an algus after all, and the Silk City had fed him enough to stay strong. But this was the King's Sword…

Am I better dead by the sword than the alternative? He backed up to the wall, waiting for an opening. Only the dagger at his waist would save him. "Let me explain myself to Ophelia." Every word came out quicker than the last. "She'll understand."

The King's Sword shook his head, increasing the pressure on Nikolaos's neck.

He never listened to reason. There was no other way.

Nikolaos jerked to the side, brought up his forearm to bat the sword away. The blade cut to the bone as he shoved it from his neck. With a stifled grunt of pain, he dropped low, using his other hand to rip free his dagger and thrust it out.

Jason stepped back, watched the dagger stop inches from his belly as Nikolaos's reach stretched as far as it could. Before Nikolaos moved again, Jason brought his sword down to slash across the back of the algus's hand.

Nikolaos yelled, failing to stifle the noise as the knife dropped from his hand and clattered onto the floor. *So fast…*

Realising his odds were slim, Nikolaos lunged to run away, but the King's Sword moved in a blink to thrust a blade in his path.

Nikolaos's sweaty feet slid across the floor. He dropped and landed with a crack. His bleeding arm stained his silken clothes and the surface beneath.

Before he could lift his head to run again, the point of Jason's sword pricked the vein at his throat.

Heavens, save me. Every one of his rapid breaths threatened to cut loose gushing crimson. He'd known it was a long shot and was tempted to ram his neck into the sword to save him the inevitable pain of a spy's death.

But he also knew they'd saved him from Margalvia for a reason not yet fulfilled.

As the two paused, the door behind eased open, releasing a flood of light.

"Nikolaos." Ophelia's voice was as relaxed as one inviting an old friend in for a drink. "I've been wanting to have a word with you."

Nikolaos gripped his bleeding arm tight, the warm fluid leaking between his fingers. He dared to turn his head to see the open doors and Ophelia's silhouetted figure in front.

"Well?" the King's Orator said. "Are you going to get up or sit there until you bleed to death?"

Unusually for him, Nikolaos deemed silence his best approach. He slowly clambered to his feet, slipping a few times in the blood, all the while with Jason's sword at his throat.

"There's no need for that." Ophelia waved a hand to the King's Sword. "I think he knows better than to try anything now."

As Jason slowly withdrew the long blade, Nikolaos struggled to put together what was happening, why the King's Orator acted as if she'd watched everything that had transpired instead of asking what in hell was going on. The friendly invite made him sweat more than a tirade would have.

Regardless, Nikolaos walked inside the room, not making any effort to avoid bleeding on the floor or the white silk rugs. *Hope the place reeks of blood after they've got what they want from me.*

The King's Orator waved over a few slaves, who already had thick bandages in hand, and they began wrapping them tightly around Nikolaos's wound. Meanwhile, the King's Sword stopped behind, sword held out and ready to bring death.

"Did you set this up?" Nikolaos asked in a tone of true contempt.

"I didn't force you to spy on me." Ophelia's face lost its pleasantness, seeming to join Nikolaos in removing the mask.

"You seem to have known I would."

"I know your reputation. You're predictably conniving."

"Predictably?"

"I'll admit I wasn't certain you'd tell the Silk Regent about Alexandra when I asked you not to, but when I learnt he'd sent out assassins, I knew I had you figured out."

The revelation that the King's Orator was aware of Nikolaos's disobedience would ordinarily have made him spew ever more lies to cover his tracks, but it hardly seemed to be worth the effort now. "It's no secret that I serve myself first, much like you, and the King."

The smile returned to Ophelia's face. "I'm glad we can speak candidly now. It makes life easier."

As would offering me a seat, but she still wants me uncomfortable. Nikolaos swallowed, knowing he could spin a tale that put the myths of the origins of Trogus and Arria to shame, but also knowing Ophelia was a greater liar still. Orators were best known for their works of fiction, and the best made tales indistinguishable from history.

"What do you want?" Nikolaos winced as a slave pulled a bandage too tight.

Ophelia strode up to him, scrunched up her flaking nose in the look one gave to a plague-ridden slave. "I want you to stop interfering, stop costing me crests to pay assassins to abandon their orders. There will come a time when I need you, and when that time comes, I'll say."

363

"When wi—"

"Until then, stay out of my way, and I may yet bestow you with the regency you so desperately crave."

Nikolaos bowed his head, cursing at his own transparency. How had he got away with it for so long if someone could know him within only a few hours of conversation? Still, his thoughts lingered on the Orator's words. He may not gain power through the means he'd anticipated, but a regent was still a regent.

Clearing his throat, Nikolaos softened his voice. "Why would you—?"

"My reasons are my own, or rather, are the King's. You'll have your uses. For now, Alexandra and Laltos will be dealt with *my* way and—"

"How will—?"

"*And* I can assure you, she and her father will not live to see the winter."

Although being rebuked, Nikolaos was relieved by the words he'd waited to hear for so long. *Finally, Lex will pay.* It was too bad the Orator's words were wrapped with condescension.

Only the thought of himself wearing a regent's crown stopped him plotting to abandon the city and the King's envoy.

45

Darius – Laltos

Darius stood gingerly, unsure whether the shout sufficiently distracted the executioner. When the man lowered his axe, Darius breathed deeply once again, then craned his neck to catch a glimpse of the woman that had yelled.

His stretching split open old cuts on his neck. Despite his tall frame, he couldn't see beyond the crowd of iron helmets and pillars in the room. Still, he stared.

"Don't kill him!" Her voice echoed in the tall roof above his head.

Easing back down from the tips of his toes, Darius turned back to Theodoros, now in no need of a glimpse of the woman. Lex's voice was unmistakable. She'd come back, but Darius struggled to think why she had left in the first place.

"Is that you, Alexandra?" the Regent asked.

The shuffling of feet murmured across the marble floors as the crowds parted for the new arrival.

Darius dared another glance, not wanting to give away the fact they knew each other but unable to resist the chance to see how she fared. Her hair was tied behind her head but with many loose strands across her face, like she'd ridden for days on a swift.

"It's me." Lex walked forward between the two lines of sour-faced men and women, slower than her usual gait, and her eyes swept left and right, as if expecting an attack at any moment.

To her left, holding her hand, walked a little girl, doe-eyed and sucking her thumb. The girl's blonde hair was dishevelled and her cheeks flushed, like she'd just dismounted too. Wearing a plain brown cloak over her dress made her appear ordinary, but Darius recognised fine clothing and quilted padding when he saw it, even if designed to look cheap. *Why hide her wealth?*

"What is it to you if I have this assassin killed?" Theodoros asked.

"I didn't assassinate anyone…" Darius muttered under his breath. It was probably best the Regent didn't hear it.

Lex avoided his gaze as she continued walking, leading the girl around him and towards her father, but she stopped a few paces short. "He's no assassin."

"You know his reputation as well as I."

Lex's jawline tensed. "I know. But he saved Selene, didn't he?"

Theodoros sighed so forcefully his thin beard rippled. "It doesn't excuse him. What's your objection?"

Her eyes met Darius's for the first time, and he looked away quickly lest the Regent see some connection in their stares. But it warmed his heart that she'd come back.

"My objection is that he's my ally," Lex finally said.

The air left Darius's lungs as he gaped up at her in shock. A glint of algor sparkled in her steely eyes, and while her left hand still clung to the girl's, her right squeezed the hilt of her sword.

"What?" the Regent yelled, along with several other algus from various angles in the crowd.

As the grumbles increased in volume, Darius wished he had the strength to help her should he need to.

"Why?" he mouthed to her.

She met his pained stare with a fierce look and the hint of a smile, as if telling him she'd fight and do anything to save his life. Why had he ever doubted her?

The Regent raised a hand and quieted the room for a second time, though Darius noted it took longer than before for the shouts to subdue to whispers.

How much of the truth was Lex willing to divulge in front of a mob about to turn bloody any second? That she'd aided him since well before Archimedes had stolen his mind?

"Explain yourself." Theodoros stood.

"I count anyone that saves my life as an ally." Lex scanned the crowds over her shoulder, the stare exuding a confidence that she'd take them on no matter how outnumbered. But despite being a fearsome fighter, even she wouldn't be able to fend off this many.

A dozen algus amongst the surrounding mob had swords drawn, not to mention the bolts of the soldiers' crossbows ready to loose.

"After he and the rakkans killed Archimedes," Lex continued, "they next turned to me. But he spared my life that day."

Don't remind them I killed Archimedes.

"And what did you give him in return?" Theodoros winced as if unsure whether he wanted to hear the reply.

Lex grimaced. "Nothing like that, Father. He took the first step to a change in the relations between rakkans and mankind."

The indistinct murmurs in the room were of a tone that suggested a scepticism born from the bitterness of decades of war. All the bitter stares were making the room spin. Darius knelt, exhaustion threatening to overcome him. *Hurry, Lex.*

"How can you trust them?" Theodoros asked forcefully.

"I've dealt with them myself. They've never betrayed me and have aided me countless times. Who do you think gave me so many kuraminium edged weapons?"

Theodoros gasped and slowly eased down onto his throne, as if about to collapse.

Meanwhile, one of his elderly algus advisors spat at Lex's feet. "We'll never stand beside those filth."

Lex glared at him as if ready to rip out his gullet.

Theodoros's stare hardened once more. "It's nothing personal, but I don't see how I can rely on them. They aren't like us."

"What if I proved they could be trusted?" Lex asked.

Theodoros's forehead creased, and he tapped his fingertips on the armrest. They stilled as he spoke. "How?"

Selene looked achingly at her father, tempting Darius to dare hope he could reason with the Regent.

Lex pulled the little girl in closer to her and wrapped an arm around her shoulders. "It's something I must show you alone."

The elderly advisor stepped forward, pointing a nobbled accusatory finger. "She means to kill you, Regent."

Theodoros narrowed his eyes. "Watch your tongue, Konon. That's my daughter."

"I must insist that we be present when these matters are discussed. It's unwise—"

"You think me so weak-minded that I can't endure a conversation with her without bowing to her will?"

"Yes."

The colour drained from the Regent's face, his stare hot with fury while his bear growled. "As I'm merciful, I'll give you a chance to clarify that remark."

Konon hobbled farther forward, circling around Lex, apparently undisturbed by the unsaid threat. Darius had seen that look in a man's eyes before—the look of a man with no fear of death—usually seen in the older generations.

"In all my years," Konon began, "I've never seen an algus father an algus. All our children are adopted, yet you've been graced with this blessing. It stands to reason that you spoil her. Anything she asks—"

"I've heard enough." Theodoros waved his hand. "Guards, remove him. And the rest of you. Out."

The two axe-wielding executioners stepped forward, each with enough brawn to handle an old man, but it was only then that Darius realised they must be algus. It was most unlike him to not see it before. He guessed when breathing felt like too much energy, sizing up opponents seemed a waste.

Most of the mob had already turned and begun filing out with hushed whispers when the guards reached Konon, who now grinned. "You see? Anything she asks."

Theodoros shot up from his chair and opened his mouth, as if ready to launch a tirade, but Konon finally turned his back and left with the others.

While her father was distracted, Lex caught Darius's eye with a soft glance, like she was trying to tell him it would be fine. If only her father hadn't just been riled up…

The doors banged shut behind Darius, leaving just him, the Regent, his daughters and the child. By the throne, Theodoros's escort shifted uneasily.

Another couple of pairs of footsteps arrived behind—the guards—who Darius had missed in his count.

369

He really was losing it, and in desperate need to lie down, but sleep would surely take him if he did, and he'd rather stay awake for what may be his last few minutes alive.

The two guards now took up post on either side of the Regent.

"I said alone, Father," Lex said.

"Don't push your luck!" Theodoros's echoing yell forced Lex to back up slightly. "You're lucky I'm indulging this frankly insulting request. Get to your point, and quickly."

Lex bowed slightly. "I never meant to insult you. You know I love you dearly. But this is a cause I feel so strongly about that I'm willing to risk the most important thing to me."

"What? Losing your father?"

"No." Lex stepped to the side slightly, leaving the blonde girl in the centre of Theodoros's glare. "I'm speaking of her."

The Regent frowned. "Who is she?"

"She's my daughter." Lex lifted her chin slightly.

"Daughter?" Darius, Selene, and the Regent exclaimed in unison.

Darius had known Lex had a son, long ago lost to Archimedes, but she'd never mentioned a daughter. He puzzled over what the girl had to do with their current predicament.

Theodoros's shocked expression soon softened to a smile. "I have a granddaughter? Why didn't you tell me?" His eyes widened, full of a caring and compassion that Darius wished he'd shown before.

Lex pulled the child back behind her once again. "To protect her."

"From Archimedes? He's been dead for a long time."

"From him and many others, including you."

The Regent's smile faded.

370

"What's her name?" Selene asked, beaming at the girl as if she were the most beautiful thing she'd seen.

"Cynthia."

The girl gazed at her mother at the sound of her name. Lex, however, never ceased staring down the Regent. In her eyes was the fierce look of a lioness about to defend her cub.

"Why would you need to protect her from me?" Theodoros asked. "Is she an algus?"

"No."

Darius frowned, now baffled.

Lex withdrew her sword slowly from its sheath. "I doubt you'll believe me unless you see it for yourself." She let go of the child's hand, and for the first time, looked at her daughter with a smile. "Darling, now's the time. Like we discussed."

Cynthia nodded and closed her eyes.

Before Darius could wonder what was about to happen, the girl's head erupted in a blaze of ferven.

Theodoros and Selene gaped.

How? The girl's blue eyes confirmed to Darius she was only half-rakkan, and he suspected he knew who the father was—the blond warlord.

Theodoros began shaking his head. "It can't be true."

"It is," Lex replied as Cynthia extinguished herself.

"You're not her mother."

"I am. Who else would she be? Why would I—?"

"Lies!" the Regent yelled so loudly Cynthia stepped behind her mother's leg.

The silence that followed gave Darius a moment to untangle his thoughts. All this time, she'd hidden it from him. His shock at her risking her own daughter's life to save him brought inexpressible warmth to his chilly bones, along with guilt for ever having doubted her.

371

But it crossed his mind she'd taken a calculated gamble to secure the First Alliance she so desperately wanted.

Theodoros's gaze shifted to Darius, algor flaring in his eyes. "Don't tell me you mated with him!"

Darius snorted. "Do I have blond hair?"

"Doesn't mean she isn't yours."

He guessed that was true. "Still, lowers the odds."

Selene was looking between him and Lex too with a grimace.

"He's not her father," Lex said.

Darius was a little relieved. He'd begun to wonder if he was to feel the brunt of Theodoros's anger.

But no sooner had he thought it than the Regent stood and began walking forward with his guards following at his side. "You're lying. She's not my granddaughter. I should kill these half-breeds and end this affair."

The Regent's escort bounded forwards, a mass of beast moving at a speed Darius would have fled from even at full strength.

Lex lifted her sword, her arm steady. "Don't think I won't fight you."

The Regent strode onwards as his guards stepped ahead of him, their readied axes beginning to glow blue.

Lex bared her teeth and drew back her arm.

Selene cried out, "You'd kill an innocent child? She has Lex's eyes. She's part of your genos. What if you're wrong, Father?"

Theodoros wavered, looked back at his other daughter, back at Lex and Cynthia, fists unclenching slightly.

Then his escort skidded to a halt with a scratching of claws.

"Stop," Theodoros yelled just before the two guards clashed with Lex.

The Regent's arms trembled, his breaths deep. He blinked twice as often as a normal man, and his eyes darted around as if being spoken to from a hundred directions. A leader with a conscience would be a first for Darius.

"Papou?" Cynthia said in a mousey voice.

At the sound, Theodoros's shoulders relaxed, and his gaze settled on her. He cocked his head slightly to the side as one did to an innocent creature.

For the first time that evening, Darius felt a little hope. Who would have thought a girl could be the one to give pause to a man so steadfast?

"She didn't ask for this," Lex said. "She never wanted to be born an exile."

"Few do." Theodoros paced forward slowly. "But I guess she is human…"

As was Darius, but that hadn't stopped them mistreating him.

Lex watched her father, hand still wielding a sword, but the old algus merely crouched with an outstretched arm, letting his silk tunic brush the floor.

Cynthia grinned and reached out from behind Lex's leg. The two relatives touched fingertips, which brought a grin to the Regent's face. "Half human…half rakkan." His smile vanished and he shot up to meet his daughter eye to eye. "No one can find out about her."

"Why do you think I hid her outside the city?" Lex said.

"You're a fool to even bring her here. Why now?"

"It was the only way you'd believe me, and the only way you'd see an alliance is in our best interests."

Theodoros paused. Meanwhile, Darius shivered from the cold of the grand room more with every passing minute.

"Think of how strong an army of both rakkans and algus would be," Lex said.

Theodoros ran a hand through his thin hair and stared at Darius.

"I trust them with my life," Lex continued. "Darius's grandfather—a rakkan—raised Cynthia."

"And I trust him," Selene said with an apologetic look to Darius.

Theodoros sighed. "I suppose he did save Selene's life. And he killed his own kind."

Lex's gaze fell upon Darius's hunched, weak figure. "Let him win the war for us."

Darius looked away, suddenly wondering whether that was Lex's focus all along. That's all he was to most, a warrior to use.

Did she care how much he hurt? Did she care that the pain weighed him down so heavily that he'd prayed for death?

"Can Darius defeat Hadrian?" The Regent's stare turned ravenous, like a starving man eyeing food.

"To beat an infernal fiend, we need one of our own," Lex said. "He'll win many wars as our ally."

Darius growled. *Fiend?* "Many wars?"

She gave him a slight raise of her eyebrows to soften the words. "The Viridian Legion is only one concern of many."

Darius's vision darkened, and he barely managed to stretch out an arm to prevent his face from crashing into the marble. He gasped. "Food… Water."

"Please, Father," Lex said.

Theodoros glanced down at him then waved to his guards when apparently satisfied that Darius posed no threat. "Release him. Bring him what he asks."

The guards looked to one another.

"Obey your Regent unless you want to wear the shackles yourselves," Lex said.

The two finally withdrew their axes and unlocked the chains on Darius's wrists and ankles. The metal had dug so deep for so long that he barely felt the difference when they were removed.

Once free, Lex quickly walked over to him with Cynthia in tow and knelt beside him, taking his head in her hands.

"I'm so sorry, Darius," she whispered. "It was all I could think to do, but she was so far away. I left as soon as possible, but your grandfather only meets me with her on the first of the month."

Her hands hurt the cuts on the back of his head, but after so many weeks without human contact, he felt safe within her grasp.

"Is she Varro's?" he croaked.

"She is, but don't you dare tell that bastard."

Darius snorted. *Typical Lex.*

One guard ran to the main doors, opened them, and barked orders to those outside. Barely a minute passed before three slaves brought in water and a steaming pot of stew.

Lex helped Darius sit up before a slave poured a mug of water into Darius's mouth. Half dribbled down his bearded chin, but the rest of the cool liquid soothed his parched gullet.

The light-headedness eased a fraction and brought his focus onto Selene's bruised face. "What about her?"

Theodoros caught the comment and turned to her. After pondering for a moment, he nodded to a guard who promptly released Selene from her cuffs.

Before even standing, she made her way over to Darius and Lex.

Still confused whether to feel love or betrayal at the sight of her, Darius put his focus back onto Lex.

"Alexandra." The Regent signalled to her to stand and came closer as she rose. "If I'm to contemplate this alliance, I must ensure the algus agree. Konon was already brazen enough to

375

speak against me. The older he gets, the more outspoken he becomes, and I'm not the only one that's had enough. Kill him."

Lex bowed her head. "I'll see to it once I've taken Cynthia to a safe place."

"Very well." He turned to his other daughter. "Selene, I need your help with sounding out the other algus. Bring your brothers and sisters too."

Darius took a bowl of broth offered by a slave and began drinking down chunks of beef and potato whole, only stopping when the urge to throw it all back up became too great. "We should send word to Margalvia. Lex, can Tiro—"

A scream echoed through the hall from behind the entrance doors, followed by scurrying footsteps. *What new hell is this?*

The two guards strode forward and planted their bodies and axes between Theodoros and the doors.

The Regent's escort stirred.

Another cry seeped into the room along with a faint crash.

"Perhaps the algus know what's happened here," Selene said. "They're coming for us."

"Impossible." Lex pulled Cynthia behind the two guards and her own tense body.

All too often Lex's words and actions seemed in opposition to each other. Darius could do nothing but sit and wait. These algus could fight and protect *him* for once.

As they all waited in a stiff silence, the doors parted slightly.

Both guards' arms bulged as they flexed and readied their axes, but they relaxed a fraction when a thin figure slipped inside then pressed the door shut with his back.

His white linen tunic was decent but lacked a certain class. *Not an algus.* As if mirroring Darius's thoughts, the guards lowered their weapons.

"Regent, they're attacking!" the man yelled, running towards them. "They're in the city."

"Who?" Theodoros stepped out from behind the guards.

"The Viridian Legion!"

"What?" Lex yelled, her breaths suddenly agitated.

Darius clenched his jaw. After all his effort spent forging alliances and seeking them out, Hadrian had come to him?

The time's come. Ready or not, Darius's chance to avenge his escort loomed.

46

Darius – Laltos

Darius attempted to stand but cursed as his thigh shook and refused to push him upwards. *Damn.* Why did Hadrian have to attack when he was crippled?

The thin man skidded to a halt in front of them. "The rakkans have breached the city's defences."

Theodoros gaped. "How? Any force large enough to breach the walls would have been seen from miles away. We heard nothing."

"I don't know. All was quiet, then suddenly they were in the palace. It was chaos. I ran as soon as I saw the ferven."

Darius murmured to himself. It made no sense to him that an army had reached them without going through the walls to both the lower and upper city.

Theodoros shook his head in disbelief. "Imposs—"

"The passageways," Selene cried with a horrified look.

"They're all blocked bar my own, and that has two on watch every night. They know to flood the passage with water if any rakk—"

"I relieved the guards so I could escape with Darius… We need swords." Selene darted towards the throne and avoided meeting Theodoros's furious glare.

"We haven't time for reprimands." Lex tugged her father's shoulder until his gaze shifted to her. "We have to get Cynthia and Darius to safety."

The fact she thought of *him* in the same breath as her own daughter shook Darius more than the impending rakkan attack.

"Cynthia?" the Regent exclaimed. "We need to raise the alarm, not run."

"Others have heard; they'll do it. These two won't survive an army of rakkans."

Theodoros pushed Lex aside with a shake of his head and waved to the guards. "One of you run to the southern tower and sound the bells. The other get to the courtyard and blow a horn lest the first fails. Take the rear exit and you shouldn't cross paths with anyone coming from the cellars."

"Father!" Lex shouted. "We can't spare them."

"Are you mad?" The Regent spun. "This city is the most important thing, and it will fall unless we rally our troops."

Selene returned with swords and tossed one to her father while giving Lex an apologetic shrug that told of her agreement with him.

The two guards sprinted away as ordered. They were out via the rear door in seconds.

Meanwhile, more cries emanated from the entrance hall at the front and grew louder second by second. Clashing swords and falling bodies sounded as if right outside the doors.

All Darius could do was sit and hold down the stew in his belly.

"We're leaving." Lex shoved Cynthia towards the back exit. The pair's footsteps tapped briskly across the floor.

Before they'd reach the exit, a crash echoed through the throne room as the main doors burst from their hinges and slammed flat onto the ground.

As the bang echoed from the walls and statues, two figures clad in full-face helmets, cuirasses, bracers and greaves made of black metal walked over the door, each footstep pounding with the weight of armour a human couldn't lift.

Theodoros's escort stepped forward until its muscled body stood in front of the Regent. The beast reared on its hind legs with a ferocious snarl.

Another crash from the back of the room made Darius's head whip around. Dozens more rakkans entered through the rear exit. Apparently they'd found a way around, despite the Regent's assurances.

By the time Darius looked back to the main door, rakkans had filed in and fanned out to surround the five of them.

Damn. If only he was strong enough to fight. He pushed his palm into the cold marble and tried to stand again, but his arm trembled, no strength within to summon.

Lex quickly stepped back with Cynthia behind. Theodoros and Selene regrouped, and the Regent's escort held its ground, growling as the five of them huddled together so close they touched.

By that time, almost half a century of rakkans had now encircled them, kuraminium blades brandished, some with ferven, others plain but ready to cut them all the same.

There were too many to fight off, even for three algus. *So, this is how it ends.* At least there was no sight of Hadrian, so it wouldn't be the fiend himself to finish Darius off.

One of the rakkans stepped from behind the others, the horns of a bull protruding from his helmet.

Darius blinked his eyes to better focus. Something seemed odd. Only a warlord wore such horns, but the figure was too small for Hadrian.

As the rakkan came closer, Darius noted a distinct swagger to the Warlord's walk and noted the three bands on his bicep weren't Viridian.

"Darius," the rakkan said, voice echoing inside his helmet. "What in hell have they done to you?"

Rubbing his eyes until they finally focused, Darius now made out the red colour of the bands on the rakkan's arm—Militia. He sighed and collapsed to the ground.

"Sulla?" Lex took a step towards the rakkan.

Sulla raised his sword, which halted her. "Hand over Darius, Blue-eyes."

"You have to stop this attack." The panic in Lex's voice suddenly set Darius's nerves on edge again. "Tell your men to fall back here and lay down their arms."

"Do you know these invaders?" Theodoros asked Lex with a scowl.

"We'll lay down nothing until we've got Darius to safety," Sulla growled.

"He is safe."

"Looks like it." Sulla motioned to a few of his men. "Take Darius away from these sharks."

As tempting as the offer to escape was, Darius held out his palm to the few who moved towards him. "Lex speaks the truth. Call your men back."

"Don't tell me they've broken you," Sulla said.

Darius snorted. "Hardly. They're thinking of allying with Margalvia."

Sulla's helmet surveyed him and Lex before turning to Theodoros. "Is it true?"

"Yes," Lex said.

"I wasn't asking you." Sulla's tone was flat and devoid of its usual playfulness.

The Regent screwed up his face, as if he had to force his next words out. "I haven't decided yet, but I'm considering."

"Then why is Darius within an inch of death?"

"It took a while to open his mind," Darius said.

Sulla slowly removed his helmet and held it to his hip while staring down Theodoros, both men unblinking at each other as the Regent's escort continued snarling.

After the pause, Sulla grunted and turned back towards the door. "Sound the horn. Call everyone here." He turned back to Lex. "But no one's laying down weapons."

"Fair enough." Lex's grip on her sword relaxed slightly.

One of the rakkans left the room, greaves clunking as he ran.

"So, these are your allies?" Theodoros said, his own fingers white around his weapon. "Who needs enemies…?"

"Time your battles," Darius said.

Sulla began pacing towards them and pointed to Selene. "Is this the algus that handed Darius over to the Laltos Guard?"

Darius didn't bother to look at her. "Yes."

"Want us to run her through?"

Theodoros flared algor across his sword, and he thrust it out between Sulla and his daughter. His escort roared and shifted in front of Selene, rearing onto its hind legs again.

Sulla paused but didn't shift his gaze from her. "Well?"

Darius would be lying to say he'd never thought of killing her during the weeks of agony. But now he met her eyes, those that again saw him as something other than a killer, the same feelings he'd had lying next to her in bed stirred.

"No," he said. "Leave her alone."

A horn blasted outside, its low, familiar tone unmistakably rakkan.

"How many of my Guard have you killed?" Theodoros asked.

Sulla shrugged. "About one for every lash on Darius's back." His grin made a reappearance.

"This is serious," Lex said. "We need to know what damage we must undo. An alliance is harder to make if you've just slaughtered half our algus."

"Fine. One algus, perhaps. A handful of soldiers. Your city's defences are pathetic."

"How did you find my passageway?" Theodoros asked.

Sulla's smile widened. "Your daughter has let us in on many secrets over the years."

"Let's focus," Lex interjected. "One dead algus is manageable. Selene, we stick to the plan."

Selene's stare was fixed on the rakkans surrounding her, as if she didn't trust them enough to blink. "Plan?"

"I'll handle Konon while you speak with the other algus."

Theodoros's blade still glowed with algor, but he lowered it while his escort fell onto all fours again. "I'm only contemplating this for my granddaughter's sake. Does Margalvia assure us of their willingness to honour an alliance?"

Sulla put his hand over his heart. "I guarantee it."

"Darius, Sulla, will you watch over the girl?" Lex finally sheathed her sword and nudged Cynthia towards him.

"Sure," Sulla said. "Why don't I breastfeed her too?"

Lex marched up to the rakkan and went nose to nose. "Cut the sarcasm. Will you watch her?"

"He will," Darius said as Sulla opened his mouth to make no doubt another sarcastic remark.

With a final click of her tongue at Sulla, Lex led Selene and Theodoros through the horde of rakkans and out of the door, followed closely by the bear.

Meanwhile, Sulla walked over to Darius and offered him a hand to get up.

Darius shook his head. "Too weak." He was fit only for lying down.

"If you don't have the strength to walk, we can carry you."

"That won't be necessary."

"It is. I lied about Margalvia. Truth is, I can't speak for Warlord Varro. We've all been exiled."

Darius snorted, at first taking it as a joke, but Sulla's stern face soon set a sinking feeling in his stomach. "Why?"

"I had a disagreement with Varro about coming to rescue you."

Darius was tempted to tell Sulla he shouldn't have, but the memories of those nights in his cell, when he'd prayed for anyone to come to his aid, soon reminded him it would have been a hollow statement. "Sulla, I…"

"No need to say anything. Margalvians defend their brothers."

All the other rakkans in the room grunted, having risked exile and death to save him. Whether that was out of solidarity to him, or loyalty to Sulla, he couldn't say, but he knew it was a camaraderie he'd always taken for granted before. He'd assumed it was out of fearing him on the battlefield.

Many times, Darius had thought Selene was the first that saw him as more than a mere warrior, but how wrong he'd been. Sulla had always been there for him, first against Archimedes, and now in Laltos. Then there was Brutus, the rakkan that treated him like a son despite him deserving less.

Yet, despite the loyalty they'd shown, he couldn't shake a gnawing distrust inside. Would everyone forsake him, as Selene had, when he needed them most? *Damned if I know.* So far, they hadn't, so he drove the doubt to the back of his mind.

"Thanks, Sulla," Darius said. "How's Lyra?"

"Up and walking last I saw." Sulla smiled. "Let's speak more once we're safe. My men will carry you."

A few rakkans came forward, but Darius shook his head. He wouldn't run away like a coward. Lyra had never run from a fight, however long the odds, and they still had options.

"No." Darius allowed one of the rakkans to help him sit up but refused to stand. "How many men do you have?"

"Around a thousand outside the city," Sulla said. "I could only bring a century through the passageway. Why?"

It was a decent chunk of the Militia, and enough to give the Laltos Guard an edge fighting the Viridians.

"I think we should stay," Darius said. "Offer Theodoros your army to help."

"To attack Hadrian?" Sulla scoffed.

Darius nodded, seeing the hatred spread across Sulla's face at the utterance of the name, a loathing he shared.

"I don't know." Sulla scratched his chin and looked around at his men. "Theodoros may be displeased when he learns the Black Legion isn't here, and we can't assault Viridia with only the Militia and Laltos Guard. Plus, I'd rather take you away from those that did this to you."

"Varro has to attack Viridia at some point, doesn't he?" Darius asked, tired of dwelling on his own safety or condition.

"We can push from two fronts." It was the best chance they had of cornering Hadrian, and that was most important.

"I'd presume so," Sulla said, "but I still wouldn't risk attacking Hadrian without Varro's backing. It might invite the fiend to attack Margalvia."

Just like I did. A wave of guilt came over Darius, but he resisted the feeling and focused on the matter at hand. "If we leave Laltos now, Theodoros will take it as a rejection of the alliance."

Sulla took another look around at his men. "What do you all think?"

One of the commanders stepped forward, fresh blood dripping from his sword. "We're always game for slaying Viridian swine."

A few of the other rakkans chuckled while others grunted in what Darius had come to know as a "yes."

Sulla smiled for a second, but it soon faded. "Viridia will be no easy task, even with some Militia. The Viridian Legion has thousands of battle-hardened warriors. Even if we breach their walls, you can't take on Hadrian in this state. We need Varro."

Darius's pride stung at the pronouncement, but he wouldn't argue. "We'll convince Varro."

"Anyway… Those humans won't be back for a while." Sulla turned to the main entrance that Theodoros and the rest had left through, doors still flat on the floor. "I'll decide what we're to do when they return. Always was better at making decisions on a whim."

Darius wouldn't argue with that and was now too spent to talk. "I need to rest. Wake me when they come back."

Sulla snorted. "Young ones these days have no stamina."

With that, Darius eased his body back to the floor. It didn't matter that the hard stone sent chills through his bony hips and shoulders; the noise of muttering rakkans faded from his mind a few seconds later.

47

Darius – Laltos

A rough shake dragged Darius out of a deep, dreamless sleep. Pain, like a tight band, clutched his head to remind him of how desperately he needed slumber. He opened his eyes to see Sulla's face hovering over him.

"Sorry," Sulla said, "I tried to be gentle, but you wouldn't wake."

Darius groaned and closed his eyes as his mind and body begged for more relief. "I can't…" Stringing together a thought seemed beyond him.

"The algus came back over an hour ago. We let you rest, but you'll want to be part of this now."

The warm, pungent smell of beef filled his nostrils, and he sat up. This time it was Selene's striking face that greeted him. She held a bowl of broth near his nose.

"I thought this might help," she said.

"Yes," Sulla muttered. "That makes up for weeks of torture, right?"

Selene frowned at him but held her tongue. Darius had thought little beyond the chunky pieces of tomato and beef that would melt in his mouth.

He propped himself up on one elbow and grabbed the bowl from her. Before Selene blinked in surprise at his rapid movements, chunks of vegetables and meat were slopping down his throat with barely a pause to chew. Within seconds, he was slurping up the last remaining dregs of juice.

He held out the empty bowl to Selene and rested his head against the floor once again. "Keep it coming." If he was ever to regain his strength to fight, he'd need to eat his bodyweight in fatty meat. Despite being a finely cooked meal, his stomach lurched, having been used to scraps for weeks, but if it took force-feeding himself to recover, then that's what he'd do.

Tightness gripped his entire body from sore wounds, and when he looked down, he realised they'd bandaged him all over. The stinging from every cut and scrape told him they'd been cleaned too.

While Selene handed the bowl to a slave girl, Sulla grabbed him by the shoulder and hoisted him to his feet so fast the broth almost shot up and onto the cow skins they'd laid him on.

"Easy." Darius blinked and swallowed a few times to stop the room turning.

As his senses slowly returned, he realised he was no longer in the throne room but in what appeared to be the Regent's private reception area. Royal blue tapestries hung over the windows and matched the fine upholstery on a series of chairs around a dark, rectangular wooden table. Yet the fabrics were worn, lighter at the bottom with stitching coming loose at the end.

Theodoros sat at one side with only his bulky escort lying beside him, while Lex, Sulla, his commanders and centurions had positioned themselves opposite. At the far end, a blazing fire gave heat to the room and sent wafts of black smoke up the chimney but left a dark mist.

"Back to the matter at hand." Sulla helped Darius into a chair before taking a seat and slouching as if at complete ease. "From what you've said, I'm satisfied the people that matter in Laltos won't murder us if we stay, Regent."

"Well, if you're satisfied then that's what's important," Theodoros said in a dreary tone. "But the others will defer to my decision. *I* speak for Laltos."

"Forgive me, but doesn't King Medus have control over Laltos?"

Theodoros's face flushed, his nostrils flared.

"Father," Lex interjected, "I think we're in danger of straying from the point at hand. We have the support of Laltos's armies, but we must now decide how we're to deploy them against the Viridians."

It was a good thing a woman of Lex's temperament was here to mediate these talks, or the men would end in fisticuffs no doubt. Hadrian should have been their primary concern, and how they'd take the fight to him instead of skirmishing over villages.

"If we're to act in alliance with Laltos," Sulla said, "I need convincing you have the resources to go on the offensive. If you were to launch an attack on Viridia, what would your strategy be?"

The thought of taking on the Viridians brought a grin to Darius's face, which he quickly covered up.

Theodoros ran a hand across his escort's head, which lay resting with closed eyes next to him. "Viridia has resilient defensive fortifications and little food in the surrounding land. A siege would be near impossible. We'd starve before them, with all the tunnels the rakkans have. And we lack the numbers to launch a direct assault."

"What if you had the numbers?"

"I wouldn't rely on them. I'd first find the Staff of Arria."

Darius winced at the memories of the goman and the blackened staff that had reduced him to a crawling insect. The longer the Waif Magician kept the Staff away from the humans, the better.

Sulla shifted in his seat with a sigh. "It'd be more helpful if you gave a straight answer."

"It's the truth."

"Then I guess the truth is you're cowards."

"Sulla!" Lex yelled.

Darius expected the Regent's face to flush again in anger, but instead he frowned. "It's true what they say of you."

"What's that?" Sulla asked.

"You have no fear."

"I've never been held back by such constraints."

The Regent suppressed a laugh. "Constraints?" His eyes scanned the room at the few standing rakkans. "Since you like hypothetical questions, answer me this. A lion happens across two boars. One has fear; the other does not. Which survives?"

"A boar can't out-run a lion. Its best chance is to stand its ground, make the predator doubt itself by doing something unexpected. If you run like prey, they'll chase you like prey."

"The boar doesn't have to out-run the lion," Darius said. "It only has to out-run the other boar."

"Whose side are you on?" Sulla asked.

"No one's." Perhaps Darius would have been best to keep his mouth shut. After all, he wanted them to show no fear to the Viridians.

"I've had enough of speculation." Lex's voice cut through the growing rifts. "Let's talk facts. We have a few hundred algus and twenty thousand soldiers, including the citizens we can call to arms."

"Fine." Sulla leaned forward. "How many heavy and light infantry?"

"Half hoplites, the rest peltasts and archers."

A spear throwing peltast would be of little use attacking a fortress, which left an inadequate number of ten thousand armoured men against an entire legion of rakkans. Theodoros was right. An assault would be pointless. Even in an open battlefield it would be difficult if not impossible, which would make convincing them to take the fight to Hadrian even harder.

"Could you rakkans breach the walls?" Theodoros asked.

Sulla scratched his head. "Normally we can breach even the thickest gates or wall in a few hours, but the Viridians reinforced theirs with kuraminium bars centuries ago. It would take a considerable number of us to melt through them, and time. We'd be best building a ramp."

"You can double the numbers we'll need then," Darius said. *As well as double the expected losses.* "It would be better to draw them out of the city."

"I don't see how that's possible," Sulla said. "Unless—"

The words were cut off as a door burst open and a panting slave ran in, sweat dripping down his tanned cheeks. He held out a roll of parchment in his hands and approached Lex. "Apologies, mistress. I have an urgent…" He couldn't drag air into his lungs fast enough and bent over heaving.

Theodoros rose from his chair. "You'd better have a good—"

Lex snatched the parchment and unravelled it. As she did, her eyes widened and her mouth fell open. "The Viridian Legion are marching on Laltos."

Darius's stomach tightened. Memories of his arm caught in Hadrian's grasp sprang to mind.

The Regent fell back down onto his seat while Sulla frowned and exchanged glances with his commanders.

"How do you know?" Darius asked.

"Varro sent word." Lex stared at the floor but finally closed her mouth with a tense jaw. "His source is reliable."

"Well, we have our wish," Theodoros said quietly. "They've been lured out of Viridia."

"How far away are they?" Darius asked. "How many?"

"Most of the legion," Lex said.

The Regent straightened his back. "Send out scouts and escorts at once. If they're marching here and we haven't seen them, it means they're moving through the hills and densest forests, trying to amass without our knowing. If they've already reached the major roads south and north, it will make evacuation difficult. We need their location."

At the order, an algus bolted out of the room and left a grim silence that painfully stretched out. The rakkans, the Regent, and other algus mulled. Darius tried to read their darkened faces, finding nothing but fear and anger amongst them.

Finally, Theodoros cleared his throat, and everyone's gaze fell on him, willing his next words to relieve the dread. "It seems our hand has been forced," the Regent said. "Laltos agrees to the alliance if Margalvia is willing."

"Sulla, we'll need your help in preparing our defence," Lex said. "No one here knows rakkan tactics better than you."

The Militia Chief looked to his commanders before letting out a sigh. "You could ride out and meet them in battle in the forests, but you'd likely be massacred. Laltos's walls would give you better odds, but even then, defence is risky if you don't have the numbers. My advice is to flee. The road south is the most obvious choice."

"Obvious to the Viridians too," the Regent muttered.

"And where will we go?" Lex cried. "Xavala? Toria? Where is large enough to house our whole city, and all the people sheltering here from their razed towns and villages in the west? No. We have no choice but to stand and fight."

A moment's pause followed where Sulla ran a hand across the scars on his chin. "Xavala's best to flee to. If the roads are too long or aren't safe, go through the mountains to the east."

Lex scowled. "They're impassable."

"Not for a rakkan. From all I've seen and heard, even combined, the Viridians threaten to overcome us. Most of you are too young, spoiled by Archimedes defending you and making you think your high walls protect you from a rakkan legion. You're wrong.

"I remember the times before the War of the Uncharted, when Hadrianus the Great almost razed this city. You've never seen what rakkans can do: smash through walls in an hour with flaming pickaxes, tunnel through rock, leap over trenches and spikes, sling boulders from far outside the range of your archers.

"Sure, harassing them with swift riders will slow them, but it won't overcome them. They're in the thickest forests, not the plains." Sulla paused for a moment as his words sank into the minds of everyone there. "We need the full might of the Black Legion. If Hadrian's marching here, then he has greater numbers than even I'd estimated. Not to mention your city is built in the shadow of the cliffs. There's no escape once they besiege us. The Regent's passageway isn't made for fleeing armies."

"We'll call our allies for aid. We can get—"

"And!" Sulla rose from his seat, fists clenched as the muscles on his forearms bulged. "I'll be damned if I'll ask my men to die defending a city that did this." He pointed to Darius, who felt all eyes shift to view his withered frame. "I'm prepared to make peace, and I'm prepared to fight Hadrian on our terms. I'll help you flee, but I won't lock myself into a trap. So go ahead and plan, but we leave tomorrow, with or without you."

Another silence followed that lingered as long as the first. Darius strained to think of any appropriate words to fill it. Sulla's mind wasn't easily changed, and part of Darius would have been glad to watch Laltos burn, the city that had heard his cries for weeks and done nothing, but then he realised there wouldn't be the time or desire for all to evacuate the city.

He recalled the slaves that would be left behind, the poor he'd seen begging in the streets that would starve if they took to the roads.

How many like Omid were here? How many would be left to be slaughtered or worse? Or if they fled, how quickly would Hadrian catch them while trekking through hilly terrain?

"Find the fastest pigeon you can," Theodoros ordered. "I'll write to the Silk Regent myself. The Xavalan cavalry are the only ones that can arrive in time to aid us."

"Better send two lest one doesn't make it," Lex added.

A couple of slaves that had been silently watching from the side scurried away while Darius continued his imaginings. The mention of the cavalry gave him a flicker of hope. Sulla didn't know of the weapons Lex had traded with the Silk City, and with the Red Militia, the defenders had the element of surprise.

Darius couldn't recover in time himself, but the thought of Hadrian filled with glee at Laltos's destruction brought bile to his throat. He wouldn't let it happen. *That fiend deserves pain and death.*

Given a battle was imminent no matter which option they took, Darius would rather give the people of Laltos a fighting chance. Judging by the disturbed yet firm looks on Lex, Theodoros and Selene's faces, they shared his sentiments.

But now, they had under a day to convince Sulla.

48

Brutus – Viridian Camp

The hiss of rain on the canopy of leaves above drowned out Brutus's heavy footsteps. With each splatter from his boots, his nerves tightened as he moved ever closer to the Warlord's tent and the queue of rakkans waiting outside the entrance.

Clasped tightly in his hand was a bunch of silver crests he'd pilfered from a legionnaire the day before. Every night he'd tried but failed to get close enough to Hadrian. But he only needed to be lucky once. Tonight was the night.

The canvas of the large green tent ahead shivered with each gust of wind. It may as well have been made from kuraminium, because outside, dozens of Viridian Guardians wandered around, raindrops dripping down the element symbols on their tattooed arms.

The Viridian Legion was fractured into smaller camps in the final push towards Laltos, marching and camping deep within the forests, fed by the hulking bags of supplies the rakkans carried.

Brutus's time was running short, but he'd managed to stay close to the Warlord.

Pulling his helmet lower, Brutus cloaked as much of his face as possible, whilst still able to see, and joined the back of the queue of rakkan warriors. Each held a gift in their hands, either grain, nuts, gold or livestock. With every step closer, more guardians stared at him with suspicious eyes.

At the front, one of the guardians slapped a bag of seeds from a legionnaire's hands and yelled, "That's chaff. Only the best of the harvest is good enough. Get out of here!"

With a scowl, the legionnaire skulked away muttering profanities. The next three rakkans fared no better, and the guardians rejected their gifts, just like Brutus's had been every time before.

The ceremony made Brutus want to vomit. Hadrian acted as if he wielded the powers of a god, or the Twin Blades of Trogus, which was absurd.

But it was Brutus's only chance to get close to the Warlord alone.

When only a few yards away and at the front of the queue, two Viridian Guardians moved to block Brutus's path.

"What's your offering?" one asked in the snide tone of a man who took too much pleasure from frustrating others.

Brutus searched their eyes, as black as their helmets, and was relieved to see they weren't the same ones he'd happened across the other nights. The pair's full cheeks and bald chins placed them as youngsters to him. It gave him more confidence. The young were more easily fooled.

"Silver." Brutus stood square, exuding the arrogance most Viridians possessed, and held out his hand for them to see. "But these are no ordinary crests. We found them in the hidden coffers of a human village. They're at least two centuries old and bear the symbols of long forgotten idols. The people said they once belonged to witches who cast spells of lost gods to bring fortune to the bearer." It was all a lie, but Brutus knew enough of history to blunder through.

"Hmm. Better than the rest." One guardian reached out to snatch some, but Brutus pulled his hand back.

"It's for the Warlord only." His voice emulated his brother's quiet, menacing tone.

"We take our cut."

Whilst true that the guardians could take a share of offerings, Brutus would be damned if he'd let two youngsters diminish his gift.

Brutus squeezed the coins tight. "Come take your cut then, but I'll make you bleed for it."

One guardian chuckled and looked to his friend, but then stopped once his eyes locked with Brutus's glower again. "Fine. Go in." He pulled back the tent flap and ushered Brutus inside.

As soon as the fabric opened, Brutus's body tensed. He dropped his right hand to his side and clutched the hilt of his dagger. Inside, a haze met his vision and brought a pungent mix of smoking herbs to sting his nose.

He rid his nostrils of it with a violent snort. The dim light highlighted every wisp of smoke, undisturbed by the gusts outside that shook the surroundings. Despite being large enough to house a few dozen people, there was only one other in there, looming like a shadow through the fog.

At the far side, Hadrian sat on a throne of stained oak and iron.

"Come, low-ling," Hadrian uttered in a deep, unworldly voice. "Earn my blessing to protect you on the battlefield."

Brutus had to suppress a snort of laughter. He instead bowed his head and wondered how close he'd get to the Warlord.

He stepped forward, each pace careful and hesitant.

"That's far enough," Hadrian said.

Pausing mid-step, Brutus slowly completed it to stand a couple of yards away, too far to reach with a dagger but close enough to toss it through an eye.

He'll dodge if I try. Biding his time, Brutus knelt and held out the wet silver in his palm.

"I heard the guardians outside." Hadrian's voice softened, almost inviting. "Is this silver really centuries old? A product of witchcraft?"

For all Brutus knew, it was older and cursed. All he saw was that it lacked the King's eagle emblem.

"Yes, Warlord."

"Such a worthy offering on this day then." Hadrian gazed up to the roof of the tent, which Brutus only now realised was open at the top, revealing the rain and stars through a gap in the branches and clouds.

"You see this, Grandfather?" Hadrian said. "We're retaking what was stolen from you. I'll make you proud."

Bowing again, Brutus turned a fraction to hide his right hand, which now reached for a dagger.

He gripped the hilt, risking a glance up to see Hadrian still staring at the sky, exposing his neck beneath his helmet.

Brutus pulled the dagger from its sheath, cursing in his mind as his hand slipped a little on the wet hilt.

"May the stars rain down their blessings." Hadrian's glare snapped back down, kuraminium once again shielding the neck.

Damn. Still kneeling, Brutus shifted his weight onto his front leg, ready to pounce.

He hoped his wife would forgive his sacrifice. In this final moment, his only regret was he'd never given her a child. But

Darius had been as good as one. She'd loved him, as had he. *Farewell, my love.*

"Warlord!" A guardian burst into the tent and tripped over Brutus on his way forwards.

The Margalvian stumbled, knife digging through the canvas floor and into the soil under his body.

"What is it, you bumbling fool?" Hadrian barked.

"The spies have seen rakkans in Laltos."

"Who? Why?"

"Margalvian Militia."

Brutus's heart sank. His kin being in the city they were about to attack was the worst news he could hear.

He got back to one knee, pulled out the dagger from the ground and held it behind his calf.

"They must intend to help," Hadrian muttered. "Summon the commanders. This demands a change of strategy."

With a last prayer, Brutus moved to leap, but a hand caught him beneath the armpit and hauled him up.

"On your way, legionnaire," the guardian said as he dragged Brutus towards the tent flap.

Brutus dug in his heels, still clutching the dagger by his leg. He looked back at Hadrian who stood inhaling heavy, angry breaths.

"Hey!" the guardian shouted. "Out!"

"My offering…" The longer Brutus glared, the lesser he reckoned his odds of gutting Hadrian.

"No more offerings," the guardian barked and shoved him out of the tent.

This time, Brutus didn't resist and stalked away into the cool drizzle once again, contemplating the fresh information the Warlord had been given.

It didn't take him long to guess who Hadrian had spying for him that could get close to Laltos—the Numbered. Many captured early in the war had been broken by pain and stress. Now they did the Warlord's bidding, but Brutus had seldom seen them, a well-kept secret, it seemed. They weren't just for spying, that was sure.

The more Brutus pondered, the more he realised how vital it was to slay Hadrian. It would have to be the next time they met, and if Margalvians dined in Laltos, then Brutus needed to ensure that was soon.

49

Darius – Laltos

Darius scoffed down his third bowl of broth, savouring the salty beef juices. Even after a day of stuffing his face, the taste hadn't yet grown old. The other rakkans along the rows of long dining tables ate with a lot more grace than he did, but damn them. He needed more, or he'd never be strong enough to fight alongside them.

Splatters of gravy stained the tablecloth underneath as juices dribbled from his chin, but he carried on regardless. After the initial shock of the Viridian Legion's attack had faded, Darius's thoughts had lingered on only one thing: revenge on Hadrian and stopping the brute's campaign of terror.

Sat on Darius's right, Sulla had long since finished his food and picked his teeth clean from what seemed more force of habit than to loosen chunks of meat.

Darius tried his best to ignore the rakkan and retreated into his mind to connect with Lyra for the third time that day.

Lyra. Tell Varro we need him. Urge him to come however you can. As he'd grown used to, his connection with her was disturbed because she was moving around—probably bouncing from the walls or on the hunt—but he hoped she'd find a way to communicate with the Warlord. *At least you're better.* They'd sent pigeons, but Darius wanted to make sure the message got there as quickly as possible.

Sulla nudged Darius from his pondering and leaned in. "Have you decided whether you're leaving with us at dusk?"

The question grated Darius's nerves, being the fourth time he'd asked.

"I'll stay with you," Darius said.

Sulla raised a hand to give him a pat on the shoulder but froze at the last second with a wince at Darius's delicate body. "Good man." Sulla gave a thumbs up to a commander across the table.

"But I don't want to leave Laltos. According to Lex, the humans will defend. The Viridians are days away, and the Regent is only evacuating a third of the city. Everyone else will stay to assist with building fortifications and then battle."

The grin that had appeared on Sulla's face turned to confusion. "But you said—"

"I want you to stay too. Let's fight the Viridians while we have the city walls to shield us."

Sulla leaned in closer and lowered his voice. "If things don't go well, there'll be no escape from this place. And need I remind you how they tortured you for weeks. Why do you want to protect Laltos?"

"Not all of them wronged me. There are plenty sitting in the gutters that didn't."

Sulla rested his head in his hand. "I know the feeling, but we need Varro."

"Let's get some air," Darius said. "We can talk more candidly alone."

Sulla helped Darius up, as his legs were still weak, and the pair exited the dining hall. They made their way through the palace halls until they reached a rooftop garden. It overlooked the lamp-lit city but was small, with room for only a wooden bench and three potted ferns.

As they gazed over the flickering lights of the city below, all Darius imagined were each flame turned into ferven-fuelled blazes devouring citizen, soldier and slave alike.

He leaned on the stone wall at the edge, and Sulla did likewise to his right.

"Sorry to be a pain," Darius said, "but with the Xavalan cavalry our odds have improved."

"They haven't even agreed to come. Is this you talking or Lex?"

She'd spoken to Darius at length about what they should say to Sulla, but Darius had resolved to make up his own mind for once. "This is me."

With a growl, Sulla straightened his back. "It's hard for me to defend a city that did what it did to you." The wall cracked under his hands, and the glow of ferven engulfed the rakkan's eyes. "It takes all my strength not to rip them all limb from limb."

As Darius stared at his friend, he couldn't believe how intensely the rakkan felt his own pain. "I want this. I want Hadrian dead. I want payback for Lyra and all the others that have suffered at his hands."

"You don't get it, do you?" Sulla's voice rose. "That's how I feel when I see what these humans did to you!"

Darius turned away, unsure how to respond. How could Sulla care for him like he cared for Lyra? He'd done nothing to warrant it besides lie and go behind his friend's back.

"Why?" Darius asked.

"You may have forgotten, but I haven't. I won't. You were like a brother to me, and you still are—even though half a century separates us. When we first met, you found me stealing a kuraminium dagger from your quarters. Back then, I was a vagrant and a thief. I could excuse it by saying I was poor or desperate, but the truth is I was just idle and aimless. Most that caught me gave me a fresh scar or broke a few bones, but not you. You signed me up for the Militia."

This was the first story Darius had heard about his old self that wasn't one of battle and conquest, the first that roused a sense of pride.

"I still see the man I knew inside," Sulla said with a warm smile.

Darius scoffed. "And what if I'm not? Would you stay and defend Laltos then?"

"I know what you're doing." Sulla turned to him, lifted his chin a little.

"What?"

"You blame yourself for all this, so much so that you'll risk getting yourself killed trying to put it right. Well, the past can't be put right. All you can do is not damn your future."

Was that true? The more Darius pondered, the more the guilt became obvious, but it did nothing to resolve their situation. Given it was only Sulla's fondness of Darius that kept him from the fight, if Darius wanted his way, he'd have to remind Sulla of the mistakes that led them here in the first place, and remind the rakkan of the dead Militia Chief he was still to avenge.

"I don't deserve your loyalty," Darius said.

Sulla raised an eyebrow. "Oh no?"

"There's something I never told you before…about what happened with the Viridians that made them attack the mine."

A darkness fell upon Sulla's expression, and for once, Darius wasn't sure of the rakkan's intentions. But he had no better idea to rile the man up, to spur him to battle. "Before I travelled there, I had every intention of slaughtering them, despite Varro's orders." While not strictly true—he'd been far more conflicted over Lex's pleas—it was close enough to the truth.

Sulla frowned, eyes fluttering as his brain put together the pieces.

"I'd heard what was happening," Darius continued, "what hell I'd unleashed on Laltos by slaying Archimedes. So I went to aid them. The Viridians didn't attack me like I said. I attacked them."

For a few moments, Sulla froze, each passing second chilling the cold glower on his face even more.

"You witless bastard." Sulla punched him across the jaw, thrusting Darius's head to the side with a crack that knocked him to his knees.

The city's lamps spun in his vision. He'd felt the strike coming in the air but had let the blow land, and he was ready to take the rest. It was the least he deserved.

"*She* put you up to it, didn't she?" Sulla snarled.

Darius said nothing. He stood back up and braced for another punch, conscious that Sulla had only put half his weight behind the first.

But the only movement from the rakkan's balled fists were tremors. "That got my chief killed. It lost us the mine... Why?"

Darius avoided his furious stare and gestured towards the city below. "For them, for my human half... I'd do the same for the rakkans." It was only then he realised that his former self had done just that. His fight against Archimedes, all the slaughtered algus in Denehill, were to protect the rakkans from annihilation.

Guess the old Darius is still somewhere inside. For the first time, he felt a kinship with the man and less like an imposter filling his boots.

Sulla grabbed him by the cloak and jerked him forwards. "Your infatuation with Lex ends now. She's warped your mind into believing her twisted plans are what *you* want. But the only cause she fights for is her own. *We're* your true friends."

Darius couldn't brush Lex aside so easily, given she'd risked her daughter to save him, but this wasn't the time to argue it.

"Trust me," Darius said, "I'll be wary of them."

"Who's 'them'?"

"Lex, Selene, any woman. I can't trust them when I feel something for them." And his distrust extended to men too after the torture.

Sulla's scars deepened as he grimaced. "The 'mindless' excuse doesn't last forever. We're all responsible for our own actions, even if we're swayed by a beautiful woman."

Darius hung his head. "Like I said, it's my fault. I made my choices."

"If you were any other rakkan, I'd break your neck. You're lucky I'm merciful. I haven't seen it, but I've heard what the Viridians are doing out west." Sulla finally released Darius and paced around the small rooftop with a balled fist, as if looking for something to smash. "Don't mention this conversation to Lex. I want her to think she's still in control, but I'll never trust her again." He shook his head. "What will Brutus say…?"

Darius hadn't even considered this story making it back to his mentor. He suddenly felt chills. "I won't tell Lex, but only if you agree to one thing."

Sulla stopped and his fists shook. "I'm in no mood for demands."

"Then think of it as a request. If we ever see Brutus again, let me be the one to tell him."

"He'll be livid…but I agree; it's better coming from you. And Varro?"

"I'll speak with him too." Trying to avoid dwelling too much on how the brothers would take the news, Darius rubbed his tender jaw, which pained him more from the touch. He must have been recovering because, previously, a strike like this wouldn't have registered above the soreness everywhere else.

"I don't suppose you've changed your mind on staying?" Darius asked, a shot to nothing. "It's your chance to avenge Claudius."

Sulla scowled at him. "Don't push me. I'll decide once we hear from Xavala on their plans." With that, he strode back inside and disappeared down the corridor.

50

Nikolaos – Xavala, the Silk City

"Send your cavalry!" Nikolaos followed the Silk Regent at the hem of his cloak, through the central aisle of an enormous stable. Rows of stalls stood full of horses and swifts of shades from brown to black. Hung over the wooden beams containing them, each had a large coat of iron scales ready. Hoplites with spears stood to attention in front of each, kuraminium edging the tips.

"I can't send riders alone," the Silk Regent replied over his shoulder, kicking away straw at his feet. "Laltos will have to defend without my help."

"You must send your cavalry." The King's Orator strode alongside him and cast her eyes over each horse. "The King wasn't requesting."

Nikolaos frowned, still uneasy every time he learned the King wanted something specific. *If it gets me closer to the regency, though…*

"If the King wants to help," Aristippus replied, "then he can send his own algus."

"Toria is too far." Ophelia's voice chilled. "The King acts through you."

"I know what you asked of me last night, but I'm sure Nikol—"

"What was said was for your ears only." The King's Orator spun and put her body in the Silk Regent's path, bringing the three of them to a halt. Her grey eyes stared unblinking at the algus, who returned the stare with a dark, furrowed brow.

Whatever was said, I'll find out. Nikolaos pondered for a second before remembering there wasn't time for puzzlement.

He strode to stand beside Ophelia and faced Aristippus with her, if only to avoid another slash to his arm in the future.

"You must aid Laltos," Nikolaos said. "Most of the city is loyal to the King and will be loyal to you thereafter." Not to mention, Nikolaos didn't want to rule over the ruins of his childhood home, over an empty bank. Its rulers needed to die, but not with the entire city.

"Liberate them," Ophelia said, her voice soft and honeyed but an order nonetheless, "and it will be yours."

The words set a stone in Nikolaos's belly. Surely, she hadn't promised the city to this algus…

Aristippus's dark eyes searched them both then rested on the King's Orator. "I'll get what you vowed? The mulberry trees?"

Ophelia didn't reply, her unwavering gaze enough to convey she was cunning but a woman that honoured her word.

"Fine. I'll do it on one condition," the Silk Regent said.

"What?"

"The King's Sword rides to Laltos too."

Ophelia smiled. "Done."

411

A greedy smile spread across the Silk Regent's face. "Then the cavalry will ride. I'll set the people of Laltos free."

The words should have relieved Nikolaos, but he could only be unnerved by the sinister grins on both of their faces.

Regardless, he made himself focus on the positive. Soon Laltos would be saved and its regent deposed. Nikolaos was one step away from ascension.

51

Sulla – Laltos

Sulla stomped down the hallway, the echo of his boots diverting the paths of passing slaves ahead of him. Dried mud trails spoiled the blue carpets as he trudged, and Sulla did his best to hammer the stains in deep with each step.

How could Darius be such a fool? The old Darius would never have acted without speaking with Sulla first. Sure, the half-man had often had his own agenda, but he'd discussed things with Sulla, or at least Brutus. Although the old Darius was still in there somewhere, the new one was developing some rather bothersome traits.

Sulla grunted. Was his judgement impaired when it came to the lad? If it were any other rakkan that had plotted to ignite all-out war… Perhaps he was best to let his commanders decide their next course of action.

It wasn't much farther until he reached the section of the palace that had been reserved for the rakkan guests. The décor was barer, with no paintings of long-dead kings or battles, only bland stone that a rakkan could crack with a single punch.

A few chunks had already been taken out of the walls by passing rakkans in heavy armour knocking into them.

Sulla spotted the wooden door marked "Parlour" he'd been searching for then slammed his palm into it.

The door swung open so violently the handle knocked another hunk of stone from the wall behind.

As the bang's echo faded, the rakkans inside the stuffy room fell silent, some with smoking pipes hanging from their mouths. So many had crammed in, from legionnaires to commanders, that most had to stand around the small tables dotted around, outnumbering the seating the Regent had provided.

Who could blame them for huddling together? Inside the rooms they'd been allocated was the only place to escape the locals staring in the same way people looked at stray dogs. Being away from the glares made it worth putting up with the smell of sweat and ash.

"All except the commanders leave!" Sulla barked.

Without hesitation, rakkans began to silently file out. *This is how loyal rakkans act, Darius.*

"What's wrong?" Atticus came forward and, as he so often did, offered Sulla a cup of firewater.

This time, the Militia Chief refused with a shake of the head. "I need a clear mind." Sulla pulled a chair up to one of the larger tables and collapsed onto it with a sigh.

Seven commanders joined him at the table while the last remaining warriors left the room and closed the door behind them.

Sulla regarded each of them, their black eyes wide with concern over his troubles. How should he phrase his dilemma, and should he reveal what Darius had told him?

"Are *we* allowed to have a drink?" Horatius asked. Brown firewater had already stained the stubble on his jaw.

"I'd rather not until we're done." Sulla swept his arm across the table and moved aside all the cups and dice that littered it. The lives of he and his men were all part of such games to the likes of Lex and the algus. To think how much he'd helped her over the years…

Although empty, the room was still suffocating and hot. The smoke snaking from the pipes left on tables only worsened the tightness in Sulla's throat.

"The Viridians are only a few days away," Sulla said. "The humans' preference is to stay and defend Laltos, and the Xavalan Cavalry may ride in support, but who knows if they'll come in time. Even with them, the battle will be a struggle. We need to decide what to do next."

Atticus took a long drag from his pipe. "You're thinking of staying to defend Laltos, aren't you?"

Sulla scanned the faces of the rest to gauge their reactions to the statement, and, unsurprisingly, they all looked as if it was already on their minds. Darius hadn't spoken to most of them as far as Sulla knew.

"My mind is clouded by everything happening with Darius," Sulla said. "I can't make this decision." For now, he wouldn't remind them that Darius was indirectly responsible for the death of the former Militia Chief. Seven commanders were a good enough number for a vote. It would avoid him having to come down on either side.

But the others all seemed afraid to speak, to move even.

"This is no trick," Sulla said. "I know this isn't how rakkan leaders usually decide, but for this, it's how I'm doing it."

"Why?" Atticus asked.

Sulla slammed his fist onto the table. "Because I said so! Now discuss the options."

Horatius leaned forward and took hold of a cup of stiff drink, but paused when he saw Sulla's glare. He retracted his hand and spoke. "If we leave, where will we go?"

"South is our only choice," one commander replied. "We have Viridians to the west, humans to the east and the sea to the north."

"But what's the destination? A thousand rakkans is a lot to feed and house, and more difficult without a city to assimilate them into."

An issue that had given Sulla many a restless night—a first for him.

"Staying means a bloody battle." Atticus sighed. "Are we all prepared to die?"

Horatius stood, much to Sulla's surprise, and clenched his wide jaw. "Do we really need to discuss this again?"

"When did we discuss this?" Sulla asked.

"You didn't," Atticus said, "but it's all we and the men talk about."

"This is our chance." Horatius held up a fist. "We'll catch the Viridian Legion off-guard and crush them. They don't know we're here. We'll stand a better chance inside the city than if they catch us fleeing south. Let's avenge our last Militia Chief."

Three other commanders grunted and nodded their heads. Sulla looked each one in the eye and saw a determination and purpose in them that he'd seldom seen since their exile.

Death held no sway over him, and it warmed him that the others were of like mind.

"If you're tired of argument then let's vote," Sulla said. "All who wish to stay and fight the Viridians, stand. If you don't, stay seated."

416

Horatius remained standing as four other commanders stood. Only Atticus and one other didn't, whose faces bore concern but no fear or anguish that the vote was lost.

Sulla picked up a cup of firewater and held it high in the air as he stood up to join his commanders.

The remaining two stood as well with a nod, and Sulla breathed a sigh of relief. If the Red Militia wanted to fight, then he was happy to fight alongside them. All that remained now was to figure out a way to tip the scales in the defenders' favour.

He downed the half-full cup in one gulp and savoured the burning in his throat. "Let's give them hell."

52

Darius – Laltos

Darius awoke to a stiff breeze washing over his bandaged body. Thin curtains waved frantically in front of two open doors that led to the balcony of the bedroom he'd been recovering in for the last few days, one of many rooms within Lex's home. His muscles tensed and he curled up, reaching for the satin covers to shield him from the chills.

"Sorry," a woman's voice whispered from across the room, much to Darius's surprise. Selene hurried to close the doors, which cloaked the once bright room in shadow. "I thought we could use a little air."

Darius sat up, glancing from the armchairs around the hearth to the bolted door. It was only the two of them. "What are you doing here?"

"Lex asked me to watch over you until she returned."

"She did what?" His knuckles cracked as he squeezed the covers in his hands. Lex and her workers had been taking good care of him and cleaning his wounds, but he hadn't spoken with Selene much since the failed escape.

His mind was a confused mess of emotion at just the thought of her.

"Lex trusts me, even if you don't." Selene walked softly towards the unlit hearth. As she did, a pteron darted from a shelf and landed on her shoulder. It took Darius a few moments to recognise Selene's escort, which sent his thoughts immediately to Lyra.

Paris flapped his scaly wings until he landed on her outstretched arms as she sat down in a chair. She avoided eye contact with Darius, which he had no qualms about. Still, he couldn't help but stare at the bruises on her face that were healing since he'd last seen her.

"Food?" he grunted.

"There's a spread of hog and bison laid out in the dining hall when you're ready."

He was tempted to go dressed in only a sheet, but judging by his joints creaking as he stretched, he needed a few minutes to limber up. "When's Lex back?"

"Any moment," Selene said, still avoiding eye contact. "She's due to finish the tour of the city with Sulla, and she wants you to accompany them for the end."

"I don't feel like a hike." The cuts on his body prickled as he hauled himself out of bed and threw on his trousers.

"It won't be long. Just the main gate left to inspect." Selene's finger shook slightly as she stroked her pteron's breast.

"What's wrong?" he asked.

She looked up at him. Her eyebrows raised when their eyes met. "Nothing."

Darius stalked over to her, scowling, which caused Selene's brow to rise further.

419

"What is it?" Darius demanded.

"It's just…I'm a little afraid."

He stopped. "Oh. Of the Viridians?"

"No…of you."

Darius scoffed. "If anyone should be afraid it's me, still in this city and at the hand of my torturers."

"I hear the anger in your voice every time you speak, see the way you can't look at me. I remember what you did to that village of rakkans."

Shaking his head, Darius turned away from her and began pacing the room to get his fatigued legs used to moving. "I don't know what to think, what to feel. You risked your life for me, but it's difficult to forget you handed me over in chains. The pain was…"

Selene stood too and flinched as if about to step towards him, but she held back. "I'm sorry I didn't believe you. But I never intended to have you tormented."

In his darkest moments in the prison cell, he hadn't expected an apology to matter much, yet now it made him want to take her in his arms and enjoy the warmth of her skin again.

A pair of voices grew in the hallway outside, and Darius threw on his tunic and cloak as they grew louder. He recognised the voices as Lex and Sulla, and the two didn't knock as they opened the door and halted in surprise when they found him standing to greet them.

By their beleaguered faces, Darius saw neither had slept much.

Lex wore her usual algus clothes while Sulla wore a thick black cloak and hood, shielding him from even the dim sunlight in the room.

"I hear you're taking me on an excursion," Darius said.

"Indeed. Let's go." Sulla turned and paced back down the hallway without a smile—another sign that filled Darius with worry.

Selene followed him, and the four of them made their way through the long halls of Lex's house to the street outside, then towards the main gate.

Darius was surprised at how well he kept pace with Sulla's hurried footsteps because at first, he'd struggled.

The group made little conversation, so Darius once again reached out to Lyra and tried to sense how she was, and how much luck she'd had with Varro.

Once connected, he felt a mild thrill and a sense of relief from her. Perhaps she'd got through to the Warlord, but it could have easily been from catching a meal. She moved around more now and had probably tired of the rations the Margalvians gave her.

Darius refocused on his surroundings again when the group arrived underneath the arched stone entryway into Laltos, where Theodoros awaited them. Like the others, he'd opted for a simpler, more practical cloak and could have been mistaken for any other nobleman without the golden threading.

The Regent dismissed the guards around him and stood silently, hands clasped behind his back.

The high gateway cast a long shadow over the cobbles below. At least two dozen men could march through side to side, and the gates themselves were not a substantial challenge for a rakkan army to break through, easier than the tall, flat walls.

Sulla shook his head. "By the Creator, this is even worse than the rest of it. How many years since rakkans attacked here?"

"A while," Theodoros admitted.

"It shows. The back of the city is well protected by the cliffs and mountains behind, but the front… You wouldn't survive a band of drunks, let alone the Viridian Legion. Do you have enough algus?" Sulla turned to Lex, who sighed with a tired shake of the head.

"We have a couple of hundred," Selene said. "Those that have swifts have already ridden west to harry their army with bows and spears. It'll thin the numbers and slow their approach while we gather the people and food from the surrounding settlements."

"So, you'll lose some." Sulla rubbed his eyes and took a few deep breaths. "This needs a better strategist than I."

"Don't forget we have a thousand rakkans of our own," Lex said. "Let us worry of tactics. You worry about pointing out the flaws in our defences."

"Do we need more flaws? They'll tear through this gate in minutes, and don't think they won't try. Your lands have too little food for them to risk a lengthy siege."

Darius's heart quickened before they'd even drawn blood. "We must slow their approach outside the city and give our archers as much time as possible."

Sulla gave him a sceptical look, like he'd suggested they try to defend with wooden swords.

"Dig trenches," Darius said. "Flood them with water from the river and have algus protect the walls of the gateway with algor. It'll give us time to spray them with arrows."

"The trenches will need to be wide and deep," Sulla said. "They may have ladders too."

"Then burn them. We have rakkans."

"They'll be made of metal."

"Melt them then."

"Kuraminium."

Darius grunted in frustration. "I doubt it. Why carry all that weight so many miles when they only expect to face humans?"

422

"Assumptions are dangerous."

"We have other defences that will work." Lex folded her arms. "Like sulphur."

Sulla swallowed. "It'll only slow them."

"I have other ways," Theodoros said.

The four of them turned at the Regent expectantly.

He walked up to the gate and slapped a hand on it, the sound as flat as if he'd struck a stone wall. "That gate is made from imported ironwood and has kuraminium bars drilled through each offset layered plank. Before that they must reckon with our ballistae, which are of my design and will have a range beyond what they've seen before. They'll be tipped with algor from channels of oil running along the battlements, as will all our arrows."

Sulla sighed as if unconvinced, but his frown eased slightly, and he stepped closer to the gate. He slammed his palm into it a few times and sucked his lips when it didn't budge.

Whilst it may have given the Militia Chief comfort, Darius still saw the substantial risk. "How long will it need to hold until the Xavalan cavalry arrive?"

"A week if they don't get delayed," Lex said.

"Too long," Sulla said, this time so loud that even the peltasts and archers farther up the street heard, which caused a few anxious stares.

Lex tightened the tie in her hair. "I know how we can get them here in time."

Every face turned to her, including Theodoros, who had a raised eyebrow but a glint of expectation in his eye.

"Dig a new tunnel through the cliff," she continued. "Not all the way through, but enough to connect it to the easier hills atop. Then the cavalry can approach directly from the east."

Darius looked back towards the cliffs. *A tunnel in only a few days? And trenches?* The suggestion struck Darius as optimistic, and a few of the soldiers around exchanged bemused glances, but Darius had heard of rakkan mining speed.

He watched Sulla's reaction closely and felt relief when he saw the rakkan's mouth curl into a grin with a nod.

"Tunnels, we can do," Sulla said.

The battle was on.

53

Darius – Laltos

A few days passed with poor news from the west. The mounted algus slowed the Viridian advance but struggled to thin their numbers given the forests. Still, the delay gave them more time to strip the farms outside the city, and gave the Xavalan cavalry longer, who Lex had informed of the new plan via her escort.

Every man, woman and boy that could lift a spade was called outside Laltos to dig trenches. With time against them, they were deepest in front of the gate. Those were filled with water, but it didn't flow across the entire front of the wall.

Darius took the time to recover, resigned to bed rest. But after a few days, he quickly tired of being confined to his room, so instead he searched out Sulla, who was overseeing the digging of the tunnel.

The hostile air hit Darius as soon as he set foot inside. With the molten rock at his feet, every breath was hot and heavy. Once deep inside, the only light came from the ferven flaring across the hands and pickaxes of the rakkan warriors smashing apart the stone ahead. Tunnels were hellish places to work, but the rakkans were at least out of the afternoon sun, and they cut through rock so fast it was a struggle for the workers to extract the loose rubble fast enough.

Sulla turned and saw him. "What are you doing out?"

"Change of scenery," Darius replied. "The tunnel is coming along well." Separate from Laltos's existing passageways, this one was tall enough to ride a horse through.

"Is it almost finished?" Darius asked. The ground sloped gradually upwards and surely had to break through to the surface soon.

"We'll see daylight within the hour. We'll start evacuating soon after."

Only the most important and wealthiest had fled so far, evading the demands to fortify the city, as the rich always did. But this tunnel would give a swifter and safer escape for the toilers.

Not everyone would escape in time, but Darius guessed that it was still better than nothing.

He ran a hand down one of the stone pillars, still hot to touch. "Did you build in the fail-safe Theodoros suggested?"

"Yes. There's a chamber below the tunnel. Knock out the central columns and this entire place comes crashing down."

"Looks like you were wrong, then. If the battle doesn't go well, we have a way out."

The frown on Sulla's face told a different story. "We're behind the palace. If the Viridians make it here, then we're already dead. Which reminds me, I need to give you your orders."

For the first time, it occurred to Darius that there wasn't anyone to issue him commands, with Varro far away. But he reckoned he owed Sulla.

"I'm too weak to join the front line," Darius said, "but I could—"

"Don't worry. You won't be near there. You'll be here at the palace."

Darius grimaced. "No one will be fighting at the palace."

"Exactly. You may be fuller in the cheeks and walking with more ease, but I've seen you swing a sword. You won't be much use in a battle, and I need a pair of rakkan eyes high that can give the Regent and commander's information on the front line."

"But I'm—"

"And, if we need to collapse this tunnel, I'll need a rakkan with the strength to knock out the pillars and fast enough to make it out alive."

With a curse, Darius looked around at the musclebound warriors and miners, knowing none moved those beefy legs with enough haste. But he didn't want to be out of the fight like a coward.

"Don't even think about arguing," Sulla said, catching his expression. "This isn't for your benefit. I need someone I can trust to oversee the battle and send guidance."

"I've never seen a battle that I remember," Darius murmured. How was he supposed to guide others when he had trouble taking care of himself and Lyra?

"Your old self had keen insights, and you can do it again. And don't forget"—Sulla's eyes narrowed, a fury in them so unusual that Darius felt himself sink—"you owe me."

As much as it would pain him to sit idly by, Darius couldn't argue with his indebtedness. "Fine. Whatever you say, Chief."

"Sulla!" A commander ran up the tunnel, panting. "The Regent sent word. Lex's escort has seen the Xavalans, numbering around ten thousand men and horse. They'll be here in two days."

The Militia Chief grinned, but a shake of the commander's head soon quashed it.

"There's more," he said. "The Viridians have reached the edge of the forest and made camp. If they set off at dusk, they'll be here in the morning."

"They won't," Sulla said. "They'll sleep through the night, when the algus riders can't see enough to harry them, then set off at dawn. Better to arrive at dusk and fight in darkness. Easier to cover your skin on the march than in battle."

Darius nodded. "Let's get moving with the evacuation then."

54

Battle of Laltos

Darius lingered at the foot of the steps of the palace, watching the once white Laltos buildings that now glowed orange in the waning sunlight. He and Selene stood rigid and silent, teetering at the edge of the royal courtyard.

Lines of women and children shuttled past the palatial pillars of the algus elites that had once protected them from the rakkans' wrath, the tunnel now their best hope for salvation. As for the men, anyone older than fourteen had been given spears, a few hours training on how to hold the thing, and pushed to the city walls.

In front of Darius, not a single head was without dishevelled hair, including some wealthy citizens with pockets stuffed heavy with coins and jewels. One woman had knotted blonde hair falling across her tunic and hugged a child in her arms while her slaves tugged bags behind. By the relief on the slaves' faces, they were just glad they got to proceed at the front of the queue with their mistress rather than be left behind with the others.

A kuraminium cuirass weighed down Darius's shoulders, but he wouldn't have traded it for the paltry scale armour most of the hoplites wore that couldn't even block the stiff breeze. Along with his helmet and greaves, it almost felt as if he sank into the stone beneath his feet, his bones compressing.

"You didn't have to stay with me," Darius said, tiring of the silence.

"I did." Selene gave him a wistful smile. "My father needs my escort to relay messages. Besides, I won't desert you again."

Even if he hadn't totally forgiven her, the sentiment stirred pangs of longing.

The spot gave them a suitable vantage point over the city below, from the greenery of the upper city to the once smoky lower city, where slaves and servants hid in nooks and cellars.

Beyond the walls, the acres of farms that fed the nation were now stained with patches of darkness drifting steadily across. At the flanks, groups of mounted algus charged in and out with bows and javelins to harry the legionnaires, but the Viridians' shields and slingers looked to spare them significant losses.

"I see a battering ram heading for the gate." Darius strained his rakkan eyes to see farther. "Along with at least half the legion. There are no siege towers or ladders."

"I'll relay it to my father." Selene scrawled a note while her pteron waited on the wall. "Let me know if you spot anything else."

Soon, only raging ferven blazes would light up the city enough for humans to see. The towers would be stained black and red with fire and blood. How he wished he could be down there defending.

The tension seized his head like a band tight around it, and he clutched his temples.

"Darius?"

He looked up and expected it to be Selene who spoke but instead met Lex's blue eyes.

"Lex." How glad he was to see her. He'd searched for her all day without success.

Along with the usual black tunic, she'd fitted a set of steel scales across her arms and shoulders.

He slipped the helmet from his head, wanting to get a clear look of her for what could be the last time.

"Are you ready?" he asked.

Lex dipped her head. "Yes, but I'll be on the battlements a mile from the gate. The fight may bypass me entirely."

Darius scoffed. "I'm not the only one set aside, then."

"My protests were firm, but ultimately fell on deaf ears. It's my father's choice."

He smiled, unwilling to pretend he wasn't relieved. "I guess it's ironic, that a rakkan we both want dead is just outside the city, yet we've been held back from the fight. Maybe he'll survive."

Lex's jawline tensed. "If he doesn't die tonight, we'll try again tomorrow. And the next day."

He grinned, the words being just what he expected and wanted to hear.

"Don't take Hadrian on alone, even if you see an opportunity." Lex gave him a concerned look before sighing and casting her gaze over the citizens still scurrying to the tunnel. "Tiro will be overhead. If he can't see, I'll keep him close to you."

If only Lyra were by Darius's side too, but his connection with her was ever more erratic. She had been restless since sensing the danger he was in. *Poor girl can't sit still.* At the thought, Darius recalled Lex's young girl.

"Where's Cynthia?" he asked.

"She's in the palace cellars. Sulla gave me a few rakkans to protect her along with one of my brothers." Her eyes met his for a few moments, and specks of algor glinted inside them, seeming to say a thousand things her lips wouldn't.

"I should take up my position." She took his hand, brushed her thumb against his with a smile before turning away.

"Lex?"

"Yes?" She looked over her shoulder as strands of her hair swept across her cheeks. He'd promised Sulla never to be swayed by that beautiful face again, but seeing it now made him doubt his willpower.

"I appreciate you always saving my neck," he said.

She smirked. The sight was so rare his mouth almost fell open.

"Let's not add another time to the list," she said. "And about what you said before. You're wrong. You're not being left aside."

"Then what am I?"

"You're with Selene. They trust you enough to help direct our forces, just as I'll be doing."

The thought of him directing anyone felt so out of place that Darius was at a loss for words. He was used to fighting, nothing else.

"May Agathos protect both of you." With a slight bow of her head, Lex turned and set off at a run down the hill.

Darius watched her go, all the way to the end of the street and round a corner out of sight.

"And you," he whispered. If she was killed and he somehow survived, he had no idea how he'd tolerate such rage. Woe to anyone he unleashed it on.

He turned to Selene, who had stood quietly, acting as if she hadn't listened in on them. The fading light set deep shadows on her sunken cheeks.

"How're you feeling?" he asked.

She frowned and looked unsettled by the question. "Fine."

Well, that's a bare-faced lie. "The Viridian Legion is about to raze your home, and you're fine?"

She sighed. "As fine as I can be, considering. Here, before I forget…" She felt around her sword belt and clasped the bear claw forever tied to it. With delicate fingers, she unfastened the leather strap and held the claw out to him. "I want you to have it for fortune."

He watched the claw swing back and forth in the wind, wondering if her fingers would let go once he clasped it. "You said it was all you had left of your escort."

"It is, but who knows what will happen tonight. I just need you to know whose side I'm on."

Darius carefully took the claw and held it in his hand, ran a finger across the slight dents in it where the beast had scratched metal or bone. It would be impossible for him to part with his last remaining piece of Lyra if, heavens forbid, something happened to her.

Still holding the claw, he took both it and Selene's hand into his own and stroked it. His touch brought a little colour to her cheeks.

She released him with a smile, and he tied the strip of leather to his belt with four tight knots.

"Thanks," he muttered as he replaced the helmet back over his head. The cold metal eased his headache. "Do you think things will ever go back to how they were between us?" He cringed as soon as the words left his mouth.

Selene sighed. "I hope so."

"Can you see me as more than a murderous warrior again?"

"Oh, Darius." She brought a hand to his neck, gave it a squeeze that relieved tension with a touch. "I already see you as more."

The reassurance lifted his spirits a little for the first time in days, and he realised how much he'd longed for her to see him as she once had.

Too bad there's little time to dwell on it. "How far away are the Xavalan army now?"

"Around eight hours, last time Paris checked."

"Damn. Then let's pray the Viridians don't breach the gate quickly as Sulla predicted."

***

Sulla strode in front of the black shield wall and cast his eyes over the corrugated face, ready to charge as soon as the Viridians burst through the gateway. Creator willing, the surprise at seeing rakkan defenders would rout the invaders.

He kicked at the curved, rectangular shield of a short warrior. "Lift it up, or they'll have your head and the man next to you."

The rakkan lifted the shield to which Sulla nodded in approval.

"Spears out!" Sulla shouted.

A series of razor-sharp spearheads jabbed between the thin gaps in the shields.

"Good," he yelled. "At ease."

The men lowered their shields and weapons as Sulla turned his gaze to the entrance into the city.

At each side of the gate, the battlements teemed with iron-capped soldiers readying bags of sulphur and buckets of oil.

Not long after he'd surveyed the defences, a series of rakkan horns blasted out from beyond the walls.

The sun had all but disappeared. Time had finally run out.

"Hear their cry!" Sulla bellowed. "Let's show those scum why Margalvia's warriors make even the demons cower!"

***

The horns' blares grew louder with every step Lex climbed until she finally reached the ramparts, panting. She pushed through the lines of soldiers to the front.

Only faint sunlight remained, enough to make out dark ripples of movement in the land outside, as if watching over the seas on a stormy night.

Drums pounded in unison. Six thousand enemies were far from the largest army she'd seen assembled, but, like the sea, she feared the destructive power within.

Of the fire pits the Laltosians had dug and lit across the fields before the attack, only a few remained alight, with more being snuffed out with shovelled dirt by the second. The rakkans' sight in the shadows was an advantage they'd utilise. Men feared nothing more than the dark and unknown.

Atop the battlements, the first row of heavily armoured hoplites was interspersed with the occasional rakkan in disguise. Behind stood archers. The men closest held their weapons tight and flinched with every boom of the Viridian drums.

"What can you see?" Lex asked the nearest rakkan.

Other heads turned to hear the answer.

"Looks like the entire legion is here," the rakkan replied in a tone that sounded a little too keen at the fact.

"How far away are they?"

"Quarter of a mile."

A couple of minutes until in range of the ballistae. Then they'd likely charge towards the trenches where the archers could thin the ranks.

"Ladders?" Lex asked. "Any other siege weapons?"

435

"No ladders, but hard to say."

"Catapults?"

The rakkan scoffed. "Rakkans don't need them. A sling is enough."

As they'd thought, but it was important to make certain.

"Load the ballistae!" she called. The crank of handles and clunk of kuraminium-headed bolts being picked up from the piles melded in with the monotonous thunder of drums from the marching legion.

"Archers, ready!" Lex cried.

Each bowman withdrew an arrow from their quiver.

The thundering drums silenced to leave only the rapid breaths of the surrounding soldiers.

All light now extinguished, the fields in front were black, as if she were blind. No moon. No flame. Only an abyss, and the low roars and clanks of metal from the invaders.

"What're they doing?" Lex asked the rakkan in a tone far more nervous than she'd intended.

"They've stopped."

"Are they in range?"

The rakkan grunted. "Hard to say. They're straightening their ranks, and troops are moving. I still see no ladders, but their warriors are spread wide."

"What about the battering ram?"

"It's on course for the gate. We have many in front of us, so prepare to…oh, hell! Slingers!"

Thousands of small flames sprung up in the field, forming a dotted line that stretched all the way from the gate to her position a mile along and beyond.

"Take cover!" Lex screamed, but ignored her own order while bodies all around dropped flat to the stone beneath.

The lights were too weak to make out anything other than the position of the front line, but all Lex cared about was whether they were in range of the ballistae. *Barely.*

She stepped closer to the rakkan who remained standing behind his kuraminium shield.

"They won't get through this," he grunted.

That's what she hoped because she needed to watch. Tiro circled above and showed her just how spread out the army was. *This doesn't look right.*

Whilst still at first, the flames then began moving rapidly in thousands of tiny circles.

"Incoming!" the rakkan roared.

Lights were unleashed and came screaming towards them.

Lex ducked behind the shield. Projectiles crashed into the wall and buildings around, so many they formed one long crack that set her ears ringing.

Chunks of stone and debris shot into the air before they rained down and filled her lungs with dust.

She coughed and dared to move her head to the side of the shield to steal a glimpse. More glowing balls as large as her fist were on their way.

She summoned the frozen touch of algor to her hand and then ducked to the ground, sinking her fingers into the oil.

As it set alight, the fluid sparked into a bright cobalt blue that spread rapidly through the trough.

More loud cracks sounded, followed by the crumbling and falling of stone.

"Load the ballistae!" she cried at the top of her lungs.

The rakkans all dipped the heads of the bolts into the algor oil then slid them into the ballistae.

A flaming rock crashed into the closest one, sending splinters flying into the surrounding soldiers. They skewered hands, punctured necks. Those closest fell with cries of pain.

"Loose!" Lex cried.

The ballistae twanged. Thick blue streaks lit up the night air as the bolts arced towards the line of flaming slingers.

More rocks peppered the buildings behind Lex. Chunks of merlons bashed into the soldiers ducking behind them while the rakkans loaded the next bolts.

Beyond the wall, the boom of metal on metal echoed across the field as the bolts reached the ranks of the Viridians.

They smashed apart the invaders' flaming shields, but half the bolts dipped and punctured nothing but earth. Other ballistae along the wall followed Lex's lead, as the other algus joined in the bombardment. Thank Agathos at least some were in range.

***

Darius watched the streaks of light, orange and blue, criss-crossing over the land outside the wall. One continuous, relentless wave of fiery balls came at the defenders, the Viridians displaying a unity and synchronisation the Laltos defenders failed to mimic.

The faint echo of stones hitting helmets, shields and bone became monotonous and grating. Ballistae responded, but more and more defenders fell with every onslaught.

"The Viridians aren't advancing on the gate," Darius said.

Selene gave him a worried look. "Really?"

Whatever Hadrian was up to, Darius was sure it wasn't what Laltos had prepared for. He began pacing, turning around with each crash of projectiles that hit the city. Before long, he'd made himself dizzy, so he stopped again next to Selene.

"Why the hell are we waiting here?" he asked. Being so far from the fight felt wrong.

"We're following orders," Selene said.

Right. The retort of every coward.

Selene grasped his wrist. "I know what you're thinking. But there's nothing you can do to help."

He felt strong enough but knew just how easily he tired. Fighting would exhaust him far quicker than he could afford.

Again, Darius watched the Viridian forces spread out across the fields. Those nearest the battering ram concentrated much less fire against the city's entrance.

"We should move some of our army from the gate," he said.

"Why?" Selene asked.

"I don't think that's their target. The ram has stopped, and the slingers aren't focusing their attacks there. Our ballistae can take care of the ram if it advances."

Selene frowned and squinted at the projectiles lighting up the sky. "Yes. Things aren't as I'd expect if the gate was their target."

"Send word to the Regent."

Selene wrote brief notes on a slip of parchment as Darius paced once again. He prayed he wasn't needed to cave in the tunnel but wouldn't hold his breath.

***

Sulla waited. His face ached from the frown it had been tensed into for who knew how long. The only gauge for how the ranged fight fared was how numerous the incoming projectiles were. Given they'd hardly changed, he guessed not great. *Come on, Hadrian. Breach the gate and stop horsing around.*

The men on the nearest battlements shouted. Some pointed to the far right while others bolted for the stairs and began racing up the street in the direction the others had pointed.

Something was amiss. Sulla broke free of his ranks of men. "Stay here." He tore down the road towards the gate and up to

439

the closest set of stairs. One of the descending archers tried to brush past him, but he clamped the man's arm tightly.

"Ouch!" the archer cried, with a wince, as if he expected Sulla to strike him.

"What's happening?"

"New orders. The Viridians are moving farther to the north."

Sulla released the man and bolted farther up the stairs until he caught sight of the fields himself. He ducked to narrowly miss an incoming stone. The shifting masses of rakkans below were marching away from the deep trenches near the gate, just as the man had said.

Holding onto a broken merlon, he leaned out over the parapet and saw a formation of legionnaires approach the city much farther along.

The Viridians leapt over the shallower trenches and clung to the other side. Others had approached with a shield wall. Every second rakkan shovelled like their life depended on it while the others raised their scuta to block the barrage of arrows now incoming.

All too quickly, the once steep side of the trenches in those shallower stretches was whittled away.

"Creator, help us," he muttered under his breath. He pulled himself back up and grabbed the nearest soldier. "You!"

"Yes?" the aged hoplite said in an anxious voice.

"Do you know the streets well enough to get me and my men close to that point?" He pointed to where the wall of shields would meet the city perimeter.

The hoplite took a quick glance then nodded.

Sulla shoved him forwards. "Then what are you waiting for?"

55

Battle of Laltos

Lex dared a glance over the ever-withering battlements. She made out only the glow of slingers still raining down fire. They'd carry on pelting until the last moment.

Amidst the barrage, she continued to take every chance she could to survey the black fields, ducking behind the closest rakkan's shield, which repelled blow after blow. The man grunted with each strike that almost toppled him.

Below, the lofted shields protecting shovellers were only illuminated by the occasional algor-coated ballista bolt or arrow that speared into either a rakkan or the dirt.

More and more invaders fell as the minutes passed, but not enough to satisfy Lex, whose eyes were ever on the trench and how much dirt they'd shovelled. *Too much.* Worse, ever fewer arrows were coming from the defenders.

She bent down and plunged her fingers into the oil again, sending a renewed wave of algor down the trough.

"Archers! Give them another volley. Hoplites, protect your comrades."

A hoplite next to her nodded and rose, lifting his sword with a furious cry. But a searing rock smashed into his helmet and cut off his shout.

His body tumbled to the ground. Bone crunched, and the stench of charred flesh made all those around recoil with scrunched faces.

Those that had looked poised to stand now hesitated, eyes fixated on the dead soldier. With only wooden shields to protect themselves, who could blame them for wavering?

The wall had taken the brunt of the damage, but the real destruction had been done to the men. In each pair of eyes, she saw the fear, the urine stains on the battlements. Their hands shook as they covered their eyes from the blinding dust.

"Come on." Lex waved at them to stand. "Laltos needs you."

The roars of hundreds of rakkans swelled from beyond the wall and stole whatever valour had remained in the hearts of the men. They needed more than courage; they needed inspiration.

Lex withdrew her hand from the trough and shook off the oil before releasing the bow on her back. She took in a deep breath. *For Laltos.* Amidst a backdrop of flaming projectiles still pouring down, she stood up tall above the parapet and lifted her chin.

The men gawped as if she'd grown wings and withdrawn a weapon of the God of Justice.

Pulling an arrow from her quiver, she set her eyes ablaze with algor and glared down at all the fearful soldiers with a grimace. "Get up and die with honour!"

She turned her gaze to the field and extinguished the light from her face. Her bowstring twanged as she unleashed an arrow into the neck of a rakkan holding his shield too low.

As her eyes scanned for the next target, a man stood up to her right, scowling. Then another to her left. Arrows appeared in the peripherals of her vision as the archers took their stations again and aimed at the shield wall.

That's more like it. She reached out with her bow and once again sent algor shooting down it and through the trough.

The archers dipped their arrowheads in and loosed a barrage of blue flares into the Viridians' shields.

The satisfying cracks and screams were a little too loud for comfort because they betrayed just how close to the wall the invaders were.

She gave a rakkan beside her a nudge and joined him behind his shield. "What do you see?"

The rakkan peered around. "They've almost finished dirt ramps into and out of the trenches."

"Still no ladders?"

"None."

The ballistae kept a steady pace but would soon run out of kuraminium-headed bolts.

Before she could give the order to switch to steel heads, horns blared from below.

The rakkan next to her squinted. "The shovellers are retreating. A few centuries have formed a shield wall, testudo formation."

"Where?"

"Right in front of us and fast approaching."

Damn that battering ram. How could she fall for a diversion?

She turned to her men and cried, "Get bags of sulphur and buckets of oil!" She caught the eye of a younger, doe-eyed archer

443

at the back, and he turned and ran like he needed no further excuse to evade the front line. Hopefully, he'd have enough sense to ask others for help. The main gate had most of their supplies.

The archers sent another volley of arrows into the frontmost group that had traversed the trench and advanced towards the wall.

When close, the shields in the formation erupted in ferven. Arrows fizzled out as they hit and bounced from the tough metal.

Damn them to hell.

The first testudo hit the wall and kept their blazing shields raised above them. None attempted to climb or jump.

The group stood still, fifty rakkans across at least. There was movement beneath, but it was hard to make anything out through the blinding light.

Lex started. They weren't coming over. "They're undermining the wall," she said to the rakkan next to her.

His eyes lost focus for a second before he gave a sombre nod to confirm her suspicions.

"How long will it take them?" she asked.

He grimaced. "Not long for rakkans. Can you protect it with algor?"

If only. "It's too far down and there are too many." Even dozens of algus couldn't nullify the ferven of hundreds.

The defenders tried to angle the ballistae down but failed. The miners were far out of their line of sight. Only algus on the ground would prevent it, but with so many in the open it would be a slaughter. Best to save their algus to defend the city in the narrow streets.

The trenches had delayed the Viridians but not enough. They'd breach the wall, eventually. All they could hope for was to slow them until the cavalry arrived. They needed the sulphur.

***

Sulla pushed the old soldier in the small of his back and thrust him through the streets. "Run like your life depends on it, man, for it does!"

They'd taken a shortcut and Sulla saw nothing but houses. So narrow were the roads they could only run with three side by side and still allow room for others to pass.

He coughed and took deep breaths, struggling from too many years without running in full armour. Perhaps his sister was right and he shouldn't have smoked so much. A young archer heading towards them caught Sulla's eye.

The boy skidded to a stop and almost tripped on a protruding stone. "You!"

Sulla didn't slow his pace and bolted past.

"Wait," the boy said, turning and easily overtaking them. "Are you bringing the oil and sulphur from the gate?"

It was Sulla's turn to skid to a halt. Metal crunched as the rakkans behind all compressed together. "Some. Why?"

"Follow me."

***

Darius hauled himself up onto the wall and stood, wobbling as he barely kept his balance with his aching thighs. A few months ago, it wouldn't have required thought.

He strained his eyes, focused on the parts of the city wall where the attackers approached.

"Do you see more?" Selene asked.

Like an extra few feet higher will help me see behind stone. "No ladders. No siege towers. No climbers." *No clue. What's Hadrian's plan?* "There's still no one coming for the gate."

He jumped down, and his knees buckled as he hit the ground, almost collapsing him into a heap of limbs and armour.

"Careful." Selene grabbed him under the arm. "You're still not strong enough for that kind of thing."

445

He took her hand for stability and found his balance only when his face stopped an inch from hers. Staring into her hazel eyes, for a second, he felt as if lying next to her in Dolthea again, but the look of pity and regret on her face soon brought him back to the invaded city.

"Why don't you sit down?" she said.

That wouldn't give him a good enough view of the battle below. "I'm fine."

She frowned and shook her head. "Stubborn as Lex."

Maybe that's why they'd been drawn towards one another.

He leant his arm-guards on top of the wall and took some weight from his legs. *Better. Now I can view the death more comfortably…*

"How long are we going to stand here and watch?" he asked.

"We aren't just standing here. Because of us my father was able to reposition his soldiers to the right place. The Xavalan cavalry will have a clear run to leave the city via the main gate and launch a sally." Flickers of the raining fire lit within her eyes. "Listen. I don't want to hurt you…"

Where was she going with this? He glanced down at her hands to make sure she wasn't concealing a dagger. "Huh?"

She sighed. "You'd be useless down there."

He turned his head away with a grunt. Perhaps a dagger would have hurt less.

"You're so weak you can't even jump from a wall," she continued. "How would you fare against rakkans stronger than stampeding bulls?"

"And whose fault is that?"

"Mine. I know. I'm just saying, Sulla ordered you here for a reason. This is the one place you can make a difference, to collapse the tunnel and cover our retreat lest we need it."

446

He growled under his breath, and she took the hint that he wanted not another word. Regardless of how weak he was, there was only so long he'd watch and do nothing.

***

Lex leapt to her feet and drew back her bowstring. Her eyes narrowed in on a slither of space between two flaming shields as she flicked the head of her arrow with her finger, coating it in algor. She loosed. The projectile darted into the neck of a rakkan, who toppled over to the side.

When so tightly packed, their reflexes meant nothing. There was nowhere to dodge to.

"Hold me," she said to the rakkan beside her, pointing to her belt.

He took hold of her while she nocked another arrow then leaned out over the parapet. At the base of the wall, the glow of molten rock made her squint. The sight of shovels and pickaxes was unmistakable beneath the Viridian shields, and she set her sights on what looked like the head of a digger through another gap.

She let the arrow fly then lurched as the rakkan violently pulled her back. Her shocked gaze met his as he dragged her behind his shield.

Three loud thumps rang in her ears. The slingers hadn't relented, despite the legionnaires below.

"Thanks," she muttered to the rakkan, bending down to send algor down the trough of oil again for the other archers.

A stooped hoplite scurried towards her and halted behind the rakkan's shield. "Algus, the sulphur has arrived."

About time. "How many sacks?"

"Enough."

She cast her gaze down to the streets behind the wall, never so happy to see Sulla's vanguard forming ranks.

Slingers' rocks bounced from their scuta while they readied for a breach.

She turned back to the soldier. "Keep the sulphur protected until it's dropped." The last thing they needed was a flaming projectile to hit them. "Toss them over onto the shields below. The Viridians' ferven will do the rest."

"Yes, Algus." The hoplite stooped again and made his way gingerly along the battlement.

Lex licked her finger and held it up, relieved to feel the cool breeze wafting away from the city. *Perfect.* The noxious gas wouldn't rebound on the defenders nor would it be swept away too quickly. It seemed Agathos watched over them.

A few yards down the battlements from her was a gap in the parapet, littered around with loose stones from where rakkan slingers had smashed it.

She pointed to tell the approaching hoplites where to make the first drops.

The soldiers already there had sense and scampered away from the area as the sacks arrived. Once clear, a hoplite pushed the sulphur to the edge then craned his neck away and shoved it over with his heel.

The thud and hiss told Lex without looking that they'd struck. Roars and the clashes of shields and armour rang out into the night. Hundreds of scrambling footsteps followed with coughing and heaving.

Hope they choke on their own blood and vomit.

A few of the soldiers cheered and hurled insults.

Lex opened her mouth to reprimand them but held her tongue. *Let them have this.* A minor victory in what may still become a colossal defeat.

She stood up, tall and proud once more, and nocked an arrow. "Show them no mercy!" Her arrow loosed from the bow and into the back of a fleeing rakkan.

Unfortunately, the man was one of only a small group that had turned their tails. Beyond a few yards, the rakkans were far enough away to escape the worst of the stench and remained tight to the wall in formation. And the burning sack wouldn't last for long.

Other algus on the battlements also stood and unleashed their arrows. Most of the guardians had now joined her from the gate, allowing her to breathe a little easier.

Through the plume of smoke below, Lex spied that the rakkans had already dug many feet down across a wide stretch of wall. Without foundations, the stone barrier wouldn't stand for long. Perhaps she'd relaxed too soon.

"Bring more sulphur!" Lex cried. "And you"—she pointed to some nearby hoplites—"all of you grab as many stones and debris as you can and toss them over the side. Let's fill the hole they've dug with what we can."

Agathos willing, it would buy them a few precious moments more. Enough time bought, and Xavala's army may arrive before the Viridian's reduced the city to rubble and ash.

56

Battle of Laltos

As time passed, more sacks arrived at the wall, and soldiers tossed them over. The yells the first few bags had provoked turned to roars of rage and frustration. Lex glanced back every so often to count the sacks and grew anxious as the pile quickly reduced.

Behind her, a rhythmic metallic thud sounded, getting louder with each iteration. The crumbling of stone and debris falling soon accompanied each.

Darkness fell on the wall like a sudden fog. Lex looked up at the sky, once lit with streaks of ferven, but now black and void. Armies only halted bombardment for one reason—to protect their own.

Her hip suddenly sent a jolt of pain. *Damn you. Not now.* She drew her sword, flared algor across it and held it over the parapet, leant out to see rakkans leaping up the wall and driving in what appeared to be metal hooks.

She extinguished her blade and turned to the soldiers still cowering. "They're halfway up! Hoplites, stand! Archers behind." The climbers had to be a reactionary move to the sulphur, rather than planned. "Keep the sacks coming."

Scanning her eyes quickly across the battlements, she saw algus at regular intervals ready their swords. They shouldn't need Sulla's Militia to hold back the few climbers. Best to leave them until the most difficult stage, when they'd hopefully take the attackers by surprise.

Catching Sulla's eye, she held out a palm to him. He nodded and turned to give orders to his men.

While she surveyed her men and began counting, a hand grabbed onto the stone merlon to her left.

As the rakkan lifted his head over the parapet, Lex spun and sliced under his helmet, rupturing the neck.

The body toppled but was soon replaced by another face. As good at climbing as rakkans were, they had no answer for the speed of an algus when deprived of their ability to dodge.

Blades all along the battlements burst into life with algor, including Lex's own. Her grip tightened on the hilt, and she drew in a deep breath.

For now, the algus had an advantage. How long would it last?

***

Sulla watched the numerous blue swords streaking across the ramparts. The algus cut down the attackers so quickly he only saw a handful of rakkans make it over the parapet. Even with his superior eyesight, most of the human guardians had melded into blurs.

They sliced open heads and severed arms as Viridians clung to the merlons. Sulla had been foolish to think the invaders

451

would use ladders, because against only a line of warriors, he now saw how the algus dominated.

The hoplites around gave the arcing blue swords a wide berth and focused on throwing more sacks. Others lit buckets of oil with algor from the trough and doused the attackers below.

Sulla turned his attention back to the Margalvians jogging past the rows of terraced buildings, all with shutters nailed closed. Each warrior brought a steady supply of sulphur and oil. Some had sacks on their shoulders, others had buckets hugged in both arms.

He could see the end of the line farther up the street. *Not long until they run out.* Sulphur didn't burn long enough.

His heart had pounded for a while, his arms and legs twitchy. It wasn't fear; it was eagerness. Who knew why his body reacted as it did, but it was always the same before a battle. Relief would only come from hacking apart his enemies.

A rakkan horn blared from beyond the wall. If the Viridian horns were anything like those of Margalvia, the pitch meant to cease.

Sure enough, soon the slashes of swords and blood stopped, and no more rakkan invaders attempted to climb over the parapets.

"Are they retreating?" a young rakkan asked hopefully.

"Yes," Sulla said. "They marched for weeks to get here, but after losing a few legionnaires have decided it's too much hassle."

Another rakkan let out a gravelly chuckle.

It was likely the Viridian Commanders never gave the order to climb the walls. Algus needed to be overwhelmed with numbers or they'd cut through you forever. If right, it meant the Viridians weren't as disciplined as he'd once thought.

"They'll still try to get through the wall," Sulla said. "But why waste fighters? They'll let us exhaust our supply of sulphur. Then there'll be no stopping them."

The young rakkan bashed a fist to his shield. "Yes, there will."

Sulla grinned, admiring the lad's nerve, but he didn't know what hell he was in for. The Militia had blockaded every street within a wide radius of the potential breach site, and it would get ugly.

The faces of his warriors suddenly glowed orange, like they faced the rising sun. Sulla looked up at the torrent of fire once again lighting up the city.

The rakkans raised their shields. Thud after thud echoed in the street. Stones battered the building closest to the wall, smashing slates from its roof and sending them down onto the Margalvians.

A flaming rock hit one sack on the shoulder of a rakkan, who fell to the ground and coughed as a cloud of smoke engulfed him.

Men yelled and turned to run, retching and grimacing. The putrid smell hit Sulla's nose, like rotten eggs a decade old. He took in a deep breath and started towards the smouldering sack.

Fleeing soldiers bashed into him as he tried to make his way to the source. His chest constricted as the air held in his lungs begged to be replenished.

Black liquid began oozing out of the bag, alight with blue flame spreading the noxious air farther. He flared ferven on his eyes so he wouldn't need to close them in the billowing smoke and finally reached the blackened bag.

Liquid gushed out as he picked it up, but the sack beneath disintegrated, spilling the mess of powder and liquid over the ground. It was useless. He couldn't throw it over the wall, so he dropped it and backed away, scraping off the gunk that spoiled his arms and armour like an infectious disease. He retched, unable to catch a breath of fresh air.

While he struggled, Lex sprang from the battlements and landed next to a rakkan carrying oil. She grabbed the bucket from him and bolted towards the smouldering mess in the street.

Bright blue burst from her hands and immersed the oil before she tossed the contents over the sulphur.

The smoke thinned. The flames ceased.

Sulla summoned a blazing film of ferven across his body. The sulphur fizzled and melted from him, dripping onto the road as he walked away in search of a place free from the stench.

"It's alight!" someone called behind. He turned to see another rakkan running away from a burning sack that had been hit with a molten stone.

"Shields up!" Sulla yelled. He ran towards the line of rakkans still carrying their loads, grabbed the first, and pulled the man under his raised scutum.

The others followed his lead, and the steady supply to the wall continued amongst a hail of molten rocks so thick they piled up on the streets.

Sulla glanced back, able to see the back of the line carrying supplies. *Almost done.* He had a warrior replace him in protecting the sulphur and ran back to the shield wall farther up the street, catching the gaze of his warriors.

Their eyes were as hard with awareness as his own. They looked ready.

Sulla raised his sword. "Our time's almost come, boys!"

57

Battle of Laltos

Lex pressed her back against a battered merlon and took deep breaths. Traces of the rotten smell still lingered in the air, but hardly enough to deter her. In front, the once white buildings of Laltos were now blackened and scarred. Chunks of stone had been cleaved from the facades all around. Some had succumbed completely and lay in heaps of rubble.

As soldiers flung the last of the sulphur bags over the wall, Lex cursed with a glance at the moon. They hadn't lasted as long as she'd thought.

Kneeling next to her, her rakkan companion stared blankly at the ground. The stone against her back shook as pickaxes struck the earth underneath.

For the first time in history, invaders would breach Laltos's walls. *Damn you, Hadrian.* If only Darius had the strength to take the Warlord on.

"Algus?" An archer long past retirement knelt in front of her.

"Yes?"

"The oil." His gaze slipped to the trough below the parapet that was extinguished.

"Of course." *Stop getting distracted.* She dipped a finger in and sent algor flaring down it again.

The archer gave her a nod and leaned over to dip his arrow. Once coated, he nocked it and stood, drawing back his bowstring. Before he could release, a flaming rock burst through his skull, and his lifeless body slumped, showering Lex in warm gore.

She slid the body away with her foot, turned the man's face away from gazing at her as if rightfully blaming her for unleashing the hell they now faced.

Resisting the urge to despair, she took her own bow and nocked an arrow. But before she stood, sounds outside the walls made her pause; hundreds of footsteps scurried in the mud along with the clanks of armour clashing.

Thud.

Crack.

The stone beneath her shuddered.

Agathos, no. She gaped at the rakkan, who now gazed up, fear in his eyes. She motioned for him to stand and he obeyed, raised his shield.

Standing up, she took cover behind him while peering below. Groups of Viridians were backing away from the wall under where she stood. Rakkans tossed pickaxes and shovels and instead drew swords. *Damn. How can they undermine so quickly?*

The thuds grew louder, followed by the rattle of crumbling stone.

She turned to face her men. "The wall's coming down!"

Soldiers and archers all spun and bolted for the staircases. Margalvians jumped from the battlements, cracking the cobbled roads with their heavy landings, and sprinted to Sulla, whose men tightened their shield wall and pressed towards the breach.

Meanwhile, the algus hopped onto rooftops and other vantage points.

Lex stood, the rakkan still beside her. "Go back to Sulla," she urged. "The algus and I will attack their flanks."

He nodded and leapt off the ramparts.

The stone beneath her feet lurched, throwing her off balance. Slinging her bow back across her shoulder, she steadied herself then sprinted along the battlements.

Rumbling swelled behind her. Vibrations shook her boots. As she leapt for the closest rooftop, the ground where she'd stood fell away with a crash of stone that echoed from the buildings in an ever-growing thunder.

A cloud of dust spewed out from the tumbling rocks and engulfed the streets, carrying with it the remnant reek of sulphur that made those around gag and splutter.

Lex coughed and closed her eyes. Each breath pulled more dust into her lungs, so she stretched her tunic across her mouth and breathed through it.

Agathos, save us. The real battle had just begun.

***

The stone beneath Darius's hands cracked as he watched the cloud of dust rise in the air. He should be down there aiding. With their most powerful defence now reduced to rubble, how long would the city hold off the invaders?

He looked back at the water clock. *Too long until help arrives.*

The last streaks from the once unrelenting rain of fire cast a dim red glow through the dust as the Viridians stopped slinging and prepared for the assault.

"How large is the breach?" Selene asked.

"Big enough."

"My father will want specifics."

Darius sighed. "Fifty yards at a guess."

Her eyes widened in horror.

"Maybe less," he added. "Hard to see at this distance. Perhaps the haze makes it appear larger."

She scribbled it down while he cast his eyes over the legionnaires outside the city.

"Most Viridians are moving towards the breach, and those at the gate are building earthwork ramparts. Advise your father to pull the forces at the gate back to the entrance to the upper city before they're cut off."

Selene shook her head. "It won't take the Viridians long to get through."

Darius prayed she was mistaken.

***

Sulla conjured ferven across his eyes to guard against the billowing dust. Viridian horns blared ahead, and the ranks of Militia in front of him twitched, knees bent and ready to charge at the command.

Not yet. Let them traverse the rubble.

The algus crouched on the roofs two storeys above on either side of the street. To the front of the shield wall, rakkans that had once been on the battlements arrived and pushed through the lines of men.

An orange glow swelled in the dust. Soon individual bursts of light sprang out, hundreds of flaming swords swinging as their wielders bounded towards the defenders.

"Militia!" Sulla's voice boomed above the cries of the invaders. "Advance!"

Roars erupted and the bang of boots on stone thumped, rhythmic and in unison as the shield wall surged down the street.

Streaks of blue light darted into the now thinning dust cloud. Projectiles silenced roars, others met flaming shields in resistance. Through the haze, the glowing figures of the first attackers formed.

"Brace!" Sulla yelled.

His men pressed together. Those at the back reinforced the front line, whose spears pointed forwards, awaiting first blood.

A line of Viridian Legionnaires charged from the dust and clashed with the shield wall. Sulla felt the jerk backwards of his men but put all his weight behind the man ahead to help.

The lofted swords of the invaders all dipped as spears rammed into their armour. Some spears found flesh and pierced arms, thighs, necks, drawing out screams of pain. Most only pricked kuraminium chest-plates. The second row of the Militia rammed their weapons repeatedly towards any exposed skin that caught their eye.

Sulla craned his neck, feeling less resistance against his pushes now. The Viridians had hesitated, slowed the charge. Some tried to stop but couldn't before spears pierced their thighs and arms.

The Militia's defensive line lurched forward a pace.

More Viridian Legionnaires flooded over the pile of rubble in the breach, forcing forward the invaders that had paused. Those with a scutum now raised them and frantically formed a shield wall of their own.

Sulla dipped his head low and pushed the backs of his men with a shoulder. *Let's crush the scum.*

The two lines crunched together and pressed. Boots skidded across the cobbles. Grunts echoed all around as the crowds behind drove those in front.

While the pushing raged in the streets, barrages of arrows and javelins darted from the rooftops as other archers and peltasts found their way up.

But all too soon, fiery rocks hurtled back at them from behind the Viridian front line.

The rakkans ahead of Sulla suddenly jolted backwards, almost sending him to the ground. He dug in his heels and pushed into the back of the closest man. Blood trickled down the street. His feet slipped on the stones.

The Militia lurched back again. Each row dug the pointed backs of their spears into the road and tried to hold the line.

"Don't give them another inch!" Sulla yelled, his voice barely audible above the deafening roars.

One Viridian Legionnaire leapt high and caught hold of the rooftop, only for his hand to be severed a second later by a waiting algus.

The same blond algus gazed down for a moment before he leapt into the sea of Viridians, followed closely by his tigress escort with fangs and claws bared.

His gleaming sword vanished behind the bodies, but the odd flicker of blue light showed he'd survived and fought. The tigress's roars carried over the grunts and shouts of battle.

My Creator. As brave as a rakkan.

The algus's assault weakened the Viridians' push the fraction the Militia needed, and they barged forwards. Clashes of metal on metal rang out as spears hit armour again.

With every passing minute the dust cleared further, showing the heap of rubble left with figures piling over it. The marauders sliced apart the few hoplites that hadn't escaped the battlements.

Crashes of what sounded like rock buckling emanated again. Sulla glanced around, but no more of the wall had collapsed.

The thumps continued echoing from the walls of the buildings around. More crashes accompanied them like pottery shattering and wood splintering.

What the...? Sulla scanned around. Behind, there were only a few Laltos soldiers wary of joining the fray. At either side, just shuttered buildings. The Militia's shield wall held strong now, but that just made him even more uneasy.

He dropped his spear and drew his gladius instead. Backing away from his men, he peered through the shutters of the building to his left. Abandoned utensils on a wooden table shook with each resonating thump.

A commander fell back with him, frowning. "What's wrong?"

Another thump came from the house to his right. *Oh, hell.* "Militia! Protect your rear!"

The back line of Militia turned and formed a new wall of shields as rakkans burst from the shutters of the buildings all around. The charging invaders trampled the hoplites behind Sulla and slashed open their scale armour.

Before Sulla could move, a legionnaire broke through the shutters on his right.

Sulla twisted out of the rakkan's path and took a step farther up the street, narrowly avoiding the thrust of a spear, but it caught his commander in the arm.

The commander grunted and batted away the weapon. But the legionnaire followed up with his shield and drove the spike at its centre straight into the commander's neck.

Sulla screamed curses. As the Viridian placed a foot forward and halted his lunge, Sulla sank his gladius into the invader's thigh.

The rakkan cried out and dropped to one knee. With his free hand, Sulla ripped the helmet from his foe's head and jabbed his sword through the eye.

He twisted the blade, feeling the edge scrape bone as he stared at his commander's slumped, lifeless figure.

He then ripped out the gladius and turned around, teeth bared, ready for more death.

Dozens of legionnaires filed out of the windows and charged at the Militia's rear shield wall, separating Sulla from his men.

He backed up until pressed against the wall of the building opposite then raised his sword. Finally, his chance to fight had come, and he eyed one Viridian in particular as they stepped out, a commander.

I wonder how many I can slay before they end me.

The commander met his stare.

Sulla held out his arms in invitation. *Come try it.*

58

Battle of Laltos

The slates underneath Lex's feet shuddered with every mysterious thump emanating from the building. Tiles slipped from the roof and were devoured by the clamour below. Another algus stood beside her. His round face was smeared with blood and gave her a worried, knowing look, as if he suspected the same thing.

Lex bolted to the edge of the roof closest to the city wall and peered down at the mass of Viridians below. A few slingers pelted rocks at her, but she dodged and glared at the warriors disappearing through holes in the sides of the buildings. *Damn.*

More crashes shook the tiles beneath her feet. She ran back across to the other edge and saw the lines of Militia that were now surrounded. Amongst the invaders, Sulla grappled with one of them, separated from his warriors.

"Cover me!" Lex yelled at the other algus. Without waiting to see if he'd heard, she flared algor across her sword and leapt towards Sulla.

While she soared, molten stones flew past but only grazed her. She landed a few yards away with a heel to a Viridian's head as she stabbed down through the collar.

After giving her a quick grin, Sulla charged at one Viridian while Lex turned and severed two legionnaires' arms with a flurry of slashes until they fell away.

Sulla backed up to her, his bloody sword held high. "Come to join me in death?"

Never. Lex turned towards the line of Militia and began slicing her way through every Viridian between them, her algor-coated sword cutting spears and exposed flesh.

All the while, the shield wall pushed towards her, their low spears piercing the invaders now pouring out of the windows all around.

Too many. A few more seconds and Lex and Sulla would be swamped.

Across the street, a rumble and cloud of dust erupted from a collapsing building, felled by one too many holes in its walls.

Lex jabbed her sword into the eye socket of a Viridian Commander, and she and Sulla finally met the shields of the Militia.

They squeezed through a gap, back into their ranks.

All sides constricted them as the Viridian Legion pressed the shield walls from the front and rear.

"Hope you've got an idea, Blue-eyes," Sulla shouted.

The air escaped Lex's lungs as the armoured bodies crushed her chest. Her chain armour dug into her skin, compressed by the stiff cuirasses surrounding her.

"Can't…brea…" Lex hissed.

Sulla's eyes widened. He grabbed her waist and thrust her upwards.

Pain speared her hip, but her chest broke free above the mass of bodies, and she sucked in the debris-filled air.

Above the Militia, she was free but also a sitting target, so she planted a heel onto the shoulder of one of the warriors and sprung herself upwards.

Cold slate met her hands as she grabbed hold of the roof and hoisted herself up.

Looking back down, she noted Sulla's eyes still gazed up at her, searching for instruction.

Think. Help me, Dianoia. No ideas surfaced. By the crashes and smoke from the streets, the Viridians had already spread out wide. Soon, only an act of the gods could save them.

***

Darius pressed his knuckles into his eyes until odd circles and shapes of light swirled in his vision. Anything was better than watching his friends die.

Weeks ago, in the torture chamber, he would have paid to see Laltos burn. Now, he wished he had the strength to prevent it. Sulla's orders for him to remain near the tunnel echoed in his mind, the only thing rooting him in place.

"I hate the dark," Selene whispered. She hadn't been able to speak properly for half an hour. "At least when the sky rained fire I could see."

The rumble of another collapsing structure finally made Darius open his eyes again.

"I hate only hearing the destruction," she whispered.

"I know what you mean." All he saw was smoke and the odd glint of algor. Sulla and his friends were dying far out of view. "There's dust far east of the breach. The Militia hasn't held there.

Tell your father he needs to pull back to the narrow roads southeast."

Selene nodded.

"The south is holding, for now…" Some algus ran back along the rooftops to the upper city, but Darius saw little to suggest the Militia were behind them in the retreat.

The streets all around threw up dust and signs of fighting. The fiercest of it still seemed to be near the breach, but he was blind to the exact position of Hadrian's legion.

Seems my usefulness is spent. "I'd advise your father to call a retreat to the upper city," Darius said. "Get word to Sulla."

"I'll try, but it's difficult."

"I swear, if your father is leaving the Militia to cover his retreat…"

Selene placed a hand on his. "He wouldn't."

How do I know that? He took a deep breath, ripping his hand away from her. "I don't see the point in even trying to hold the upper city."

"Me neither."

He paused, having expected her to push back. "They'd all be best withdrawing directly to the tunnel."

"Given the speed they've rampaged through the lower city, I agree. I'll let my father know."

The stiff wind brought the thick smell of embers and melted stone to his nostrils. He gazed up at the water clock and cursed at the hour. "Where are the Xavalans? Their scouts should have arrived by now."

Selene gazed back at the clepsydra too and frowned. "I don't know. Perhaps they're having difficulty finding the tunnel."

Darius doubted it, but then was lost as to other explanations. Plus, he was tired of watching clouds of smoke for hints of what happened below. "I don't think there's any more we can do here.

466

Let's go through the tunnel and see if we can hurry the Xavalans along."

Selene nodded.

Darius took a last look across the war-torn cityscape. *Sulla, I pray you get out of this one with nothing worse than scars.*

***

Brutus rubbed his neck to ease the tension that almost prevented him from turning his head. The Viridian Legionnaires in front of him stood in silence, eagerly waiting for the order to advance through the breach in the city wall.

Hadrian watched the destruction with a sickening grin of satisfaction. To his sides, rows of Viridian Guardians stood with their tattooed arms brandished.

If Brutus could have, he'd have rammed his sword in the Warlord's throat and to hell with the consequences, but if Darius had failed to best Hadrian, then what chance did he have?

"Move inside!" a commander called, signalling to Brutus's century. "Push through that rakkan line of defence."

Brutus closed his eyes as he tried to suppress the ferven welling inside him at the thought of his brothers dying while defending.

Before he could compose himself, the surrounding warriors began their march. Pushing down his rage as much as possible, Brutus strode along with them. The rubble of the wall slowed them a little, but soon they'd clambered atop and were ready to enter the city.

Brutus paused at the highest point that gave him an unobstructed view of the streets to each side. His gaze fixated on the shield wall defending the main road into Laltos, on the visors that covered the faces of the warriors. *Margalvian armour.*

The other streets had similar defenders desperately pushing against the tide of invaders. The red bands on the defenders' biceps angered Brutus even more.

Viridians had burst through the buildings, climbed the roofs, and surrounded his friends who were hopelessly outnumbered.

He couldn't let them die. He pushed past the warriors in front of him, ignoring their grumbles of annoyance, and headed straight for the closest building. The row of terraced homes extended all the way to the defenders and beyond, and he quickly counted the three houses until the first line of defence before diving through an existing hole in the wall.

Inside was a chaotic mess of half-burnt scrolls, charred stone, and seared corpses. He pushed on through, using the holes in each internal wall.

Other warriors brushed past him to continue to flank the Militia, but he paid them no mind. Fighting them now would only get himself killed.

When inside the house closest to the front line of the invaders, he peered out of the grated shutters and made sure the street was crammed with Viridians.

It was, so he sheathed his sword and placed his hands on one of the inner walls. Ferven spread across the stone like elongated fingers and sank into the weakened stone.

He shoved, and at first met unyielding resistance, but eventually part of the wall softened. Stone above cracked away and fell to rubble.

He repeated the act on every interior wall he found, always at the strongest points. The creaking of stone and wooden beams above were a pleasure to his ears.

Finally, when there were no more interior structures to weaken, he placed his hands on the exterior wall.

On the other side, the yells of Viridian Legionnaires and smashes of swords against shields and spears pierced through.

The wall sank under his palms.

One of the rakkans running through the building stopped. "What're you doing?"

Brutus pushed harder, spread out his arms to coat several feet of the wall with vines of ferven, just like the Viridian would have done to the foundations of Laltos's walls.

A protracted groan emanated from the house.

A crack of stone sounded above his head.

Slates crashed from the roof onto the helmets of the legionnaires outside.

"You fool," the rakkan said, raising his sword.

Before he could approach, the exterior wall shifted down. The melted, blackened stone buckled.

The rakkan turned, ignoring Brutus, and instead sprinted back out as Brutus held his forearm above his head and bolted after the man.

***

Sulla turned to the quaking building to his right. Dust and stones crumbled from its front wall as if the earth shook beneath it. *What the…?*

He opened his mouth to issue an order, but the wall cracked and was already tumbling over towards the Viridians beneath before he could yell.

Hundreds of crashes fused into one ear-splitting bang of stone. Roars cut off, screams silenced.

Then another dust cloud choked the defenders' lungs as they continued to thrust out spears to those invaders still standing, reeling from the collapse.

After the haze settled, all Sulla made out were a pile of stones and buried legionnaires.

469

Now's our chance. "Militia!" Sulla called. "Sound the horn to retreat. Fight your way back to the upper city."

The horns blared before he'd finished the words.

Lex and the other algus above increased their barrage of the invaders as Sulla's warriors began pushing back. They met weaker resistance that their shield wall smashed through and trampled underfoot. Behind, more booms of falling houses swept up the street.

Sulla glanced back at the new clouds of dust covering more of Hadrian's warriors. The Creator was smiling on them today.

As they pushed through the streets, other groups of Militia that had escaped the fighting joined them. Sulla couldn't count how many he'd lost, but it was many. *Hurry, Xavala.*

59

Nikolaos – Xavala, the Silk City

Nikolaos poured another two cups of wine from the amphora and handed one to the Silk Regent. As usual, slaves had laid out a vast swathe of fruits on the table of Aristippus's chambers for them to pick at. Accompanying them were only two algus guards standing behind the Silk Regent's chair.

Nikolaos sat down in a seat opposite and raised his cup. "To the liberation of Laltos."

Aristippus smirked and took a sip.

"Your horses will arrive soon." Nikolaos tapped his foot repeatedly on the carpet. "I'm impressed you convinced Ophelia to send the King's Sword with your cavalry. Jason hasn't left my side much since rescuing me." How Nikolaos enjoyed his freedom again.

"Oh, it was nothing," the Silk Regent said in a voice as smooth as his clothes.

Nikolaos frowned. "So, what agreement did the two of you make?" It was the first time Nikolaos had dared ask, for the King's Orator had seldom left the pair alone.

Aristippus chuckled and took a large gulp of wine. "I suppose it's fine to tell you what Ophelia's real plan is now." He quickly glanced at the guards over his shoulder, as if to check they were still there. "You don't have time to send them warning."

"Warning of what?" Chills made the hairs on Nikolaos's neck rigid.

"Laltos will be liberated," the Silk Regent continued, "from both the rakkan army and the traitors that control it. I have no love for the King, but when the alternative is banding with rakkans and the King offers me riches instead, my hand is forced. A poison runs through Laltos's veins, and who knows how deep it has reached? In the King's mind, the city is best razed."

Nikolaos leapt to his feet, wishing he had a weapon instead of only being able to ball his fists.

Before he reached the Silk Regent, the two guards drew their swords and stepped forward.

"You'll murder the whole city?" Nikolaos shouted. "What about the Bank?" *How can I be regent of corpses and empty coffers?*

"Murder?" Aristippus's smile widened. "In Xavala, a regent cannot murder, for he writes the law. Laltos's leaders should have been as cunning as I. Perhaps then they'd have lived.

"I don't have friends there, and Laltos is only worth what's in its coffers to the King. The people are just hungry mouths to feed. Once ransacked, the King will take everything in the bank, and in return, I'll grow my own mulberry trees. The Scorched Forest will bloom once again."

Nikolaos lunged and punched for the Silk Regent's jaw, but a guard darted between the pair and smashed him in the chest with a fist.

472

Nikolaos fell backwards and toppled over the chair, spilling a mess of grapes, berries and wine over his tunic and burning face.

He hit the floor and groaned, squirming for a moment before he stopped and stared at the sky-blue ceiling. *What have they done?*

60

Battle of Laltos

Darius whipped the reins of the black swift and urged it on up the sloping dirt. Selene held tightly to his waist, preferring to be a passenger while travelling in what was the pitch black for her.

The boot-prints left by those fleeing Laltos through the tunnel had created a muddy path through the mountainous terrain. An actual road would have made travel much swifter, but something about the unspoilt hills around told Darius these reaches had seldom seen a man.

His rakkan eyes, helped by the moon's shine, gave him a full view of the landscape ahead—smooth crests with grass and heather up their sides, rolling one after another like waves on a stormy green ocean, spotted with patches of white flowers like froth in his imagination's eye. It was too bad the numerous mounds blocked him from seeing any Xavalans.

"Are you sure this is a swift?" he asked. It had yet to display the pace he'd seen in others.

"Be grateful we found any," she replied.

"Might have been faster walking it," he muttered.

Selene rapped his chest. "Do you ever stop complaining?"

"I'll stop when I have no more reasons to grumble."

"Then stop. Paris has seen a mass force on the other side of the hill. It must be the Xavalan cavalry."

At last. They carried on up the slope. The silence of the mountains would usually be peaceful, but all it left were the memories of crashes and cracks of yielding stone and armour with each of the horse's snorts.

As they reached the peak, thousands of figures came into Darius's view in a shadowed valley below.

He smiled weakly, allowing himself to take a few easy breaths. He pulled the horse to a stop and took in the sight before him.

Organised groups of mounted figures moved swiftly up the lengthy hill towards them. The whole force was led by a large heavily armoured unit. They'd opened a gap between those lagging, who, besides being farther back, looked less organised than the formations at the front. At full pace, the cavalry would be in Laltos within the hour.

Selene flared algor across her arms and began waving the army towards them while Paris landed on her shoulder.

Darius made out the spears and shields of mounted hoplites along with the black leather of algus—hundreds, as promised.

Behind, it seemed as if the disordered group weren't moving at all. Moreover, he now noticed there were no horses among them.

That's odd. He strained his eyes. Those behind were still. They didn't even seem to be standing, more like they were lying on the ground. No glint of iron in the moonlight came from the figures. *No armour. No weapons.*

While Selene waved, the ranks charged ever faster up the hill, and algus raced ahead, riding swifts.

Darius twisted in the saddle and grabbed Selene's arm. "Stop!"

She extinguished the glow and frowned at him in confusion.

"They've killed them all! We need to get back."

"Killed who?"

"The people fleeing Laltos."

Selene's mouth fell open. "No…"

Darius jerked the reins with his right arm, turned the swift around, then kicked his heels into its belly.

The swift bolted forwards, finally living up to its name, and forced him to hold on with all his strength. Their pace built on the downward slope with the rapid pounding of hooves, faster than Darius was ordinarily prepared to risk.

"Why would the Xavalans do that?" Selene asked. "Are you sure it wasn't the Viridian Legion?"

"Unless Hadrian has cavalry, I'm sure."

Selene squeezed his waist tighter. He looked over his shoulder and saw the first riders fly over the crest of the hill. *Damn. We have to get back…*

And do what? Cave in their only chance of escaping Laltos?

The ground levelled out for a while before they began climbing the next hill, one of many in a series they needed to traverse before they reached the tunnel. *With my luck, Hadrian will be standing in wait.*

As questions circled in his mind, the drumming of hooves beneath his horse slowed. Its breaths grew louder and faster with every heartbeat.

"Faster, boy," Darius said. A glance back revealed dozens of algus racing down the hill.

He ripped the sword from his scabbard, praying he didn't have to use it because the heavy kuraminium strained his forearm without even swinging. "Keep going, boy. Prove I was wrong about you."

61

Battle of Laltos

Lex stood in the gateway with the weight of many eyes on her back from men atop the walls of the upper city. As an algus, she'd had little difficulty in making her way across the rooftops—other than resisting the urge to turn and slay every Viridian she found—but had lost sight of Sulla and his men in the dust before falling back herself.

She scanned the straight cobble road ahead for movement but struggled to see anything through the thick haze of smoke. Along each side were small trees outside buildings deliberately built low to prevent easy access to the inner walls.

Still, the ramparts either side of her hadn't the height of those that had been breached. *They won't last long.* Soon, the smoke plumes filling the sky would spread here along with the Viridians.

She clenched her teeth hard. *Come on, Sulla. Hurry.*

"We should close the gate," Gorgias said from behind her.

"I heard you the first time," she replied slowly. *Coward.* Algus that hid in the upper city whilst the others fought hadn't earned an opinion in her view.

Still, every passing minute told her he was right.

As she was about to concede and order the gates barred, figures fronted by rectangular shields turned from one of the side streets ahead and rushed up the road towards her.

Soldiers all along the wall readied their spears and archers drew back their bowstrings.

"Don't shoot. It's us!" Sulla called in the distance.

Lex took a deep breath and turned to meet Gorgias's sweaty face. "Prepare to close and barricade the gate."

He scuttled off while Lex quickly cast her gaze over the rakkans. As the faces of haggard warriors moved past her, she checked the coloured bands on their arms and made an estimate of their number by counting groups of ten. *A couple of hundred at most.* At the rear, Sulla pushed the last of his warriors through then stopped beside Lex.

"Where's your rearguard?" Lex asked.

"We're it." His face was cut and bruised, eyes heavy with defeat.

"You look how I feel." Lex put a hand on his shoulder and urged him inside the ironwood gate before her men began barricading it shut.

Her father waited with a few of the other algus farther in at the main square, debating with furrowed brows in the shadow of the Dianoia fountain that no longer flowed.

"Where's your defence?" Sulla asked Lex. "The Viridians are only a few minutes behind us. They slowed when they found civilians cowering in their dwellings."

Lex gritted her teeth while Theodoros paced towards them alongside his armoured bear, who shook his soot-covered head.

The Regent's chainmail hung low under his tunic, and the thick grey cloak across his shoulders was held only by a string across the neck. "Over half the algus are dead."

"Only half?" Sulla said. "Lucky for you…"

Theodoros's eyes filled with sorrow as he looked the rakkan in the eye. "Darius says its best we retreat and leave via the tunnel."

"They'll raze the city, plunder the vaults…" Lex's voice trailed off. No words were strong enough, *vile* enough to convey how she felt. Her hands shook. The rage inside threatened to burst out, algor leaked from her fists, but she'd keep it buried as long as she needed to. Her men needed a leader, needed hope, not an algus narrowly clinging onto her stability.

"The last of our soldiers and algus are making their way to the palace," Theodoros said. "We should join them."

Sulla nodded. "Don't need to tell me twice." He set off with long strides, leaving Lex and her father to watch the kuraminium braces being secured diagonally across the gate by a few of Sulla's warriors.

"It will hold them long enough," Theodoros said.

The rumble of boots pounding on the cobbles outside grew. Archers atop the battlements nocked arrows and loosed. Algus and hoplites gripped their swords ready.

"They'll scale the walls," Lex said. There was no sulphur to save them now.

"These soldiers know their fate," Theodoros said. "Come." He took her hand and dragged her away towards the palace, his escort bounding behind them.

Lex couldn't help but gaze back at the gate as they ran, at the frantic shots the archers now unleashed. Chances were these brave men would fall before the Xavalans arrived to save the city, but their fight wasn't in vain. *Don't fret, brave soldiers. Soon, you'll be avenged.*

***

Darius yanked the reins, pulling the swift's head to the left and narrowly out of the path of an arrow. Its gallop grew weaker by the second as the dirt trail passed underneath. Only a few hundred yards separated them from the black hole of the tunnel, but at this rate, his stallion would collapse.

To the rear, at least two dozen algus had pulled away from the main group and closed in on horses frothing at the mouth. Selene had felled a few with her bow but not enough to make a difference.

Darius's horse shrieked as an arrow pierced its backside, but it kept going, though now with a limp hindering every step.

"Just a little farther, boy. You can do it." It was fortunate horses couldn't sense the doubt in his voice.

Only a few seconds more and they'd be swallowed by the tunnel, but what then? He'd rather be buried alive than either of the armies kill him. Whatever his thoughts, Darius wouldn't stop fighting until his last breath.

An arrow pierced the horse's head and its legs buckled. Darius had just enough time to shift his sword before he was jolted forwards and over the horse's dipping head.

Selene tumbled into him, his battered body breaking her fall, and ended with him squashed into the dirt with a grunt of pain.

Her weight shifted from him in a heartbeat. Then an arrow thudded against the back of his cuirass. Rolling over, he freed the sword still clutched tightly and watched Selene parry a few slashes from a short algus that had dismounted.

Another pair aimed arrows at Darius with algor glowing from the tips.

481

He paused. *Wait for it.* The air shifted as the projectiles launched from the algus' bows.

He pushed himself aside, out of the path of one, and thrust his sword flat into the path of the other. Summoning ferven, light burst from his blade and burned the arrow shaft to ash soon after it hit. At the same time, algor flared from his eyes.

Selene parried the short algus's sword and kicked him in the groin.

The others fidgeted on their horses with nervous glances towards Darius, seemingly unwilling to dismount and face the dreaded half-breed.

Selene took her chance to back up to Darius as he stood and sent ferven dripping from his sword.

One of the algus nocked another arrow with a twisted snarl on his face and loosed.

Rather than dodge, Darius summoned ferven across his cuirass and let the arrow ricochet from it.

The algus looked to one another, then behind them at the other horses still racing from farther away.

"What's wrong?" Darius shouted with a grimace, backstepping. The fear in the men's eyes was familiar.

"You won't best him," the short one muttered. "Let's leave him to the King's Sword." They all glanced behind again.

Selene gasped, grabbed Darius's hand. "Run!" She bolted for the tunnel, but Darius let his hand slip through hers and instead stepped backwards, unwilling to shift his gaze from the surrounding algus. *They'll charge as soon as I turn.*

Those that had dismounted scrambled back atop their armoured horses. After a distance had built up between them and Darius, they whipped their reins.

On second thought… Darius turned and sprinted after Selene but was unable to match her pace. The tunnel loomed. Behind, more horses thundered ever closer again.

He stole a glance back, expecting to see a horse's head an inch from his face, but was relieved there was still smoky air between them.

At the forefront of the riders, a hooded algus bounded on a grey steed.

Before the algus could catch them, Darius and Selene dove into the mouth of the tunnel. She conjured algor to guide her path, lighting it up for Paris, who zipped low past them flapping his scaly wings. The jutted ceiling above and pillars of stone scattered around wouldn't be enough to stop the galloping algus, but Darius hoped it would at least slow their galloping a fraction.

He broke a few pillars with his sword as he ran, eventually smashing a large one that brought a boulder crashing down over half the path and scattered rocks across the rest. He grinned as he saw the horses behind slow to a sluggish pace, but his relief was short lived. Each of his breaths became deeper and deeper. His throat closed, muscles ached.

"Selene," he wheezed.

She turned, dropped back, then slung an arm across his back and pushed him along. Her tight grip pulled the scabs from the wounds on his skin, but all that mattered was reaching the column underneath that kept the tunnel standing. Collapsing it was the only way to stop the Xavalans.

Movement ahead caught his eye. Tens, hundreds even, of dark figures running towards them, soon followed by the growing rumble of their footsteps. When a few of their eyes glowed with ferven, Selene skidded to a halt.

"Don't worry," Darius croaked. "They aren't Viridians." Most of the figures' armour wasn't bulky enough.

483

Darius soon made out the black tunics of Laltos's algus flapping as they ran. Near the front, Lex loped and quickened her pace when she spotted them.

"Where have you been?" she snapped as she reached out an arm to halt the pair mid-stride.

"The Xavalans are coming," Selene said through her panting.

Lex smiled. "Thank Agathos."

"No," Darius said. "They've killed the civilians that fled."

"What?" Theodoros's bark echoed down the tunnel, drowned out only by his bear's growls.

Lex's smile fell, and she cast her forlorn stare down the passage that had once been their promise of freedom. "No…"

"We don't have time to debate it." Darius grabbed Lex's shoulder and turned her back to the city, pushed her onwards. "Get back into Laltos, and I'll bring the tunnel down behind you."

She glanced around at her men and cursed. "Turn back!"

Word filtered through the ranks, and soon they sprinted back.

"We'll have to escape through my passageway," Theodoros said as they ran. "Go to the palace then follow the corridors down to the cellars."

"We'll break back through the wall if we can't get to the entrance." Sulla pushed through the hoplites and took Darius by the arm.

"That's as good a plan as any." Darius focused on the sides of the tunnel, searching for the narrow hole that led to the chamber underneath that housed the supporting column. Lex, Sulla and Selene followed him while the rest of the army bounded.

After a run that stole Darius's last remnants of energy, they reached the hidden offshoot and tore down the spiralling passage, into a hollowed-out space below.

Two large pillars of rock stood at the centre with a kuraminium pickaxe propped up at the far side.

"I hope your architects calculated right," Darius muttered to Sulla as he went to retrieve the tool.

The rakkan's face was sullen.

"You should get out now. You'll be too slow." Darius took the wooden shaft in his hand.

"Wait," Sulla said. "Maybe we shouldn't."

Lex and Selene glared at him.

"They're coming to kill us," Darius said. "Jason's with them."

Lex swung her head to him with a fear in her eyes that even the battle hadn't brought out.

"Perhaps Jason's the only one that can kill Hadrian," Sulla said with a hateful scowl. "Let the Xavalans fight them."

Darius should have balked, but the thought made him pause. The image of Hadrian and the Viridian Legion being slaughtered suddenly roused an angry satisfaction in him.

"They'll kill all of *us* too!" Selene cried. "Don't be such fools."

"It's our choice, Dar." Sulla stepped towards him and put one hand on the pickaxe. "We've already lost most of our warriors. Let these armies kill each other. The few of us left will get out through the Regent's passageway."

Darius met his eyes. "For Margalvia's sake?"

Sulla's mouth formed a wicked grin. "Exactly."

Filling Darius's mind were Hadrian's cries of pain as algus cut him down—revenge for Lyra, revenge for the rest of the innocents wronged. Darius's heart wouldn't be satisfied until he witnessed it.

Lex grabbed his collar and pulled him aside. "Don't listen to him, Darius. We still have people here, and they have a chance of escape. But they can't flee algus. The Xavalans will slaughter them."

Her eyes were wide, pleading. All this had started because he'd been swayed by her beautiful gaze, yet he couldn't help but ache to please her.

He pushed her aside and stepped away to get space to think. Too bad he didn't have time.

Sulla shook his head. "I'd better leave while I can. I hope you see sense." He shot Darius a last hard stare before sprinting back up to the tunnel.

A stiff gust brought the echoes of shouts and cries down the spiralling passageway and into the chamber from above, the shouts of those same people that stood no chance if Darius didn't stop the Xavalans.

He paced over to the column with the pickaxe in hand.

Lyra, should I do this? He reached out to his escort, but she was focused on something else.

To hell with it. He'd listen to himself for once. He'd survive, get strong, then kill Hadrian with his own hands.

Dismissing further doubts, he raised the pickaxe. "Run."

Lex and Selene looked up, relief on their tired faces, before they joined Sulla and darted for the passage back to the tunnel.

***

Brutus ducked through the stone entrance into a house and slammed the door shut. He snapped the bolt lock across then pressed his back against the thick wood and braced it so strong a battering ram would struggle to get through.

After witnessing the hell outside, his blood boiled with rage, and *he* was a battle-hardened warrior. *Only the Creator knows what the people of Laltos feel.*

Closing his eyes, he tried to imagine himself back home in Margalvia, safe, relaxed beside his wife, but a woman's scream outside dragged him from the fantasy.

He opened his eyes and took in the room before him, an outsized kitchen of a merchant of Laltos. A few utensils hung around the dome-shaped clay oven and, as he scanned, a pair of eyes in a darkened corner caught his attention.

He focused his sight, revealing the shape of a cowering woman cradling two small infants. Her rough skin was too pockmarked for a citizen, and the tattered, dreary clothes she wore confirmed she was a slave.

"Don't be afraid." Brutus stepped forward and raised both hands, forgetting the blood-stained hammer in his right.

The woman's eyes widened and focused on the weapon as he quickly dropped it to his side. "I mean you no ill will. I only want respite."

Brutus had been in the thick of battle before, with so many bodies at his feet he couldn't walk, but never had he been in the raid of a city. The true horrors in men's hearts were unleashed when all law was absent, and it took all his restraint not to join the few Laltos soldiers hopelessly trying to defend the upper city. He'd survived his attempts at help, barely. Then he'd stayed as close to Hadrian as possible, looking for an opening to end this, but he'd failed miserably, as he so often did.

The woman in the corner pressed her eyes shut and squeezed her children so tightly she risked suffocating them.

My words won't soothe her panic. After a while she'd realise that if he was going to do something, he'd have done it already.

"Warlord!" a rakkan yelled outside.

Brutus ducked, before remembering a solid wall separated him from the street.

Hadrian's reply was sharp. "Where are they retreating to?"

Brutus crept up to the door and pressed his eye to the keyhole. Through the billowing clouds of black smoke, he saw Hadrian's tall figure, white-hot fervern raging in his eyes.

A smaller commander bowed in front of him, face blackened from the soot and ash. "Into the palace, Warlord."

"Perhaps that human soldier spoke the truth," Hadrian growled. "The passageway he mentioned must lead outside the city."

"Y-yes." The small rakkan took a step back. "The legionnaires can make chase."

"No. Push the humans back with a number small enough to capture any algus they can. We only have a dozen Numbered in chains so far. We'll never find that witch at this rate."

Brutus started. He'd guessed the Viridians were capturing algus for spying and battle. Yet now he knew exactly who Hadrian spoke of—the Waif Magician. Suddenly it made sense why he'd want algus, but that didn't tell him anything of why he so badly wanted to find the witch.

"The rest of the Legion will move outside the city," Hadrian continued. "We'll find whatever hole they emerge from."

Brutus prayed that Hadrian was mistaken but knew all too well the passageways existed. Brutus's best play was to withdraw with the rakkans and hope to divert them away from the few passages he knew the location of.

The Warlord stomped up the street, out of Brutus's view, while the other rakkan barked at two centurions. "You heard him. Relay the orders to the other commanders."

As the two centurions withdrew, the commander took the time to search around until his grinning face fixed on the door Brutus crouched behind.

Brutus stepped back.

A few silent seconds passed before the deadbolt rattled as the rakkan tried to open it. Before Brutus could reach for his hammer, the bolt sprang off and hit his cuirass as the door thrust open, bringing fumes with it.

Brutus coughed as the man stepped inside. It only took a brief scan of the room for the intruder's eyes to home in on the cowering family.

"I didn't know this house had already been claimed." The rakkan gave Brutus a toothy smile. "Care to share?"

Brutus scowled. "I found her first." The words were insolent given his legionnaire disguise, but he'd be damned if he didn't protect an innocent woman.

Rather than pull rank, the commander pouted in a false sad face. "How about you take her, and I take the others?"

Externally, Brutus made sure not a muscle flinched as bile rose in his throat. It was time this city saw at least one instance of retribution this day. "Fine. But close the door. I don't want a crowd."

The rakkan grinned and turned to shut the door while Brutus bent down and picked up his hammer. He slipped it behind his meaty thigh before the rakkan turned around and eyed the children hungrily.

Brutus stepped behind him, the commander too focused on his prey to notice.

"They're so young," the rakkan whispered.

Brutus raised his weapon, drew back, eyes fixed on the back of the rakkan's skull. "Too young." With gritted teeth, he swung and unleashed his fury.

62

Battle of Laltos

Darius summoned the anger within him and watched ferven crawl down the pickaxe and engulf the head. With a cry, he smashed it into the pillar, knocking out a third of it with the blow. His next strike shattered the remaining rock.

The stone ruptured overhead. A deep crack spread farther by the second. Darius bolted for the passage and made his way up as the booms and crashes echoed all around him, collapsing into what could become his grave.

Once hurtling through the main tunnel, huge chunks of the ground sank away from his feet, taking pillars and walls with them. Cracks burst through the ceiling, sending dust into his eyes, forcing him to conjure ferven so he could keep them open.

As he ran, he smashed the pickaxe into more pillars along the way, to hasten the downfall. One after the other burst into fragments but drained more of his strength.

Soon his heaving chest couldn't drag in dusty breaths deep enough to satisfy his lungs.

It wasn't long before he caught up with others fleeing. Everyone sprinted for the exit: men and rakkans that had lagged along with the Xavalans hunting them.

Darius barged through as many as he could, tripping a few Xavalan algus along the way, before he finally got free of the tunnel and emerged into the smoky night air.

Clouds of dust and rocks poured out of the passage as a final thunderous bang shook the mountain.

In front of him stood the palace. Behind, rock. The only route away would have been to either side, but some rakkans had already punched a hole directly into the building.

The Xavalan algus that had made it through the tunnel didn't hesitate and slashed apart the people closest.

Darius gasped to catch his breath as he cast his eyes over the scene, alarmed that most of Laltos's algus already seemed to have fled. *There's enough Xavalans to kill us all.*

Xavalan algus cut through the Militia and soldiers. All hoplites and rakkans fled to the hole in the palace's side where only Lex, Selene, and the few remaining algus clashed with the Xavalans as they came.

Among the group, Darius recognised Gorgias's flushed face, the man finally wielding a sword alongside his wife, Fourteen.

Darius dropped the pickaxe and drew his gladius. It immediately felt heavy in his hand. *Damn it.* The sprint had sapped his energy. Whatever use he'd served in this battle was now done.

Hundreds of roars echoed from his left. He turned his head, and a wall of kuraminium shields met his vision, flooding from around the building. The grass underfoot shuddered as the Viridian Legion's charge built more and more pace.

Darius sprinted as fast as he could, tailing at the rear of the group of people from Laltos. It wasn't far to the hole, but a Xavalan algus lunged in front of him and blocked his path.

His sword met the man's shimmering blue weapon, and he shoved the algus backwards, straight off his feet.

Thank the heavens I'm still strong. Because he wasn't fast.

Selene fought her way over to him, cutting through the chainmail of two of the algus, and pushed him towards the hole. "Go!"

A few paces later and he was through the jagged gap, back into the wide marble-floored halls that now echoed with the sound of fleeing footsteps.

Lex soon followed him along with Gorgias, Fourteen, and the other algus, most of whom wasted no time in sprinting away.

Sulla and a few of his men greeted them inside with raised shields and spears, ready to cover the retreat.

"What took you so long?" Sulla asked.

"Where's Selene?" Darius searched around to see only Lex, Gorgias, and Fourteen left, along with a few Militia men.

"Selene's coming." Lex bent over, breathing heavily as Gorgias helped her to her feet. "She's outside."

As Darius stepped to find Selene, she sprang through the gap with her escort close behind.

Finally, they were all there but would soon be followed. *Block the hole.* Darius rushed forwards, between Selene and Fourteen, but before he reached it, an algus stepped through and brought him to a skidding halt.

The man wore a white, hooded tunic that cast his eyes in shadow, and he grasped a thin algor-coated sword as long as his leg. *Jason.*

The King's Sword suddenly thrust his blade at Darius.

He brought up his own sword to block, but Jason had feinted and brought the blade around to strike his other side.

Selene shoved Darius away and parried the swing herself while Paris zipped towards the algus's head.

The shove threw Darius off balance, and he stumbled a few yards back before falling to one knee, vision shaken. *Damn.* Why could he never help when it mattered?

Sulla came forward and grabbed his arm, hauled him up. "I've got you."

"Run!" Selene cried as Jason dodged Paris's swoops and slashed at her again.

Fourteen lunged and blocked Jason's sword, saving Selene's neck, but Jason twisted his blade and freed it enough to stab into the Numbered's heart.

Gorgias screamed as his wife's face flushed deep red with a grimace before she collapsed to the floor.

Darius lifted his sword and stood, ready to rush forward, but Sulla's grip tightened on him. "No." He dragged Darius away. "We have to go."

Selene swiped at Jason, forcing him to step back to the hole while Paris darted from high towards his hooded face again.

Before the pteron reached him, Jason shifted to the side and sliced his blade through the winged creature.

Black blood hung in Darius's vision as it splattered over the algus's tunic. Memories of Lyra flashed through his mind.

Selene yelled with a contortion of pain and fury, then lunged for the King's Sword.

Jason sidestepped, gave her a push as she missed him and tumbled forwards.

Her auburn curls were the last thing Darius saw as she stumbled through the dark hole into the cataclysm outside.

Lex rushed towards Jason, but one of Sulla's men reached out and caught her arm in an iron grip. The rakkan scooped her up, despite her struggles, and carried her away at pace.

"Selene!" Darius pulled at Sulla's hand. The rakkan's feet slid across the floor with a screech. Darius had more strength than Lex to resist, but still not enough.

All thoughts of Selene's betrayal, and the pain she'd caused him, evaporated. He had to get to her.

While they struggled, Jason's head turned towards them.

"We can't take him, Dar!" Sulla cried, desperation in his voice.

Shouts and the clash of metal on metal rang from outside, only swelling Darius's terror.

The King's Sword spun to face the hole just before the wall smashed away. A testudo of Viridians burst through, crumbling stone beneath their heavy stomps.

The air left Darius's lungs. *Selene…*

A teary-eyed Gorgias sprinted away while Sulla and his other men wrapped an arm around Darius's shoulders and dragged him and his gaze from the fight.

Flashes of Jason's blue sword reflected from the floor and walls, but Darius couldn't look back, and instead he stared into nothingness as they took turn after turn, left, right, down stairs, following a trail of muddy footprints all the way to the cellars.

Racks of wine barrels as tall as him flitted past in a blur. All his mind focused on was Selene and the legionnaires that had burst through the wall. He didn't know the odds she'd survived their arrival, and he couldn't help but want to turn around. Why was he still running?

Face it; I'm too weak to help her. Hadrian had likely got his hands on another he cared for. He clenched his jaw so hard it pained his teeth.

The warrior holding Lex finally released her near a large wine barrel at the end of the room. She scowled at the rakkan but didn't sprint back. Instead, she pulled at the wooden face of the barrel. It swung open to reveal a dark, empty interior with a staircase descending from the bottom.

If only the footprints leading up to it weren't there, it would have been well concealed. *May as well have left them a map.*

While the rakkans ducked inside, Darius glanced back from the way they'd come, unable to do anything but imagine Selene caught in the grips of the Viridians. She'd be better off dead; shouldn't he try to find her?

"Don't even think of it." Sulla grabbed him by the collar.

Before Darius could protest, Sulla shoved him inside the entrance.

Lex followed and closed the facade behind them.

Sulla kept a hand to his back, and Darius loathed himself for how little he resisted.

He conjured a little ferven in his eyes to shed light on the stairs ahead. Usually he preferred to use algor to light his way, but when enraged, ferven came with ease.

After a few steps, he sensed Lex had stopped and looked back. She'd paused at the top of the staircase. Her hands trembled.

"Go on," Darius said to Sulla. "We'll follow."

Lex took a few deep breaths, with only hate in her eyes. Darius dared not so much as breathe too loudly lest she snap at him. The air smelled wooden and festered in the confined space, with a lingering whiff of the bloody men that had passed through before them.

Finally, Lex began walking with the same blank, numb face he'd seen after Omid had died. "I hope Jason can delay them long enough."

Darius's voice was barely a mumble. "By the look of it, if anyone can, it's him." He didn't know whether he wanted the King's Sword to succeed or not. The man that had sent Selene to her fate didn't deserve to live.

As Darius stared at Lex's weathered, defeated gaze as she walked, he saw her failure for the first time. He'd always assumed her plans would work—perhaps that's why he'd always listened when she'd asked a favour of him—but now he saw the truth… She was as fallible as the rest of them: Sulla, Brutus, Selene, Theodoros and even Varro too.

Lex upped her pace down the steps. They made haste on the haphazard stairs and into a narrow dirt passageway which sloped down and descended too deep for comfort, where the air became humid and all the more nauseating. His tolerance grew so thin he thought of pinching his nose, but finally the ground evened out and sloped upwards.

Soon, they met with the back of the thin crowd of soldiers making their way through. Despite the destruction no doubt still happening above them, it had faded into a distant rumble. Now all they heard were the footsteps ahead and the occasional cough.

A little while longer, the weak moonlight glowing in the sky became visible ahead.

Darius tensed. *What awaits now, God of Justice? Escape or death?* The lack of ringing in his ears from clashing swords was a good sign, but he didn't dare relax.

They emerged from the passageway at the side of a hill littered with short trees and shrubs. Most of the rakkans and Laltos Guard were together in small, separate groups within the brush, muttering to one another, preparing whatever bags they had, and bandaging the leaking wounds of those fortunate enough to have survived.

At the centre of the men, a stern-faced Theodoros argued with other algus while the Regent's escort bared its teeth.

Darius scanned around. *So few of us left?* So many fallen, yet one troubled him most.

He clasped the bear claw hanging from his belt and turned to Lex. "Do you think Selene…" His voice trailed off as he saw the pity in her gaze at his naïve question. "What now?"

For once, she looked as if she had no machinations in her mind and shrugged with a hollow stare.

While Darius searched for words of comfort, a child cried out, "Mother!"

Cynthia ran through the mud and jumped straight into Lex's arms. She hoisted the girl up, enveloped her in an embrace with eyes flaring blue in a way Darius knew blocked tears. At least they'd saved one innocent.

Bashes of stone sounded behind where Sulla's men caved in the passageway. Meanwhile, Darius and the others made their way over to Theodoros who paused his mutterings.

"Don't stop on our account," Darius said.

Theodoros shook his head. "The Margalvians want us to travel to your rakkan city."

"Sounds good," Sulla said. "It's not like we can be finicky."

The Regent looked to Lex, but she just stared with Cynthia in her arms, as if unaware of anything they'd said.

"Alexandra?" he said.

She blinked. "Yes?"

Darius grunted. "There's no time to stand and squabble. The Viridians could be right behind us."

Theodoros sighed and closed his eyes. "Margalvia it is then. We'll tell any other refugees that fled in the last few weeks to head there."

Sulla turned before the Regent had finished and began waving signals to his commanders. The rakkans hurriedly secured their weapons and belongings, then started filing through the foliage towards the south.

Theodoros relayed orders to his soldiers and the civilians that remained, then the groups followed close behind Sulla's men.

Darius stayed beside Lex as they walked at the rear of the group, slowing every time she looked over her shoulder at the rising billows.

The shelter of trees was thinner than the smoke in the air, and it didn't last long. Soon they made their way exposed in farmlands. Only the rise and fall of the landscape gave them a little cover, but it did nothing to block the whiff of sulphur carried through the haze blowing from Laltos.

The group walked through a shallow groove in the earth, flanked on all sides by slopes coated in shaking plants and dulled white flowers. Behind, the tallest hill now failed to cover the burnt, collapsing towers.

This time, when Lex moved to look behind, Darius wrapped an arm around her shoulders and held her gaze forwards.

"What's done is done," he whispered. Their time for justice would come, he prayed.

Lex's head dipped.

The lights bursting from the city reached the hills either side of them and played tricks on him. Shadows flickered. On the hill to his right, the lurching plants mimicked figures moving through them, despite only being knee-height. Across the whole crest, a cloud of grey smog hovered low and made it look as if an unbroken row of men slowly amassed.

Darius halted. As his eyes focused, the rows of shadows formed into a wave of black helmets, worn by warriors now standing on the ridge.

Lex stopped beside him. "What is it?"

This time his struggles for breath weren't from exhaustion. On their right side, the armoured mass spread farther out by the second, and none of those travelling in front of him had turned their heads to see.

He took a few wary steps towards the unfamiliar figures and strained his eyes. He saw what he feared—helmets extending down low over the chin, helmets of the Viridian Legion.

63

Battle of Laltos

Darius shoved his fingers in his mouth and whistled, but only a few humans closest turned their head. Only the rakkans would see, and they were too far to hear. Lex stared at him with a bewilderment on her face that slowly melded into fear.

With ferven in his throat, he took a deep breath and unleashed a bellow that pained his chest. This time Sulla and his men at the head of the marching group spun. Some held their hands up as if to chastise the lunacy of whoever was making the racket. But one by one their heads swivelled to the hill. Almost the whole damned legion was there.

Darius's eyes narrowed on a giant figure marching down the slope towards them. Thick muscles on his thighs bulged with each step and the mass of warriors followed.

Darius grabbed Lex's arm and pulled her across what would soon be the front line of their defence. "Make a shield wall facing me! Archers behind them."

The human soldiers, half dazed by shock, haphazardly arranged themselves. The weaklings wouldn't last a minute.

Sulla's warriors raced into formation in front of as many humans as possible.

Before Darius and Lex could reach the Militia Chief, Theodoros stepped out from the crowd and stopped them.

Darius seized his shoulder. "Hadrian is coming down—"

"I see the shadow of the army." Theodoros shook his head. "There's no use fighting."

Darius had to stop himself from slapping the old man. "Then die without getting in my way."

Lex rapped him on the arm, but at the same time, she turned her nose up at her father. "We can't give in."

"Surrender is our only option," Theodoros said. Behind him, a few algus had emerged from the crowd and looked at Darius and Lex with glum faces, as if of the same mind as the Regent. Following them, the Regent's beastly escort walked out, the iron plating on his dipped head almost slipping off.

Darius didn't need to look at the Viridians again to know he was hopelessly outnumbered.

"Feeble humans!" Hadrian's yell paralysed the scrambling defenders. "Come, Regent. Parley. Let's end the battle. I'm feeling generous."

The Viridian Legion front line halted, out of reach of spears but well within range of slingers. Hadrian stood out in front of his warriors, exposed but enjoying every second with his swords held out wide in mockery, daring them to try something.

Theodoros turned to one of his algus, a striking dark-haired woman with deep frown lines.

"What kind of leader wants to parley in the open like this?" he asked.

The algus frowned. "One that knows no one can kill him."

Darius scoffed then growled. If only he were at his full strength…but doubt rose when he remembered their last encounter. *Maybe not even then.*

"I'll go," Theodoros said. "Better I do it alone, lest it be a ruse. An old man is no significant loss."

Lex scoffed. "I'm—"

"Don't even think of arguing. I'm too stubborn and tired. No one is to follow me. If we cannot agree terms, your best chance is to fight here, united."

Lex frowned and opened her mouth to say something but stayed mute under her father's resolute frown.

The Regent began walking towards Hadrian when the Warlord pointed over to Darius. "Bring the mongrel with you."

Lex grabbed Darius's wrist. At full strength he'd be tempted just to seize a chance to run Hadrian through with a blade, and to hell with the rules of parley, but he wasn't even close to full strength.

Theodoros glanced back to him. "Stay where you are. The miscreant can go and drink from a latrine." With a hint of a smirk and no trace of the same unease that grew in Darius's belly, the Regent turned and made his way towards the towering warlord. Only his bear marched at his side, now with its head held high and snarling. As he strode up, the bottom of his cloak soaked up the dirty mud on the slope.

Darius held the bear claw on his sword belt. Perhaps he should have insisted on going with the old man.

The Regent stopped just out of reach of Hadrian's swords. His thin white hair and grey cloak swayed in the smoky breeze. It made his slim figure appear all the feebler next to the Warlord and the rows of spear-wielding warriors behind him.

"Why didn't you bring the Dreaded one?" Hadrian asked.

"He speaks for no one. I'm in charge here."

"Who leads the rakkans then, old man?"

Theodoros glared. "What is it you want?"

"First things first. Kneel."

The bear growled, and the Regent made no movement. "Kneel to whom?"

"Your new god." Hadrian raised his voice to a roar. "All of you, kneel!"

Darius scoffed. The sulphur in the air almost made him retch—or was it Hadrian's insistence on worship?

A hoplite next to him began to drop to a knee, but Darius grabbed him and hauled him back up. "Get up, you dolt."

Meanwhile, Theodoros lifted his chin. "You're as mortal as the rest of us. I kneel before no creature."

Hadrian stepped forward and pushed the point of his sword into Theodoros's belly. The two leaders glared at each other, the only movement being the Regent's cloak twitching in the wind.

"Fool," Hadrian spat. "You're lucky I want something more than your adoration."

"And what's that?"

The Warlord's head turned towards Darius. "The mongrel. Alive."

Darius lowered a hand to the hilt of his sword and glanced over his shoulder at the empty hillside inviting him to flee. They'd never catch him, but then what would happen to the others? This would probably be a good time to cut his own neck.

Theodoros took a step back from Hadrian's blade as the Warlord watched, fire beginning to rise and glow in his eyes.

"And what will become of my people?" Theodoros asked.

"We'll need them to work the farms and raise the cattle we've just reclaimed."

"Live as slaves?"

"Be thankful you won't starve, as we've had to endure."

503

Starved? If only the Warlord's thighs weren't so thickset, Darius might have believed he'd missed even a single meal in his many decades.

Theodoros's hand hovered at his side. His cloak brushed back and forth over his sword in the wafts of air. He flicked the fabric away from the hilt subtly, but Darius saw Hadrian's eyes flit down to it for the briefest of moments. *Don't try it, old man.* The warriors behind the Warlord raised their weapons.

Theodoros's words quietened. "I'll die before I call you master."

"As you wish."

Theodoros went for his sword, but not before a hundred spears flew from the front rank of rakkan warriors.

The Regent dove to the side, as far as he could stretch. But the projectiles skewered his chest, stomach and legs.

Lex screamed in fury, dropping to her knees, as the kuraminium spearheads dug into the soil, leaving Theodoros's lifeless body suspended in the air.

Blood trickled down the shafts.

The Regent's bear roared and lunged head-first at Hadrian.

The Warlord caught the animal in mid-air, a hand clamped on the upper and lower jaw.

Thrashing, the beast's body collapsed onto the ground. Its furry mass rippled frantically as the pair wrestled. Roars of anger transformed to roars of pain until a crack of bone rang out. With a ferocious yell, Hadrian ripped the animal's lower jaw off and snapped its neck backwards.

The brute kicked it away with a smile, leaving the dying escort to writhe weakly in the dirt. Mud stained its fur black as its wriggles got ever slower, much like Lyra had once been left.

Darius clenched his sword so tightly his hand trembled. "I don't care if we die, as long as we take that bastard with us." He dragged Lex up by the arm and stared into her eyes with a fire that finally lit up her own. "Do you want to mourn? Or do you want revenge?"

She flared her nostrils and gave him a stiff nod.

Hoplites around held out their shields into a wall, mirroring the Red Militia's formation. Darius was thankful at least Sulla looked ready to fight to the death.

Archers nocked arrows.

Hadrian and the Viridian Legion pointed their swords and spears, raised their shields.

Drums pounded. Legionnaires stamped their feet in unison. If any of the defenders had somehow kept an ounce of courage, this was enough to drive it away.

Darius glanced at the other algus, but they had their heads turned in all directions, apparently searching for escape routes. Was there no one left to instil courage in these humans? Lex looked ready to fight but little else. Theodoros was dead.

With a grimace, Darius stepped forward. *Looks like it's up to me.* It was time to be like the old Darius they spoke of.

He pushed aside the soldiers ahead of him and walked out beyond the front line, glaring at Hadrian for the last time before one of them was dead. *Agathos, if you're there, I beg you to make his death as painful as he deserves, whether it be tonight or not.*

Both the Red Militia and remainder of the Laltos Guard stared at him expectantly. The air stank of soot and fear. Did they expect him to give a speech?

He conjured ferven in his throat, forced a deep breath, then unleashed a ferocious roar.

The defenders beheld him and their eyes finally filled with fire, metal and resolve.

He took another deep breath and yelled, "You didn't think you'd live forever, did you?"

The furore that came in reply pained his ears, shouts of anger and pain released. "Fear not, brave men," Darius yelled. "For tonight, you won't die alone, but with me. Fight with all you have. Let's take those brutes with us to hell!"

The roars in reply carried on long after he'd exhausted his breath.

Rakkan horns blared from all angles, both from the Red Militia and the Viridian Legion in front. Darius's energy rose, as if feeding from the sounds. It felt good. Was this why Hadrian lusted after ovation?

Darius reached into his mind, to Lyra one last time. *I tried, girl. Sorry I wasn't strong enough.* He sensed she heard him, and she sent him energy, agitation, the will to battle. *Stop fighting when I'm gone. Live.*

Still, he sensed urgency in her.

He turned to face the wall of defenders with a raised sword, to begin the final charge, but he stopped when something caught his eye.

A black shadow raced down the hill, too short to be a man, and soon he made out four feline legs.

His stomach sank, chest constricted and left him short of breath. *Lyra? You fool! Go away!*

After taking one step towards her, he paused again at what he saw behind her. Figures lined up across the crest of the hill. *Damn. They're behind us too?*

Horns blared from the unknown warriors, and the humans turned around at the sound. Darius listened and tried to separate the tone from the noise. It didn't sound Viridian.

A tall figure wearing a horned helmet charged with a tight formation of warriors sprinting behind. They wore the familiar rakkan bands around their biceps, but to Darius they looked as black as old blood. *Varro?*

Hadrian roared. He barked orders at his warriors, but none of them moved. The Viridian Legionnaires gaped at one another then back at the approaching mass.

"Fall back!" Darius pushed the shields of the hoplites, who turned without hesitation. Shouts of the retreat spread quickly, and soon they all flowed backwards, except for the Red Militia whose shield wall stood fixed and braced in a rearguard.

They readied spears and drove the bases into the ground, but the invaders still stood paralysed as Hadrian smashed the helmet of one of those closest.

It snapped them into action.

The Viridian Legionnaire cried out and began charging down the hill. Once a few started, the rest followed, and Hadrian sprinted to the head with his swords flaming and outstretched.

Without a shield of his own, Darius ran over to the closest line of Militia and stood behind, peering over his shoulder.

Lyra had almost reached him. Varro was still a minute away. The Viridians, seconds. What's more, Hadrian's giant figure bounded directly for him.

Lyra. Turn back. Now! She ignored him and skidded to a halt in the mud by his feet.

He wrapped his arms around her, shielded her with his back, and pressed his heels into the ground.

The Viridian Warlord smashed into the shield of the rakkan in front with a deafening clank of metal. Sparks flew as the warrior toppled backwards into Darius and knocked him over.

His elbows hit the cold mud as he rolled forwards and scrambled back to his feet. As he did, Lyra scurried away a few yards and turned back to pounce.

Don't you dare attack him!

The Warlord's growls filled Darius's ears above the clamour of battle before he turned, and his eyes caught sight of the fiend again.

Hadrian cleaved the head from a Militia rakkan between them then kicked the bleeding corpse towards Darius.

Blood splattered across his face as he batted away the head with his sword. *Deep breaths.* All he wanted to do was wipe his brow, but instead, he held out his gladius, arm already tired.

A blue arrow streaked from behind him and grazed Hadrian's helmet as the Warlord lurched to the side. Another darted in. Hadrian flared ferven and blocked the projectile with the flat of his blade.

Darius dared a glance behind him. Lex stood behind the wrestling warriors with a bow stretched in her arms, another blue-tipped arrow ready to fly.

The Black Legion closed in behind. Darius swung back around and lunged towards the defensive warlord.

Hadrian blocked his first strike. Darius's sword bounced off and vibrated as if he'd hit a wall. A fiery growl crackled from the Warlord's mouth as he dodged another arrow and took a huge swipe at Darius's head.

Unwilling to test his ability to block, Darius ducked and stabbed for Hadrian's thighs, aiming to rend the rakkan just as he had with Cordus.

The Warlord lifted his shin and blocked the sword with a ferven-coated greave before he kicked out and narrowly missed Darius.

Darius backed off, already panting for breath.

A wave of Black Legionnaires burst from the edges of his vision then collided with the Viridians. The thunderous crash of metal rang in his ears as the Margalvians pummelled them backwards, some off their feet, trampled underfoot as the surge continued.

But Hadrian and a few men stood firm in the gap the Black Legion had left for Darius and the other Militia.

Darius ran to Lyra and planted his body above her while Hadrian swatted away the closest warriors, slashing necks and thighs in a series of strokes.

The surge slowed as the Viridian Legion dug in and finally stymied the Black Legion's advance.

Soon, Darius was surrounded by a mass of sparring warriors.

Trickles of red spread across the soil and coalesced around Darius's boots. He swallowed. *Keep it together.*

Hadrian's helmet turned to him again, and the Warlord charged and swung for his midriff. This time he couldn't dodge, so he thrust out his sword to parry.

The blow drove his own weapon back against his armour and almost threw him off his feet, but Hadrian pulled away and narrowly dodged another arrow from Lex.

As the pair parted, a Viridian Legionnaire charged into the fight with a gladius in one hand and a hammer in the other.

Darius braced, expecting a stab from the rakkan, but instead, as the legionnaire ran past the Warlord, he raked his blade across the back of Hadrian's leg.

The Warlord growled, too slow to dodge the strike but swift enough to swing for the legionnaire's neck to counter.

His sword smashed into the bottom of the helmet, flinging it from the Viridian's head, and sent him to the ground in a daze.

Darius stared, not believing what he saw. "Brutus?"

The shout drew Brutus's gaze, who gave a grin when they locked eyes.

But behind him, Hadrian moved, unhampered by the shallow wound on his leg, and swung at the Margalvian's exposed head.

"Watch out!" Darius shouted as he surged forward with Lyra at his side.

Brutus ducked. Hadrian's sword sliced hair and skin from the top of his scalp, but the Margalvian didn't flinch and spun with his hammer arcing towards the Warlord.

As Hadrian dodged, Lyra pounced and bit his arm but only caught the armguard.

Only then within reach, Darius flared algor across his gladius and stabbed at the Warlord's neck.

Hadrian dipped his head, let the point of the blade deflect from his helmet as he shook his arm, trying to fling Lyra free. But she held tight while clawing at the rest of his armour.

Darius and Brutus attacked again, and this time Hadrian moved Lyra between them like an escort shield and forced both to avert their strikes.

Darius cursed. *Let go, Lyra!* She finally obeyed his order and scurried back to his heel, which brought a chuckle from the Warlord's throat. "Cowardly escort."

Unable to contain his rage, Darius lunged at the Warlord with a flurry of swipes that struck only armour.

Another of Lex's arrows soared between them that Darius barely avoided slipping into the path of.

"Get away, lad!" Brutus called as he stabbed his gladius.

Hadrian parried and knocked the sword from Brutus's hand, forcing the Margalvian to step back.

Darius's reactions were slow, his body weak. *Damn this infirmity.* Hadrian had seen it and realised he needn't even dodge.

Darius's grip on his weapon was loose. But he couldn't live with himself if he left Brutus to fight alone.

So Darius lunged again and swiped at Hadrian, but the rakkan parried his sword with such force that his gladius flew to the ground to join Brutus's.

The Warlord brought his blade back across and stabbed towards Darius, but Brutus shoved him away, clean off his feet.

Tumbling through the air, Darius watched as Hadrian's gladius and Brutus's hammer swung in unison towards the other.

The spikes of the hammer cleaved a chunk of skin and muscle from the Warlord's bicep, while Hadrian's free arm thrust a gladius into Brutus's thigh.

Darius hit the bloody mud while both bellowed in pain and stepped back from one another. The Warlord growled and pressed his fist to the deep wound in his other arm.

Brutus's own grunts were swallowed by the clamour of war.

The Margalvian dropped his hammer, fell until his backside struck the mud, and all Darius could do was watch.

Taking advantage of the blows, Lyra pounced with jaws wide, ready for Hadrian's limbs.

He backed away, but his eyes tracked her every movement in a manner Darius knew were looking for the single opening the Warlord needed.

Enough, Lyra. Protect Brutus. If it gave the rakkan a fighting chance, it was worth it.

She retreated to the Margalvian, who now sat with his head hung low. Blood gushed from his leg, his half-closed eyes fading all the more.

Darius swallowed. Hadrian had made another he cared for bleed, and again it was Darius's fault. He hadn't been strong enough. As always, it was others risking themselves for him. He had to stop this fiend.

Blue-headed arrows darted towards the Warlord and forced him to dodge and block more.

Darius turned to see Lex loosing as fast as she could. It would give Darius the space he needed to get Brutus clear.

As Darius moved to run to his mentor, his vision darkened. A Black Legionnaire beat him to it, stooped beside the rakkan and pressed a hand to his gushing thigh.

Around them the battle raged, but the Margalvians held their own.

Some Viridians turned and began fleeing up the hill.

The Black Legionnaires chased after them, cut through their backs and ankles without mercy.

With a snarl, Hadrian ignored his men and the incoming arrows, and he charged at Darius, a fiery gladius drawn back with his one good arm.

As Darius moved his sword to parry, the Warlord feinted then thrust his blade towards Darius's midriff.

Darius flared algor across his cuirass as the blow landed and took the wind from his lungs. His armour vibrated like a bell as he fell backwards, barely managing to turn his shoulder and roll away from the Warlord's follow up stab, which sank into the dirt.

As Darius rolled through the blood and mud, fighting back the vomit, he hit the greaves of another warrior. He looked up, relieved to see the black bands across the bicep, and calmed further that they numbered three.

"Varro."

64

Battle of Laltos

Darius pushed himself free of the ground and to one knee. There wasn't a soul other than Varro that he'd be more pleased to meet in that moment.

The Black Warlord's helmet didn't turn to acknowledge him, the visor across the face instead fixed on Hadrian.

The Viridian Warlord's left arm hung lifeless at his side, with blood dribbling from his wound. He glimpsed briefly over his shoulder at his routing warriors. Some had stopped at the crest of the hill and once again pelted the area below with rocks before Black Legionnaires reached them.

"Kill him, Varro," Lex shouted as she loosed another arrow at Hadrian.

She was right. The three of them had a chance, and it had to be fast because Brutus was bleeding out.

Hadrian swiped away the arrow with his flaming armguard. Varro began striding forwards. Rocks struck the surrounding ground, but his unflinching walk continued. Meanwhile, Darius got back to his feet, grabbed the spear of a fallen enemy in one hand and a shield in the other. Holding the scutum in front of his head, he moved to Hadrian's flank, fighting back a faintness coming from either his weak body or the blood that coated it. Clank, clank, clank sounded as slinger stones struck his shield.

Lyra stood beside Brutus. She eyed Hadrian.

Don't you dare. Darius continued stalking.

The Viridian Warlord backed up a few paces and looked between Varro and his routing legion as if torn.

Fight. Let us strike you down. But if he ran, Darius was ready to hamstring him. He'd chase the brute to the edge of the world if he had to.

Varro's walk suddenly burst into a sprint. The unexpected movement caught Darius by surprise, and he belatedly hurried his move to Hadrian's flank. Varro's blades shimmered with thin flames as he leapt and soared towards the Viridian Warlord.

Lex loosed an arrow.

Darius flung his spear at Hadrian's chest.

The Viridian Warlord erupted in ferven. He let the projectiles strike his armour before bringing up his sword to block Varro's double chop.

Darius winced at the bright light. Vengeance was within reach, and he closed in while Varro unleashed a flurry of strikes with a speed that almost matched an algus.

Hadrian held his own but parried and stepped farther and farther back with each block, the last strike forcing him down to one knee.

They almost had him. Bending down, Darius picked up another spear from the blood-soaked ground. The red mess dripped from his fingers as he held it up and prepared to toss it, but his vision lost focus. After a shake of his head, he flung the javelin towards what he saw of Hadrian's figure.

The focus returned to his eyes enough to see his spear miss, but he watched Varro cut Hadrian's right knee.

With each step towards the warlords, blood squelched inside Darius's boots. His vision blurred again. *Damn you. Not now.*

A stone struck his helmet, dazing him, and he almost fell to the soil.

The slingers on the crest focused all their fire on Varro, and rock after rock hit his armour. The Black Warlord paused to dodge the projectiles, and Hadrian seized his chance to turn and hobble up the hill.

Darius lurched forward shakily as a second stone caught his shin.

Lyra bolted, still eyeing Hadrian, as if ready to chase.

No!

As she ran past, Darius bent down and grabbed her. He pulled her tight to his body, shielding her from another couple of slinger rocks that hit his shoulder. Despite the surrounding death, her warm fur brought a calm he'd craved for too long. *I won't risk you again.*

Varro turned and made a signal with his fist to his legion. A few seconds later, a Margalvian horn blared to which the Black Legionnaires slowed their chase.

All Darius could do was watch Hadrian stagger up the hill to rejoin his army. Remnants of the Viridian Legion scrambled to catch up to their scattered brothers, as their warlord disappeared behind the crest.

Darius's stare was interrupted when the Black Warlord hauled him backwards with Lyra still tight in his arms.

"Fall back," Varro ordered.

"You're letting him escape," Darius roared.

"We don't have the numbers to chase. They've routed. Fall back."

"But Lalt—"

Varro bashed the flat of his sword against Darius's helmet and set his ears ringing. "Fall back!"

Darius grunted, wondering if this was the same rakkan that considered each decision for an age back in Margalvia. "We need to get Brutus. He's here, injured."

Varro froze for a moment, eyes black inside his helmet. "Where?"

Darius didn't answer and instead responded to the question by running in the direction he'd left his mentor. He scanned the piles of bodies for a familiar face while Varro followed closely.

Eventually, they spotted Brutus lying in the trampled grass. A rakkan still tried to stem the blood from the thigh wound, but it gushed between his fingers.

The stench filled Darius's nostrils, but he held his breath and knelt down, regardless. With only a glance at the wound, he knew it had severed the thickest veins, drenching the rakkan's legs.

It took all Darius's strength not to turn away—not because of the gore but because of the guilt at knowing it should have been him.

"Darius," Brutus said weakly, eyes turning to him before shutting again.

"I'm here." Darius swallowed. He took the rakkan's hand tightly but only felt a feeble squeeze in return. "'Twas a nasty wound you gave Hadrian. Saved our hides." Appropriate words seemed to seldom strike Darius when they mattered most.

Brutus rasped as he grimaced and clutched his leg. "He…got lucky." Brutus's grimace eased, and his eyes faded as if his pain no longer registered. He whispered, "I want…Varro—"

"I'm here, brother." The Black Warlord knelt beside him in the mud.

"Hadrian's after the Waif…"

Darius frowned. "Don't speak. Save your strength."

Brutus's head fell to the ground, which smeared it in bloody dirt. But Varro took it and held it still, giving it a shake to rouse him. "I'm here."

"Varro? It's cold… So cold."

"Don't be afraid, brother."

"I am… It's cold…" Brutus's last whisper faded, and his head rolled back again.

"Brother…" Varro muttered.

Still gripping Brutus's hand tightly, Darius gave the rakkan a shake, not believing it until he felt the once strong-arm limp and lifeless. "Brutus…I'm sorry," he whispered, hoping the man heard him in whatever afterlife there was, but knowing how insignificant and perhaps insulting the words were.

At the thought, the anger of battle that had boiled inside him was replaced with only a numbness intensified by the wind.

He lowered his head, unable to take his eyes from the smeared face of his mentor and unwilling to catch Varro's eye.

One more death my choices have caused. And who knew where Selene was, whether she was even alive… The slashed body of the woman in the village all that time ago came to mind. She'd born such a resemblance to Selene. He wasn't sure whether to pray she was dead rather than in Viridian hands, rather than suffer the pain and despair he had in Laltos and worse. Was loss unavoidable? After all, the decisions of everyone else seemed to result in death and destruction too. But that didn't make Brutus's lifeless gaze any less acrid.

"That's two brothers you've cost me," the Warlord growled. "Another woman you've widowed. If you hadn't provoked

Hadrian… You deserve a punishment I'm too honourable to inflict."

As Varro's words trailed off, Darius had no defence, and even if he had, he wouldn't have uttered it, knowing he deserved the sickness now in his stomach and more. He braced for a sword to the back of his neck, almost wishing it would come to end the pain, but felt nothing but a gust carrying the stink of gore.

Without another word, Varro began ripping the ties on Brutus's armour, pulling it off piece by Viridian piece while Darius stared so lost in thought he didn't notice Sulla approach until the Militia Chief spoke.

"Oh…hell," Sulla muttered. "Hate to interrupt but we need orders."

When Brutus's body was stripped of Viridian armour, Varro slid his arms under his brother and picked up the burly warrior.

A few Black Commanders and algus ran to join them, among them Gorgias and an older woman Darius had seen before.

"The Viridians are in full retreat," she said, "but they still hold the city."

"For now," Sulla said. "The Xavalans will ride around the mountains and come to finish their task."

As much as Darius wanted to rush back into Laltos to find Selene, Sulla was right. If she'd survived, he'd never get to her, and Varro had been in no mood to chase even before Brutus had…

"Now isn't the time to reclaim the ruins," Varro said quietly, hidden gaze still seeming to linger on his brother's face. "We march to Margalvia."

"Yes, Warlord." The Black Commanders ran off barking orders while the algus exchanged disgruntled glances before setting off too.

"And you." Varro turned to Darius, dipping the horns of his stained helmet. "I'll allow you to return with us as a last courtesy to my brother. Then, my patience is spent. You'll take all you own and leave my city for good."

Given the circumstances, Darius shouldn't have expected less. Ordinarily, the words would have struck him with more force than Brutus's hammer, but after the torture, then losing Selene and now Brutus, exile barely registered. Even Lyra pressing her cheek into him did nothing to bring the usual warmth inside.

His known life had begun waking with no place to call home, and now he was back where he started, unsure whether the man he stood as today was better or worse than the wretch back then.

Without another word, Varro began walking up the hill with his brother's dripping body cradled in his arms.

Darius froze, staring at the sunken mud where Brutus had lain for who knew how long, as recent events tried but failed to sink in.

Before he'd realised, tears welled in his eyes and fell from his cheeks mixed with grime and blood. Weeks of hurt, worry for Lyra, betrayal, longing and loss overtook him, unable to be shut out any longer. He barely noticed the gore soaking into his trousers.

Lyra pressed her head to him again, and he wiped his face, brought his attention back to the moment. After regathering himself, he stood and took Lyra into his arms.

He sensed her sorrow stemming from his own angst. *Don't worry, girl. We'll figure out what to do next.* His first thought was to find Selene, but he was too much of an exhausted mess to string a plan together now.

After taking all the time he dared, he made his way after the Warlord. Lyra squirmed but he held her tight as he cast his gaze at the Black Legionnaires and Militia hurrying up the slope, then at the bodies he stepped around. Some still writhed, but most didn't.

The high Viridian death toll brought little consolation.

As he neared the crest of the hill, he saw Lex dragging her feet through the flattened dirt, her head hanging low and dishevelled hair falling across her face.

The retreating Black Legionnaires stomped around the slow-moving algus, with the last of them leaving her alone and silent. Meanwhile, Darius placed Lyra down and gave her a pat before nudging her to go to Sulla.

She did as instructed, which left only Darius and Lex trailing at the rear.

Darius waited a moment, trying to pull together words that might ease her pain, but he doubted even a skilled orator could succeed in that. After a few moments, she looked up, her gaze going immediately over her shoulder to the dull flames and smoke from Laltos.

The soot across her face reflected the despair in her eyes. His body and mind may have been a tortured mess, but he wouldn't want to trade places with her right now. He'd lost a father-figure, but she'd lost the real thing and more.

"Lex, we should hurry." It was difficult to keep his voice low and gentle for her because of the hurt still twisting his insides, but he managed it.

She nodded faintly but made no obvious effort to speed up. The other warriors, hoplites and algus were already forming new groups on the hill.

Darius placed a hand on her arm. His touch drew her stare towards him.

Her lip quivered. "Where's the justice?"

As far as Darius had seen, this world had none. He remembered back to when he'd once asked *her* about justice and wondered whether the answer she'd given would offer any relief. "Perhaps the judgement hasn't yet come."

Her face twisted into a grimace. Her right hand shot to her neck, ripped the chain from around it then threw it into the dirt. "Hope is for fools." Then, she threw off his comforting arm and strode up the hill.

He bent down and picked up the pendant from the mud, wiping the small figurine to show the silver Agathos. "Where were you when we needed you? When Brutus needed you? When I needed you?"

. . .

Silence—the God's answer to every question, every call for aid, it seemed.

He glanced back at the ruined city and suddenly froze. He recalled a desperate plea he'd once made in his cell, a plea for judgement to fall on his torturers. Had that prayer been granted?

He murmured, staring at the pendant. *Perhaps.* Who was he to question what was just? He slipped it carefully into his pocket before taking off after Lex. *She may forgive you one day, Agathos.* And who knew, maybe Darius would too.

65

Darius – North of Margalvia

Being without enough shelter, food or accessible water left the thousands in the group afraid, surly and bitter. The remnants of Laltos travelled south with the Black Legion, through the sparse forests and grasslands, while avoiding the roads the Xavalans might use to get to Laltos. Their movement wouldn't go unnoticed, but Darius hadn't the energy to let it concern him.

Lex barely spoke as they walked together, and Darius waited for the right moment to tell her of his exile, and perhaps go his own way, but found no heart to do it.

After days of travel, they made camp in the small hours once again. When what tents they had were set up, warriors went to scavenge food while Darius and others settled around a fire.

He held his hands out by the flames and rubbed his palms together, more so to keep them busy than from the cold. With the energy of battle long since faded, he had the irresistible urge to fidget, which was only calmed when Lyra lay next to him with her head in his lap.

The black, charred logs from the chopped-up tree still produced flames as high as his head when seated, through which he saw Varro—who had yet to say a word to him since exiling him.

Joining them in silence by the fire sat Lex, Sulla, Gorgias, and an older but striking woman Darius had learned was Gorgias's mother, Hera. Her dark hair matched the heavy makeup outlining her eyes, which made her stare more piercing and menacing.

For almost an hour they watched the flames writhe in the stiff wind that swept across the plains.

Cynthia squirmed in Lex's arms and sighed.

"Looks like it'll be a cloudy morning when the sun rises," Sulla said with a sigh.

Always him that likes to disturb the quietness.

"We'll risk travelling through the day then." Varro still wore his helmet, no doubt to show all who was in command. "Let's hope the clouds last all the way home and we don't lose hundreds of men to sunstroke like we did coming."

Darius knew the comment was intended to pile more guilt on him, and it worked.

"Are we welcome too?" The scars in Sulla's face deepened with his grimace, as if expecting a rebuke to the question he'd avoided asking until now.

Varro shook his head. "I came for you, didn't I? Margalvians defend their brothers."

Sulla grinned for a few seconds before it fell away again, likely recalling all that had fallen doing just that. Darius had said nothing of his own banishment, and had no plans to, knowing Sulla had enough to deal with.

"What's Margalvia like?" Gorgias asked, nervousness in his voice.

"It's not so bad," Darius said. "As long as we find food regularly."

"We have space for you now, since many are dead," Varro added.

Gorgias gave his mother a fearful stare then pulled his cloak tighter around his body.

Another that fidgets. "Don't fret," Darius said. "They say I lived there since I was a boy, and they didn't eat me."

"You'd be a little coarse for my liking," Sulla said. "I'd be on the latrine for a week."

Gorgias's mother turned her head from the sordid talk and cast her gaze across the hundreds of Laltos soldiers and citizens left, still keeping distance between themselves and the Margalvians. After Theodoros's death, she seemed to have taken it upon herself to speak for Laltos, and neither Lex nor any algus had objected.

"It's gracious of you to offer us shelter, Warlord," she said, "but we must decide where our people wish to reside in the longer term."

"One step at a time," Darius said, echoing his thoughts on his own future.

"Margalvia is the best place for us." Lex stared blankly into the flames. "We'll rebuild our strength. We'll reform our strategy. Then we'll win the war."

Like they had an army left that could achieve anything beyond harrying or espionage…

"We can't be slow about our next move," Varro added. "If Hadrian is after the Waif Magician, I want to know why."

Darius thought back to what Brutus had said before he died. It confused him as much now as then. "Any ideas why?"

"A couple," the Warlord said. "I think it's the Staff of Arria he wants, and not for battle."

"What else is it useful for?"

"Didn't you read the scroll Brutus gave you?"

Darius lowered his head. He'd had plenty of time to read it so far but hadn't taken his mentor's advice, like many times before.

Crackles and spits from the fire filled the air between them.

Gorgias snorted. "I hope the Magician slays the lot of them, then Xavala and Toria too."

"Xavala will be crushed, one way or another," Lex spat.

"They'll all pay," Varro said, deathly certainty in his voice.

Darius didn't know where he now fit into this. Whatever he did next was up to him, and his thoughts had lingered only on Selene since Laltos.

As far back as his memory stretched, he couldn't recall a time when he'd been in charge of his own destiny, or really wanted to be. He'd bent to the will of others countless times, but following Varro and Lex's instructions hadn't ended well for him.

And now, he was cut loose. Was it time to try another way? Having people gape at him in awe on the battlefield, and listen to him, had been a little intoxicating.

Gorgias nudged Darius's shoulder. "Do you hold a grudge for what we did to you?"

Darius was taken aback at the question. Was Laltos's destruction enough? The stench of sulphur and stone still burned his nostrils, yet the anger was hard to let go, despite the devastation of those that had wronged him. "Help me kill Hadrian and you're forgiven."

Gorgias's nostrils flared, and even Hera's eyes filled with rage at the mere mention of the name. "You have my word," he said, "and my sword until the Warlord falls or I do. Then we'll move onto the King and his algus that killed my wife."

Lex's jaw clenched, which told Darius she too was far from giving up. She'd finally got the alliance she'd wanted, but when they next had a quiet moment together, he'd ask her whether it was worth the cost. He hadn't even considered it worth Lyra's brush with death, let alone the tens of thousands in Laltos, Selene, Brutus…

Darius watched Lex's hate-filled eyes with a new unease. What kind of woman would emerge from this despair? Judging by her callousness before—when she'd had more to lose—her lust for revenge would be unrelenting, much like all the others around the fire.

On that, Darius was with them. Whether exiled or not, he'd see Hadrian's end.

66

Nikolaos – Toria

I should kill them all for what they've done. Nikolaos stirred the strongly brewed tea round and round in the pot on the table in front of him. Sat high atop his balcony overlooking Toria, he watched the ignorant populace go about their dealings on the banks of the sprawling network of canals, much in the same way he had every day since his arrival.

In the capital, the King had spun the tale of Laltos as one showing the consequences of rebellion, but the jubilant atmosphere that had taken hold upon the news of the destruction finally seemed to have died, much to Nikolaos's relief. How could they do it? As much as he hated them for it, he had no option but to remain subservient to the King for now.

White tarnflower petals floated on top of the now lukewarm brew, and it reminded him of the years of his youth spent searching for and picking them in the mountains behind his home city, often with Lex, who'd made hairbands of flowers from them until she outgrew the practise.

No one else would enjoy that luxury. Only Laltos dried the tea correctly. This might be one of the last sips of it he took before the Empire's stocks ran out, but he couldn't bring himself to drink it because it reminded him even more of the childhood home he'd dreamed of ruling, that now lay in ruins. Plus, the evening was too stifling for tea.

"I see you're now partaking of weaker drinks," Ophelia hissed behind him. "Ran out of firewater?"

Nikolaos didn't bother to turn around, now used to the King's Orator arriving uninvited. "I felt like clearing my head." How else was one to survive in a city with no allies?

The woman made her way before him. "The King has a request to make of you."

After destroying my home, leaving me nothing to rule over? It was a good thing Nikolaos was used to cloaking his reactions, or the contempt would be all too evident on his face. "What request is that?"

Ophelia smiled and motioned for a slave to bring across a chair. She waited for a frail boy to slide it under her before sitting. "Aren't you glad to finally learn the reason we rescued you?"

Nikolaos turned away from her, but she continued, "It seems that a number of people from Laltos escaped."

What did it matter? Nikolaos shrugged. "Even the tightest net will let a few fish slip through."

"Well, these evasive fish have taken refuge in Margalvia."

The spoon slipped through Nikolaos's fingers and splashed tea over the table. Why did traitors always seem to prevail? He sat back with his best attempt at indifference.

"Fortunately for us," Ophelia continued, with barely contained glee in her eyes, "I have bait that will let us hook the rest, and their Margalvian protectors."

If she were so shrewd, she wouldn't have to ask for his assistance. "I don't see how I can help. I've never been fond of angling. Too much patience required."

"That's a pity, for you will need patience for this task."

Nikolaos picked up the spoon and stirred. He evidently had some patience, as he hadn't thrown his tea over her tunic yet.

"Jason," Ophelia called towards the door behind.

Nikolaos had the presence of mind not to drop his spoon again, but his tea-stirring ceased. Once in Toria, he'd seen little of the man.

He turned to see the grey-cloaked King's Sword walk onto the balcony with an auburn-haired woman held loosely by the arm.

A gasp escaped Nikolaos's mouth. "Selene?"

Her hazel eyes and crooked, broken nose were in stark contrast to the clean and pressed cloak falling from her shoulders. She stopped and looked him up and down with a frown.

"They captured you?" he asked.

Selene gazed at him with puzzlement, as if unsure whether he'd spoken to her or the vacant space behind. It was an oddly familiar look to Nikolaos, but he couldn't recall what it reminded him of.

"This is why I was told to keep you alive, even after you spied on me." Ophelia smirked. "The King needs your help."

Nikolaos scoffed, too numb to bother wondering how anyone knew the King would need his help now.

"If you think I'll torture her, then think again," Nikolaos said.

The King's Orator grinned more widely. "You can give us nothing we don't already have. We want you to train her and ensure that she acts and speaks exactly as Selene once did."

Despite the bewilderment surely present on Nikolaos's face, Ophelia paused. With searching eyes, Nikolaos stared at Selene again and tried to penetrate the confusion on her face. "Selene, what's wrong?"

"She doesn't go by the name Selene, yet. Call her Six."

The air atop the balcony stilled.

Now he knew that look. *The Numbered*. But Nikolaos had watched Archimedes die. No other gomans had crossed the Aretean Sea, had they? Was it the Waif Magician? "How…?"

"I think it's obvious how." Ophelia leaned across the table, and all humour fell from her face. "The King has many resources at his disposal. This one is a well-kept secret for a variety of reasons. Jason will accompany you at all times from now on, and if we so much as suspect you've shared this information, you'll beg for death."

With a swallow, Nikolaos nodded weakly. "Understood. But why tell me?"

"To subdue her we've had to remove a lot of her memories," Ophelia continued. "You're the best one to prepare her."

"Prepare her for what?"

The smile returned to Ophelia's face.

Other books in the series:

A Mark Of Gods

Prequel to the Rakkan Conquest series

Available for FREE at AndyBlinston.com

They sentenced his brother…

…but the boy never touched that panther.

They know the truth. Even the reigning algus gods wouldn't have been foolish enough to invite such wrath.

In a city ruled by the sword and spear, Javad's dreams of freedom in the eastern sands are fading. His brother is condemned and would be lucky to hang. But slaves are never lucky, and someone worse than a regent or king has been wronged.

Darius, the Slayer, is coming.

Even the gods flee.

All Javad has to face him are his lock picks, his hope in justice, and the heart of a warrior.

Follow Javad and his brother in this short story of underdogs against a corrupt system and a legendary adversary bent on revenge.

Printed in Great Britain
by Amazon